THE HOUSE
OF THE FALCON
AND OTHER EXOTIC PLACES

THE HOUSE
OF THE FALCON

AND OTHER EXOTIC PLACES

HAROLD LAMB

WILDSIDE PRESS

CONTENTS

INTRODUCTION, by Karl Wurf 7

THE HOUSE OF THE FALCON 9

THE DEVIL'S BUNGALOW .174

THE DESERT DRIVER 218

INTRODUCTION

Harold Albert Lamb (1892–1962)[1] was an American historian, screenwriter, short story writer, and novelist. He was born in Alpine, New Jersey to Eliza Rollinson and Frederick Lamb and was the nephew of the architect Charles Rollinson Lamb. He attended Columbia University, where his interest in the peoples and history of Asia began. Lamb's tutors at Columbia included Carl Van Doren and John Erskine. He received a Guggenheim Fellowship for twelve months, starting on April 1, 1929.

Lamb built a career with his writing from an early age. He got his start in the pulp magazines, quickly moving to the prestigious *Adventure* magazine, which became his primary fiction outlet for nineteen years. In 1927 he wrote a biography of Genghis Khan, and following on its success turned more and more to the writing nonfiction, including numerous biographies and popular history books, until his death in 1962 in Rochester, New York. The success of Lamb's two-volume history of the Crusades led to his discovery by Cecil B. DeMille, who employed Lamb as a technical advisor on a related movie, *The Crusades*, and used him as a screenwriter on many other DeMille movies thereafter.

Lamb spoke French, Latin, Persian, and Arabic, and, by his own account, a smattering of Manchu-Tartar. During World War II, He was an OSS agent serving in Iran, which deepened his understanding of the Middle East and its people.

LAMB'S FICTION

Although Harold Lamb wrote short stories for a variety of magazines between 1917 and the early 1960s, and wrote several novels, his best known and most reprinted fiction is that which he wrote for *Adventure* between 1917 and 1936. The editor of *Adventure*, Arthur Sullivant Hoffman, praised Lamb's writing ability, describing him as "always the scholar first, the good fictionist second". The majority of Lamb's work for *Adventure* was historical fiction, and it can be thematically divided into three broad categories of tales:

1. Stories featuring Cossacks
2. Stories featuring Crusaders
3. Stories with Asian or Middle-Eastern Protagonists

Lamb's prose was direct and fast-paced, in stark contrast to that of many other contemporary *adventure* writers. His stories were well-researched and rooted in their time, often featuring real historical characters, but set in places unfamiliar and exotic to most of the western audience reading his fiction. While his adventure stories had familiar tropes such as tyrannical rulers and scheming priests, he avoided the simplistic depiction of foreign or unfamiliar cultures as evil; many of his heroes were Mongolian, Indian, Russian, or Muslim. Most of his protagonists were outsiders or outcasts apart from civilization, and all but a very few were skilled swordsmen and warriors.

In a Lamb story, honor and loyalty to one's comrades-in-arms were more important than cultural identity, although often his protagonists ended up risking their lives to protect the cultures that had spurned them. Those holding positions of authority are almost universally depicted as being corrupted by their own power or consumed with greed, be they Russian boyars or Buddhist priests, and merchants are almost always shown as placing their own desire for coin above the well-being of their fellow men. Loyalty, wisdom, and religious piety is shown again and again in these stories to lie more securely in the hands of Lamb's common folk.

While female characters occasionally played the familiar role of damsel in distress in these stories, Lamb more typically depicted his women as courageous, independent, and more shrewd than their male counterparts. Their motives and true loyalties, though, remained mysterious to Lamb's male characters, and their unknowable nature is frequently the source of plot tension.

Lamb was never a formula plotter, and his stories often turned upon surprising developments arising from character conflict. The bulk of his Crusader, Asian, and Middle-Eastern stories (as well as the latter stories of Khlit the Cossack) were written in the latter portion of his pulp magazine years, and demonstrate a growing command of prose tools; the more frequent use, for example, of poetic metaphor in his description.

Writers influenced by Lamb's work include the creator of Conan the Barbarian, Robert E. Howard (who described Lamb as one of his favourite writers), Malcolm Wheeler-Nicholson, Norvell Page, Gardner Fox, Thomas B. Costain, Harry Harrison, and Scott Oden.

—Karl Wurf
Rockville, Maryland

THE HOUSE OF THE FALCON

CHAPTER I
THE ROOF OF THE WORLD

Men drop out of sight there. This one did. Or, no, I shouldn't say that. He went up out of sight. You see, he was carried.

Yes, right out of the city up toward the top of the world—at least that's what the natives thereabouts call the mountains, where the spurs of the Thian Shan meet the Himalayas. About five thousand men saw him go.

And not one of 'em cared to follow.

They were natives of course, all sorts—Chinese, beggarly Sarts, Mussulman traders, Kirghiz shepherds and what not. He was a white man. The other Europeans in Kashgar were all in the new city, the Chinese city, where the *taotai* and the missionaries are. He had come to the old city of Kashgar, by the dried-up river. He rode—uncommonly well, they say— across the wooden drawbridge and under the arch into the thick of the bazaar section.

Not that he'd lost his way. In fact he seemed to be looking for some one in the bazaar where he must have known there were no foreign barbarians— only the natives. His horse was dark with sweat land he was covered with dust. There was a good rifle slung over his shoulder and a native servant followed him. So the white men in Kashgar, when they heard what had happened to him, thought he must have been a big game hunter.

Still, they couldn't understand why a hunter should off-saddle and go wandering through the bazaar as this one did guided by his servant. White men, even *ovis poli* and wapiti hunters, are not frequent visitors in Kashgar, you know. It's a city on the old caravan route from China into India and Persia. It's sort of stuck up there under the hills that overlook Tibet, Turkestan and Kashmir, and the hills themselves are rather a no man's land—tribal areas.

I have said he was looking for something, or some one. And he didn't find what he was looking for. That seems to be clear. So he let his servant take him to a *serai*, an inn for travelers in the bazaar quarter. For a hunter he was traveling awfully light, and with no heads at all in his baggage. He'd made a long trek, too, judging by the condition of his beasts.

It sounds just like a story, of course. The white man—we'll call him that for want of a better name—was sitting in a corner of the *serai* with his back to the mud wall smoking a pipe and watching the other inmates—a fine lot they were, too—when a big black-faced native in sheepskins, blind in one eye, got up and went over to him.

"*Effendi*," the fellow said, "your slave who is the dust beneath your feet (he meant himself) has heard that there is danger and trouble in store for you here. Will the *effendi* ride hence at once and swiftly?"

The white man laughed and said he liked it where he was. At this the chap of the sheepskins went out of the *serai* and began to run as if the devil were after him, through the twisting alleys of the bazaar, out past the mosque and up the road to the hills.

He didn't stop running as long as he was visible from the balcony where the *taotai*, the governor, was having dinner. They noticed that, because those natives never run unless necessary, and then they ride.

In an hour, after he'd eaten a little dinner, the white man was knocked out. Not actually, of course, but by fever or food poisoning. It was so quick in coming, it must have been poisoning.

He still sat in the comer of the *serai* with his rifle across his knees and his face drawn with pain. He couldn't move except to put his finger on the trigger of his piece and watch the crowd in the *serai* with his eyes. This was necessary, because his servant had left him and he hadn't tried to get word to the few Europeans who were near by in the new Kashgar.

Perhaps he did try to get word to them; still, there was no evidence that he did. A Kashgar crowd is harmless for the most part; but not when a foreign barbarian with his kit and rifle is helpless in their hands. Well—this chap kept watching the crowd and the crowd watched him. Waiting for him to die, most likely, so they could appropriate his kit and rifle.

Evidently while he was still alive they didn't dare touch him. And it wasn't dark yet. The Chinese governor, who was very conscientious—a fine fellow and a scholar, too—and investigated the affair to the best of his ability, says that this was before the *namazgar*, the time of evening prayer for the Moslems who made up the greater part of Kashgar.

Apparently the white man made only one remark.

"Where is Jain Ali Beg?" he asked—referring to his servant.

The *serai* keeper swore afterward to the governor that the servant had run away, perhaps because he scented trouble in the air.

So the white man sat there, poisoned perhaps by the Moslems of the bazaar. So the governor said; but a Chinese official hates all Mussulmans. Then a curious thing happened.

Those in the *serai* heard the trample of the camels of a caravan outside, in the alley. They heard the bells of the camels. And the leader of the caravan, the man who holds the nose cord of the first animal in the line, was the one-eyed chap in sheepskins.

The caravan had come down the road from the hills. Nothing unusual in that, of course, because caravan transport is the only way of moving goods in Central Asia and a half dozen of 'em go through Kashgar every day. But this particular caravan didn't have any boxes or anything but a score of dark-skinned hillmen for riders.

It might have come in to the bazaar to load up—only it didn't. The caravan moved down out of the hills in the dust, to enter the bazaar. It stopped just for a moment outside the *serai*, and the riders took the white man away with them.

That was exactly what they did. Set him on a camel; then the whole string turned and went off with the one-eyed beggar in the lead. They had crossed the old bridge over the moat and disappeared into the dust before the bazaar knew what was happening.

At that, the natives of Kashgar gave the caravan a wide berth. There wasn't a soul in the alleys when it went away. Every one had popped into the open shop fronts or under the sun mats. They seemed to be superstitious about it and the Mussulmans related something to the *taotai* about a caravan that came from nowhere and went nowhere.

Yes, that particular white man went up out of sight. At least, he was never seen again.

Now, what do you think of it all?

CHAPTER II

THE LISTENER

"Now, what do you think of it all?" repeated Whittaker. He rubbed his bald forehead with a plump hand and cast birdlike glances at the girl beside him.

Whittaker flattered himself that he could tell a good story well, and that, having trotted over most of the globe, he had good stories to tell. Moreover the finest young woman of the Château had been listenings to him attentively.

In the upper corridors of the Château music echoed from the orchestra of the ballroom, popular music with a tang to it. Whittaker's eyes had watched the girl's slippered foot tracing a dainty accompaniment. But she had smiled away several men who had come up to urge her to dance—had refused them, to listen to him. Whittaker glowed.

"Did it really happen, Mr. Whittaker?"

He liked the way her words slurred together softly, after the manner of the women born in the South of the United States. Whittaker believed that he was an excellent judge of women. So he permitted himself to admire the girl's tawny hair, dressed low on her neck, almost touching her bare shoulders.

She carried herself devilishly well, he thought, and had a haughty eye. Came of one of the oldest Southern families, Kentucky, he believed, and knew it. Her father was rich. They went the round of Fifth Avenue, St. Augustine, the Riviera, and Canada—the Château, at Quebec.

"Of course, Miss Rand," Whittaker was aggrieved. "You know Major Fraser-Carnie, don't you? Well, when you see him, ask him about it. He told me the story. And I"—he looked up hopefully—"I have arrived at an explanation."

Leaning back comfortably in the settee Whittaker contemplated Edith Rand, who, with gray eyes half closed, was staring out of the drawing-room window at the lights of the Château terrace.

Beyond the lights, the mist over the broad bosom of the St. Lawrence was luminous under an invisible moon. But Edith Rand did not see that. She was wondering why the man in the chair by the fireplace within a few feet of them was listening so intently to what the globe-trotter was saying.

She knew he was listening because his cigarette had burned his fingers and he had dropped it hastily. He was playing solitaire on a green card table drawn up before his chair and was making palpable mistakes.

When the chatter of people passing in from the dining-room or leaving the ballroom had drowned Whittaker's voice, the man had leaned ever so slightly nearer. She wished he would turn around.

"Most people would say," Whittaker argued, "that the natives of the caravan—the one that took the white man away from Kashgar, you know—were robbers, brigands from the hills. Kashgar is north of the English lines in upper India, and it is full of outlaws."

"No," said Edith Rand. "You said they only took the man himself, not his belongings."

"Precisely—exactly what I was going to point out." Whittaker joggled his eyeglass triumphantly. "Now I have heard other people say that the whole queer event was a conspiracy. The white man in short was an outlaw, as well as the—caravaneers. That was why he lurked in the bazaar instead of going to his own countrymen in the modern city of Kashgar.

"But my own opinion, my dear Miss Rand, is this. *My* theory is that the white man was carried off as a punishment for some crime he had committed. A crime against the natives, you know. Robbed a temple, or—ah—something of the kind. One-Eye—the chap of the sheepskins—drugged him and then went to fetch his gang. Helpless under the influence of the drug, the white man was borne away to his fate. Eh, what?"

Edith Rand was silent. She had observed that the card player had returned to his solitaire with fresh enthusiasm; he was placing red cards upon black, quite correctly. He had even lit another cigarette.

"And now," continued Whittater, convinced of the success of his narrative, "we come to the sequel. You remember that the white man's servant, Jain Ali Beg, ran away from Kashgar and was missing—for some time. A year later he turned up at one of the English Stations in the Kashmir hills five hundred miles away to the south in upper India. Major Fraser-Carnie, your friend, saw him.

"Jain Ali Beg," nodded the globe-trotter, "was arrested. Doubtless, you wonder why. He had in his possession the personal effects and the rifle of his master—claimed they had been given him by the white *effendi* before his master was carried off. But Fraser-Carnie had no doubt that Jain Ali Beg robbed the man."

As Whittaker said this Edith Rand saw that the listener laid down his cards entirely, with the game half finished, and began to tap upon the green surface of the table with blunt, powerful fingers.

"And Jain Ali Beg was glad to be arrested. He had been running away because he was very much afraid. Not of arrest, but of something in Kashgar. Perhaps, of the caravan. Picture the scene to yourself—a lonely hill station with the British officer standing at the door of his quarters talking to the fear-sick native.

"The next moment Jain Ali Beg was lying on the doorstep, knifed. And the murderer who had come up behind the house was my friend of the sheepskins—One-Eye, the personal conductor of the caravan. The queer chap actually took the pains to explain why he had killed Jain Ali Beg. He said:

"'For the space of three moons I have followed in the tracks of this one'—he pointed to the body—'to give to a faithless servant the reward that he has stored up for himself.'

"Then One-Eye vanished around the bungalow and, by George, the native servants of the station refused to try to follow him! They said a curious thing. They said:

"'Sahib, when the lightning strikes, does any one follow?'

"And that," Whittaker concluded triumphantly, "that, my dear Miss Rand, was precisely what the natives of the Kashgar bazaar said when the caravan came and carried off your white man. Strange, what?

"Are you sure," questioned a quiet voice beside them, "the man was really dead?"

Edith Rand observed that the card player had turned and was looking at them fixedly, his brown face serious.

"Eh, why—he was stabbed four times about the heart, as dead as Mahomet—"

"Not Jain Ali Beg." The card player shook hi head impatiently. "The man in Kashgar."

The stranger pronounced the native names in a certain sonorous fashion quite different from the flat phrases of Whittaker.

"Oh, the hunter." Whittaker rallied to the defense of his story. "Well, there's not much doubt that he is dead, after all that. He was never seen around there again, of course. You see there was something spooky about that caravan. You don't think he isn't dead, do you?"

The card player smiled. "A case of *corpus delicti* is sometimes difficult to prove," he observed. And now his glance rested on the girl, keenly appraising, as if he were probing for what might be in her thoughts.

Then his smile changed and he stood up, his dark eyes intent upon her. Few men failed to render tribute to the beauty of Edith Rand. His brows raised tentatively at Whittaker.

"Pardon me," the globe-trotter obeyed the signal with some reluctance. He felt that the spell of his story had been shattered. "Permit me, Miss Rand, to introduce Edouard Monsey."

With a ready courtesy the newcomer bowed over Edith's hand. In spite of his almost perfect English the girl felt that he was of foreign birth. She was vaguely surprised that Monsey should be an acquaintance of Whittaker—although her companion seemed to know everybody. For the past hour she had fancied that Monsey had been wholly absorbed in hearing Whittaker's story.

She had seen the man at intervals about the Château—during rides along the heights, and once when she was walking alone along her favorite promenade on the ramparts. On that occasion she had been aware that Monsey had followed her with his eyes.

"I have had the pleasure," remarked Monsey, "of meeting your father, Miss Rand, in the Château. We had something in common, you know. He is going to India on business."

He looked at her questioningly.

"Daddy will have to take me," she drawled. "He would be right lonely without me. I always go with him. Mr. Whittaker was trying to frighten me with his stories—"

"But it was true," protested that gentleman. "It was quite true."

Monsey shrugged. "Kashgar is hardly India, my dear chap. Calcutta, or Kashmir for that matter, is safer than New York."

Edith turned to him impulsively. She was an uncommonly outspoken person, as her aunt, who was traveling with the Rands, had frequently reminded her—with the added prophecy that her disposition would undoubtedly get her into trouble, unless she married first.

But the girl was quite heart-free and she was tremendously content with the path in life that Arthur Rand, her father, had opened for her. She liked to wander, to see things, and to ask questions.

"Are you from India, Mr. Monsey?"

Instinctively she felt that she should say "Captain Monsey," the man was so plainly a former soldier. His accent hinted at French schooling; the name might mean anything. India, to Edith, represented a pleasure spot frequented by likable men who played polo and owned horses—the girl had been brought up to love horses.

Monsey hesitated momentarily, looking at her.

"I have been there," he said, and changed the subject, requesting the favor of a dance. "A privilege so great that only the necessity of your coming departure emboldens me to ask for it. Miss Rand, may I be permitted to say that you dance as well as you, ride, and that is—perfectly?"

It was one of the requirements of her world that she should do so—the festive world that was her birthright.

Edith could appreciate the formal courtesy of the stranger, Monsey. It was that of the elder school of French gentlemen. But, even while the music called her, she found that her mood had changed.

"Let's walk up to the ramparts," she cried "I visit them every night, and sit on a wonderful old cannon. If you don't mind—"

As she tripped through the lobby with Monsey at her side, her quick eye sighted letters in the array behind the desk in the pigeonhole that belonged to her. Mail always held a fascination for Edith and she could not resist claiming the letters, handing them to Monsey for safe-keeping.

Clouds were passing over the surface of the moon, rendering the light on the wooden steps fitful. When they ascended from the last platform four hundred feet above the roofs of the river front, a fresh breeze touched their faces.

"Do you not find it dangerous?" Monsey asked curiously. "I should think your aunt would object—"

"She does," absented Edith, "that's why she is not invited."

The girl perched herself on the bole of an obsolete cannon that rested its muzzle on the grass near by. She patted it in friendly fashion. "Old war dog, I wonder did you growl at enemies in your time? Do they have forts like this in India, Mr. Monsey?"

Standing beside her, he could see the girl's form against the sky and admire the light that glinted in the tangle of her hair. A remarkably willful person, he thought, wishing that he could gauge her mind.

"I have heard there are many such in northern India in the mountains. You will doubtless visit them, because the early summer heat will be oppressive in the south."

"Major Fraser-Carnie lives in Kashmir, I think," she nodded. "We will visit him for a while—until Daddy has finished his business in Calcutta."

Inwardly she was wondering why he parried any direct allusion to India. She remembered now that her father had mentioned meeting a man in the Château who had come not long ago from that country and who had given him some useful information. Monsey, she reflected, did not seem inclined to give *her* useful information.

"If you are in Kashmir, Miss Rand," he observed after a brief silence, "you will doubtless be in Srinagar. I have already assured your father that I may have the pleasure of meeting him there. Business"—he laughed— "recalls me from my—ah—vacation, I believe you call it—yes?" Monsey tapped the pocket of his dinner jacket. "I have here a summons to return. It is my misfortune that I must hasten by the most direct way, the tiresome C.P.R. boat, while you will cross from New York."

There was something fantastic, it seemed to Edith, in the thought of any one's taking a vacation from India in America, even in quaint Quebec. And Mousey did not appear to her to be a business man. Of course he might merely be cultivating her to gain the good will of powerful Arthur Rand—

"In Srinagar," his low voice went on, "you will grant me the happiness of the dance that *kismet* has denied me here?"

"Yes, of course."

"Ah, you will not forget? Kashmir is the garden of India: Srinagar is the jewel of Kashmir."

Monsey was speaking to her of the Himalayas, of floating pleasure palaces of dead kings, and the shrines of the hills that were built before the coming of Europeans. They were walking back slowly toward the stairs, and Edith was wrapped up in his description of the place she had looked forward to seeing. A cloud was passing over the moon's face.

The girl was at the edge of the parapet and she stepped out upon what she thought to be the head of the stairway. A high-heeled foot slid over the brink of the height and she fell to her knees.

All the blood seemed to leave her heart, and every nerve tingled with swift pain. She cried out as she slipped downward and glimpsed the docks in the shadowy darkness below.

Then she felt an arm about her shoulders. Monsey's sharp exclamation of alarm penetrated the roaring in her ears. He must have thrown himself down on the grass beside her.

By degrees that seemed to Edith infinitely slow the grasp on her shoulders tightened and she was drawn up. Above her the stars danced in a maze of light and a dozen moons circled the sky.

She was standing again in the grass, well back from the edge, Monsey's arms around her, and his face peering into hers. "Thank you," she heard herself saying quite calmly. "I was very foolish—" She drew away, leaning against the cannon for support.

"It was my *kismet*," he nodded, "that I should be of aid to you. Now you will not forget the dance at Srinagar. I must see you again." His voice, always low, was little more than a whisper. "Because I shall not live until then."

Edith was repeating to herself that he had saved her life. He had acted promptly, at great risk to himself. The man seemed to think only of her.

Yet, even while thanking him, Edith was conscious of a strong feeling of aversion. More than his last words offended her. The young girl was sensitive to impressions. Something, perhaps, that she had seen in his face repelled her.

* * * *

When she returned to her room Edith glanced through the letters that Monsey had given back to her, a note from a school chum, invitations. One missive caught her attention. It was a single sheet of blue paper, and the envelope from which it came had already been opened. On the blue sheet several lines of meaningless characters peered at her.

"How strange!" Edith whistled softly, a habit of hers when puzzled.

The odd lettering was very neat—pothooks, dashes, and scrolls, all following each other in regular succession. It was not shorthand. Nor was it any language with which Edith was acquainted. But underneath it she noticed some penciled words in English.

Her smooth brow wrinkled as she reread the penciled phrases which were evidently a translation of the message.

The Falcon is on the wing, searching the City of the Sun. Take care.

It was like poetry, she thought—like a bit from the *Rubaiyat*. Or was it a code? Her father had used code at times—writing apples when he meant profits, and plums instead of losses, and so forth. Yet here the second line seemed to make good sense as it was.

The phrase "City of the Sun" had been scratched out and "Srinagar" substituted. Was this code? The word "Srinagar" gave her an inkling of how the blue sheet had come into her possession.

For the first time she inspected the envelope, the open envelope from which she had taken it. It was addressed to Edouard Monsey, the Château,

Quebec, Province of Quebec, Canada. In one comer was the legend, "To be held until called for."

A foreign stamp was attached, blurred over by an unreadable postmark. The writing on the envelope was English, but angular and stilted as if penned by an unfamiliar hand.

Edith replaced the blue sheet, and rang for a boy. To him she delivered the missive with instructions to take it to Mr. Monsey and say that he had given it to Miss Rand by mistake that evening.

It was clear that Monsey had handed the blue letter to her when returning those she had given him. She regretted that she had, unwittingly, read his letter. When she tried to put it out of her mind she found that she could not do so.

What a queer phrase—the Falcon! She had always connected the word with knights and the days of chivalry. Were there falcons to-day? Or was it a kind of code word for something else? Edith did not know.

"It must be code, after all. He said he had received a business letter," mused Edith, drowsily, and straightway went to bed and to sleep.

* * * *

By now the lighted windows of the Château had blinked into darkness. The twisted streets of Quebec had long been silent. The pleasure-stage was deserted by its guests, the curtain drawn. Players and attendants alike slept.

Somewhere in the old French city under the height chimes rang out from a cathedral tower. Answering bells sent their notes forth under the stars. A chorus of ironlike harmony welled from invisible sources.

Though the pleasure-stage was dark in the hours before dawn, the chimes of Quebec did not sleep. The roofs of the city were still, under the eye of the moon. A solitary note of carriage bells struck into the chimes—from the slope of a dark street.

Monsey, who had been dozing, dressed, in his chair, swore softly and leaped to his feet.

"Confound the bells!" he muttered, lifting clenched hands to his head.

In the confused instant of wakening from heavy, troubled sleep he had fancied the chimes were human voices. Into his senses had come the distant, wailing cry of cloaked muezzins summoning to prayer and shouting forth the salutation to a prophet.

He had been dreaming, and the effect was still strong upon him. He fancied that cries of anguish were ringing in his head—cries drowned by the clamor of huge trumpets lifted to the skies.

"Horns of Jericho!" he exclaimed, and this time he did not speak in English.

His fancy still retained the echo of the chimes distorted into another sound—the summons of ten-foot trumpets reverberating from the impulse of the lungs of powerful men, and reëchoed from distant hillsides as if from cliffs in the sky. His memory pictured hooded heads raised to the first light of dawn, and lips murmuring age-old prayers.

The carriage bells of Quebec had taken the semblance of camel bells of another country that jangled as long-haired beasts pad-padded over the snow to the *hoa-hoa* of caravaneers.

Then he glanced from the window out over the mist-shrouded river, laughed, and stretched.

"Nerves, by Jove! Didn't know I had 'em."

CHAPTER III
THE GATE

It was at Baramula, which is the beginning of the real Kashmir, that Edith Rand saw the watcher at the gate. At least so she christened him to herself.

The girl and her aunt, Catherine Rand, had been sent to the hills by Arthur Rand at the first contact with the lifeless heat of Calcutta. A Southerner by birth and an easy-going gentleman of the old school, he could not permit the women to face the climate of southern India which was like a fever breath compared with the heat of Louisville in midsummer.

His florid face had been almost purple when he kissed Edith good-by on the platform beside the carriage of the Punjabi Mail. Edith had not wanted to leave him. She knew that he was not well—this knowledge had made her determined to come with him to India.

Moreover Edith fancied that the business venture that brought them to India had not been going well. Letters from home had hinted at a stock market slump and she knew that her father had invested heavily.

But the Southerner, reluctant to worry his daughter or his sister, had smiled and said that he would join them within a few days in Kashmir. He had handed Catherine Rand her inseparable traveling companion, a pail of assorted medicines dear to her heart, wrapped in a black doth, and waved good-by.

"My dear," admitted Edith's aunt, as the guard closed the carriage door, "no one can do business in this Turkish bath. It was fortunate that I brought my medicines. I fear that we all shall need them. Your father is not well. He should never have come."

This had filled Edith with vague foreboding, a feeling that Arthur Rand was concealing his worries from her. Murree and the fresh air of the hills after the long train journey had revived her, and the joggling carts that conveyed them to Baramula fascinated her.

They had passed through the gateway of Kashmir, threading mountain passes, while cold winds bearing scent of pines, jasmine, and acacias swept down on them. They moved in the shadow of cliffs. Vines and wild flowers almost touched their hats as they passed by.

It had cast a spell upon Edith, a sleepy, pleasant kind of spell. She yearned for a horse to ride among the mountain paths. Two English ladies, officers wives, who were with them had smiled at her indulgently. The American traveler, they thought, was a beautiful girl; they wondered just how she would fare in the army circles at Srinagar. When she inquired if it were called the City of the Sun, they responded that the natives interpreted its name so. They spoke of it as "Sreenugger."

At Baramula the tongas had halted to change horses. At once a crowd of natives pressed around them, shouting, pushing, bowing. Bearded Afghans elbowed tattered Turkomans aside; slim Paharis gestured frantically beside squat Kashmiri traders with arms full of shawls; handsome Central Asian Jews pleaded with great play of brown eyes for the *khanum* to notice the unrivaled excellence of their heaven-devised silks; self-appointed interpreters cried loudly that the *mem*-sahibs should not fail to avail themselves of their matchless services. Pockmarked beggars in garments that were miracles of rags continued to wail for the never-ending *baksheesh*.

All—except the beggars—deprecated any idea of reward, and asserted boldly and bodily their high integrity and the encomiums heaped upon them by previous travelers. Noisy recrimination on the part of the tonga drivers against the horde of rivals added to the confusion.

Through the mass of natives a carriage drove up behind splendidly matched horses, scattering the ranks of the beggars. A diminutive, uniformed figure dropped instantaneously from the seat beside the driver and sought out Edith Rand. The military atom bent a turbaned head and raised slim hands, crying in very fair English:

"Major-Sahib Fraser-Carnie presents compliments. Is this the American Missy?" Adding complacently, "I am the orderly of the Major-Sahib, Rawul Singh."

Edith was about to follow her aunt into the carriage, while Rawul Singh attended to the forwarding of their baggage on the tongas, when a man stepped from the crowd and thrust his arm over the carriage wheel. The action surprised the girl, unaccustomed to the manners of the native servants.

She saw that the man was as tall as the Afghans, but of a more powerful build. His impassive broad face was the hue of burned wood. Slant, black eyes were bent submissively before her. Yet she had the impression that he had been looking at her intently for some time.

The aspect of the native was somber—one arm resting across the heavy, gray woolen coat over his chest, his big head surmounted by a round, black velvet cap. A scar, running from mouth to eye, increased the grimness of the intent face.

Just for an instant the eyes of the man sought hers. Then, with a bow he was gone. Edith fancied that he was still watching the carriage from the crowd. As they sped away she looked back and thought that she saw him climbing into one of the tongas.

She forgot him almost at once, in the glory of the drive along the valley beside the flooded Jhilam that muttered through its gorge at their feet. Those who have once entered the paradise of Kashmir do not soon forget the gateway.

Edith laughed with the joy of it, seeing gray clouds twining among the mountain slopes behind them. The edges of the cloud bank were touched with a fiery purple from the concealed sun, when—as if an invisible hand passed across the face of the sky—the sunlight was blotted from their path.

The horses quickened their pace as the Afghan driver cracked his whip and Rawul Singh spoke sharply in Turki:

"Drive, son of a pig! Would you discomfort the guests of your master?"

He glanced back reassuringly and met Edith's flushed, delighted countenance. "Verily," he observed to the muttering Afghan, "this young *mem*-sahib has no fear of a wetting or a storm."

Edith laughed as the carriage swayed and rattled onward, happy in the rush of air, exhilarated by the challenge of the wind. Dust eddied around them, and the poplar trees that lined the road turned their pale leaves restlessly at the breath of the storm. In a few moments the temperature dropped many degrees.

As the first heavy drops of rain fell, they swept under the trees that almost covered one of the outer avenues of Srinagar, in the growing darkness. Lightning flashes dazzled them, while a peal of thunder brought a quick response from the apprehensive Miss Rand.

Just as the thunderstorm broke, the carriage jerked to a halt. Rawul Singh sprang down and led the two women up a steep flight of steps in a grassy slope. With the orderly almost carrying her aunt, and Edith running ahead, they gained the shelter of a wide veranda as the rain pelted down.

A white figure strode down to meet them, and the girl was assisted up the veranda steps, breathing quickly with the effort of the climb. In the darkness of the house a voice spoke close to her ear.

"You have come to the garden in a storm. Perhaps the gods are angry."

Edith almost cried out in surprise. A glimmer of lightning showed her the dark countenance of Edouard Monsey. Blackness closed in on them again. A curtain of rain descended upon the bungalow, and the road became a mass of mud. Edith heard her aunt stumble on the porch.

For an instant she wondered whether they had come to Monseys quarters instead of the major's. Monsey wore an undefinable air of ownership. She shivered slightly, chilled by the sudden cold. By now the full force of the thunderstorm had swept upon them. The mat blinds rattled with the impact of the wind gusts. Lightning flickered incessantly, revealing the Afghan, water dripping from his beard, staggering up with their hand luggage.

A spattering of drops that was almost a spray ran along the porch, and Rawul Singh led them inside, lighting lamps that trembled in the air currents.

"Is this the house of Major Fraser-Carnie?" Edith asked Rawul Singh quickly, drawing away from Monsey, and arranging her disordered hat. "Aren't we going to a hotel?"

The orderly glanced at her curiously, and Monsey replied. The major was detained at the cantonment, settling some affairs of the natives. Fraser-Carnie had arranged to take up his quarters at the Residency, and they were to have full possession of the bungalow—Fraser-Carnie's bungalow. There was no good hotel, he explained.

Monsey turned to go and in so doing spoke to Edith.

"You have not forgotten your promise?"

She shook her head and watched him depart, somewhat surprised that he should go during the storm and without waiting for the arrival of the major.

The shower had passed over Srinagar; the level sunlight shone on a freshened vista of poplars and the water-stained wooden bungalows of the European colony when Fraser-Carnie appeared to pay his respects.

Major Alfred Fraser-Carnie was ruddy and gray-haired. He was good-natured, in a heavy kind of way, and not talkative until aroused to the proper point. Well past middle age, he still made a presentable figure on a horse.

Moreover, he did not shun an occasional sally into the polo fields of the northern stations to keep himself fit. A surgeon, attached to a cavalry regiment, he had labored conscientiously at his profession, a labor increased by his own hobby—gathering material on the tribal customs and environment of Central Asia. For many years he had been looked upon as a total loss by marriageable ladies of the cantonments, who spoke vaguely— as if by way of excuse—of an early attachment which the major had been unable to forget.

He greeted Catherine Rand with unaffected heartiness, mentioning his remembrance of former visits to Louisville, and took Edith's hand in his, looking long into her face.

Edith was the first to finish dressing for dinner, and tripped downstairs to find the major. Now that the storm had ceased a ruddy light was flooding the house, and the blinds and mats had been flung open. In a near-by compartment she heard the servants moving about, setting the table.

On the threshold of the room she paused with a quick breath of surprise. Framed against one of the French windows opening into the veranda she saw the figure of a tall native that was unmistakably familiar.

The man had been bending over some objects on the window seat, and now he straightened, casting a startled glance over his shoulder. In the brilliant light she could see the scar that ran from eye to cheek quite plainly. It was the native of Baramula, the watcher at the gate, as she had christened him whimsically.

With a leap he cleared the window seat and disappeared out on the porch, as a great, shaggy mountain sheep might vanish from sight of a hunter.

"What in the world!" thought Edith, because it was quite clear that the man had no right to be in the house. Going directly to the open window she looked out on the lawn, but saw nothing more of the uncouth visitor.

Having assured herself of this, she glanced down, wondering what the native could have been doing in the room. A thief, perhaps, she thought. Yet his bearing had been more bold than furtive, and certainly he had tried to take nothing with him in his flight.

Quickly she glanced around the room, with a woman's keen eye for details in a strange house. She saw neat disorder. Trophies—fine heads of mountain sheep and elk—hung from the walls. Twin collections, European and native, of weapons were ranged systematically on either side of the stone fireplace in which a blaze crackled cheerily.

Comfortable wicker chairs, bookshelves filled with much-used volumes, green cotton curtains—all this was quite homelike.

On the window seat under her eyes stood a bamboo box filled with a varied assortment of objects: some stained clothing, a tarnished telescope, a notebook carefully tied up, and a volume of poetry. On the clothing was pinned a slip of paper.

"Belongings of Donovan Khan," she read.

The two words did not seem to fit; the "khan" did not match with "Donovan." Beyond this there was nothing unusual in box or contents. Edith, perceiving this, felt a trifle embarrassed, as if she had been spying unwittingly on another person.

Probably, she reflected, the big native was a servant of the place—one who was not allowed in the front portion of the house. Edith, unfamiliar with the customs of the people of Srinagar, did not wish to play the part of a busybody. It was quite a trivial thing, she thought. And she said nothing at dinner that evening to the major about the scarred native.

Once when Fraser-Carnie's eye traveled to the box she fancied that he smiled.

"I have a duty to perform. Miss Rand," he observed. "A mutual acquaintance, Whittaker by name, a very talkative chap you know, has written me. His stories are quite a religion with him and he complains that you did not believe one of his yarns." He glanced quizzically from the attentive girl to her aunt. "About the man who was missing from Kashgar, and all that. It's quite true. There is his outfit, in that box."

He nodded at the bamboo chest on the window seat.

"Then, his name was Donovan Khan?" Edith asked.

"Quite so, to be sure. Donovan Khan."

Edith was interested. For the first time she felt the reality of the odd story Whittaker had told. At the Château she had hardly thought of it as true—until Monsey had chimed in. Monsey ? She frowned.

And then she drew a startled breath. Whittaker had said that the native who had been leading the caravan at Kashgar, the one who had killed Jain Ali Beg, had been blind in one eye.

It had just occurred to Edith that the big native who visited the drawing-room that evening had not seen her until long after she had seen him. Then he had turned clear around to look at her. There had been a scar, running from his mouth to his eye—the eye that must be blind.

"Edith, my dear," her aunt was staring through her lorgnette, "you are not ill, are you?"

She shook her head, laughing. "Only excited, Auntie."

Major Fraser-Carnie had said that the Kashmiris were harmless as kittens and quite all right. Edith told herself that she was a silly goose. There must be more than one native in Central Asia who wore gray sheepskins and was blind in one eye. For all she knew there might be hundreds.

CHAPTER IV

THE SELLER OF RUGS

"Once a Tartar emperor made it the heart of his kingdom, dust and ruins now. Then the tidal wave of the Osmanli Turk swept over it, and that, too, is gone. After that a Czar and his Cossacks reached out hands, greedy hands for it. *Pouf!* The wind of Asia, the ghost wind—*tengeri buran* the beggars in the hills say—that wind blew, and now the Czar is hoist with a petard and his soldiers are either dead or farmers, my dear Miss Rand."

Fraser-Carnie reined in his horse to point with his riding crop up at the overhanging vastness of the Himalayas. Underneath the forests of the foothills—rising green shoulders, buttresses of the Titan masses above them—Srinagar, the City of the Sun, looked very tiny indeed. And compared with the great peaks that loomed behind the foothills, Switzerland itself, thought Edith, was a toylike place.

Edith's eyes were somber. She threw back her head upon her strong, white throat, looking up at the statuesque boles of the pines that were scarcely smaller than the redwoods of California. She sniffed the pungent fragrance of the *deodars*.

"It *is* a garden, after all!" she cried.

Fraser-Carnie glanced at her appreciatively. He relished their rides together. Edith was a horsewoman born, and the major liked that.

"Kashmir is the garden," he murmured. "Up there it's rather a wilderness, I fear. The law of the white man no longer holds good. Since the War, the tribes are their own masters. What poet said, 'Fate has turned a leaf in the book you and I cannot read'?" He paused to light a cigarette and tossed the match away moodily. "Up yonder, somewhere, Donovan Khan dropped out of sight."

Edith was still gazing at the snow peaks. They fascinated her. There seemed to be no life in them. They loomed against the hard blue of the sky like bulwarks of Jotunheim. What was beyond them?

"I thought at first," Edith smiled whimsically at her own fancy, "that Edouard Monsey might be Donovan Khan. He was so interested in Mr. Whittaker's story. I just wondered, because I like to play at dreaming."

"Dream, by all means, dear child. After all, is it not the stuff our life is made of? Eh, what? Monsey, though, is scarcely the Khan." He eyed her appraisingly. "Curious thing, about a year ago Donovan Khan himself dropped in at my diggings up Gilghit way for the night. He claimed he was looking for some one at Sreenugg'r. I've seldom met a man I liked more. The politicos were furious when I didn't arrest him or some such thing."

"Why?" Edith was surprised. She felt very much out of touch with all that was happening in this place. It was so different from the world in which she had lived and moved.

"Why? Well, all of India would have thanked me for delivering Donovan Khan to the army. Five years ago, just when the War began, Donovan Khan took himself off from here, to go hunting, he said. Since then we've heard of him occasionally amomg the tribes. Periodically he seems to vanish. He knew the tribes as no other man in India did—"

The major broke off, to puff vigorously at his cigarette.

"Jain Ali Beg who went West said to me more than once that Donovan Khan, his master, had the aspect of one who hunted, although he never killed game except for the pot. Also that riders came from the hill villages—men of a race strange to Jain Ali Beg—to follow Donovan Khan; and there was much fighting. There would be."

"It's all so strange," thought Edith aloud.

"Riddles? Not altogether"—again the officer checked himself. "The Viceroy doesn't let us tell everything we hear. But this man was up to something, on his own. Up yonder, you know. He gathered power to himself, and his followers named him Khan—at any rate, until that caravan called for him at Kashgar. It looks to me as if the hillmen had sent a funeral cortege for him."

He spoke half jestingly, but Edith caught the thoughtfulness that underlay his words. Her brow wrinkled as she remembered the letter addressed to Monsey that she had seen at the Château.

A falcon. A search in the City of the Sun—Srinagar. Sheer nonsense, unless it was code. What had Fraser-Carnie said that reminded her of it? Something about searching—she could not place it.

"Have you," she asked, "a servant with a mark on his face under one eye? He frightened me once."

Fraser-Carnie glanced at her strong, young figure, erect in the saddle, at her friendly, gray eyes. "I hardly fancy you are easily frightened, my dear Miss Rand. By Jove! If you *should* see a big hillman with a face like a dog, blind in one eye, tell me. He's a murderer, you know. The Maharaja—ruler of Kashmir—has a sense of justice. Which reminds me that I am taking you to the Maharaja's ball, in two days."

The Maharaja was giving the ball to the members of the British Residency and Fraser-Carnie was among those invited. Monsey would be there. And she had promised a dance—

"Speaking of your admirers," grumbled the major, "here comes one now, unless I am mistaken. The Russian chap, Monsey."

Edith turned in her saddle and saw Monsey cantering after them, well mounted and well dressed as he always was. Fraser-Carnie looked at her quizzically.

"I owe him," she confided quickly, almost defensively, "a debt."

"Then, my dear young lady, pay it"—her companion spoke sharply—"and wipe the slate clean."

"Why?" she whispered under the beat of the nearing hoofs.

But the major was silent and greeted Monsey with a curt nod. As if by general consent the three quickened their pace, the two men taciturn, the girl smiling. It was clear to her that Fraser-Carnie did not like Monsey. She wondered why.

And then, abruptly, her horse shied. Edith, clever horsewoman that she was, had him under control in a moment and looked to see the cause of the animal's fright.

At the roadside lay an ugly sight, the half-decayed body of a sheep from which a half dozen wide-winged, bald-headed birds had soared up at their approach, startling the horses.

"What are they?" Edith asked, nodding at the carrion birds that were circling now overhead, waiting for their departure. There was something foul and evil in their slow movements.

"Vultures," responded the major briefly. But the girl barely heard. She had seen Monsey's eyes widen and his lips twitch.

"Birds of prey of the basest sort," repeated Fraser-Carnie and this time he, too, glanced at Monsey.

"Are they called falcons sometimes?" She turned to the major.

"Rather not. Falcons, my dear young lady, are a sort of hunting bird, used by the natives hereabouts, especially in the north. An old custom, you know, favored by the hill chiefs."

* * * *

At the door of the bungalow Fraser-Carnie made his adieus, saying that work claimed him at his quarters. Monsey, however, lingered. Miss Rand, Edith learned from the boy who took their horses, was out. Monsey accompanied her up the porch steps. Here Edith halted, stifling an involuntary exclamation of surprise.

In the shadows of the veranda a white figure rose before her. It salaamed respectfully and revealed itself as a turbaned Mussulman.

"O, will the mistress of the house see what her servant brings?" the figure said in fair English. "I am Iskander, seller of rugs."

Edith seized this pretext to avoid being alone with Monsey and ordered Iskander to bring his wares to the upper porch. As she passed through the drawing-room she could not resist stealing a glance at the window seat where the box containing the belongings of Donovan stood. She saw her companion follow her gaze and eye the box inquiringly.

Iskander, rejoicing in the favor of the white woman, lost no time in showing his goods. Rugs of every species from Persian to Chinese and rare silk objects were spread on the floor of the veranda as if by magic.

The Russian, who plainly had something on his mind, seemed determined to outstay the merchant; but when Edith purchased a small rug and began trying on the soft gray and blue Kashmiri shawls, he rose, knowing that the Mussulman would remain as long as there was a prospect of further sales. Edith, intent on her selection, nodded farewell. Monsey, however, took her hand and held it.

"I will claim," he whispered, "the promised dance. I will ask it, at the ball."

"Yes," she responded quietly, withdrawing her hand. Iskander glanced from one to the other with veiled curiosity.

"In the garden of the palace I will show you the beauty of our paradise," he smiled, and was gone.

She listened to his departing footsteps, as he strode down the stairs to the floor below and out on the lower porch. When he had disappeared under the trees, Iskander rose from where he had been squatting on the floor.

Edith, trying a fabric of the finest Kashmir wool on her slender shoulders, felt the Mussulman draw nearer. Iskander towered over her. His servile attitude had been flung from him like a discarded cloak as he stretched out a lean hand toward her swiftly. She was surprised to see the costliness of his white silk vest sewn with pearls and the jewels that gleamed under the dark throat.

A strange merchant, she thought fleetingly. Then she saw that Iskander had stooped over the scattered rugs—again a soft-tongued barterer of his wares.

For the first time she noted that Rawul Singh stood in the doorway. He spoke authoritatively to Iskander. The merchant departed with many compliments and effusive thanks, wishing her the happiness of pleasurable dreams.

A moment later when Edith descended to the drawing-room to look for a book she found that the box containing the belongings of Donovan Khan was no longer in its place. Rawul Singh said that no one of the household had removed it.

The girl thought of Iskander who might have conveyed the box from the bungalow wrapped in some of his rugs. Still, it did not seem reasonable that the seller of rugs would have stolen such a valueless thing when articles of silver plate and the collection of weapons had been left untouched.

Had Major Fraser-Carnie sent for the box? Rawul Singh said not, adding that the house servants, though of insignificant worth, were faithful to their salt. They would not steal.

Somewhat worried, Edith asked the orderly to report the incident to his master. It was a trifling matter—one of those details that vex because they defy explanation.

And the worthy Miss Catherine Rand was still more vexed the next day when she decided she had a headache and sought her cherished medicine pail for a remedy. None was forthcoming: the pail and its medicines had disappeared from her room.

Convinced that some native maffia had designs upon herself and Edith—who had just left for a boating tour with Monsey on the lagoon of Srinagar—Catherine Rand dispatched a house boy for the major, requisitioning her three words of Hindustani for the occasion.

"The *burra sahib*, you stupids! *Ghee!* And the boy, notwithstanding her request for clarified butter *(ghee)*, read the mind of the *mem*-sahib with the intuition peculiar to Orientals and brought Fraser-Carnie posthaste.

The major questioned his servants briefly and turned to RawalSingh, speaking in Kashmiri.

"So, the hillman, blind in one eye, has been seen near the bungalow again even while you were seeking him in the bazaar."

The orderly bent his head.

"Then, sahib, I have blundered. Yet, who can separate one sheaf of grain from many, or one drop of water from a stream ? It is in my mind that he is a caravaneer of an upland caravan that has been seen within a few days near Gilghit. More I know not."

"Then give over the search to the native police, and whenever I am not with the young *mem*-sahib do you accompany her. Her safety I give you as a duty. This is understood?"

Rawul Singh salaamed. Hereafter, should any harm fall to the lot of Edith Rand, the Garhwali, corporal in the Siwalik Rifles, would be as a man without honor.

That night after Edith had retired to her room she could hear the orderly pacing the veranda. She did not go to sleep at once. Her aunt had kept her up late discussing the matter of the missing medicine chest.

The memory of the native with the scar stooping over the kit of John Donovan was strong upon her. The major had called him a caravaneer, and a caravan had taken Donovan Khan away. To the hills.

The events of the day had tired her; the continued absence of her father filled her with misgivings. Monsey had proposed to her on the lagoon; and as he spoke, her dislike of the man had grown upon her, as at Quebec.

He had said that he loved her, needed her. Her refusal seemed to affect him strongly. His savage anger at her words had aroused Edith's rebellious spirit.

Drowsily Edith smiled at her own musing and fell into a troubled sleep. Vivid dreams thronged in upon her.

Visions of the splendors of the carpets of Iskander ibn Tahir passed before her unconscious eyes. The white-garmented Arab salaamed to her, rising abruptly, after the manner of dreams, from the piles of his own goods. Then Iskander's swarthy face grew black—as black as the storm clouds that passed over the city of the hills.

The Arab seized her in an iron clasp. Edith had the tormenting sensation, familiar in a nightmare, of wanting to cry out and of being unable to utter a sound. Quite as a matter of course the veranda of the bungalow faded from her vision and the bare slopes of the Himalayan foothills took its place. The carpets of Iskander lay stretched before her, and each one seemed to be a shroud.

Edith, still held by the Arab's remorseless hand, stared at the carpets. Under them veiled forms lay motionless. She felt very helpless.

Then she saw the sharp face of Monsey, smiling at her in friendly fashion. Again, the girl tried to articulate—to tell him that she was held a captive above the carpets. In the queer fantasy of the dream, Monsey bowed politely and passed on, unheeding. Sheer terror gripped the girl, and she fell to weeping—not so much, she thought, on her own behalf as because of what lay under the carpets. She was very, very sorry for the things, whatever they were.

She could no longer see Iskander, although his hands still held her. But the face of the tall native of Baramula peered into hers. He spoke, and never had Edith felt such utter distress as at the sounds of his heavy words.

"These are no longer alive!"

And at the words, the man with the scar pointed to the forms covered by the rugs. Edith felt that in some manner he was kin to the passive figures. Then he stooped to raise one of the rugs with a gigantic hand, and Edith cried out frantically—

She was awake, her forehead moist, and her thin nightgown cold with perspiration. Huddled, the girl brushed back the damp hair from her brow and stared up into the blackness of her room.

The nightmare had been very real. She still heard the terrific words—so they seemed to her—of the strange native ringing in her ears. With a whimper of subsiding fear the girl cuddled down in her bed, listening to the stentorian breathing of the sleeping Miss Rand.

Awake in the dark, Edith was thankful to hear the quiet footsteps of Rawul Singh on the veranda below her, and to know that the orderly was keeping his nightly post.

CHAPTER V
ALAI BALA SLEEPS

It had rained and ceased raining that evening as it usually did in Srinagar. Mist, tinted flame color by the setting sun, was twining around the rocky base of Jyestharudra's pinnacle. The melancholy call of the boatmen in the *doongas* came over the water as Monsey drifted about, alone except for his paddler, on the lagoon.

Edith had left him in a black mood. He lay back on the cushions of the *doonga*, his powerful body tense, a cigarette half bitten through in his nervous lips. Overhead the panoply of sunset, spreading across the arch of the sky, reflected itself on the lagoon.

Boats moved slowly under the rickety bridges. Not without reason is Srinagar called the Venice of India. Distant spots of purple that were iris beds growing over graves winked down at the twilight city.

While Monsey meditated, the ragged Kashmiri boatman propelled his craft slowly toward the bazaar quarter with its yawning shop fronts, its raft of vessels crowding together, and its poppy-covered, tumbledown roofs.

"Where will the sahib go?" the man ventured at last, feeling the inner impulse of hunger.

"To purgatory, or Abbas Abad's," growled Monsey. "Take your choice."

A moment later the gondola drew up at a painted flight of steps. Glancing about the canal keenly, Monsey left the boat, tossing its proprietor a coin. Stepping forward with the assurance of one who knew the way, he entered a ramshackle wooden structure that had once been a bright pink but was now the hue of a very dirty and diseased carnation. Stooping under an openwork balcony he pressed onward in semidarkness rife with a pungent odor.

This smell came from a native woman lying huddled on some mats, puffing a spluttering opium pipe with a child at her breast Monsey kicked the woman aside, the movement drawing a wearied cry from the baby. To silence it, the Kashmiri placed the pipe at its lips. A single breath of the smoke and the child subsided into a drugged sleep.

Monsey ascended a dark flight of steps to an upper room lighted by a yellow hanging lamp and apparently without access to any fresh air. On a bundle of quilts in one corner the form of a girl was coiled—a satin-clad form with spangled, velvet bodice and flooding brown hair escaping under a cap of tarnished cloth of silver.

The pale olive countenance of the woman—a Georgian—was lax in sleep—it might well have been judged pretty otherwise. Circles were under the closed eyes, stained lips parted over fine teeth. An aroma of musk and rose scent exuded from her body. Mingled with the stale perfume was the stringent fragrance of a Turkish hubble-bubble, at which a man puffed. He glanced at Monsey casually, from half-closed eyes.

"*Nasha* or opium ?" he remarked.

"Neither," said Monsey curtly. They both spoke Turki. Apparently they were on familiar terms. The man's face was the hue of the girl's, only the skin was creased and pinched as if from exposure to hot winds. His heavy eyes were bloodshot; a red fez rested on straggling, curly black hair.

"As you please," he muttered. "What was your fate?"

Leaning back on the quilts, he eyed the gurgling water pipe. His dress had once been immaculate white duck, girded by a brilliant shawl belt. The open collar disclosed a round, muscular throat rising from a stout chest.

"An evil one. Abbas." Monsey sank upon the quilts and tossed away the burned stub of his cigarette savagely. The woman stirred, opened tired eyes, and hunched away from the men, to fall into her disturbed sleep. "I played my cards and they lost. I tell you, they lost."

"I hear. It is fate. Did you think the beautiful *Americain khanum* would want you for a husband?"

"Why not?" Monsey scowled. "Other women have loved me—and they were better than this—"

He looked at the drowsy woman sardonically. The Turkoman—he was actually an Alaman, a Russianized Mohammedan of the Turki race—shrugged powerful shoulders.

"I saw her passing in the boat, my friend. Nay, I believed not she would be a wife to you. Who was the native soldier?"

"Orderly to the British major—the son of a dog. He will not leave the woman."

"Therein he shows his wisdom." Abbas bared stained teeth. "So they do not trust you, despite your French manners and your patrician Russian birth? Eh?"

Monsey—perhaps the name had once been spelled otherwise—looked up coldly. His dark eyes were dangerous. "At least," he smiled, "I know my own birth. *I* am not a jackal, born in a gully."

Abbas Abad Mustieh'din exhaled the smoke from his lungs and his faded eyes blinked. *"Khei'leh khoûb, Effendi, khei'leh, khoûb!"* he murmured. ("Very well, my good master, very well!")

"Nor," continued Monsey ironically, "am I a monkey, clad in the garments of gentlefolk, my betters."

Willful and domineering, he was irritated at himself, at Edith Rand. The remarks of Abbas had added fuel to the fire. Like many men of narrow mind, the Russian lacked humor. He was not a man to swallow a jest lightly. With his faults, however, he was not lacking in courage. He faced the Alaman, smiling but watchful.

A dull red flooded into the seamed countenance of Abbas. The artificial pride, common to those who mimic the personality of their superiors, had been touched. One powerful hand clasped the turquoise-inlaid hilt of the dagger in his girdle.

Monsey dropped a hand into the pocket of his jacket and waited. The pocket bulged, and the bulge pointed toward Abbas. For a long moment the Alaman eyed his friend, the coat of his friend—under which he knew a serviceable revolver was turned toward him—then his brow cleared and he raised an empty hand, palm up.

"Bismillah! Why should I cut open your throat? I need you. You need me. But keep your tongue in your mouth, or one day it will be slit—thus!"

Monsey had relaxed his vigilance for an instant at the overture. The dagger of Abbas flashed out and passed across his companion's breast.

Monsey stared down grimly at his jacket. The cloth over his heart had been slit deftly, yet he had felt no prick on his skin.

Abbas replaced the knife in his girdle, grinning, well pleased with himself. He clapped the stem of the pipe to his lips and inhaled, slapping Monsey on the knee with his heavy palm.

"Eh—you have seen what you have seen. Be wise, oh, be wise. By the seven hells of purgatory, you are no fool. Or I—Abbas Abad—would not walk in your shadow. Come, my cherished gentleman. Hearken. Have you given up your lust for the girl? Are you willing to listen to the wisdom of Abbas, your friend? I, who sent you a letter clear across the ocean—I, who paid a scribe well to write your name and address in English. Would I have done that if I had not wanted you? The time is ripe for us to sell our merchandise. Aye, the markets of Samarkand and Kashgar will pay good prices for women. And for such a one as yonder *Americain*—"

"Bah—I tell you she is mine. Abbas, would you fly a falcon at a hare when a young deer is marked down?"

"Why not, my Excellency? We must eat. We have no money."

"Abbas, you are a fool. The American father is rich. He can pay—more than the price of six light-haired Georgian women at Stamboul." The Russian's dark eyes were calculating. "He would fill both your hands with gold pieces."

The Alaman grunted skeptically.

"What would it avail me, if my head were cut off? The days are past when we might garner white women openly for slaves." He shook his head. "Nay, I will take a serpent from its hole with my bare hand, but a white woman I will not touch. With my own ears I heard the cannon of the French warships battering the gates of Constantinople. The Protector of the Faithful is but a shadow and the cloak of Islam is rent asunder. I know, I know."

"All this," said Monsey impatiently, "is idle talk. Abbas, there is a place where the hand of the Englishman does not reach. You know, for you lay hid there many months."

"Above?" Abbas pointed upward and to the north.

"Aye—beyond the Hills. Once the Cossack posts were set there, like the links of a strong chain. Now, the chain is broken. The tribesman grazes his cattle over the ashes of camp fires. The priests of Islam chant their prayers unheard, save by true believers. You have seen that. Abbas!"

"It is true."

Monsey tapped his chin reflectively with lean fingers.

"No American consul is within a thousand miles. Do you think I am a child, wet with mother's milk, to want to make the American girl a slave to sell at a price? Not when I love her, as I do. Allah, and all his saints!—she is beautiful. I have been thinking."

The Alaman was silent, pondering. Monsey, who had been the link by which he sold the choicest of his women to be "servants" of the Russian officers on the border during a former régime, never spoke idly. The dissolute gentleman—once an officer himself—had profited much by Abbas. But the shrewd merchant was cautious lest the whims of his companion should involve him in needless trouble.

"Once beyond the Kashmir frontier, we would be safe, Abbas," muttered the white man, "Fraser-Carnie—a disciplined numskull—would not dare send any of his few men into the Hills—if, indeed, he could trace us. The Kashmir government would not bother its head. And we would return the woman—"

He shrugged.

"For a price," grinned Abbas. "Oh, undoubtedly we would."

"Rand would pay the price. He could. I tell you, I want the woman."

"For a time—yes. You tire of them quickly. As I have seen."

"Abbas, you are a thrice-born fool. Think you I would run such a risk ? Nay, my plan is otherwise."

"I heed. Excellency!"

"If we carry off the woman—you and I—there must be no accusation of brigandage. Am I a bazaar thief, or a lawless hill chief? I tell you, I will marry the American woman. I will find means to make her submit. A missionary can be found in Kashgar. By God, Abbas, do you think I would have risked my neck to come back here, if I had not seen her and wanted her at Quebec?"

The Alaman listened intently. For the first time he seemed to approve. "This is wisdom—perhaps," he grunted. "Speak!"

Monsey's expressive eyes glowed. After his fashion he loved Edith, and her curt dismissal of his suit had angered him. "After the marriage we can talk terms with the father. If he will not pay well for his daughter's freedom, he will pay to have her restored to him. I will see to that." He laughed and stretched his arms, good-humored again. "Abbas, my dog, luck is setting my way again. I shall do it."

"Who knows what is before him?" The Alaman shrugged. "There is much danger and also much profit at stake. Has your wisdom found a way to take the woman to the Hills?"

"Said I not my star was rising, O one-of-small-wit? To-morrow night is the ball of the Maharaja. I am bidden, because of"—he hesitated and his eyes darkened—"old ties. Well, it is our *kismet*. I shall dance with the woman. She has promised, and she will keep her word. The father has not yet arrived; the aunt is a fool. We will walk in the garden, she and I—"

Glancing around cautiously, he lowered his voice. Abbas bent his bearded head to listen. For several moments Monsey talked, gesturing vividly, his purpose strong upon him. An able man, strong-willed, he had gambled with the finer ties of life—rank—honor. Now his mind was twisted, his thoughts bent inward. Perhaps Abbas Abad was the better man of the two. He at least had not forsaken his heritage for a mess of pottage. He had never been otherwise than he was—a slave dealer, of Asia.

"This is wisdom," muttered the Alaman, "and our need is great. Yet the danger also is great."

"Abbas, my luck is good. I feel it. Come, we will try the dice of fate! This woman of yours has slept through our talk. She would not have wakened if I had slain you. We will hear what she has to say—"he touched the passive girl with his foot, then shook her by the shoulder. "Confound your opium, Abbas! Alai Bala!"

She stared up at him sleepily, too drowsy to rise. The Alaman looked on curiously.

"Alai Bala!" commanded Monsey, "hearken! Your master and I are of two minds. Shall we abide in this hole or ride to the Hills?"

The girl seemed not to comprehend. She shook her head slightly.

"Speak, my pretty parrakeet," purred Abbas. "Come, my gentle dove, my jewel of jewels, my priceless pearl of beauty! You have heard, O offal of the bazaars, harlot—scum of paradise, my saintly *houri*—"

"The Hills," murmured Alai Bala wearily. "This is an evil place: let us ride to the Hills—"

She sank at once into her interrupted slumber, her *kohl*-stained face pallid, and her breathing laboring from tormented lungs. Monsey nodded agreeaby.

"My luck holds."

Abbas glanced up shrewdly. "You would have let her decide, *effendi!*"

Monsey turned away. "Certainly—as I said."

He disappeared down the stairs. His footsteps died away and the room was silent except for the gurgle of Abbas' pipe. Presently the shrill cry of the sick child sounded from below. It ceased, and Alai Bala twisted uneasily in her sleep.

Abbas looked from her to his pipe. The murmur of the chanting boatmen came to his ears, mingled with another chant.

"Allah il akbar," came the murmur. "Allah, the Great. There is no god but Allah—"

It was the hour of sunset prayer.

CHAPTER VI
THE GARDEN

Edith had never been quite so happy as the night of the Maharaja's ball Major Fraser-Carnie had announced that Arthur Rand was near Srinagar—the mail tonga had come in a few hours ago and its driver brought the tidings.

Relieved and excited at the news, the girl had donned the gown that was her father's favorite, the blue-gray ball dress she had worn at Quebec. The pleasure of the coming occasion added its glow to her cheeks and her eyes sparkled.

"Ripping! Oh, I say, you're absolutely splendiferous, and—all that, you know." Fraser-Carnie, who had blossomed forth in dress uniform, added his compliments to the purring approval of her aunt, at the carriage. Rawul Singh strutted behind his beautiful charge, supremely unconscious of the envy of the other house servants.

Edith smiled at the major joyously as the carriage rolled forward between the poplar avenues, following a line of European carriages of visiting native potentates.

> *Sultan after sultan with his pomp*
> *Abode his destined hour and went his way—*

Miss Rand murmured the quotation.

"Quite so." The surgeon's ruddy face reflected a shade of anxiety. Almost to himself he quoted another couplet, but Edith's quick ear caught the words:

> *The Sultan rises and the dark Ferrash*
> *Strikes—and prepares it for another guest*

The flush of evening lay again upon Srinagar; the sky was flaming from the gateway of the departing sun. Mists were gathering in the hollows and creeping together along the plain, as if tenuous spirit hands were gripping each other.

The mists half concealed a caravan of animals winding along a path outside the city. Edith could see only the heads of horses and the cloaked forms of riders. It was as if beasts and men were swimming in a gray sea in the evening calm.

Like an echo from another world, she heard the faint sound of tinkling bells wafted from the caravan—the *hoa-hoa* of drivers. A hooded wagon rumbled in the mist. Barely could the girl see the moving shapes, so swiftly did the wings of evening fall.

She wondered briefly if the cavalcade included the tonga of her father. Then she reflected that he would approach Srinagar from another quarter. She looked up. Her aunt had neither seen nor heard the caravan.

Edith glanced back at the path in the mist. The riders and horses were almost invisible. Dimly the hood of the *ekka*[1] moved along jerkily. Then her own carriage swerved into a drive, and the Afghan servant and Rawul Singh shouted as they almost collided with a vehicle coming from the other direction.

Through the garden the bulk of the sprawling, ill-designed palace confronted them. Edith was claimed joyously at the entrance by her new friends, the young subalterns. Fraser-Carnie expostulated good-naturedly and they all laughed.

Whole-heartedly, she threw herself into the tide of the evening. Dances were begged and allotted; Fraser-Carnie insisted on the first waltz—although reminded by his brother officers that he had not danced in public for half a decade. Edith was presented briefly to her host—a sallow-faced, smiling little man in evening clothes that did not quite fit.

"It's so good of you," whispered the girl, "to do all this."

She gave the officer's hand a quick pat, and he glowed. He managed the maneuvers of the waltz much as he would the evolutions of dress parade. Edith, however, was too much interested in the spectacle of the native dignitaries, the watching British matrons, the active junior officers, to care.

Her eager eyes danced as they took in the vista of the moving throng on the polished floor, the arched corridors decorated with immense festoons of acacias and honeysuckle, the great divans where hill chiefs in native dress sat painfully erect with their retinues behind them. She hummed lightly in the air of the orchestra—a favorite British cavalry quickstep.

"It's glorious," she exclaimed. "I do hope Daddy comes in time."

Major Fraser-Carnie halted precisely at the end of the music, his ruddy face a shade redder and perspiration on his bald forehead. He bowed.

"Your wish. Miss Rand," he observed, "is my pleasure to fulfill. I go to make inquiries—"

Time passed. Partners came and went—to return again. Edith had not seen Monsey yet. A young subaltern escorted her to a balcony overlooking the garden of roses where the dark surface of a round lake glimmered faintly.

Perching on the stone railing, a scarf flung over the flimsy ball gown, she stared out at the sentinel-like trees rising against the sky. It was chilly and a fresh wind was lifting the branches of the trees below her, setting the tiny globes of the lanterns to dancing.

---

1   Two-wheeled native cart

The last thing Edith wanted was to be left alone. She listened sympathetically while the young subaltern described the miraculous floating gardens of Akbar, the pleasure palace of the dead emperors. She liked the witchery of the darkening garden, she liked the subaltern, and the music—

"My dance, I believe. Miss Rand."

At the first strains of the music beginning anew, Monsey had appeared behind them. Instinctively Edith yearned to restrain her former partner who now bowed, preparing to leave. Then she rose quietly. After all, she had promised.

So she walked back to the ballroom, her hand on Monsey's arm. It would soon be over. Then she could enjoy the evening.

Monsey had placed his arm lightly on her waist, and she swayed to the rhythm of the music, when a voice spoke at her side.

"*Mem*-sahib, pardon!"

Edith turned inquiringly, to see Rawul Singh stiffly at attention. Monsey wheeled on the Garhwali, his lean face dark.

"It is the order of the major-sahib," Rawal Singh bowed apologetically. "He has sent a message."

Monsey would have spoken angrily, but the girl was before him. The appearance of the orderly made her heart leap. "My father—he is here?"

Rawul Singh shook his head.

"This is the message, my *mem*-sahib. The major begs the *mem*-sahib to come to the bungalow. There your father waits. He has come in a tonga, and he asks for you."

Placidly, the orderly met the glance of Monsey. Both men waited for the response of the girl. Edith had a swift impulse of alarm. Why had not the major and Arthur Rand come to the palace? Why had they delayed in summoning her? And why had not Fraser-Carnie come for her in person?

The uncertainty passed quickly. Her father was tired after the journey. He had never cared for entertainments. Fraser-Carnie had remained at the bungalow to keep his guest company until she should come. That was it.

"My father is well?"

Anxious to be reassured, she asked the question of Rawul Singh, forgetting that the orderly had not left the palace.

"*Mem*-sahib, I do not know. I have not seen him."

Of course! She ran to where she had left her scarf and snatched it up, anxious only to be gone. There was no reason for her to be alarmed on behalf of Arthur Rand. But, womanlike, she wanted to assure herself of that at once. She did not even wait to speak to her aunt.

It was a slight matter. But this eagerness of Edith to see her father, and her failure to tell Miss Rand, had in reality an important bearing on what followed. With the scarf in her possession, she was turning back from the balcony when Monsey confronted her.

"Your promise?" he inquired evenly. "You must finish your dance with me. Rawul Singh can wait."

Edith met his glance fairly.

"It will be over in a minute," he urged, "and I will take you to the bungalow in my carriage." She hesitated, and he resumed impatiently, "Rawul Singh can accompany us—if you wish."

"But my father is waiting, Mr. Monsey."

"And I have waited. Since—Quebec."

Monsey's hand stretched out for the scarf. The girl drew it closer over her bare shoulders.

"You will not deny me the dance ?"

"Yes—for the present."

"Then I will escort you to the bungalow." Swiftly, he shifted his ground. "Surely you will not refuse that, Miss Rand?"

His words were ironical, challenging. But Edith lifted her head purposefully. "My father has sent for me, Mr. Monsey—"

"And you—"

"I am going to the bungalow—with Rawul Singh."

He drew back, his dark eyes gleaming. Edith passed from the room, followed by the orderly. At the stairs she glanced back. Monsey was no longer to be seen.

She would not wait for Rawul Singh to find the carriage and bring it to the main entrance. Instead she accompanied the orderly out upon the drive, where groups of native servants and drivers stood about lanterns. A puff of wind smote at the bushes beside the road, chilling the girl who had come without sufficient covering.

"Hurry, Rawul Singh," she urged, "find the carriage."

He ran ahead shouting among the idlers. She pressed after, not wishing to lose sight of him. They were nearing the outbuildings where the palace stables were located. Figures of natives gave back respectfully at her approach. She heard voices, in the darkness, almost drowned by the rising wind.

A lantern, held by a bearded Kashmiri, flashed in her face. She could no longer make out the form of the orderly, and paused, uncertain. The rumble of wheels sounded in front of her.

Two horses trotted out of the gloom. The lantern flickered away from the girl, not before she had seen the bulk of a wagon and the white tunic of its driver.

Then powerful hands grasped her from behind. She was lifted bodily from the ground. A deep voice grunted a command, at her ear.

Other hands groped for her from above. Startled, the girl cried out. "Rawul Singh!" And again: "Rawul Singh!"

There was no answer. The wind had ceased abruptly, and the night was still. Edith felt herself drawn into the vehicle. She struggled, knowing that this could not be the Fraser-Carnie carriage. A hand, rough and odorous, pressed over her mouth, and she was laid swiftly on some yielding substance.

Again the voice spoke angrily. A whip flapped. Edith was conscious that the wagon lurched forward, gathering speed. She heard the beat of hoofs, and struggled again, violently, in the hands that held her.

The cart shook from side to side. Edith was dumbly surprised that it should be so dark—until she heard tree branches brush over a covering of some kind, near her head. Her blunted senses told her that she was held firmly, a man's powerful knee prisoning her legs.

By now the wagon must have attained swift headway. It jolted and bounced painfully.

Then, slowly, at first, came a scattered rustle an the roof of the vehicle. It increased to a rattle—grew deafening. A damp breath of air swept her face. Across her vision flashed a veiled gleam, followed by the rumble of thunder almost overhead.

The thunderstorm had broken.

CHAPTER VII
INTO THE UNKNOWN

Edith had been sole ruler of an American home and an American father. Now for the first time in her existence she was deprived of personal liberty.

During the long hours of a stormy night she was held captive in the racing cart. The man who sat beside her in the darkness under the hood only placed his hand upon her when she struggled. Edith could not see him— except as a vague, cloaked shape during the intermittent flashes of lightning that cast a lurid half-light into the cart.

Once she screamed vigorously. Only once, because a heavy wad of felt was thrust against her mouth and kept there. The girl could not loosen the grasp that held it, and the overpowering scent of grime and mutton tallow gradually nauseated her. Her dainty lips and teeth never had been so outraged before. When her head drooped and a despairing murmur escaped her, the felt was removed and the solitary guardian resumed his vigil.

Twice when the cart first started its journey she had tried to rise and spring out. She was by no means a weakling. An active and athletic life had made her muscles supple and firm. Each time, however, the watcher as if guessing her intent had pushed her back upon the cushions in spite of kicks, scratches, and vigorous blows against his bony face. Edith wondered if he were made of iron.

After the second attempt she lay quiet, panting and furious. At intervals the cart stopped briefly while voices sounded obscurely by the horses; chains jangled and horses neighed near by. Then they went forward at a faster pace. Edith guessed that fresh horses had been harnessed to the *ekka*—the native cart.

Plainly, they were traveling swiftly. But in what direction she could not know. Had there been a mistake? She felt not. The men in the cart must have seen her face by lantern light before they seized her.

Was Monsey responsible for the whole thing? She thought he was capable of it. Who else would dare to lay hand on her? For a fleeting moment she considered the native visitors at the palace, even the raja. But it did not seem reasonable that they would try to abduct her—especially at the palace.

Where was Rawul Singh? Why had he not answered her? She dismissed the suspicion that the message delivered by the Garhwali had been a pretext to make her leave the ball. Rawul Singh was faithful, and he must have been near her when she had been carried off. Why had he made no effort to help her?

It was impossible for her to understand yet that she was leaving her father. Major Fraser-Carnie, and Aunt Kate.

Every sense, however, told the girl that the hooded cart was pelting through the rain-driven night at a reckless pace. Its sway and lurch shook her roughly, dulling her perceptions. She found it almost impossible to think. A blanket was wrapped around her shoulders. Until then she had not noticed that she was shivering. "I'm so thirsty," she murmured petulantly.

A figure on the driver's seat stirred. There was a movement, a gurgle of liquid, and a cup was thrust against her lips.

Edith tasted its contents suspiciously. Then she took the cup and drank. It was good water, rather musty. "Some more," she commanded.

She had emptied the cup a second time before she reflected that some one in the cart must understand English. Edith sat up and looked over her shoulder, hugging the blanket to her.

"Who are you?"

Like the glimmer of a will-o'-the-wisp, the lightning flickered, revealing two huddled shadows on the driver's seat. They had not moved at the question. Her voice rose angrily, almost hysterically.

"Take me back to the major-sahib—at once. You must take me to Srinagar! You must—"

A lump rose in her throat. Edith began to cry, overmastered by sheer helplessness.

By degrees the rain ceased. A fresh, cold wind sprang up, shaking the hood of the *ekka*. The thunder had rolled away, like some sportive, muttering giant betaking himself to distant skies. The blackness around Edith changed to a somber gray. She could make out the cloaked form of her guard, a massive bulk wrapped in sheepskin. She sat up, peering at him.

The scarred face of the native of Baramula met her eyes.

Dawn flooded the interior of the hood suddenly. Edith could hear the twittering of birds near by. And the cart jolted to a halt, while the heavy breathing of spent horses reached her ears.

A voice close at hand was repeating unknown words monotonously, sonorously. The girl stirred her numbed limbs and climbed stiffly forward upon the empty driver's seat.

She looked out upon a verdant mountain slope. The level light of new day revealed towering mountain peaks snow-capped. A flock of sheep were feeding about a broken-down hut that looked for all the world like a *chalet* of Switzerland. Steaming horses hung their heads over a muddy road that was more like a trail. Beside the road two small carpets were placed and on them turbaned figures raised lean arms. The driver and his companion were praying. It was this prayer Edith had heard.

The taller of the two men rose to his feet, and, seeing her watching, salaamed.

"Iskander!" she cried.

The seller of rugs inclined his head respectfully; his elegant attire seemed none the worse for the bad night. "Good-morning, *khanum*," he said quietly. Edith stared at him. She wondered if she looked as disordered as she felt. She was trying to read his face, but found the task singularly difficult.

"Madame will have her breakfast," observed Iskander in his excellent English. The girl saw that the other native—a withered satyr of a man— was building a fire. Edith was hungry. The smell of boiling coffee attacked her with a vital pang. Thus, she resolved to breakfast before speaking her mind to Iskander.

Heated *chupatties*, fruit and coffee refreshed her. Her chin rose a notch and she summoned Iskander with purposeful calm. Her gray eyes were coldly alight The storm was about to break.

"I have you to thank for the cup of water—last night?" she observed.

Iskander bowed.

"Then," she went on, "you heard me call to you. Why did you not turn back at once to Srinagar?"

Again the Arab bent his head. His aristocratic features were inscrutable.

"I regret," he said, "it could not be."

"You will do it now—at once!"

The gray eyes were tempestuous, the beautiful face flushed. Not many women could have passed through such a night and looked as attractive as

Edith Rand. The discreet gaze of the Mohammedan seemed to suggest as much.

"I am sorry," he responded politely, almost absently.

Edith flared into angry scorn. She stormed, threatened, abused. She warned Iskander that Major Fraser-Carnie would most certainly avenge the insult to her. The Arab's dark face was blank under the lash of words. Edith checked herself—suddenly, realizing that she was making no progress.

"My father will shoot you for this, Iskander," she said slowly.

The man's brown eyes sought hers curiously.

"A life already has been spent," his voice was stern.

The girl caught her breath, wondering what he meant. Abruptly Iskander stepped from her view and the powerful native climbed back into the cart. A lurch, and the ekka started again upon its course—away from Srinagar.

Throughout tormented hours of a long day Edith was jolted ceaselessly upon the floor of the cart. She lay passive, white-lipped. Resolutely she fought off weariness, determined not to sleep.

It was evening when the cart at last halted again. Edith was weak with hunger and fatigue. Iskander's bearded face peered in at her keenly and the Arab gathered her up bodily in his arms. When she pushed away from him and gained her feet on the ground, he spoke gently.

"Madame must have a bath. Then dinner will be served."

Bewildered by the ordeal of the day and night, Edith saw that she was being led to a small, whitewashed *dak* bungalow. It was evening and she could barely make out her surroundings; but in a neat room stood a tin tub filled with warm water. Iskander pointed to a pile of clothing on a chair.

"It would be well to change," he suggested respectfully. "The night in the upper Hills will be cold, very cold. We cannot stay here."

With that he left her, closing the door after him. Edith's woman soul yearned for the tub, but she was resentfully unwilling to bathe. She took up the clothing and was surprised to see a stout walking suit of her own, with shoes and woolen stockings. Her tam-o'-shanter was there, as well as a linen waist.

Edith appreciated the advantage of changing from the flimsy ball gown to a serviceable attire. Feeling utterly weary, she even indulged in a hasty wash—and donned the other suit.

Iskander smiled approval when he saw her changed dress. He did up the discarded gown skillfully and announced that dinner waited in the main room of the bungalow. Food and the warmth of a fire at her back brought irresistible drowsiness. Reaction claimed her at last. As she stared at the white figure of the Arab, it seemed to grow until it filled the room. Iskander's eyes peered into hers.

"You will sleep, madame," she heard him saying. The outlines of the room faded. She felt herself slipping into a comfortable void, deliciously restful.

"You will not need opium—tonight," Iskander was murmuring. Edith lifted her head in an effort to shake off the overpowering drowsiness. And the Arab again picked her up in his lean arms, carrying her out into the cold night air to the waiting cart.

Powerless, the girl subsided on the cushions, pillowing her head on her arm. Again the native tucked the blanket about her, and once more she felt the familiar shaking of the *ekka*. Edith tried desperately to collect her thoughts.

The last thing she had seen was—she was certain—the medicine pail of her aunt, as it was placed beside her in the cart.

Surely she had been mistaken. She almost laughed at the thought. Poor Aunt Kate without her medicines! Why, she would be positively ill if they were not returned to her. She must speak to Iskander about it Then he would go back…back…

She slept.

It was long before she wakened. Dimly she was conscious of daylight and the monotonous rumble of wheels. Edith asked for water sleepily. Instead, a cup of cold coffee was presented to her lips. Strong coffee, she thought, for it tasted bitter and made her head swim. Swiftly, without effort, she slipped off again into stupor.

Vague impressions crowded in on her. Always the cart raced forward. She saw the scarred face biding over her—heard the musical voice of Iskander. Once she looked out into a sea of mist She was very cold…

Another time the cart was standing still in what seemed a red inferno. Demoniac forms peered at her from the walls of the inferno. Her lungs labored for air. Edith hid her face, not knowing that she was in a valley walled with red sandstone from which the glare of the sun was reflected from rock pinnacles and grotesque shapes carved by the erosion of water throughout innumerable years.

She did not know that she was passing through a lofty altitude where breathing was difficult, and that the snow peaks she had once seen from a distance were close overhead—

Iskander understood well the uses of narcotics, and was aware that sleep alone would retain the strength of the woman through the continuous stages of a racking journey.

When Edith climbed at last from the *ekka*, assisted by Iskander, she saw that the cart was drawn up beside the kneeling forms of a long line of camels. Near the shaggy beasts stood natives staring at her. In the hand of one she recognized the familiar black medicine pail.

"So it wasn't a dream after all," she thought. "Poor Aunt Kate. She will have to do without her medicine pail!"

CHAPTER VIII
EVENTS OF A DAY

Methodically Major Fraser-Carnie arranged the papers on his desk and glanced from the distressed countenance of Miss Catherine Rand to the handsome features of Monsey and the grim, bearded face of the Afghan driver of his own phaëton. The American woman and the Russian were seated in front of him; the native stood at attention by the door.

For once the worthy major's ruddy cheeriness was replaced by a keen and somber gravity. He had his report to make to his superior officer, and— he was very fond of Edith Rand.

Miss Rand sat very erect in the canvas-backed camp chair. Double misfortune had descended upon her within the space of a few hours.

"I *did* see her for a moment in the ballroom, Major. Edith was standing with Mr. Monsey, Then Rawul Singh came up and spoke to them. At that moment the dancing began again."

Almost absently Fraser-Carnie nodded. Miss Rand closed her thin lips severely, feeling that she had been snubbed. She demanded that Fraser-Carnie go at once to the Maharaja and request that a search be made for her niece. And she threatened to wire the American consul somewhere in India—she did not know where.

Fraser-Carnie answered her quietly, aware that she had been under a strain.

"My dear Miss Rand, the raja is quite ignorant of the disappearance of your niece. I can assure you of that. The servants at the carriage entrance did not see Miss Edith leave the palace. But those at a side entrance opening into the drive did see her. She went very quickly along the roadway, following Rawul Singh."

Monsey leaned forward.

"Your pardon. Major. Why do you not question the orderly?"

For an instant Fraser-Carnie glanced at the man who had interrupted him, then continued calmly.

"That was just before the storm broke. A Kashmiri horse boy gives evidence that a two-wheeled vehicle left the drive at that time, going at a round pace. The boy swears it was a covered, native cart, without a lantern. Several men were in it. I have had—ah—inquiries made among the guests of that evening. No one claims knowledge of the cart."

"Rather, no one admits it, Major," put in Monsey smilingly. "Now what does Rawul Singh say?"

He spoke lightly, as one entirely disinterested in the proceedings. Major Fraser-Carnie folded the paper he had been scanning and met the other's stare fairly.

"Rawul Singh was found dead in the rhododendron bushes beside the carriage drive at the palace at dawn," he responded.

"Oh!"

Miss Catherine Rand had recourse to the salts. Monsey looked interested.

"You connect the death of your orderly with the disappearance of Miss Rand?"

Fraser-Carnie smiled, a trifle wearily. He had been up all night with a patient at the bungalow.

"Rawul Singh had his orders—not to leave Miss Rand. He would obey orders, you know."

"Yes, he would do that." Monsey's voice was uncertain, as if he were thinking quickly. "May I ask—how he died?"

"Stabbed in the back, and his throat slashed. Quite clearly he was attacked in the road, for we found blood stains there. These led us to look for the body in the bushes. It was thoroughly wet, having been exposed to the rain during the night, so the murder must have taken place during the time of the ball." The officer took up his pen. "Dhar Beg!"

The figure of the Afghan stiffened.

"Did Rawul Singh come to you among the carriages last night?"

"Sahib, he did not come." Dhar Beg was the son of chiefs and he had been a noncommissioned officer in a native regiment. Wherefore, his words were prompt and to the point.

"You did not see him seeking the carriage?"

"Nay. A storm was arising, and I was leading the horses to a covered place. Sahib, I thought Rawul Singh called to me once. I did not answer, being busy with the beasts. But, later, I went to see if he had called and I did not see him. There was much confusion because of the coming storm."

"Know you aught of this cart?" Fraser-Carnie and Dhar Beg were conversing in Hindustani.

"A cart—nay." Dhar Beg plucked at his beard shrewdly. "But a carriage passed before my sight, rolling swiftly."

"What carriage?"

"The same, sahib, that nearly ran us down, owing to the thrice-cursed arrogance of its driver, when we first entered the palace grounds. I knew the horses."

"Do you know the owner of the carriage?"

Before the Afghan could answer, Monsey, who had followed the conversation, broke in. "It was mine, I believe."

"Ah. But you were not in it?"

"You have heard my testimony."

Monsey was quite at his ease now. He had come to the quarters of Major Fraser-Carnie fully understanding that he must answer for his whereabouts the evening before. And he had made it clear that he had not left the palace until some two hours after Edith Rand had been seen with him. What was more to the point, his story was verified by certain native dignitaries and British officers whose word was better than a bond.

Well aware of the hostility of Fraser-Carnie, reticent though the Briton was, Monsey enjoyed his advantage; his alibi was complete. Perhaps for this reason he insisted on making his testimony as formal as possible—as if he had been charged with complicity in the matter of Edith Rand.

"Then," inquired Fraser-Carnie, ignoring the other's tone, "who was in your phaëton?"

For just an instant the black eyes of the Russian flickered. Whereupon the Afghan drew a deep breath and glanced at his master.

"The driver, my friend, Fraser-Carnie," responded Monsey carefully. "I had sent for the carriage to escort Miss Rand back to the bungalow. Unfortunately,"—he shrugged—"she chose to go with Rawul Singh."

Dhar Beg waited until the speaker bad finished, then let out pent breath.

"Sahib," he addressed the major, "the carriage came not to the palace entrance but went swiftly from the stables out the gate."

"After the two-wheeled cart had passed out."

"As the sahib has said."

Fraser-Carnie glanced inquiringly at Monsey.

"You said the phaëton called for you at the drive entrance?"

"I did not enter it. Because Miss Rand—she had gone." Just a trifle, Monsey's slight accent thickened. "So, I dismissed the driver."

"Who returned to the stables?"

Monsey was quick of thought. At the card table he seldom hesitated. Nor did he hesitate now.

"Yes, *monsieur*—I believe the chap drove around the drive, however, to arrive at the stables."

Fraser-Carnie glanced at Dhar Beg. It was not an easy matter to give the lie to a white man; but an Afghan has principles of his own and he generally lacks fear.

"Sahib, with my eyes I saw the carriage roll from the palace gateway and it did not come back."

This time the major nodded slightly. By long experience he knew when Dhar Beg was telling the truth. All that he had learned, however, was that the carriage had left the palace grounds shortly after the cart. Monsey rose.

"My dear fellow," he observed idly, "am I answerable for the route followed by that scoundrel who is my driver? Was I or was I not at the palace during the whole of the evening?"

At this Miss Rand announced that she must return to the bungalow. Fraser-Carnie ushered her to the door and commanded Dhar Beg to escort her. Then he swung around on his remaining visitor, gnawing at his white mustache.

"Monsey!" His full voice rang out sharply. "Where was your friend Abbas Abad last night?"

The Russian stared, and the skin of his face darkened.

"Abbas Abad? The Alaman drug seller of the bazaar? Why do you call him my friend?"

"On the testimony of Rawul Singh."

"Really?" A hard smile crept across Monsey's thin lips. "I fancy your orderly was mistaken." To himself he muttered: *"Les absents ont toujours tort!"*

"Was Abbas at the palace last night?"

"Dear Major, where was your watchdog? I do not follow the nightly prowling of the scum of the bazaar."

The British officer paced the narrow confines of his quarters, glaring at the more nimble-witted man, much as a caged lion glares at its keeper.

"I think you do, sometimes," he admitted frankly, "when there's a chance of money in pocket."

Monsey's hand twitched toward his coat and his smile was wiped out on the instant. But he had broken the gentleman's code so often that he could well afford to overlook one other insult. Besides, he realized that he held the whip hand. Fraser-Carnie was helpless to accuse him of any wrongdoing. Nor could any blame be affixed to Abbas. So he smiled, although his eyes blinked.

"Each to his taste, my dear chap. You Englishmen have a saying—'Trade follows the flag.' *Voilà!*" He lowered his voice earnestly. "Fraser-Carnie, you cannot afford to offend me. Have a care what you say. Remember this: I did not kill your orderly nor did I abduct Miss Rand. But, through this man Abbas I believe I can trace her—perhaps. Do not forget that."

"Ah. You can find her?"

"I do not know—but—I will see. If you have—patience—I will make inquiries, now."

He bowed to the steady-eyed Briton. "Is the inquisition over—the *concours* at an end? Yes? Then I have your leave to depart."

"By all means," growled the officer.

CHAPTER IX

ABBAS ARRANGES

In the roadway without Monsey gritted his teeth and spat heartily.

"Idiot! Donkey with ears a yard long! *Cochon! Canaille!* Oh, what a fool. By all the saints and the ninety-nine holy names of Allah: his brain is transparent as the monocle in his eye!"

Thus muttering he strode to the canal bank and hailed a passing gondola. Making sure, without appearing to do so, that he was not followed, he directed the paddler to the bazaar quarter.

Monsey did not go to the house where Abbas sold his poisons, but landed at the silk shop of a Bokharan Jew. Pushing impatiently through a splendid rug hung as a curtain, he confronted the squatting proprietor who was deep in talk with Abbas Abad. The Alaman had buttoned the open flaps of his dirty drill suit and boasted a new pair of English boots, but he lolled over the spluttering water pipe, very much at his ease. Like the Turkish dignitaries he sought to ape, he was solidly fleshed and eager to gratify his senses; unlike the average Turk, he was active in the brain cells, energetic when it was necessary, and possessed of unusual strength in his massive figure.

Monsey dismissed the Bokharan with a jerk of the head, and took the precaution to stand near the curtain until he was satisfied that no one lingered on the other side.

"What luck?" he demanded of Abbas.

The Alaman grinned, picking at yellow teeth.

"Patience, my Excellency. Am I not a splendid man-of-business? By Allah, I am!" He slapped his girdle until it chinked. "Gold, silver. I would take no paper bank notes. We have enough—"

"For a good outfit—good horses, guides, and followers?"

Abbas nodded complacently.

"Am I not Abbas Abad, who once made a fortune out of nothing in Khokand and Baku? Nay, my own men will guide us."

"How many? Are they well armed?"

"Is a beetle ever without his shell? Eh? They are as many as the fingers of two hands, less one—Sarts, godless thieves—one or two Tartars, dogs without wit but hardy—a cousin of mine who would rip up his grandfather for a silver ring. These will suffice until we reach Kashgar."

"And this Bokharan advanced funds?" Monsey nodded toward the curtain behind which their host had disappeared.

Again Abbas patted his girdle.

"*Khosh!* I persuaded him, and he gave a letter to his uncle in Kashgar who will aid us—with more money. There we will have many friends, of other days."

"All this without security. Abbas?"

"Aye, Timan is generous."

"Look here!" Monsey scowled at his companion. "If you are lying, I'll stretch your hide over the doorpost of Yakka Arik."

"Excellency mine, would I embark upon a journey where I did not smell a profit at the end? Would I have slain the rat of a Garhwali if I were not in earnest?"

"That was a blunder!"

"Now, by the prophet's beard," growled the Alaman, "how was I to know that the woman would be whisked away from under my eyes while I was attending to the affair of the dog of a Rawul Singh? Eh? I have not the eyes of a cat, so I did not see the cart drive up."

Monsey shrugged his shoulders.

"You blundered. I brought you to the palace in my carriage, so that you might seize this woman. You saw the girl and the soldier outside, in the roadway; you were a fool to slay the man before seeking Miss Rand."

"Ah-h-h." Abbas Abad grinned. "Shall I, who am no man's fool, take a wolf cub from under the teeth of a grown wolf before striking down the stronger one? The Garhwali was active and swift as a snake."

"But you saw the woman put into the cart?"

"Aye."

"And the cart was that hired by Iskander ibn Tahir in the relay station?"

"Aye. likewise—for my ears are keen—I heard the Arab shout to his men." Abbas Abad paused to spit, then nodded with great self-approval. "Monsey, my friend, verily your luck is good. For lo—the woman is taken, and not by us. Now we have but to take her from those who hold her"—he laughed gleefully—"and Iskander, that dog of a desertman, he is a fox that I can trail. *Maili barlik!* (Everything is prosperous!)"

He leaned forward to slap the leg of his companion.

"Monsey, *effendi*, in your carriage I followed the *ekka* without the gate, through the lanes of this accursed city, and up into the northern road to the first relay of horses. By the winged horse of Afrasiab, they went swiftly. Come, in the name of Allah, we must lose no time. All is ready. Oh, I have not been idle. I and you, also, know whither that fox of an Iskander will run to earth. By riding certain sheep paths, we can overtake them."

"And then—"

"The Arab will have but one or two men and the woman will encumber them. O Most Generous and Most Wise, have you forgotten that in the uplands we have a mighty following who will come at our summons? That, and a little gold, of course. When I sent the *firman* to the *effendi*, I sent also a little whisper to these, our allies of the uplands, where there is no law save that of strength. Now they await our coming. They know where the fairest women of the Sayak village or the Kirghiz hamlets are to be found, and where they may be sold at the highest price. Aye, with the *Americain khanum*—"

"My wife. I tell you, I will marry her, and then sell her back to her father, who will be fool enough to take her."

Abbas nodded readily.

"The wisdom of Iskander was no greater than that of the *effendi*. Aye, by pretending to seek for the woman on behalf of the British pig—for a little price, to lull his suspicions—we will cause him to wait here idly."

Attentively, Monsey had followed the complacent words of the Alaman. Now he checked Abbas.

"Will you take Alai Bala?"

"Nay." The Alaman took up the stem of his hubble-bubble. "She abides here."

"I could make a place for her in our party—she rides well."

"Nay," said Abbas sullenly, "those sons of many jackals, my men, would not respect her." He fancied that Monsey found the Georgian attractive.

"Well, then, where will you leave her?"

"With Timan, the Bokharan. He will keep her."

Monsey frowned irritably. It was significant of the relations between the two that the Alaman was obdurate in trifles, whereas he recognized the superior leadership of the Russian in weightier matters.

"So long as you are certain you can overtake Iskander at Kashgar—well and good. We will leave before sunset."

"*Effendi* mine, my men can trail a marmot through hell. They know the hills yonder as a Tartar knows his sheep."

"But first," murmured Monsey, "I shall visit the American father. Abbas, these American fathers have nothing but their children in their hearts and their purse strings are open to the touch. Be ready with the horses in an hour and take heed that the British major sees you not."

"Nay, the eyes of the man are closed, now that Rawul Singh is dead—"

But Monsey had stridden from the curtained chamber. Abbas Abad yawned and stretched, binding his girdle more tightly about his stout body.

"*Sa'at*," he murmured, "it is the hour of commencement. Eh, but that Russian milor' has wits—little else he has, but wit—yess! He is not one to sleep when the dogs are a-prowl, by Allah, no. He is useful. Ohé—Alai Bala! My parrakeet, my soft pigeon. Have you forgotten the voice of your friend and father?"

He stepped into an arched hallway leading into the rear of the shop. At a curtained recess he paused prudently. Timan was a Bokharan, and the rooms beyond were those of his women. Even though the two were firm friends-which was the case—it would have been a mortal offense for the visitor to enter the space beyond the curtain where the women lived. To speak as he did was daring enough. Abbas heard Timan curse in his beard, and grinned softly.

"Alai Bala," he called, "be kind to your new master. He is a righteous man. Verily, an honorable man. Abide here and think not of the hills and pathways of the uplands."

Leaning forward, he listened shrewdly. He heard a half-sob, then the growl of a man's voice in an angry whisper. The whimper of Alai Bala came to him faintly.

"…you swore…we were mounting to ride to the hills… I would ride to the hills and the valleys of Khorassan…"

"Kaba-dar" (have care), grumbled the heavy voice of Timan.

"Dance lightly for Timan, my delightful pigeon," added Abbas. "Bathe in musk for his pleasure and scorn not the kohl. O weep not, for I said to Timan that you were a rose of beauty. But now we go—the effendi and I—to take another rose." He muttered to himself as he slipped away from the curtain: "May you cost the Bokharan a pretty penny for your opium—that he suspects not. However, a bargain is a bargain." Whereupon he slapped his girdle and listened to the chink of coins, well pleased with himself and the world.

He had been paid a good price for the woman. That price he would double in his claim upon Monsey for the money spent on their journey, and he would get a half of the profit from the blackmail received from Rand.

So Abbas Abad was well content. Not so very often had he been able to kill two birds with one stone and pluck the feathers of both in this fashion.

"Maili barlik," he repeated.

* * * *

"Missing?" Arthur Rand was in bed with a high fever in his room at Fraser-Carnie's bungalow, but he rose on an unsteady elbow. "Edith is missing from Srinagar and I wasn't told?"

Monsey glanced around warily. He had taken some pains to find the American alone; he feared that the others's high voice might attract attention.

"Your daughter was carried off by some natives at the Maharaja's ball last night. Fraser-Carnie's orderly was supposed to be with her. I have had some dealings with a—trader of the bazaar, Mr. Rand. I believe he can trace Edith—"

Abruptly the American sat up, his face flushed and his mouth drawn into a hard line.

"Mr. Monsey, I have heard you call yourself a friend of my daughter. Yet you sit here and talk, while natives no better than negroes—negroes—make away with Edith! Damnation!"

At this Monsey stiffened in disagreeable surprise. He had not counted on the hot anger of the Southerner.

"Indeed, sir," he hesitated and then smiled, "to organize pursuit of these bandits it is necessary to bribe and bribe well, also to get together horses and men. Unfortunately, I have no ready funds. So I was forced to come to you."

"Money," the American repeated slowly. "How—how much will you need?"

"Perhaps four hundred pounds. Better, six hundred." Monsey was weighing his man in the balance, shrewdly.

"Three thousand dollars. Confund this fever! Mr. Monsey, if I could straddle a horse I'd light off after those scoundrels with my gun in my hand. Why, I've paid three thousand dollars for a single race horse in my time."

He stretched out a trembling hand. "You don't know, Monsey. I—I've had news from home. I am bankrupt."

Lying back on the pillow he pressed his hand against his eyes. "A year ago I could have borrowed ten times three thousand dollars on my word alone. But—I reckon they'd want security now, and I have none. Fraser-Carnie—no, if he has not sent after Edith, I cannot ask it from him."

Monsey's eyes hardened. The cards were not falling as he supposed. Rand could not pay blackmail or ransom. "I wouldn't go to Fraser-Carnie," he suggested quickly. "But perhaps I can manage—"

To be sure, he reasoned, blackmail was not to be thought of now. But—there was Edith. Was it not his luck that had taken the girl beyond the borders of civilization, where a man could keep what he could take?

"Perhaps I can borrow among my—my friends here, Mr. Rand. Of course in time you will be able to foot the bills. Your assurance—"

"Anything, anything!" cried the Southerner, a new eagerness in his feverish voice. "Pay a ransom if you must. I will make it good."

Monsey smiled fleetingly. Good! He would have this to hold over Rand. Meanwhile he would find Edith. She would be his.

Monsey's memory dwelt hotly on the girl's delicate, friendly face, on her warm charm of manner—little tricks of personality that carried intimate fascination—and, most of all, her pride. After all, fate had been kind to him.

CHAPTER X
CONCERNING A YASHMAK

"Whither?"

That was the question Edith Rand asked herself ceaselessly, and there was no answer. More than two weeks had passed, she calculated, since her abduction. Her first long sleep and the spell of unconsciousness that followed had confused her count of the days.

She had asked Iskander the question, and he had replied:

"To one who waits."

That was all. But Edith, watching keenly, had noticed two things: this caravan, the one that had come to meet her, was not an ordinary caravan; and it traveled in haste.

Moving upward along rocky defiles that skirted the glacier slopes of the mountains where the route was marked along by ibex horns upright in the snow and by an occasional native shrine adorned with fluttering rags, they had met at times other caravans.

Always the other caravan had made a detour into screening timber, or down into blind gorges. More than once the girl was sure she had seen native shepherds fleeing away from them.

Again, a leper beggar sitting at the roadside had groveled in the dust when he sighted the brown men of the caravan.

Puzzling the matter, her quick eyes had noticed certain differences existing between her caravan and the others, seen at a distance. While the approaching strings of camels kept to the majestic, supercilious gait of the loaded Bactrian animal, hers pressed onward swiftly; while the others were conducted invariably by a patient, plodding Mongol, hers was led by Iskander on his active horse; the others enjoyed a raucous escort of mongrel dogs; no dogs followed Iskander's beasts, nor were there any bells to give out a rusty *clang-cling*.

There was something methodical in the speed with which the camels and the wiry, brown-skinned men passed over the waste of the Himalayas, heads down against the winds that buffeted them, drawing their gray woolen garments closer when the sudden hailstorms burst from an angry sky.

They were fearless, but fear was written in the faces of those who saw them pass.

"It's so pitiless," she had murmured to herself—wonderingly.

Iskander, sitting his peaked saddle with centaurlike grace, seldom glanced behind. Often she searched the back-trail down the gorges below which lay the City of the Sun, and her heart sank when she saw that they were not followed.

She hated Iskander.

In the soft-mannered Arab she recognized the personality that played the part of her master. To be sure, it was Iskander's attentive care that kept Edith so well. He seemed to understand her needs without being told. Her food he inspected carefully; every night he saw to the erecting of her stout felt tent, braced on willow poles, the earth beneath it covered with splendid rugs and *numdahs*. A clean mattress had somehow been procured for her use, and the blankets were of the softest Kashmir wool. Always, men went ahead to pitch the tent and light therein a fire among stones skillfully arranged—a fire that had rid itself of smoke and subsided to comfortable embers by the time she arrived at the camp site.

Edith knew, that while she slept, Aravang—the big man with the scar— or Iskander himself watched before the entrance of her shelter. By now it was clear to her that Iskander and the others intended no immediate harm to her. In fact, the girl had never feared them. Raised as she had been in an environment of total safety and comfort, it was inconceivable to her that these men should molest a white woman.

To Edith Rand they appeared as unruly servants who had rebelled against their mistress—except for Iskander. Aravang was a hideous sort of watchdog, more her slave than guardian.

"So, *kapra wallah*," she had ventured after long pondering, "you are not even a merchant, a seller of cloth—but a slave, to Monsey."

It was a bold stroke. Experience had taught Edith that the Arab was most outspoken when angered; her own pride goaded her to anger him. Her scorn was by no means a trivial thing, and more than once she had fancied that the inscrutable Iskander had writhed mentally under the lash of her words.

Now he had urged his horse to her camel's side—a horse never willingly approaches a camel—and Edith had found time to admire the splendid ability with which the man handled the beast.

"No! God forbid!" he had scowled. "I am as my father and his father before him—a soldier."

By this Edith was reasonably sure that Monsey had had no hand in her abduction. At his ease, the liquid-tongued Oriental baffled her; provoked, Iskander was an open book to the quick-witted girl.

If not Monsey—who? Who was the one that awaited her? Iskander? Hardly. In spite of his boast she felt that the Arab was the agent of another man. Once, when she had overslept—the exertion in the high altitude always made her intensely drowsy from sunset to sunrise—he had upbraided her vehemently through the tent.

"Are you a sultan's favorite, to linger in this manner? By the honor of Tahir—uprise and haste! On the sword of my fathers have I sworn that

I would bring you, in time. We are late—late. If we are too late you shall know sorrow."

It was the inborn arrogance of the Mohammedan, who is monarch of his womenfolk, breaking through the studied courtesy with which Iskander had sought to ease her journey. And it stirred a thrill of revolt in Edith's breast. She had remained where she was, lying in the blankets.

Iskander's will matched her own. He had ordered Aravang to take down the tent and to pack it; then to remove her outer garments from her side.

Edith had watched this, dangerously quiet.

"Now," he had said calmly, "you will clothe yourself in garments of my choosing. If you refuse, you will ride as you are—tied to a camel's humps. Decide!"

The girl had stood up, in petticoat and underclothing, her long hair whipping about her in the wind and the sun beating against her flushed face. Iskander studied her with the measured glance of the Oriental philosopher who reads a woman's beauty as a priest reads an open book.

"Coward!" she had gasped. "Boor! Thug!"

She had stamped her stockinged foot and Iskander's dark face became a mask of stifled vindictiveness. The word "thug" in India has a meaning deeper than in our language and symbolizes something below human caste. It acted upon the Arab as acid upon water.

He had thrust the apparel he held about her bare shoulders. "Are you without shame, woman? Have I read you wrongly?"

She saw that he had given her a cloak with a hood to cover her hair— also a woman's veil for the lower portion of her face.

Edith had promptly torn off the offending articles. She had never seen the usually emotionless Arab so aroused. Fiery oaths fairly flew from his twisted lips, and his black eyes snapped furiously.

"Once you were a European *madame*," he observed, "Now, you are otherwise. You will obey me, and I command that you shall be robed in decency—thus. In the path we follow a woman covers her face—thus."

Whereupon Edith tossed the veil into the dying camp fire.

"And I will not—thus!"

With tightly clenched hands and rigid lips she faced Iskander, whose lean face darkened with anger. In his hand he held a knotted whip. At once he lifted the whip. Edith's eyes blazed. She did not shrink back, but looked full into the Arab's eyes. For a long second her gaze challenged him hotly, but his eyes did not soften.

Then came Aravang between them. The big native spoke vehemently to Iskander, gesturing much with powerful hands. He seemed to be arguing something feelingly.

The Arab lowered his whip and swung away, to spring into the saddle of his horse. At this, Aravang held out the cloak and hood to Edith, signifying by dumb show that she should put them on. His dark, oxlike eyes wheedled her mutely. He looked so ridiculously unlike a lady's maid that Edith smiled and put on the garment. For the time being the question of the veil was ignored. But, later, Edith donned the Mohammedan *yashmak* of her own accord.

For a while she wondered at the necessity of the cloak. Being quick of thought, however, she did not fail to see that Iskander wished to disguise her.

So it was to escape prying eyes as the caravan flitted among the defiles— no longer ascending, as she noticed—that Iskander had given her the cloak! Then either one of two things had happened: they were pursued, at last; or they were approaching some point where Edith might be observed and her presence might provoke curiosity.

Drowsily Edith wondered whether she herself had not changed in aspect; the life of the caravan had become her life. She wore the cloak quite naturally.

She was always sleepy. If it had not been for her bodily strength, bred of an active outdoor life, the girl would have sickened and, perhaps, have died before this. Cold head winds, the swaying motion of the clumsy beast, the inevitable smells—one by one these things had stripped the softness of life's luxury from the girl.

From day to day she had dreamed, in a kind of stupor, of her other life, of the warmth and tranquil friendship of Louisville. Momentarily she had expected to awaken to see her servants about her—but only the brown faces of the caravaneers met her eyes, and she shrank from the camel and the rough food.

In this coma of fatigue the girl's innate vitality had come to her aid. Her cheeks became firmer, her eyes brighter. The mocking illusions receded— thanks to the constant care of Iskander.

One day she observed a box strapped on the side of the camel in front of her. She knew that box. It was the one containing the kit of Donovan Khan.

"Iskander," she smiled, "are you a thief as well as a—thug?"

The seller of rugs looked up warningly. He saw a rosy face, brown-tinted by sun and wind, turned toward him under shadow of the burnoose hood—a face rare as the wine-inspired art of a Persian painter. So he looked away. The woman was unveiled and she was not for him.

"That box," challenged his prisoner. "You took it from the house of Major Fraser-Carnie."

"Yess, *khanum*—madame."

"Why?"

No answer. Long ago Edith had discovered the uselessness of asking direct questions. Dissimulation is second nature to the Orient. So she probed for information as a skilled fisherman casts a light trout fly.

"And you stole the medicines of the *mem*-sahib, my aunt. So, you are no soldier, but a thief!"

Inwardly she was wondering what the seller of rugs could want with two such articles as the box of John Donovan and the medicines of Catherine Rand. If she knew this she would know something of Iskander's purpose—

"Yess, *khanum*, we took them, Aravang and I. But it was not stealing. It is the word of God that a thief must eat the dirt of his dishonor." He nodded reflectively. The seller of rugs was in a philosophical mood that afternoon and his philosophy was a trenchant thing. "We took them because we could not buy them—in Srinagar or elsewhere. Likewise—and it is different as day is from dark—we took them not for ourselves but for another."

"Who?"

No answer, except an indulgent smile. Edith had committed a second breach of Moslem manners—the question direct.

"The medicines are for you to use."

For her use! The girl wondered at first whether the remedies of her aunt had been purloined against possible sickness on her part. Yet she was conscious of a deeper meaning in the man's words. The Arab expected that the time would come when she herself would have use for the medicines. Either that or she must administer the remedies to another person.

"As for the other box," the scion of Tahir resumed, "before our coming to the City of the Sun it was stolen by a faithless servant. Yess, Jain Ali Beg tasted the punishment he had stored up for himself—Aravang saw to it. We are carrying the box to him who owned it, before Jain Ali Beg stole it. Am I, then, a thief?"

"Why, perhaps not."

Here Edith had her first insight into a curious code of ethics—a code that was not her own, but one that was ancient as the hills under which they were passing. The son of Tahir might regret stooping to theft. His righteousness, however, was satisfied. And his pride. Certain things—and they were many—Iskander would have died rather than do.

Like the girl, he had an unyielding pride. Edith hated him cordially, yet with a good deal of respect. His unfathomable fatalism depressed her.

"Donovan Khan," she said. "You are going to take the box to him?"

For a long moment Iskander's brown eyes sought her gravely.

"What is written is written. And who can read what will come to pass?"

"A white man?"

"Once. Now—who knows?"

"You mean that Donovan may be dead?"

"It is all in the hand of God." The Arab swept a wide-sleeved arm against the infinite blue of the sky. "Dono-van Khan is like to the eagle that flies from mountain crag to tree top. Who will know when he is dead? Sometimes is he called *khalga timur*—the iron body—and sometimes—"

"The Falcon?"

Iskander almost started. His words had recalled to Edith the message received by Monsey in Quebec—*the Falcon has taken wing*. Her response had been intuitive. Why were men—certain white men—termed eagles or falcons, in the Himalayas? It was absurd.

Monsey's letter had said that the Falcon was searching Srinagar. For what? Fraser-Carnie had related that Donovan had been in the City of the Sun. A sudden thought caused her to catch her breath.

"Tell me, Iskander," she cried. "You took the medicines, because they could not be bought. Why did you take me?"

They were rounding the broad base of a pine-clad mountain—its summit invisible above vistas of barren cliffs, mist-shrouded. And above the mist stretched expanses of moraine.

As they came to a bend in the trail Edith saw some distance below and to the right the flat roofs of a town, looking for all the world like miniature clay blocks sprinkled in a sandy plain. Delicate minarets rose over the roofs: she could discern the sweep of a city wall.

Now, she had no means of knowing—for Iskander did not see fit to enlighten her—that they were rounding Mustagh-Ata, the "father of mountains," and were looking down on the roofs of Kashgar.

"You were beyond price," observed the Arab gravely. He seemed anxious to screen her view of the town, and presently the vista of the roofs was blotted out by clumps of dry tamarisks.

Edith leaned down and boldly caught his rein.

"You must answer," she insisted, hungry now for a crumb of assurance. "Is this friend of Fraser-Carnie, sahib—this Donovan Khan—dead? Did he not ride after a caravan of—of spirits?"

Iskander laughed, baring white teeth.

"Eh, I was in that caravan. And these"—he indicated the tired camels and the gnomelike natives—"also. This is the caravan that came for Dono-van Khan. Now," he gathered up his reins, "it is time to halt."

Whereupon he trotted away to view the site selected for that evening's camp. Edith gazed after him hopelessly. So she was part of the caravan that had mystified beholders in the hills! Fraser-Carnie had said that Donovan Khan was a power in the hills. Was he master or slave of the caravan? Where was he? Was he alive or dead?

At all events, she reflected, Iskander and Aravang were assuredly living men. And the camels and other natives were alive. But what had the Arab meant when he said that they might be too late?

And why did the caravan hasten so—flitting among the defiles of the silent mountains?

All at once she felt very lonely, very much disturbed. It was a misty evening, but the sun did not flame on the rolling clouds as at Srinagar. She had the fleeting illusion of having stood on the mountain slope before.

Immediately, as if it had been waiting for just this moment, a sinister fancy gripped the mind of the girl. This was the mountain slope of the dream—kthat night in the Srinagar bungalow!

It fastened upon her vividly—she recalled the implacable grip of Iskander, the hidden forms lying on the ground under the carpets, and the terrific voice that had cried, "These are no longer alive."

And here before her was Iskander with his carpets.

Edith shivered, cramped and numbed by the long day's ride. Yet the evening was far from chilly. Waves of heat emanated from the plain of sand below. The twilight air was hazy; somewhere behind the great mountain she knew that the sun was setting in a red ball of flame.

Bravely she tried to throw off the deep impression of the dream as she approached the tents and the vague shapes of the natives moving about through the smoke of fresh fires. She thought of the hidden bodies of the dream. Then a startling thing came to her. Iskander, many days ago, had said:

"A life already has been spent."

Then another voice, this time not an echo of memory, came to her ears.

"Missy *khanum*. O, missy *khanum!*"

Startled, the girl turned her head. No men of the caravan, as she knew, were behind her—merely the two led camels carrying food, tied nose to tail with her own. And the native on the camel in front of her had neither spoken nor looked around. Plainly he had not heard the low words.

Some twenty yards away in the sand on the slope below the caravan track was a thicket of stunted tamarisks. The branches of the nearer bushes had been carefully parted and she saw a native gazing at her and beckoning. It was not one of the followers of Iskander.

Seeing that he was noticed the newcomer put finger to lips and held back the bush further so that Edith could see a white horse, saddled and bridled but without a rider. The man of the tamarisks pointed to the horse and to her.

"Missy *khanum* (young lady mistress), you come—come queek, bime-by, yess!"

He was a stout, powerful fellow in a dirty white suit with soiled crimson sash and a red fez. Grinning, he released his hold on the tamarisk which flew back into place, concealing him.

Edith saw that the native in front of her had moved his head idly, not quite certain whether he had heard anything or not. She sat her camel rigidly, her pulse pounding, and breathed a sigh of relief as the caravaneer ahead of her, seeing nothing untoward in the tamarisk clump, turned back to the more interesting spectacle of the camp fire and its heating pot of meat—now near at hand.

She bit her lip from sheer excitement. Friends were near at hand! The native who had signaled to her must have been sent by Major Fraser-Carnie or her father. They had managed to outstrip the caravan to the city that lay under the base of the mountain. The man and the horse had been waiting in concealment for her coming.

Stiffly the girl clambered down from the camel after it had knelt. Every member of the caravan was busied setting up the tents or unloading the beasts. Aravang was making up her own bed. Iskander she saw beyond the camp engaged, after his custom, in evening devotions at the sunset hour. That she was watched she knew; but she had long been free to rove around the camps, and the tamarisk clump was not more than a hundred yards distant.

The depression caused by Iskander's speech and the memory of her own dream made the unexpected prospect of liberty all the more alluring. It did not occur to Edith to hesitate, now that rescue seemed at hand. Who could have sent the man with the white horse, except her friends?

Walking to the fire, she picked up an empty water jar and looked around, as if seeking the well that experience had taught her must be near the site of the camp. As carelessly as her rigid limbs permitted, she moved slowly in the direction of the tamarisk grove.

A horse, and a real city near at hand! She wanted to fling away the jar and run. Instead, the girl paused to glance back at the tents. Aravang, shading his eyes against the sunset glow, was watching her. As she looked he beckoned imperatively. Edith measured the distance to the yearned-for thicket and decided that she was halfway to her goal. Whereupon, drawing a deep breath she dropped the jar in the sand and ran, blessing her short walking skirt.

Aravang's shout reached her ears, without inducing her to look around. Gone was the stiffness she had suffered on descending from the camel—gone, her customary quiet. Edith fairly flew over the sand to the tamarisks and darted in among them.

A hand reached out and grasped her arm. She was drawn toward the waiting horse by the native and assisted bodily in her leap into the saddle.

The horse reared, but Edith—expert horsewoman as she was—had the reins in hand in a second. The man pulled the beast's head about, and pointed down a gully hidden by the scrub and leading away from the camp.

"Kashgar!" he cried. "You go queek as hell—yess!" He slapped the horse on a hind quarter and Edith started down the gully at a swift trot. She saw the native turn and dive into the thicket on the further side of the gully.

CHAPTER XI
EDITH RIDES ALONE

In the varied collection of guidebooks and tourist schedules in the possession of Miss Catherine Rand there had been one pamphlet that described briefly the location, climate, picturesqueness, points of interest, population, and means of travel of the mountain city of Kashgar.

Four kingdoms, said the guidebook in florid phrases, met at the center of the Himalayas. But the makers of maps hesitated over the Himalayas. They were a no man's land. Only in Kashgaria did the slovenly, quilted, musket-bearing soldiers of the Celestial Republic emerge from guardhouses of mud and cry "Halt!"

But the guidebook did say that there were two Kashgars, two cities: the old and the new, some five miles apart. In the new were progressive Chinese merchants, silk-clad magistrates, and the Taotai with all his pomp and power; likewise Samarkand and Punjabi traders, two isolated but indefatigable British missionaries, and even a native officer of British India who acted as a makeshift *chargé d'affaires*.

Edith Rand had not seen the guidebook. She was ignorant of the nature of the two towns of Kashgar. Iskander of Tahir would have said that destiny drew her to the older city, away from the men of her own race.

To tell the truth, Edith came to the crossroads leading to the two towns and chose the walled town swiftly—swiftly because she feared pursuit, and because the wall suggested to the girl, who was not acquainted with the vagaries of architecture in the Orient, more of a sanctum than the rambling streets of the modern Kashgar.

Not that she fancied, even in her agitation, that the men of the caravan were immediately behind her. Experience had taught Edith the utmost speed of the powerful Bactrian camels, and the length of time needed to propel, beat, and curse the protesting beasts into momentum; and Iskander's horse, even if the Arab had set out at once on her track, was tired. The white stallion was fleet of gait. The high-peaked saddle afforded the girl a rough pommel for her knee.

Her spirits rose as rider and horse swept downhill through broken brush, past cypress clumps tranquil in the quiet of evening, into the dust haze that hung over the sandy expanse, with its spots of verdure lining rough canals.

The beat of the white stallion's hoofs struck an echo of joy in Edith's heart. She was free! Surely, there would be somebody in Kashgar to appeal to for protection from Iskander—local authorities, perhaps even Arthur Rand.

They had passed outlying huts by the canals where ragged children stood at gaze, peering through the soft dust which is ever in the air of Kashgar. The stallion's hoofs left a trail of denser dust. Now, he slowed obstinately to a walk, panting and grinding at the bit.

Edith urged him on under an archway through the wall of the town. They pounded over a ramshackle wooden bridge which spanned the ancient moat under the wall. And a myriad smells assailed horse and rider. Edith grimaced and the stallion fought for his head.

It was by then the last afterglow of evening. Purple and velvety crimson overspread the sky. Stars glimmered into being and slender minarets uprose against the vista of distant mountains. There was a great quiet in the atmosphere; but in the streets of the old city of Kashgar pandemonium reigned.

Into a narrow alley, flanked with canopies stretched across the odorous fronts of booths and stalls, the horse paced protesting. Figures stepped aside reluctantly, only to hasten after. Glancing back, the girl saw that a crowd was following her—a crowd made up of motley and grotesque forms: smocked, wizened Chinamen; sheepskin-clad, swaggering youths, hideously degenerate of face; bulky women with giant, gray headdresses; half-naked urchins—all shrilling and chuckling in a dozen tongues and with a hundred gestures.

Laden donkeys pressed against her knees. She heard the curses of the donkeys' owners. Peering about for sign of a clean and European-looking house, she saw only square gray and brown huts of dried mud with some loftier edifices of blank stone walls.

A yelling lama, beating about him with a heavy staff, his body grotesquely dressed in white and black squares of cloth with a peaked cap of brightest orange, pushed her horse back, staring at her with a louder yell of surprise. Behind him grunted and squealed a line of laden camels, tied nose to rump. Dust swelled and swathed all in the alley.

In a fury of irritation at the camels, the white stallion backed obstinately against the open front of a structure covered with grass matting from which lights gleamed. In the reflection, Edith could see a leprous beggar mouthing at her.

"*Baksheesh*—plentee *baksheesh*. O my God! *Baksheesh*. O my God!"

This parrotlike ritual emerging from lips half eaten away from the toothless mouth was his one stock in trade. Perhaps this unfortunate plied his trade solely with the missionaries. But in Edith's appearance, he sensed the opportunity of a declining life.

No!" she cried, motioning him away frenziedly. No *baksheesh*." To the crowd she appealed eagerly. "English! Where are the English? Don't you understand? Does any one speak English? *Sahib log!*"

A Chinese merchant of the higher ranks would undoubtedly have gone to Edith's help, from various motives—perhaps from the instinctive good manners of his race. A Punjabi would have defended the girl against a mob, so strong is the bond between Briton and Indian. Even a group of Afghans might have assisted her boldly, enjoying the excellent pretext for beating the despised Sarts and Chinese and perhaps letting a little blood. Later they would have claimed a small ransom from the *chargé d'affaires*.

But there was no Afghan to take the center of the street against the throng of bazaar scum, indolent Sartish townsmen, idiotic Taghlik shepherds, and staring, ignorant Kirghiz, and all manner of diseased filth.

All were intent on her, all gazing, all talking. She could not move the white horse forward against these *trouards* of the bazaar of a—to all intents—mediaeval city. Instead, her mount backed against the reed matting that covered the enclosure front.

A fat man in a fez ran out in his slippers and started a tirade against the invader of his premises. Then, seeing the American girl, he fell voiceless, with his great jaws agape. He backed into the house, through the matting, still staring.

"English! I will pay!" Edith faced her tormentors stoically. "Oh, can't you understand? Go—*Boro! Boro!*"—a phrase borrowed from Iskander, in anger. "Take me to the sahibs, the *effendi!*"

She paused, biting her lips. The bleared eyes stared through the dust, emotionless. The passing camels coughed and grunted. Vile odors swept into the girl. From behind her through the matting billowed a pungent scent of frying fish, mutton fat, dirt, smoke, stale human breath wine-laden, and a penetrating, sweetish aroma she did not recognize as opium.

"Nakir el kadr!"

A voice bellowed near her. At once a snapping, snarling chorus of dogs arose as the curs of the alley felt encouraged to annoy the frantic horse. Edith saw a beast with the body of a dachshund and the head of a mastiff snap at the stallion's flank; a brown mixture of terrier and setter with a Pekingese tail slunk near her. A giant wolfhound bared vicious teeth.

The mob paid no attention, never ceasing to watch her.

It was hideous for Edith to think that in another street Englishmen might be sitting down to dinner, or the governor of the city dining upon his terrace. Perhaps an American missionary was walking near by. She could not move toward them—if, indeed, she knew where to go.

For the first time in her life Edith knew the meaning of real fear. Long-nailed hands felt of the silver that ornamented the elaborate saddle of the horse; a greasy, pudgy fist clutched suddenly the bracelet on her arm and wrenched it off. A parchment-hued face, wrinkled and evil as sin itself, peered up at her, a claw-like hand holding a paper lantern to her face. Other lanterns moved jerkily along the alley as their owners joined the assembly of spectators.

Then the voice bellowed again behind her. The wrinkled face spat, and vanished. The thieving hands fell away reluctantly. She saw the man in the fez bowing and holding her rein. He pointed into the house. Edith shook her head. Bad as the alley was, she preferred it to the walls of such a building.

Whereupon the fat man jerked down a portion of the matting, revealing a spacious room with a stone floor and a huge pot hung over a fire in the great hearth. Shadowy figures of veiled women were visible, and one or two men, also stout, sitting against the wall on cushions. It seemed to be an inn, and the perspiring proprietor made a herculean effort at English, or rather European speech.

"*Serai*—yah! Entrrez, surre—verree good, my word! *Serai*, good, yah!"

But Edith would not forsake the vantage point of her horse. Her woman's wit assured her that afoot she would be helpless in the hands of the mob.

Instead, she signed to the *serai*-keeper to send away the mob. He nodded readily and pounced upon a half-naked boy to whom he whispered urgently. The youth slipped out into the shadows of the alley. Edith noticed this byplay but could not judge whether evil or good inspired it.

Then the fat innkeeper summoned the sitting men with a single word. They leaped up, grasping staves, and flew at the throng. It was fez against turban, with objurgation rising to the roofs of the alley, slippered feet planted against broad buttocks and staves thrust into spitting faces.

Apparently the alley scum were not disposed to fight for the chance of plundering the girl. They seemed listless in defense as well as attack. The men from the inn cleared a small ring around the now passive horse and squatted there, apparently to wait.

To Edith the pause was intolerable. She could not ride free of the alley. The tired horse would not budge—disliking, beyond doubt, the presence of skirts upon his back. The actions of the *serai*-keeper suggested that he had sent for some one. For whom? Iskander?

Edith decided to wait and see. Every muscle in her slender body ached with fatigue. She dared not dismount to ease her cramped limbs.

Where were Iskander and Aravang? Had they traced her to the walled city? She hoped that they had taken the other turning. Every minute increased the suspense.

Then swaggering men bearing scimitars pushed through the throng that gave back readily. The leader of the file gripped Edith's reins and led the stallion into the *serai* and she recognized her friend of the tamarisk grove. At this, the innkeeper placed matting across the front of his room with care. One of the newcomers with bared scimitar remained at the entrance.

"Mees Rand!" smiled the man at Edith's side, adding to himself: "Verily is the luck of Monsey good, for here is the woman herself, alone and quite harmless."

In this fashion he of the leadership, the soiled fez, the immense shawl girdle and the very dirty drill suiting introduced himself—Abbas Abad, just arrived in Kashgar—and gave sharp command to one of his men to seek out Monsey in the new town.

To Edith, it was clear that Abbas Abad was turning a deaf ear to her pleas that he take her to the sahibs—if, indeed, he understood.

Her heart had leaped when she heard her name spoken. Eagerly she stared at Abbas, trying to place him. Then her heart sank.

The whole appearance of the man—oily black hair, moist, bloodshot eyes, and flabby mouth—was against him. He met her gaze boldly and grinned, muttering to himself.

"Who is your master?" she asked.

Abbas shrugged his shoulders, not understanding. When Edith drew back, he gripped her arm in an iron clasp and pulled downward. Instinct warned the girl to keep to the saddle. Abbas only grinned the more and dragged her down with the calm assurance of a constrictor coiled about a gazelle. She slid from the saddle. And Abbas passed a tentative hand across her slim shoulders and the breast of her jacket, after the manner of a skilled Kirghiz feeling a sheep.

"If the American father will not pay," he muttered to himself, "you will be worth much—much, but otherwise. A beautiful slave."

Edith shrank back from the smiling Alaman in angry revolt. The followers of Abbas looked on apathetically but with some curiosity at the dilemma of the white woman. Usually in Abbas' seizure of women there had been wrangling and a price to pay. This was different. They gazed idly at the girl's flushed face and indignant eyes.

She saw the *serai*-keeper approach Abbas servilely and the Alaman toss him some silver coins. It was as if a price had been paid for her capture. The cold expanse of the wall touched her back and Edith leaned against it wearily, as she understood the true nature of these men and the futility of her escape.

Hopelessly, she scanned the smiling Abbas, the leering innkeeper, the two armed followers—and she saw Aravang standing inside the matting.

It did not take an instant for the girl to make up her mind which of her captors was preferable.

"Aravang!" she called appealingly.

The sentry at the matting touched the newcomer warningly and motioned to the alley. By way of response the scarred follower of Iskander gripped the guard of the scimitar, jerked it from the man, struck him viciously with the hilt between the eyes, and leaped toward Abbas.

Edith stifled a scream and watched, absorbed by the swift flash of weapons and leap of bodies. She saw Abbas bury his knife in the arm of Aravang—saw Aravang fling a useless sword at the remaining enemy with his left hand and spring to grips with the powerful Alaman.

For a moment the two muscular bodies swayed and trampled across the floor, the men cursing and panting. One of Abbas' men gripped Aravang from behind. Whereupon Edith's guardian—for now she thought of him so—thrust Abbas away, to reel back to the opposite wall. Then the other assailant, gripped by the back of the neck, flew head over heels to the floor. Aravang sprang to the hearth and flung a blazing log at Abbas, who dodged. Seeking a new weapon, the scarred champion of Edith bellowed defiance and seized the great black pot from its rests.

"Sayak!" he roared.

Abbas caught up one of the low tabourets that stood in front of the cushions by the wall and advanced on Aravang, knife in hand. The pot of steaming meat and boiling water was hurled, but the table resisted it and the next moment Abbas was on his foe, stabbing and grunting with rage.

Aravang was thrust back, moaning, almost into the fire. He looked over the shoulder of his assailant, motioning, in spite of his own peril, to Edith to run from the room. But even if she had had command of her limbs, the two men of Abbas were hovering about the hearth with drawn weapons. The *serai*-keeper lurked cautiously by the door, wishful to keep intruders out, but with a keen eye for the safety of his own skin the while.

With a cry Edith covered her eyes with her hands. She had seen Abbas' knife flash red in the firelight—with a redness that was not of the fire. She had seen the mute appeal in the eyes of struggling Aravang.

Two shots roared in the narrow confines of the room.

Startled anew, Edith dropped her hands. She saw Iskander's tall form framed against the mats, a smoking revolver in his hand. The Arab's face was utterly tranquil, save for a slight smile and a certain alertness of the keen eyes.

The two followers of Abbas staggered and slumped slowly to the stone floor, their hands groping and their mouths wide in dumb amazement.

Abbas himself turned from Aravang to hurl his knife. Seeing the flash of steel, Iskander swayed aside, so that the hurtled blade barely tore the skin of his side, pinning his cloak to the matting. He wrenched himself free at once, but Abbas had vanished into a curtained archway. Nor was the innkeeper any longer to be seen.

Iskander cast a brief glance at the two bodies, moving slowly on the floor and shot a question at Aravang. The big native bared his fine teeth in a smile and shook his head. Then the Arab took Edith by the arm.

Revolver in hand, he led her out of the *serai*. The white stallion had galloped free during the struggle. Iskander strode through the alley, followed by Aravang, whose strong frame seemed able to stand upright and walk in spite of the stabbing it had endured.

Edith was silent, feeling very much as she had felt once when her father caught her playing truant from school and escorted her home. Dim forms emerged to look at them and the dog pack gave tongue.

They passed under grotesque wooden arches, between tumble-down huts, across a turgid canal on one of the curving Chinese bridges, and came to the shadowy bulk of a waiting carriage.

Into this Iskander thrust Edith with scant ceremony. There was a roomy space about the rear seat, covered with straw. Aravang lay down at once and Iskander, who had jumped upon the front seat beside the driver, called back softly for Edith to sit in the straw until they were free of the town.

With Aravang beside her, she would have no chance to leave the carriage. But Edith did not intend to try. What she had seen in the eyes of Abbas and his men had struck deep into her consciousness.

"Allah!" muttered the Arab impatiently.

But there was the flash of a match and the driver—a bearded giant with bronzed, high-cheeked face, and enormous sheepskin hat—lit his pipe with care. This done, the Kirghiz leaned back indolently and cracked his whip.

The four-horse *tarantass* sped through the night, under the stars. As they went, the driver rumbled a kind of song in his throat. He seemed utterly indifferent to the horses who plunged forward into the dark. Again they were going up and by the feel of the wind and sight of the stars Edith fancied they were on their former course, to the north.

Once when they stopped long enough for a man by the roadside to pass something to Iskander—something that very much resembled the medicine pail—she ventured to speak.

"Poor Aravang," she observed to the Arab. "Can't we stop at a house to see how badly he is hurt?"

"A house? Before long we will come to one that is yours. Until then you must sleep. Sleep! Aravang has said he will not die."

The callousness of the words chilled Edith more than the growing cold into which they plunged headlong. A hand touched her and she started. Then, since her nerves had suffered, she almost cried—out of pity. The injured Aravang was trying to place his heavy coat about her as a covering against the cold.

CHAPTER XII
THE COUNTRY OF THE FALCON

From the dawn of the next day Edith wore the *yashmak*, the light veil that conceals a woman's face from the eyes down.

She had put it on voluntarily, and she dressed Aravang's wounds— deep gashes in the flesh of his body—of her own accord. As she suspected, the medicine pail had accompanied them. The big native was immensely surprised and grateful at this attention; and Iskander watched her efforts attentively, without manifesting disapproval. In fact, he seemed pleased.

A fortnight ago Edith would have sulked in the carriage—would have considered the injuries of the two men—Iskander had wrapped a scarf about his middle over the cut in his ribs, and refused curtly her offer of aid—as only partial punishment for their crime in carrying her off.

Now she had seen two men die in as many minutes. The vision of the two men lying on the floor of the *serai* would not leave her memory. And she did not want Aravang to die. The native of the scar had befriended her, and she felt that she had an ally, even if a humble one, in him. Iskander spoke of the incident only once.

"That dog of an Alaman, you know him?" He glanced at her searchingly. Iskander had ceased referring to her as *Khanum*—lady. "He knows you?"

"Who?"

"Abbas Abad, the Alaman slave dealer—he that did this—" pointing impatiently at Aravang. "You fled to him. Why?"

"No, Iskander," she had made answer quietly, "I do not know of him. He offered me a horse. In the *serai* he called me by name—"

"Hai!"

It was a short, bitter expletive, wrung from the Arab. "Do not be so foolish again. You cannot escape. So," he went on almost to himself, "Abbas Abad knew that you were with the caravan. He must have others with him, since he dared lift hand against the caravan. For he has not forgotten our law—blood for blood, a blow for a blow—"

At this he fell silent, gazing keenly about the mountain slopes. The aspect of the countryside had changed. The barren gorges and black torrents had given way to sparkling valleys where the early sunlight glimmered on white carpets of dew. Occasionally the *yurts*—round felt tents—of a nomad settlement were to be seen, where small, muffled girls astride huge oxen stared at them, and cattle, children, and dogs littered the lush grass in happy confusion.

Tranquil Kirghiz bargained with their driver for relays of horses. They threaded sunny gullies, crashing through willow clumps and shallow, pebbly freshets, following an invisible path that was not the least semblance of a road. The rock shrines had given way to tiny blue and red mosques.

Edith wondered whether they had crossed the roof of the world to the region behind the Himalayas, and decided they had. She had seen a corpulent Chinese mandarin—at least he resembled the pictures she had come across, of mandarins—joggling along behind a shaggy, miniature pony, with a coolie running ahead. Endless flocks of sheep scampered away from them.

"Where," she remarked, emboldened by the fresh sunlight, the intoxicating air, and the recovery of Aravang, "is the house that is to be mine, Iskander? You said we were coming to it."

The Arab pointed up into the mountains they were ascending.

"There. In Yakka Arik. But the house belongs to your master, to one who is a master of many men."

Bewildered and disturbed, the girl could only say: "My—master?"

"Yess. If we are in time, and he is still alive. Then you may become a favored slave, or perhaps a wife. You are fair of face."

Stung, Edith sat up rigidly.

"I—a slave?"

Iskander shrugged.

"Or whatever your master wills. How should I know his mind?"

"And if"—Edith pondered former words of her captor—"we should find that this man is dead?"

"Then you would be less," the Arab indicated the flying dust of sand under the carriage wheels, "than that." Whereupon he turned his back deliberately, and Edith sank back upon the straw, biting her lips. A hand touched her sleeve and Aravang was upright on his elbow, his scarred face close to hers.

"Dono-van Khan," he whispered.

It had not occurred to Edith that Aravang understood thdr words. But there was an unmistakable gleam of intelligence in the native's dark eyes. "Whom are you taking me to?" She barely breathed the question.

"Dono-van Khan—John Dono-van."

"The man you call the Falcon?"

Aravang hesitated as if pondering the meaning of her words. Then, with a warning glance at Iskander's back, he nodded.

The tawny head of the girl sank upon her arms as she tried to think. They were taking her to John Donovan. Why? She did not know. The only certainty was that she was being carried to the house of the white man who—so Fraser-Carnie had said—had allied himself with the natives and was a power in these lawless hills.

The *why* burned into her thoughts. She felt very helpless. It was as if a chain bound her, a chain of many links. The medicine pail that she was to use was one link; the death of Jain Ali Beg, who had been called a faithless servant, was a link; the jealous care of her captors who slew men to safeguard her; the anxiety of Iskander—

There were so many links. Abbas Abad, who seemed to be an enemy of Iskander. The Alaman had been seeking her. Again the *why* confronted her. But of one thing she was certain.

Much as she hated Iskander, she dreaded more the man called Abbas Abad. And she felt a greater hostility toward the unknown Donovan Khan. As the hours passed, she fed her anger against the white man who had been the cause of her abduction from the world of her father and her aunt—the life of her own people.

The chain—as she fancied it—was drawing her into another world, into an environment where the realities of yesterday were the unrealities of to-day—where men knelt daily to pray like children; where hidden hatred and open loyalty were part of the new religion; and where death passed almost unnoticed.

Unknown to herself, Edith was changing. The girl's inherent vitality was gathering to meet the demand of the new life. The scornful indifference of Iskander was a bitter tonic to her pride. False vanity and the sense of security fell away from her spirit like tattered fabrics of last year's ball dresses, cast from her body. It was well that this was so.

For Edith had entered the gates of the unknown world of Central Asia, where she was to play her part in a stern drama which was, after all, no drama but inexorable reality. She had been one of the ruling spirits of the world of civilization; here, she was no more than a child, and a very ignorant child.

She started when she first heard the trumpets. They had been out of Kashgar about two days when a distant blast of sound came to her in the still air of evening. At times very faint, now and then the sound swelled strongly as if the hidden trumpeters were summoning her. A gigantic sound, vast and calm as the cliffs under which they were passing once more.

Iskander glanced at her, his dark eyes alight under the hood with a kind of grave, sardonic humor.

"They are calling you. Mees Rand, always they call—these trumpets of Yakka Arik—to the stars, to the earth, and to the spaces of air. Yess. But now it is you they are calling." He touched the driver on the arm. "Hasten. Oh, hasten. It is late, late, and the sun sets."

To the girl he added:

"Dono-van Khan has a name for them. He calls them the trumpets of Je-richo."

They were rushing along the edge of a chasm. Peering from the side of the carriage, Edith could see only the darkness of a vast gorge, filled with clouds of vapor. Faintly she distinguished the glimmer of cascades and the black surfaces of pools. Vultures hovered over the mist.

"Yonder is their home—the watchtower of the Vulture," said Iskander, who had been observing her. She made out a gray, walled building, squat and ugly on the summit of the cliff across the chasm to the west. From the walls a ruined tower uprose.

In the glow of the sunset the black bulk of the tower was outlined distinctly. Edith fancied that it did resemble the nest of some bird of prey. An empty nest For the wind-swept walls appeared desolate.

"No one is there," she murmured. The aspect of the deserted tower had oppressed her.

"Once," Iskander shaded his eyes, to gaze intently into the sun, "our enemies, Abbas Abad and his master, watched from the tower when they came to prey upon Yakka Arik. Now the kites have flown far—far. Yet it is in my thoughts that they will come again, to settle upon the tower. If so, there will be war again—"

Twilight closed its wings about them and the carriage plunged forward as the cliff trail wound downward toward the ravine and they left the watchtower on the heights behind them, to the left. When the gray stone structure passed from view some two or three miles to their rear, they came to a narrow, timber bridge spanning the rapids.

Out upon this bridge the carriage rumbled, guided by the reckless skill of the Kirghiz. Midway across it halted. Edith heard a sharp challenge from the further side and saw lights move out to meet them as Iskander answered. The Arab signed for her to step down and she faced a group of harsh-featured men, some bearing torches and some a vehicle strange to her—a palanquin.

An armed native waved the drowsy Kirghiz back, and the girl was assisted into the chair which at once moved forward. In its shuttered darkness Edith could see nothing. But she had caught a glimpse of what lay beyond—and above—the guarded bridge. In the afterglow of sunset she saw the expanse of a sheet of water open out, a lake ringed about by very high mountains—on its shore the lights of a village.

Voices reached her ears, above the *pad-pad* of the bearers. She was conscious of the scent of water, of seaweed and even fancied that she heard waves lapping along a shore. How could there be a seashore in the mountains?

Yet the murmur of water persisted, and the fragrance of pines struck into her senses. "I reckon I've crossed the Rubicon," she reflected. "And I'm going to Yakka Arik, Iskander says. I wonder if it's his home town—"

A final, short blast of the trumpets interrupted her thoughts.

"Hasten!" Iskander called angrily.

The palanquin moved forward more jerkily and after an interval it halted.

Iskander opened the shutters and assisted her to the ground.

She was in a garden of some sort, because directly in front of her a white kiosk loomed, with flowers clustered at its base. They had passed through the wall, and now Iskander stalked to the kiosk, motioning her to follow.

They entered the small, arched doorway of a house. A red lamp, hanging overhead, revealed a stone hall, the floor covered with fine rugs. At the end of the hall the Arab drew back a damask curtain from a wide aperture. He beckoned her impatiently, his lean face rigid with anxiety. Edith walked forward slowly into a lighted room.

Three men, seated on cushions, looked up at her. Somewhat they resembled Iskander, being more richly clothed in heavy silks, wearing silver ornaments. One, a withered bulk of a man whose voluminous cloak dwarfed lean limbs, spoke to the Arab.

Iskander touched her arm and whispered:

"Look!"

She followed the direction of his eyes. On a couch at one side of the chamber a man lay motionless. A shrouded lamp at his head barely revealed a blanketed form. Edith stepped nearer, peering at the face.

She saw a white man, whose cheeks were wasted, whose eyes bore heavy circles. A brown beard covered his chin. The eyes were closed. The brow was furrowed as if in pain. Edith held her breath and watched, but she could see no movement of the chest under the blanket. The man's face was marblelike in its stillness.

"Dono-van Khan," said Iskander.

CHAPTER XIII
A LAMP GOES OUT

There was complete stillness in the room as Edith stood beside the form of the white man who was called Donovan, and Khan.

She scanned the unconscious face again attentively, noting the finely shaped head, the handsome mouth and brow. The man was young, and very much wasted by sickness. The lean cheeks still bore the brown hue of exposure to the weather.

Edith turned to the Arab, forcing herself to speak. "Is he—dead?"

Before answering he bent over the sick body, his eyes gleaming intently. He touched a finger to his lips and held it over Donovan's mouth. Then he turned to exchange a swift question and answer with the withered watcher on the floor.

"If any can tell, *he* is the one." Iskander indicated the seated man of the aged face and beadlike eyes. "He is the master of healing substances, who can count the sands of life."

"What does he say?" Edith framed the question gently. She sensed the anxiety of Iskander, the patience of the silent watchers—the vital importance to them of the life of the white man.

"The sands of life have not run out. And the wine vessel that held the wine is not broken." Iskander spoke slowly, with a kind of thoughtful exultation. "He who knows the sickness of the spirit has tended Dono-van Khan skillfully. We have come in time."

Edith glanced swiftly at the Mohammedan physician. He was regarding her steadily, his dried lips framing soundless words. The other two, heavier men, bearing the stamp of authority, waited patiently. Edith's keen wit told her that they expected something of her, particularly the physician.

"Mahmoud el Dar," Iskander spoke her thought, "the *hakim*. He is wise, very wise. There is no wisdom like to his."

A breath of air passed through the stone chamber. The candles in the lamps flickered. And the shrouded light by the couch went out. It left the face of Donovan dark.

"*Hai!*" muttered Iskander and two of the three watchers echoed his exclamation. The fatalism inbred in all followers of the Prophet had taken fire at the darkening of the lamp. Edith was alert, sensitive to all that passed in the chamber. She understood that her own life, to these men, was a slight thing beside the life of John Donovan.

In the stone room of the garden house, isolated in the impenetrable hills, Mahmoud and those with him had treasured the life in the sick man, guarding it against her coming. Why?

Mahmoud spoke.

"He says," interpreted Iskander, "that the lamp was truly an omen. Yet not, of itself, an omen of death. Mahmoud is very wise. He says that a new lamp must be lit by your hand. Obey."

As if she had been a child obedient to an older person, Edith took the bronze lamp the Arab gave her, and with a wisp of cotton ignited it from another candle. Then she removed of her own accord the shrouding cloth. Holding the bronze lantern, she turned to Iskander.

"Tell me what you want done," she observed.

By way of answer, the Arab gave a command and Aravang appeared carrying a burden which he set down beside Edith. It was the familiar medicine pail, still covered with its black cloth.

"That is yours," Iskander pointed to it, "and you alone—among us four—understand its use. I have seen you tend the wounds of your servant, Aravang, when he was hurt at the inn."

He nodded thoughtfully to himself, choosing his words with care and speaking the precise English that he had learned—as he had once admitted—when attached to a native regiment of the British army during the Persian campaigns of the Great War.

"Of his own accord, Mees Rand, did Dono-van Khan come to Yakka Arik. No other ever came willingly into the barriers—no other *multani*, foreigner, at least. Because of certain things unknown to you it is necessary to kill those who spy upon Yakka Arik. Yet we had heard of Dono-van Khan, and once before then he had aided us. So we bargained with him, or he did with us, and we Sayaks helped him to fulfill his mission in the Hills. Now, he must fulfill his half of the bargain. He has given his word. We are waiting. And he is very ill. He must be made well."

Edith was silent, looking at him questioningly. She wondered why Iskander called the sick man "khan" and why there was a barrier about Yakka Arik. The casual manner in which the Arab mentioned death as a penalty rather took her breath away. What manner of men were these who called themselves Sayaks? And what was Donovan?

"In the time before the first of last winter," continued her interpreter, "Dono-van Khan again was brought here by one of the caravans to this house which is his home. But this time there was a heavy fever in him. An enemy of the Sayaks who knew that he meant to aid us poisoned him in the Kashgar bazaar. Because of the sickness, Mahmoud kept him here and we sent Aravang for his belongings that were left with a servant at Kashgar. The servant was faithless and it came to pass before long that Aravang tracked him down and punished him fittingly."

Edith thought of Major Fraser-Carnie's narrative and sighed. She was gaining a first insight into the new world of Yakka Arik. It was hard for her to understand.

"When the winter was passing, the fever grew and he was very weak. Mahmoud's remedies no longer availed because of a strange thing. The sickness was of spirit as well as body. Dono-van Khan had received word that the doors of his home in England were closed to him. He was very lonely and this weakened his spirit."

Iskander stroked his beard thoughtfully, glancing at her to make sure that she understood.

"Mees Rand, what do physics—even the substances of Avicenna—avail when the mind itself is ailing? Mahmoud desired above all things to save Dono-van Khan, and I also—who am his friend—desired it. But to the white man this house was not like his home. Then out of the wisdom of the ancient Mahmoud came a thought. It was that the spirit itself of Dono-van Khan must be healed."

Iskander Khan Edith regarded as a pagan, with blood on his hands. Aravang, she thought, was no better than a murderer. What made them so anxious to aid the sick man? She looked from Mahmoud, now heating something in a bronze bowl over the brazier, to the still face of Donovan.

"It was the wisdom of Mahmoud," the mild voice of Iskander went on, "that sent me to Kashmir—to heal the loneliness of the white man. I went to find a spur for his spirit—a spur that would drive away the dark angel of death. The spur would be a woman of his own race and rank. The sight of her would make him wish to live. Aye—she would nurse him and make this place a home."

"And so—"

"You are here." Iskander folded his arms, a brief hiss of satisfied personal pride escaping his lips. "*Zalla 'llahir alaihi wa sallam!* The will of Allah is all-in-all. Behold, the sickness is of the spirit and so also is the spur. *Hai*—you are beautiful as a keen, bright sword. I have watched you, and I know—I know."

Mechanically Edith placed the lamp by the couch and faced the Arab. She had been hurried hundreds of miles over mountain paths to serve Donovan—the man they called Dono-van Khan. At this thought she flushed and bit her lip.

"Why did you choose—me?"

"*Hai!* Does the falcon pause when a thrush is in sight? I chose the first white woman, strong, and fair of face. Likewise, it was said in Srinagar that you were skilled in tending the sick *mem*-sahib."

Edith smiled bitterly, reflecting how it would astonish her worthy aunt to learn that her fancied ills coupled with the exaggerated respect paid the medicine chest had helped to carry off her niece. Iskander had seized her—daughter of Arthur Rand and an American citizen—as lightly as he would have pinioned a struggling bird, as callously as he had slain the two men in the Kashgar bazaar.

She looked into the faces of the three. Iskander and the stout chieftain were conversing, utterly oblivious of her. Only Mahmoud regarded her intently, much in the manner of a surgeon surveying the subject of an experimental operation. A surge of rebellion swept through her.

Another woman, less proud, might have congratulated herself on the temporary respite offered. But it was not in Edith's nature to be grateful for immunity or to forget a wrong done her. She was the daughter, young in years, of an aristocratic family, and her pride was still to be reckoned with.

The pride of the Rands was not easily dealt with.

"The skill of Mahmoud guarded the life of Dono-van Khan for the space that I was gone," Iskander was saying, "and now that my task is finished, yours is to begin."

The hands of the girl clenched at her side; her body quivered, and her flushed face became all at once quite pale.

"Do you think that I shall obey—you?"

Mahmoud looked up from his task, struck by the change in her voice. Iskander rose from the stone flags and took a silent stride toward her, snatching from her the *yashmak* and cloak, baring her set face and torn traveling dress. In front of her eyes he lifted the whip that he still retained.

"Aye, you will obey."

His burning glance probed her, angrily. Her rebellion had stirred his hot temper.

"You think I will be a—slave, Iskander?"

The Arab was surprised that she smiled at him so coldly. Women of his race did not defy their masters. A lash of the whip, he thought, would wipe out the smile. And Edith read his thought easily.

"If you strike me, Iskander, I shall kill you."

She had not meant to say just that. A month ago she could not have said it. But she knew that it was true. Every fiber in her body was strung to revolt. Every instinct of nature was up in arms against the man who had said he was her master. She heard Mahmoud speak quickly and saw the Arab bend his head to listen.

Edith felt all at once very unhappy and friendless. Bodily weariness beset her; even the aspect of the unconscious sick man appeared to her threatening—as the aspect of the other shrouded forms of the mountain side that had once entered her dreams. And, as in the dream, she wanted to cry out, to waken. The room, with the cloaked figures of the men, seemed at that instant as unreal as her dream of a month ago. Iskander addressed her quietly.

"The master of wisdom has spoken anew. He says that if you are unwilling to aid Dono-van Khan, you will not avail to heal his spirit. Of what use is a blunted spur ? Mahmoud asks that you look carefully into the face of the sick Dono-van Khan and consider that, if you do not heal him, he may die."

Still angered, she would make no response.

Iskander motioned to the bed and withdrew slightly, eying the girl curiously—trying to understand the mood of the white woman that brooked no mastery.

After a space his scowl lightened and he grunted to himself.

"By Allah, the steel of my choosing is good."

By the bright glow of the lantern she appeared as an image of sheer beauty, her wide eyes fixed on the sick man from the tangle of gleaming hair, her splendid body swaying with swift, troubled breathing.

As Edith studied the unconscious face, reading the shadows under the closed eyes of Donovan and the message of the set mouth through which breath barely stirred, her mood changed. After all, the woman was very much like a child.

And the instinct of womanhood—compassion at the sight of pain—was strong. She saw the head of the sick man move uneasily and his hand twitch on the blanket. Hesitantly, she took the hand in her own. Color flooded her cheeks and her eyes brightened.

"Tell me what I can do for him," she said to Iskander.

Under his mustache the Arab smiled. Verily, he reflected, Mahmoud was the master of wisdom: he had read with a single glance the heart of the woman.

But under the compassion that had come to Edith Rand was another feeling. Donovan Khan seemed to be a leader of these men—Sayaks, or whatever they chose to call themselves. He had been the cause of her seizure. On his account Iskander had made of her what was little better than a tool, a slave.

If he lived, Donovan Khan must atone for the wrong done her.

CHAPTER XIV
THE BRONZE BOWL

"Dono-van Khan lies in a stupor," explained Iskander, "and Mahmoud knows that he must be aroused, so that he will exert his strength—the strength of the iron body—to live. When he wakens you must speak to him, and make him understand."

Edith nodded. She had often heard physicians discuss the benefits derived from the determination of a patient to recover, in a dangerous stage of weakness. She watched curiously while Mahmoud pottered about his bowl.

She had always fancied that Arabian physicians and Hindu yogis—she was somewhat vague as to the difference—practiced by means of native spells and incantation and such things. Now she learned from Iskander that the bronze bowl contained merely a heart stimulant.

To Iskander, however, the arts of Mahmoud were little short of miraculous. Later, Edith came to understand that the physician's name was feared even in Kashgar as being connected with the caravan that had become a superstition in these regions.

While the Arab chieftain raised the head of the sick man from the bed, Mahmoud calmly adjusted the lamp to throw a strong light on Edith. Following out his directions, she seated herself on the bed, taking Donovan's hands in hers.

"When Dono-van Khan drinks," added Iskander, "he will waken. Then you must speak, so that he will desire to live."

Edith assented, appreciating the necessity for rousing the patient. She watched Mahmoud turning the bowl of brown liquid in his fingers that were so thin the wrinkled skin seemed stretched tight over the bones. She held her breath as he pushed open the lips of the unconscious man. Then, taking a strip of clean cotton from his girdle, he dipped it in the bowl, squeezing drops of the liquid through the set teeth.

Undeniably, she thought, the man was skillful. She wondered faintly at the assurance of this wrinkled man of medicine who used remedies not in the pharmacopoeia of European doctors; the conviction grew on her that Mahmoud, not Iskander, was master in Yakka Arik. The other native had left the room.

Mahmoud uttered a low exclamation as Donovan's teeth parted, and straightway fell to stroking the throat and eyelids of his patient. Edith saw a flush come into Donovan's cheeks and perspiration start on his brow.

The eyelids flickered and Mahmoud drew back with a sign to Iskander. "Dono-van Khan sees you," whispered the latter to Edith. "Now you must speak to him."

Gazing full into the blue eyes, heavy with fever, that wavered as they sought her, the girl fumbled for words.

"John Donovan!" she said faintly. "John Donovan!"

The eyes of the sick man fixed upon hers and she thought his lips framed an exclamation. A sudden impulse drew the girl nearer to her patient.

"Please," she breathed anxiously, "please hurry up and get well. I am going to nurse you."

Iskander touched her arm.

"Say that you need his protection, Mees Rand," he whispered. "Then the spirit of Dono-van Khan will fed the spur."

"I want you to help me, Donovan Khan," she cried. "You will help me, won't you?"

Donovan raised his head slowly and looked around inquiringly at Mahmoud and Iskander, his gaze returning to the girl. After a moment he closed his eyes. At this, the physician motioned her away and Iskander murmured.

"Inshallah!"

Edith was aware that Mahmoud worked steadily over Donovan, rubbing his limbs skillfully, and moistening his brow. Some of the candles had gone out, leaving the stone chamber in semi-gloom except for the couch. Time passed slowly while the physician hovered over the couch and Iskander remained sunk in thought. Outside the curtained entrance she heard the footfalls of some one, perhaps a guard. But no one entered. Presently Mahmoud covered the sick man very warmly with thick woolen robes and beckoned her.

"Sit by the bed," instructed Iskander, "and when the white man arouses, speak to him again. Do not leave him. If he wakens and looks for you and sees you not, he will believe that what has passed has been a dream, what you call a vision, Mees Rand."

Mahmoud glanced at her warningly.

With that the two left her in the stone chamber. Edith did as she had been told, perching herself on a carved tabouret to watch and wait. She saw that Donovan was breathing very slowly and weakly. He seemed unconscious. One hand lay outside the coverlet. Edith regarded it tentatively, then took it in her clasp.

Very insufficient and hesitating she felt, watching the wasted face of the white man. She distrusted her own ability to help in any way. But she had come to believe in Mahmoud's skill.

Hope was arising within her. Before her eyes Donovan had emerged from the last stage of exhaustion. She prayed that he would live.

The light across the bearded face before her was changing. Looking up, Edith perceived that the embrasures of the room had turned from black to gray. The room grew colder. Then she started upright.

So near it seemed almost over her head came the blast of the trumpets.

The clarion note rose and fell, now beating at her senses, now dwindling away into space.

The half light of early dawn was creeping into the stone chamber. And Donovan's eyes had opened and were fastened on her.

Edith caught her breath, uncertain whether to remain where she was or to call Mahmoud. She decided to remain. Iskander had been positive. But the girl was troubled by the great need to serve the sick man. Mechanically, she patted the hand she held.

Donovan looked at her steadfastly, at her face, and the hand that stroked his gently. Soon she saw that his lips were moving, and bent nearer to listen. Her quick ears caught the words.

"Who—are—you?"

Edith wondered what to say, her pulse quickening as she hesitated.

"Miss Rand," she ventured finally, and felt that it was absurdly formal and purposeless. Donovan appeared to ponder it. She wondered if he had heard. When his eyes closed she was alarmed, and tugged at his hand. At this he looked up and she sighed with relief.

"Please don't go to sleep again," she cried softly. "Don't you understand? You must get well—to help me."

He was silent at this, as if the words had been too much for his weakened comprehension.

"Help you?" he murmured, eyes closed.

"Yes," she breathed.

Silence followed, but she knew now that he was awake, groping slowly for thoughts, striving to connect ideas with a kind of patient, dogged determination. Edith understood now why Iskander had remarked upon the strength of John Donovan.

"You must rest," she warned.

He was quiet for a long time. Chin on hand, she gazed out into the circle of the window over the bed. No glass was in the embrasure, and the morning breeze swept mildly into the room. She could see the red flame of sunrise painted on the shape of a wandering cloud. The sky was fast becoming blue. Edith was cold and very tired.

"Help you," the murmur reached her again. So faint that she wondered if she really had heard it. The brow of the man was puckered as if in an effort of the mind. Edith realized that this must not be permitted. So she began to stroke his forehead with her free hand. This seemed to calm him. Before long Donovan's breathing was regular and she knew that he slept. But she did not leave his side nor release his hand.

The struggle of the past night had wrought upon her strongly. The reality of John Donovan was becoming part of her life. A deep, contented glow was in her breast, arising from the consciousness that she had helped him. She had done what Mahmoud had asked of her. She already felt a sense of ownership in the sick man.

She did not hear Mahmoud and Iskander approach when the sun was well up. Mahmoud stood beside his patient and peered long into the lean face of the white man. Edith waited, with all the anxiety of a novice nurse in the presence of a noted surgeon.

Presently Mahmoud glanced at her, gestured idly, almost contemptuously at the pail of medicines that still rested by the bed, exchanged a few words with Iskander, and walked from the room.

"Dono-van Khan is in your care," interpreted the other. "And you may use the remedies of the white men. Now you must eat and then sleep. Dono-van Khan will live."

CHAPTER XV
QUESTIONS AND ANSWERS

Edith Rand knew little of medical practice or theory. In truth, she was aghast at the responsibility that Mahmoud had thrust upon her woman's shoulders. Vainly she appealed to Iskander, who came in from day to day. The Arab shook his head.

"Mees Rand, the will of the *hakim* is not to be denied. His work is done. Does a learned reader of the Koran stoop to a book of verses? Not so."

Left to herself, Edith ransacked the contents of the medicine pail and her memory at the same time, studying labels, and trying to guess the condition of her patient. After long deliberation, she reached the decision not to administer any drugs to Donovan until he should be stronger. Which was, perhaps, the wisest thing she could have done.

For days the stone chamber was her world. Aravang had arranged a couch for her near the brazier. He brought her meals to the door regularly, and the girl was grateful for the fresh fruit, the light wines, the well-cooked mutton and rice, even though seasoned in a manner strange to her.

It was quite clear that she was not expected to leave the chamber, for a native remained always on guard at the door. The masters of the house had dedicated her to the service of John Donovan.

And Edith devoted herself to her task. Racked by the pangs of inexperience, she lived in fear that her ignorance would result in harm to the sick man. So she became doubly watchful.

Not many women, with Edith's heritage of luxurious life, would have entered whole-heartedly upon the care of a man whose condition made constant demand upon their strength. But Edith, remembering the summer in Louisville when she had tended her father, put thought of self aside. Her natural sympathy was touched by the spectacle of Donovan's effort of recovery. Her pride spurred her on when she recalled Iskander's curt command to her.

More than sympathy or pride, however, was the new feeling of anxiety aroused in the girl. The safety and health of a fellow being of her own race rested in her hands. For perhaps the first time in her life Edith Rand was face to face with suffering and human need. The love of her father for the girl, the good-natured devotion of her aunt, the care of the old servants of the Rands—all these were now lost to her.

She stood alone. The men of Yakka Arik ignored her. To all intents she was a slave. And there was no telling what the morrow might bring.

The man became the only reality in her world. And she spent her strength in his care. When she slept, she was surprised to discover that Aravang slipped into the room and watched by the bed of John Donovan. At times, too, the scarred native would appear silently as always and offer by signs to assist her in her work.

To Edith it seemed that Aravang was grateful for the treatment she had given his wounds. But there was no mistaking the devotion in the brown eyes of the big attendant. Aravang had attached himself to the girl, and from that time on he devoted himself to her service as faithfully as the negro retainers of the Rand family in former days.

Days passed—every twilight and sunrise bringing its melody of the great horns. At first the girl had been startled. Later, she waxed curious as to the meaning of the trumpet call. But, as yet, she felt no desire to inspect what lay beyond the walls of her room or to ponder upon the nature and situation of Yakka Arik and its masters.

"He will know," she thought, of John Donovan.

Thus she gave freely of woman's tenderness—her hands more gentle, perhaps, than the hands of experience. Feeling that her care was insufficient for the need of the sick man, she frequently prayed at night, brief prayers whispered into the darkness. And, under Iskander's mask of unconcern, she knew that the Arab longed for Donovan's recovery and that others also waited patiently.

And day by day the shadow of death removed farther from John Donovan. Came long hours of utter lassitude when the flame of vitality glimmered low and the man's pulse was barely to be felt. The heaviness passed from the eyes that always watched Edith, and he gathered strength before her eyes.

To Edith, unaware of the resiliency of these men whose home had been the mountain heights, it seemed more remarkable even than the stolid hardihood of Aravang, whose wounds were barely healed.

* * * *

The time came when Donovan insisted on talking. Until then, he had been content to watch her. Now he raised himself unsteadily, and Edith hastened to place pillows behind his back.

"I never believed in miracles," he murmured. "Will you tell me—where you came from?"

His voice still had the low note of weakness, and he paused often. It was a quiet voice, deliberate, musing—as if its owner was more accustomed to communing with himself than others.

"Hush!" said Edith reprovingly. "You are not well enough to talk."

Donovan smiled, and when he smiled the gaunt face lighted up and tiny wrinkles appeared at the eyes. She liked his eyes.

"You are—well enough to answer. I want to know why—you are in Yakka Arik."

Edith noticed that he pronounced the name in the sonorous fashion of the natives. She smiled back. "To take care of you."

"Me?"

A slight frown creased his brow as he pondered this slowly. Almost to himself, he muttered.

"And I thought you were not here. A splendid spirit. Angels might come to Yakka Arik—more easily than white women."

Worriedly, Edith surveyed him, chin on hand. For comfort's sake she had dressed her hair low on her neck, and she wore a silk scarf—a donation from Aravang—about her much enduring shirtwaist. In the absence of mirrors—she had been unable to make known her great need of such an article to her faithful attendant by signs—she did not realize how becoming the effect was. John Donovan looked at her long.

"Because," he resumed, "I thought those horns were Gabriel's, you know, when I wakened that time, and I was quite certain that you were an angel. Didn't you wear a gold halo?"

Edith thought of the lamp that Mahmoud had held close to her hair, and for the first time in many days she laughed—from sheer amusement touched with real pleasure. "You worried me at first," she admitted—"talking about spirits. Indeed, I'm nothing at all angelic: I'm quite alive and real. I've told you my name, to prove it—Edith Rand."

"You are Edith Rand?" Donovan looked up in quick surprise. "Of course, I remember now you told me the name, part of it." He was silent, occupied with his thoughts. At such times, as the girl was beginning to notice, he seemed to forget her entirely. "But you are too young. Strange—I thought you were dead."

This remark startled her and she wondered if her patient was really free from fever. "Perhaps you are thinking of my mother," she responded gently. "She had my name and she left us many years ago. But she was never in India."

"Fate plays strange tricks," he said, and was silent again.

At this point Edith ended the talk by the simple expedient of leaving the couch.

It was the next day that Aravang brought an offering—the box containing the kit of Donovan. He set it down by the couch and departed. Edith had not thought to ask for the box—did not know, in fact, that it had reached Yakka Arik.

Donovan surveyed it curiously. It was a bright, sunny day and the fresh breeze swept the room, bearing with it the scent of jasmine and honeysuckle mingled with the fragrance of the pines. Something of the vigor of the mountain air seemed to have entered into John Donovan.

"Strange," he remarked "Now where did that come from?"

"From the same place I did."

But he was not to be put aside.

"I want to know, Miss Rand. This box was in the care of a certain Jain Ali Beg."

The name recalled the story of Major Fraser-Carnie to the girl. She hesitated whether to tell her patient. He was growing petulant, however, at being silenced.

"Jain Ali Beg was killed," she said, "by Aravang."

"Ah. Your servant?"

"No. One of the—the Yakka Arik men. The one that brought the box."

"A Sayak, then. I think he introduced himself to me in a Kashgar *serai*. Ah, perhaps he imagined Jain Ali Beg poisoned me. It would be like Jain Ali Beg." Donovan pondered.

"At Gilghit—Major Fraser-Carnie's house. Iskander stole—took—the box from Srinagar and brought it here with me."

"So Iskander brought you." Donovan's eyes became grave. "Miss Rand, I must know what has happened. Much depends on it. More than you know. You must tell me everything."

His insistence was more than the irritability of the sick. It was authoritative, urgent. She related briefly all that had passed from the night of the ball in Srinagar until now, leaving out Monsey and the hardships she had been forced to undergo; also, the affray at Kashgar.

The story had the effect of silencing Donovan. He listened intently, almost avidly, interrupting frequently. When she had finished, he lay back with closed eyes, thinking.

Edith waited, idly trying to draw the scarf about her shoulders so as to cover the rents in the worn waist. It was a torment to the girl that she had nothing to change to; because she had not wanted to ask for native garments—had not thought of it, in fact, during her care of Donovan.

"Oh, for a needle and thread," she sighed.

"There should be a sewing kit, in my box. Look and see."

Readily, the girl obeyed. Womanlike, she craved the means of sewing. Likewise, investigation of the box was not without its inducements in satisfying curiosity.

Various articles of corduroy clothing were on the top of the box. Then a rusted telescope appeared, the book of poems—Shelley. Edith was a trifle surprised at this. She had not connected such reading with the stern personality of the sick man of Yakka Arik.

Followed a worn notebook, a bag of native money, a complete shaving and toilet set in a handsome leather case, and then the housewife. This Edith appropriated gratefully. She would have liked, however, to go to the bottom of the box.

"Was Iskander followed from Srinagar, Miss Rand?"

The sudden question startled her. "Why—no. I don't think so. Certainly my father and the major could not have known of my—trip." Tactfully she refrained from the use of a harsher word.

"Yet you did not get off without a fight." Seeing her surprise, he added: "Aravang and Iskander both have been wounded. You see, Miss Rand, I have been listening to the men talking outside the door."

Pressed in this manner, she described the events of the Kashgar alley, trying to conceal her own peril. She had the feeling, however, that Donovan was piecing out from his own mind the omitted portions of the story.

"Describe the leader of the men at the *serai*—Alamans, I fancy from your version."

Edith did so and was surprised anew at the effect of her words. Donovan flushed, his eyes hardened, and he drew a quick breath. Then his glance sought that of the girl.

"You say Ab—the man knew you."

"He called me by name."

"By name." Donovan shook his head moodily. His lean face was still sharp with aroused feeling. "Then the Vulture has marked you down and followed you from Srinagar. He knows you are here."

"Now," Edith commanded, fearing that her patient was beginning to talk wildly, "you must rest. I had no idea you had been sitting up so long."

"The Vulture!" The word was torn from the lips of the man. She stared at him in dismay. "Each thing you have told me weighs—more than a handful of gold. I tell you, I must *know*. Send Iskander to me."

"Indeed not!"

Donovan's broken phrases were curiously framed, as if he employed a tongue partially forgotten. But there was no mistaking his interest, even concern. By way of answer he summoned Aravang in the native's dialect.

Aravang left the room and before long Iskander strode in, taking in the scene at a glance, and measuring Donovan as swiftly. He paid scant heed to her.

"Please, you will overtire yourself!"

But Donovan shook his head impatiently. While Iskander knelt on a convenient carpet, cigarette between his lips, the two men talked in a language the girl recognized as that of the Arab. Donovan asked many questions and Iskander replied deliberately.

"They will follow her to Yakka Arik," she heard him say once, in English.

Seeing that she was temporarily forgotten, Edith retired to her couch in the opposite corner, not without a provoked pout. She busied herself with her new trophy, the needle and thread. It was long before Iskander left, as silently as he had come. Donovan lay back, thoroughly tired.

"I don't understand," she heard him mutter. At this, she went to him and adjusted the pillow and blankets. Then she bathed his face and hands.

"If you try to think and—and worry, I'll be ever so angry!" she warned.

His eyes met hers, and he smiled.

"Thanks, awfully. You're splendid, really. I wouldn't trade you for—a real spirit of paradise."

Early that evening Aravang entered and hung a silk curtain about the corner where her bed was. Then the native busied himself in cleaning out a square depression in the stone flooring—something that had puzzled Edith more than once.

Very soon she learned the purpose of the hollowed stone. Aravang carried in a full jar of fresh water which he poured into it, then another and another until the small tank was full. Edith surveyed the addition to her quarters with bewildered interest until she heard Donovan's voice.

"You may not know a Sayak bathtub when you see one, Miss Rand. It is somewhat chilly. You will find some extra soap in my box."

Edith pounced upon the prize. The attendant did not cease his labors until he had brought several long and finely textured veils of many-colored silk. These he laid on the bed, with a grin—adding thereto a package that Edith recognized as her discarded ball dress. "Ladies' tailors are lacking in Yakka Arik, Miss Rand," Donovan explained from his side of the room, "but you may be able to do something with this stuff and a little sewing."

Then Edith understood that Donovan had thought during his interview with Iskander to mention her own needs.

That night the girl labored long by the light of a lamp. Donovan's quiet breathing told her that he was asleep some time before she had finished. The room and the hall were quiet.

With a smile of whimsical appreciation she surveyed the result of her efforts—a brilliantly colored nightgown of priceless silk. Putting out the lamp she undressed and slipped into the tank.

It was, as Donovan had prophesied, rather chilly. But it was water and she had soap. Edith did not mind the cold. Two months ago she would have exclaimed at the thought of such a bath. Now it was luxury.

Nevertheless, she was glad to scramble from the tank and dry herself on some strips of clean cotton. Then, with a sigh of satisfaction, she slipped into the new nightgown and nestled among the blankets of the couch. She was refreshed and rested beyond words.

In spite of this she lay long awake, looking out from the oval embrasure, her thoughts dwelling on many things, the recovery of John Donovan, and the spirit of mastery he had promptly exhibited. She puzzled briefly and fruitlessly over his statement that a vulture had pursued her from Srinagar. Uppermost in her mind, drowsy by now, was the fact that he had taken thought for her comfort.

So also had Iskander, in the past. And they were both her foes. Had she not a reckoning to settle with them ? Undoubtedly!

CHAPTER XVI
PANDORA'S BOX

It was a breezy, sunny noon when the midday quiet rested on the house that Edith had her first glimpse of Yakka Arik.

Donovan had suggested smilingly that she might not be so closely guarded as she suspected, and that there was a fine view from a terrace opening from the second story of the stone dwelling, also that she looked peaked from long confinement indoors. It was time, said he, she began to take care of herself a little.

"Don't bother about the *yashmak*, either," he laughed, his grave face lighting up, "you won't scandalize Iskander and the rest. They are mostly at church."

Vaguely, Edith wondered if he was jesting. Was there a church in Yakka Arik? She asked Donovan. His smile faded.

"Rather. Not much else."

So Edith ventured out into the hall, feeling a strong sense of guilt—as once when she had been a girl in short skirts and had stolen into an orchard forbidden to her. It was a relief that no one confronted her in the hall or on the winding staircase. Her pulse quickened as she stepped through a pillared, cloisterlike room and out upon a wide balcony. There she drew a deep breath.

Almost to the courtyard of the house stretched the blue surface of a small lake. Its tranquil depths reflected the panoply of white wind clouds overhead, and the lofty summits of the snow peaks that had closed around the woman since she had left Kashgar. Near at hand, the mountain slopes were a dense mass of pines. The fragrance of these woods had reached into the sick room.

Around the border of the lake Edith caught glimpses of flat-roofed stone dwellings, much like the one she occupied. The lake and the houses, set in the depths of the bowl-like valley, were dwarfed by the vast heights above. It was very warm, surprisingly so, and peaceful.

Across the lake were stretches of pasture land. The girl could make out flocks of sheep, tiny gray bodies moving very slowly, watched by an occasional white-tunicked native. Also horses, and a species of longhaired oxen strange to her. (These were the yaks of Central Asia.) Low wooden structures opening upon the pastures revealed themselves as sheepfolds and stables.

The valley extended north, beyond the lake, and here were squares of tilled ground. A gusty breeze bent the surface of ripened grain in long ripples. She could not see above the tilled land because the ground broke up into trap rock, the outcropping of which extended to the hills that pressed in on the valley upon three sides.

What surprised Edith was the complete quiet of the place. With the exception of the sheep boys, some men fishing in a flat skiff near by, and an occasional man walking barefoot between the houses, the place had the appearance of being deserted.

She had looked for the camels of the caravan. They were not to be seen. Nor could she make out the road by which she had come in the night. Paths ran along the lake shore and from house to house; but there was no trace of any road leading away to the north.

"How stupid of me," she reflected. "I must have come up from the south."

The lake was not round; it ran in a long oval under the mountains. She looked to the south. At a distance of perhaps half a mile the valley turned sharply around the shoulder of a mountain. At this point was a building larger than any at the nearer lake shore. It rose, however, from the water's edge.

It was a sheer walled edifice of gray stone. By shading her eyes and straining her sight Edith could make out a lofty arched entrance, a round dome, and twin, spirelike towers rising from either side the arch.

She fancied it resembled the pictures she had seen of Mohammedan mosques. The spires were like the minarets she had glimpsed during the evening when they approached Kashgar. But the walls merged into the gray wall of a cliff behind the edifice. The deep shadow of the lower gorge through which she had been carried in the sedan shrouded the spot. If she had not been looking intently at the place, she would hardly have noticed the mosque at all. Edith realized that, to reach the village, the palanquin must have passed through the mosque.

A wide-winged bird swept low over the lake, circling around the skiff of the fishermen. It moved lazily on the air currents, a black and white creature of the air. It was not a crow, nor an eagle. Yet it must be very large.

Edith perched herself on the stone railing of the balcony and gave herself up to the grateful flood of sunlight and the survey of her new surroundings.

Even now she felt that she was watched.

Coming from the long isolation of the sick room, she felt as if she had reentered life itself. A new life, tranquil, yet vitally significant. Srinagar and Quebec and Louisville were not a part of this world. Her father and her aunt were incredibly distant. She tried to think of the place of the lotus-eaters, the poem of Tennyson—

"What is the verdict?"

Edith looked up, and was surprised to see Donovan, supported by Aravang. Over his free arm the grinning servant carried a plaid steamer rug and a takedown armchair. She did not know Donovan at first.

During her absence he had managed to have himself shaved, and his disordered hair trimmed. A clean white shirt, a neat flannel jacket and white flannel trousers completed the metamorphosis. His mustache was altered into almost military smartness, and the growth of beard was gone. Only the blue eyes and the lean brown cheeks were the same.

"Oh," cried Edith, "you shouldn't be outdoors. You will take cold."

Donovan smiled, or rather the lines in his cheeks deepened and the wrinkles about his eyes crept into being. "Really? I'm quite accustomed to—outdoors. Besides, I've had a cold bath."

She recalled his first speech, and clapped her hands.

"Bravo! The verdict is: excellent. How did you do it?"

"Do what? Oh." Donovan sank into the camp chair Aravang had adjusted. "I meant Yakka Arik, not myself, Miss Rand."

"But you are wonderfully clean. I'm growing envious."

"The explanation is simple. A good native barber may be had in Yakka Arik—thanks to the Sayak rule of half-shaven mustaches and hair, following the Mohammedan custom. I had my own kit."

"A mirror! Have you a mirror, Mr. Donovan?" She held her breath.

"Oh, yes. And the rug and chair emerged from my box."

But Edith had sprung to her feet. "I must have the mirror!"

Donovan held up a protesting hand. His keen glance dwelt briefly on her face, flushed by the sun. Edith had been busy with her new-found sewing materials and had fashioned a light blue smock out of Aravang's offerings of veils—also a loose girdle of the same color and a light scarf.

These served to use in place of her outworn shirtwaist. Her natural taste in dress made them becoming. The girl was a splendid picture, her fine hair hanging loose to her slender shoulders and her eyes alight with good humor.

"Please!" Donovan said gravely. "Some women may need a mirror, but you—" He fell silent. "You are—"

His voice sank, yet Edith's quick ears—and it must be confessed that she was listening acutely—caught the word "matchless." It was her turn to pause. Into the eyes of the man there had sprung a glow that was not a reflection of the sunlight.

Your box is a regular treasure chest," Edith changed the topic, and did not know that her bare throat and her face had turned a shade rosier. "What else have you hidden in it?"

"Pandora! I forbid you to look." Donovan spoke lightly, his eyes still resting on the glory of her hair. Yet he meant what he said. It was characteristic of the man to expect attention and obedience when he spoke. This naturally piqued the girl who did not understand that those who have been much alone in the waste places of the world have become a law unto themselves.

Not that Donovan was silent with her. He loved to hear her talk, enjoying her low, almost drawling voice and her quick wit.

The man was a puzzle to Edith. Seemingly an ally of the natives of Yakka Arik, his name was still known throughout India. When he shook off his mood of silent introspection, his manners were those of a gentleman. He was educated, possessed a taste for Shelley, Lamartine, and Catullus—a combination of the poets that took Edith out of her depth. Yet he seemed to be little more than a wandering adventurer—certainly without home ties.

"Don't you realize," she pointed out, "that it is dangerous to forbid a woman to—look?"

"But the box is my treasure house. I do not intend to be plundered."

"What if I look for the mirror?"

"I cede that to you. Aravang has put it in your—apartment."

They were speaking lightly, avoiding—as Edith thought—^the mention of the realities of Yakka Arik—her captivity, his status in the world, and what the future held in store for her.

A shadow passed quickly over the balcony. The black bird had flown above them, circling idly. The man noticed it, as he did everything. On first coming to the balcony he had scanned the valley with the interest of one who looks for other details than scenery.

"What do you think of this?" His hand swept along the valley, much in the gesture used by Iskander. Edith surveyed the lake seriously, chin on hand, perched on the balcony rail.

"It is quiet. It is so shut in by the mountains. I think I have never seen anything quite so wonderful."

"Would you think so. Miss Rand, if you knew that this Arcadia was in reality a kind of garden of Hesperides?"

"A hidden garden? Or do you hint at forbidden fruit?"

"Both, Miss Rand. The Sayaks guard the location of Yakka Arik with blind zeal. The less you know about the valley, the better for you—"

The fragrance of flowers clung to the balcony. Edith could see the delicate blossoms of the wild rose in the open meadows. Jasmine and acacia were growing near the house. The whole vista was a garden of some sort wherein life was warm. But the Overhanging snow peaks seemed to mock the brightness of the lake—as if the garden spot were flowering only for a brief interval, and soon to be again in the grip of winter.

Edith nodded, dwelling on Donovan's words. She could hear the murmur of hidden cascades and the purring of millstones in the village near by.

"The Sayaks believe that Allah—God—put the warm springs here for their use. They bathe in them, you know. Their religion prescribes absolute cleanliness, especially before prayer."

"Then Aravang isn't a Sayak." Edith turned to him curiously. "What does the word Sayak mean?"

Instead of replying, Donovan adjusted the folds of the blanket thoughtfully.

"The Sayaks," he said, "are followers of a certain religious sect. Kind of Mohammedans, you might say. That is their mosque."

He indicated the gray building at the lower end of the lake. Edith had the feeling that he was putting her question aside.

"As for Aravang," he added, "the beggar is a *kul*, a servant or slave. He happens to be a Dungan—a Chinese-Taghlik type."

Edith recalled the difficulty Major Fraser-Carnie had experienced in placing the man with the scar. So Aravang was a man of two races, and most probably a murderer. She had not been able to forget this.

"He is allowed a lot of liberty. Miss Rand, because of his strength as a warrior and because he handles falcons well."

At this Edith smiled provokingly. Donovan was trying so palpably to lead her away from the subject of Sayaks. "You don't answer my question at all, Mr. Dono-van Khan"—watching him, she saw his brows go up at mention of the name—"and I'm angry. I'll give you another chance to redeem yourself. What is Yakka Arik?"

Donovan pointed to the lake.

"That is Yakka Arik!"

"Indeed! Then I suppose the fish are Sayaks." She frowned at him determinedly. "And that building down at the end there is nothing more than the village meeting house in spite of its being so carefully camouflaged, and in spite of the fact that practically all the men and women of this quite *ordinary place* spend hours there every day?"

"It's my fault that I'm so bally poor at explaining. Quite right. That's the church, and everybody except the *kuls* and the guards—" he broke off hastily. "Everybody, that is, of the Sayak creed is there. Otherwise, you would have to put on your veil, and I would be most unhappy."

Just a little her frown unbent, and then tightened. She would not let him change the subject again. Edith was accustomed to find out what she wanted to know.

"You are not nice, at all. I want to know *what* that mosque really is and why there are guards here. Oh, I heard you."

At this, the mask of moodiness fell over the man's lined face. He surveyed the still surface of the lake in silence. And when he spoke, he seemed communing with himself again.

"The mosque? Yes, that's the trouble, the mosque. It's better, far better that you should not know all about that. I want you not to know. It's your best chance. Iskander and the rest won't say anything. Aravang can't— much. By the way, that fellow will serve you faithfully. He worships you, as—many do."

Edith went straight to the point of this. Her inborn sincerity yearned for plain words of truth; likewise she wanted him to have confidence in her.

"Why don't you want me to know?"

"Because," he observed slowly, "I know. That's the reason I'm here. Not that I blame *them*. After all, it was my own doing. Curious thing, fate. It's like black care behind the rider—can't escape it, you know." His blue eyes brooded. "After all, they have made me their friend. Mahmoud and the others. But Mahmoud, of course, is the leader in brains. And he, like the other Sayaks, is aflame with religious zeal. No, Miss Rand. So long as you know nothing of the mosque, its meaning, or the true location of Yakka Arik, you have a good chance—"

"To escape. And you?"

Unconsciously she held her breath. At last they were facing the question that was vital to both.

"I? Don't worry. Oh, they are fair, very fair. Besides," he was pondering aloud, "they need me. I must do something for them. That's a card in our hands to get you free. But you must not go to the mosque or ask questions, as you are apt to do."

Edith felt aggrieved and not a little hurt. Woman-like, she desired to hurt him in like measure. She had been looking forward to the moment when they could confide in each other. And now—

"Mr. Donovan, I was carried here by these—friends—of yours away from my father. I don't know why. And now I'm kept here in Yakka Arik. Really, I'm a prisoner. Why? I've been wanting to know, to ask you about it all. I've waited all this time to hear you explain everything. And now you say I'm asking too many questions."

CHAPTER XVII
ARAVANG EXPLAINS

Donovan sat up suddenly and gripped the arms of his chair as if confronted by a new and disturbing thought.

"You think, Miss Rand, that I am responsible for bringing you here? No. Mahmoud and Iskander planned that while I was ill."

Edith was well aware of this, but a provoking of obstinacy kept her from acknowledging it. After all, she thought, she had not accused him of it.

"Please understand," he said slowly, almost painfully. "I would give an arm if you had not been brought here. Miss Rand, you held me back from death. I—I was probably headed for a Sayak grave—so Iskander says. Tired, you know. When your face came before my eyes and I felt your hands clinging to mine—"

"You didn't!" A rosy wave swept to the roots of Edith's hair. "You—you must have dreamed that. It was Mahmoud who saved you."

He was silent, bewildered. He had not meant to hurt the girl, was longing instead to comfort her. But his character was not schooled in the varying moods of woman.

"No, you were the one. You asked me to help you. It brought me back, to want to live. Don't you see? You were an angel. God knows, I've cursed the men who brought you here." Bitterness crept into his low voice. "It's been another misfortune that came of my mission here."

"Please don't say that." Edith did not like to see Donovan so downcast. The man was strong—a leader among his kind, she had felt. Now he seemed to abandon his thoughts to moodiness on her account.

"It's the truth. I've nothing left, no ties or hopes, except one. And that you would despise, I think. Yes, you would. You are too noble-hearted to do anything else. But, then you don't understand." His jaw thrust forward and one lean hand clenched. "Still, I will give my life to get you out of Yakka Arik and back—home. Yes, home. I haven't been home for seven years. Well, no use thinking of that or wanting to go, when I have no home. You have."

By a wayward twist of memory the thought of the young British subaltern at the Maharaja's ball came to Edith. The officer had craved sight of those he had left in England. "It must be terrible—to have no home," she murmured.

"Terrible? No. It is just being alone." He replied to her with an effort, his mind clearly on other things. "But to lose the others—that is hard." Donovan was speaking now with strong feeling held in check. "During the War my father and brother went West. There were only the three of us, you know."

"Oh!" Edith felt a quick impulse of sympathy. She tried to think of a consoling word, and was silent. John Donovan, gazing out forbiddingly at the lake, seemed to repel any such advance.

The girl had realized for some time that he was an Englishman. She wondered if he, like his brother, had been in the army. She believed that was the case. Certain mannerisms, a habit of authoritative speech, attention to the little things that go to make comfort out of hardships, indicated that this was so. But he did not care to speak about himself.

Edith bent a tendril of hair about her finger and released it—a habit of hers. Donovan watched her passively. During his illness the two had been brought closely together. A word, an inflection, or a gesture meant much.

"You think, then," she mused, "that it will be hard for me to leave Yakka Arik."

He pointed up at the hills that surrounded Yakka Arik on three sides. "I must tell you how useless it is to try, Miss Rand. A cordon of armed guards extends all around us, each sentry within sight of his neighbor. Where they are posted in the forest, a swathe has been cut in underbrush from one to the other. I have seen graves in those cleared spaces, where visitors came unbidden to steal through the lines."

"But at night—it might be possible to escape then."

"Nature has provided against that. Any one fleeing in the dark would fall into the ravines or be caught by the cataracts. At best only a little ground could be gained before morning. Then the men in the upper lookouts on the summits would spot you. After that, you would be tracked down."

It was hard for Edith to realize that she was actually a prisoner, guarded by invisible eyes. She did not know how bitter the tribal feuds of these mountains had been, and how keen were the eyes of the sheep hunters who nursed long muzzle-loaders on dizzy elevations. Inexperienced in this new life, she refused to accept Donovan's warning, believing that he had not been wholly frank with her. "There must be some way in—and out—except across the bridge at the lower gorge and through the mosque!"

Donovan smiled thoughtfully. "Once," he observed, "a man entered Yakka Arik through a sheep path, that skirted the mosque by a ravine, under the sentinel. The Sayaks call him 'the Vulture.' Now, his life is forfeit if they ever find him and his followers. And I rather think they will."

Edith shivered, as the menace that lay behind the sunny aspect of the valley assumed reality. "Oh, it is terrible!"

"Life itself is terrible sometimes, Miss Rand. But Yakka Arik assumes the guise of terror only to protect itself. What is strange to you is commonplace to these men. Really, they only follow tradition, and the law and faith of Yakka Arik are older than our faith, and"—he spoke musingly—"the two are not so different, after all."

The girl, gazing down the lake, saw a throng issue from the arch of the mosque. A many-colored group of men, women and children emerged into the village streets. The mosque *did* seem a little like a church, with its Sunday worshipers. Only the worshipers went every day. "It looks so like a big cathedral," she reflected aloud. "I wish I could understand!"

Donovan nodded sympathetically.

"Right! Only the whole of the valley is the cathedral, Miss Rand. We are in one of the holy spots of ancient Asia itself—as ancient as the Tartar hordes that once were driven past here by the Chinese, who built the tower on the lower ravine. Remember that these mountain places are considered sacred by the natives."

"I thought no Mohammedans ever lived above the Himalayas." Edith was guilefully seeking the forbidden fruit of knowledge which Donovan had denied her.

"Your wisdom is too young, Miss Rand. The forefathers of the Moslems, the Uigurs and the Tartars had their birthplace in upper Central Asia. And they had Yakka Arik. Now they come here from Arabia, Turkestan, and the corners of Asia. The Arabs, Persians, Uigurs, Taghliks, and not a few Afghans ride here in the pilgrimage caravans—"

"Sometimes called the 'caravan of the dead'?" she put in.

Donovan looked at her sharply, and a hard mask settled on his lean face.

"Those who ride in the caravan of the dead have offended against the law of Yakka Arik. God grant you never come to know its meaning—"

He fell silent, his hands gripped tight together, sunk in meditation. Edith was startled by the gravity of his low voice. She half put out her hand to touch his, then drew back.

"I am so glad that I found you here," she said impulsively. "Mahmoud and the others frighten me. They never even look at me, and I am sure they have no sympathy at all. No one, even, except Iskander, comes to the house." It was her way of offering him peace—with honors—of asking him to trust her.

Donovan replied abstractedly, without weighing the possible effect of his words: "You see, it's my house, given me because they've made me *khan*—equal in rank to Iskander. They don't look at you because you are unveiled in the house, and they don't come here on that account—because, of course, they consider that you are mine and it's contrary to the old Moslem law to visit where the women of the house can be seen."

Edith caught her breath. So she was merely the property of Donovan Khan! The Sayaks thought of her as his wife or—or slave! She recalled the words of Iskander.

"Indeed," she observed frigidly, "haven't you told them that I am an American? They must know I have friends, who may trace me to Kashgar—"

Donovan shook his head thoughtfully.

"Any place but Kashgar, Miss Rand, where the Vulture roosts just now. You are safer here. As for your nationality, if you will pardon me, it is unknown here or in Central Asia generally."

"Is it?" Edith tossed away the tendril, feeling provoked the more because instinct told her this was the truth. "We shall see. They may learn what an American father will do for his daughter. But these Sayaks—why do they keep me prisoner? For ransom?"

"Indeed not."

"As—as hostage?"

"Nearer right. Not exactly."

"Then what? You won't tell me!"

A shapely foot in a native sandal—Edith's shoes were being preserved carefully against future need—began to tap the stone floor of the balcony. Donovan noticed it with appreciation. Everything about her, he reflected, was dainty. He did not interpret the animation of the foot as a sign of danger.

"Your *friends* seem to me very much like heathens, Mr. Donovan, in spite of your defense of them. And I think that church is a *bad* place."

"Well, they think of us as infidels. Yet, Miss Rand, the mosque and the man who lives within it is one of the safeguards of Christianity. He is the one more than any other whose friendship I must keep."

Craftily she sought for information about this man.

"He is not a Christian, is he? You always say, 'Perhaps'." Edith wanted him to understand that he had not made peace. "You never say what I want you to."

Donovan smiled doggedly. He did not understand the mood of the girl—that she wanted him to confide in her, comfort her.

"Remember," he observed bluntly, "Mahmoud has done much for me. And Iskander saved you—your life at Kashgar. He did the same thing for me, too, at Kashgar, when the Vulture's friends pretty nearly succeeded in poisoning me."

"But they are murderers and—and brigands. Aravang killed your servant."

He sighed. How was this girl, fresh from the outside world, to understand the men of another race and the rigid laws of Yakka Arik?

"They have their code. An old one. Miss Rand. Before the coming of Christ it was that of Christians. An eye for an eye—a blow for a blow." Donovan pointed suddenly to the mosque. "That is not an evil place. It is a temple of faith, and faith is not an evil thing."

"Then why can't I go there? To this man who is your friend?"

Anxiety flashed into Donovan's tense face. Edith mistook it for anger.

"Because I say so! You must not try to learn the secret of the Sayaks."

The familiar ring of command was in his low voice. The girl's chin went up stubbornly and the gray eyes became cold.

"Very well," she said.

Donovan nodded in relief. He did not understand that, instead of consent, Edith's words meant that she was fully determined to disobey him. She would go to the mosque. Nothing would prevent her, now that Donovan, who should—so she reasoned—have been frank with her and trusted her instead of his Sayak friends, had forbidden it. And at the same time she would appeal to the man of the mosque to help Donovan and herself.

Unaware that Edith had made up her mind to do the very thing he was most anxious she should not do—the thing that could ruin her prospect of escape from the lake, Donovan proposed that they should go below to their quarters.

"I'm devilishly hungry," he said cheerfully, "and Aravang must have lunch ready. I think I smell baked fish."

"I'm not hungry," she assured him coldly.

The girl remained on her perch when Aravang appeared for the sick man. Later, when Donovan sent the native to convey to her by signs that lunch was waiting, she shook her head.

For the first time she noticed that Aravang had a large bird on his wrist. It was a goshawk, hooded. Its powerful claws gripped a glove on the man's hand. The slave started at sight of the girl.

Aravang had evidently planned a little of his favorite diversion, while his mistress was below stairs. Edith stared at the falcon curiously, surprised at its tameness. Hawks, she had always thought, were wild and not subject to domestication. Its hooked beak and sharp talons appeared menacing.

Suddenly she beckoned the native.

"Aravang," she said, "I know you are not as ignorant as you want to seem. You know some English. Even if you can't speak it very well. Now, please pay attention. No one else will tell me anything. So you must."

The falconer grinned, one hand gently Stroking the feathers of his pet. He could not have understood Edith's words, but he was obedient to the change in her voice. She faced him, one finger raised, as if he had been a child.

"Now listen." Edith spoke very slowly and distinctly. "Aravang, who is Dono-van Khan?" She lifted her brows and pointed to the stairway. "Who is he?"

"Dono-van Khan."

Edith was momentarily halted but not defeated. "Is he a real khan? Is he a khan among the Sayaks?" She nodded toward the distant mosque.

An expression of apprehension crossed the man's open face. He cast a wary eye at the stairs. "Sayak, no," he muttered. "Khan, yess."

Edith understood by this that Donovan was not a member of the religious brotherhood of Yakka Arik, but was held in esteem by them.

"What is a khan?" she whispered. "A chief?"

The last word did not penetrate to Aravang's understanding. He shifted his feet uneasily, handling the bird. Then he made a vocular effort.

"Mees *effendi*, Mees Rrand." He planted a fist on his own chest. "Me—*kul!* Dono-van Khan—*manaps*."

"What is that?"

Aravang was stumped. He could not explain. He shook his shaggy head and extended a pleading hand, to show his helplessness and his desire to serve his mistress. Then his broad face brightened.

"Manaps," he repeated and pointed to the hawk.

"A falcon?" She recalled that Iskander had termed him this, and she thought of the blue letter that had come to Monsey—The Falcon is on the wing."

So, Monsey had been warned that Donovan was alive.

At this, Aravang excelled himself. He drew an imaginary sword and swung it viciously at an invisible enemy, repeating the native word, as if it were a charm. He darted a scarred finger at the mosque from which the throng of men and women was still emerging.

"Iskander, Dono-van Khan, *manaps*. Mees *effendi*, thus—you look!"

Abruptly, he whisked the hood off the goshawk and slipped the silver chain from its claw. For a second the falcon hesitated. Then, with a whirr of wings, it soared up from the balcony.

Edith watched it circle into the sky with the velocity of an arrow. The only other winged thing in sight was the black vulture, a carrion bird. Ordinarily, perhaps, the hawk would not have attacked such a thing. But now it was ravenous, having been starved by Aravang to the proper point And the native had trained his birds well.

In the space of a few swift moments the falcon had got above the vulture, which now began to fly toward the pines, evidently sensing some danger; and Aravang's pet had flashed down, striking the black bird with beak and tearing claws.

Edith saw the dying bird fall into a garden not far away. The hawk circled down close upon it. She looked up. Aravang had gone to redeem his pet.

In the room below the girl found Donovan standing by the table where the lunch was set. He had not touched the food, waiting until she should came.

His lean face, and bright, deep-set eyes made her think of the hawk.

CHAPTER XVIII
THE STONE CHAMBER

For the next few days Edith was very busy with needle and thread. She had Aravang bring her one or two garments of the Sayak women, explaining to Donovan that she needed a pattern for her dressmaking.

She would sit by the embrasure of the stone room on an ebony bench, her slippered feet crossed on a splendid Persian rug, her loose blue smock stripped back from her forearms. Softly, she hummed under her breath, while the needle flew.

Donovan, now able to walk with a makeshift cane, was frequently absent. He had long talks with the leaders of the Sayaks. Once Edith saw him from the window, passing through the garden with Mahmoud. She returned to her singing and her new dress. Donovan sick had been the object of her care; Donovan convalescent was quite a different proposition.

"By Jove!"

It was the man himself, pipe in hand, leaning against the doorpost, his eyes on her. Not often did he come to the stone chamber during the daytime. He considered the room as Edith's, and he was careful not to intrude unless some occasion warranted it. How was he to know that she missed him: at least, she assured herself, it was the empty house she dreaded. Nothing more.

During the last days Donovan had been more silent than ever. He walked much, sometimes with Edith, in the garden. At such times he was shy and self-contained. But now, his eyes had lighted up, and a smile softened his clear-cut mouth.

"By Jove, you *do* seem a medieval matron, with your—ah—tapestry and your hair loose on your shoulders like that. You have no idea how beautiful you are!"

Edith drew a quick, startled breath, and her hands flew to her hair. He watched her coil it dexterously, admiring the play of her slender arms and firm fingers.

How graceful she was, he thought! How childlike in her clear-eyed honesty and friendliness. He appreciated the sterling quality of her pride and fearlessness. Yet it was not for that he loved her.

John Donovan worshiped the slender slippers on Edith's feet. Sight of the woman's fairness wrought in the lonely man a silent longing aid, more than this, an all-powerful awe. This was the reason he had been absent from the stone room so much. He was afraid his presence might disturb Edith, perhaps annoy her. He was happiest when they walked in the garden.

Resolutely he tried to keep from thinking of her—something that was as impossible as to keep from breathing—or dwelling on the happiness that her stay in the valley had brought to him. His task was to safeguard her.

To Edith, the long absences of the man and his silence when with her were things that troubled her. Frequently, when he was gone, she spent hours in trying a new adjustment of her Sayak garb, or a fresh manner of dressing her hair. She sang to herself at times. Often she frowned, feeling so much out of Donovan's life and the events that passed in Yakka Arik.

Now a tantalizing smile twitched her lips.

"Have I aged so much? I don't feel at all matronl."

"Oh, I say. The tableau resembled a sketch by Tintoretto or Paul Veronese. Really, you are no more than a child. Twenty-two, at the most—"

"Twenty," corrected Edith, biting off a thread tranquilly. She surveyed the nearly-completed garment with satisfaction. Donovan watched her, drawing at his pipe, which—unknown to him—had gone out.

Covertly Edith stole a glance at the precious mirror that she had adjusted near her bed. A skilled finger poked a straying hair into place. Outwardly she ignored Donovan. Of course.

"You know Veronese, Mr. Donovan? I adore Masaccio. His figures seem really like men and not just splendid counterfeits." A subtle undercurrent of meaning ran through her words. "They are—so honest and—and frank."

"Really?" He was absorbed in the turn of her wrist as she drew the thread through. "Oh, that Masaccio chap has strength, no end. But Veronese is—ah—luxurious."

"Am I, then, an image of luxury?" She laughed. "Behold a poor beggar maid, forced to make her own clothes, and wash them, too. And a prisoner in a pagan castle. Just how much liberty have you and Mahmoud and Company decided to allot me?"

"All you desire, within the barriers and outside the mosque."

"Suppose I go climb the mountains?"

"In those?" His pipe stem indicated the slippers that barely covered the soles of her stockinged feet. "Besides, you would be turned back by the guards in the passes."

"Haven't you the password?"

"There is no password."

A shadow crossed his expressive face. "The Sayak chiefs are in council and within a day or two there may be fighting in the hills. There are rumors that the Vulture is spreading his wings again. Until the—uncertainty is over you are safest here. I want you to trust me, Edith."

It was the first time he had called her that. The gray eyes glanced at him fleetingly, then fell to her work.

"Who is this Vulture, Donovan Khan? A tribal chief?"

"Rather more." He hesitated and Edith thought of the black bird that had passed over the lake.

"Aravang says you are a falcon."

"I wish I had wings."

"But falcons are horrid, destructive things."

"Sometimes they kill what is fitting." John Donovan fell into one of his frequent moods of introspection. "Certain things have no right to live. Destiny, in its course of life, adjusts that. Now, a vulture, flying over that sheepfold across the lake, should be killed."

A new thought startled her. "Donovan Khan, will you be in this feud—in danger?"

He paused to light his pipe, and then spoke casually. "Danger? Well, you have no cause to worry, Edith. And after all this bother is over and I have made good my promise to the Sayaks, I will ask your release from Yakka Arik and learn what *kismet* has in store."

She started. Monsey had used that word. Donovan went on amiably:

"I'm awfully grateful to fate that you came instead of—another." He frowned swiftly. "God knows, I don't mean that. I wouldn't have you here—"

"So you don't like me, after all!" Edith laughed whimsically. "I was just thinking, Donovan Khan, that my aunt would envy me. Behold, personally conducted, I have visited and seen the sights and people of Central Asia. Hotel accommodation was provided me free of charge. I have toured what the guidebooks can the roof of the world, and in conveyances that poor Aunt Kate never dreamed of."

So infectious were her high spirits the man laughed with her. Their eyes met and held. Each had a message for the other. Edith's laugh ceased. She looked away and as she did so, he saw that she had flushed.

In this one moment the two castaways were brought together. They had read understanding in each other's eyes. And this was the time when the girl needed the comfort of the man's confidence.

It was the last moment of pleasant *camaraderie*. Neither one could know of the shadow that was dosing in upon Yakka Arik, or the events that were to be set in motion by Edith's own willfulness. Nor did they realize how great would be their need of each other.

Womanlike, Edith hastened to speak of other matters.

"You are as bad as ever, Donovan Khan. You have changed the subject altogether, with ruthless damage to my curiosity. Now, how did you come to know who I was when I first told you my name?"

"That is not my story, Edith. But after I undertook this thing for the Sayaks—" he broke off. After I started on this venture, I stopped at one of our advanced posts, an English station, for supplies and weapons. There

I spent the night with a fine old chap. He was practically alone at the station. We fell to talking. First about the service, you know, and then about ourselves. He seemed to be lonely."

Donovan paused, with his habitual reluctance to explain anything about himself.

"This man was a friend of your mother. He had been often in your United States, and visited her home. Said the hospitality he received was a kind of landmark in his life. He—loved your mother and asked her to marry him. But he didn't win out. Another man, you know. It was a fair field and a good fight, he said."

Edith was intensely interested.

She understood now why Fraser-Carnie had befriended her, knowing that the old officer cherished the memory of her mother. It was clear that he and the adventurer—so she thought of her companion—had met at Gilghit.

"So Major Fraser-Carnie was your friend, too," she mused, and then added impulsively, "I feel sure he and my father will trace me to Kashgar, in time, and then they will come here—"

"Not without a guide from the Sayaks themselves. From the tower itself, down the ravine, Yakka Arik can't be seen. And then there are the guards."

Edith was immersed in her new thought.

"But you say that Iskander is master of the armed guards and that you have equal rank with him. Donovan Khan, surely this man in the temple who has authority, as you say, even over Mahmoud and Iskander, must be peacefully inclined—if he is really a priest. Can't you ask him to make peace with the person you call the Vulture and to send word to Major Fraser-Carnie?"

"No, Edith. I have never tried to see the *hadji* of the mosque." Donovan did not want to explain that, in her present situation, any attempt to get the girl out of Yakka Arik must fail; and he knew that she would not understand the impossibility of checking the feud of the Sayaks against the man he had called the Vulture.

In the annals of the Moslem tribes of Central Asia there is a wrong that calls for vengeance, calls for what is termed in their own language the "pursuit of blood." It is a wrong that is handed down from father to son, and to grandson; a wrong that stains the honor of a man—and they hold personal honor very high—until it is wiped out.

And Donovan, in making good the task that had brought him from India, had paid a price. He had given his pledge to the Sayaks to aid them in striking down the Vulture and his mates. This had kept him an outcast for the last years and once, at Kashgar, had nearly resulted in his death.

Thus Donovan had widened the slight breach between him and the girl, without knowing it. How was he to understand her swift impulses and her yearning to be trusted?

Perhaps if she had not loved John Donovan she would not have sacrificed him and herself to the anger of the Sayaks.

CHAPTER XIX

NEW ARRIVALS

The day after their talk, as soon as John Donovan had left the stone chamber—Edith was careful to ascertain this by intensive listening behind her silk partition—the girl hurried through her breakfast.

Then, moved by a long-considered impulse, she rifled the forbidden box of its telescope. Putting on her *yashmak* and concealing the fruit of her theft under her cloak, she tripped out of the house, through the courtyard and garden and up the slope that led to the pine forest.

Edith ascended the mountain side steadily until she reached the shadow of the great trees. Here she pushed forward between rocks and thorn patches to an open grove. Then she surveyed the trees with a speculative frown. They veiled her view of the valley.

Lack of resourcefulness was not one of her failings. She selected a sizable hemlock, with branches conveniently low to the ground, tucked her skirt more firmly about her waist, and began to climb.

The sticky surface of the hemlock stained her fingers, and the loose needles fell into her hair. She kept on until she reached a larger branch, where, through an opening in the trees, a clear view down the valley was afforded.

Edith breathed a sigh of satisfaction, and began to adjust the telescope. A ray of sunlight flashed on the lens. This flicker of light from the branches of the hemlock caught the eye of a man who lay hidden in the tamarisk clumps a short way up the mountain side.

He was a broad, squat fellow in dirty woolen garb, a long musket slung over his shoulder. From the shelter of the tamarisks he was keeping a keen watch over the valley. The man had seen a movement in the hemlock, but had attributed it to the flutter of birds. Now, however, he pushed his gun further behind his back and began to crawl quietly downward, passing from thorn patch to tamarisk clump and gliding across the stretches of open grass.

The watcher had not far to go. He moved with the stealth of one whose fear of observation had ascendancy over his desire to spy. A heavy-footed, evil-faced native, evidently a Sart, and a Sart upon a mission.

Owing to her interest in the panorama of the valley, Edith did not notice him. The telescope was powerful, and she could discern plainly the details of the hidden mosque. Its doors were closed at this early hour; but she could see the crimson and blue coloring of the gate arch, and certain robed figures moving on the balcony over the arch.

From this she turned the instrument down the lower valley. The gorge was revealed to her, and she drew an excited breath at seeing the gray tower perched on the cliff, rising over the steaming vapor that welled from the hot springs in the stream winding down the ravine bottom.

The square, barren tower appeared as desolate as ever, at first. The girl, however, had strong, young eyes and the telescope brought the scene on the cliff summit close before her vision, even at the distance of some three miles.

So she saw the small dots that came into view around the foot of the tower. By gazing intently, she glimpsed horses and men. It was impossible to make out the clothing of the men, yet Edith fancied that they did not resemble those she had seen in Yakka Arik.

While the girl gazed, the Sart gained a vantage point where he could see the hemlock. Straightway, after he had stared long at Edith, he fell to scrutinizing the neighboring forest as if to make certain she was alone.

Unconscious of another presence, Edith felt the surge of rising excitement. Her sally to the mountain side had been inspired by the hope of inspecting the mosque and its entrances without being seen by the Sayaks.

The sight of men at the tower stirred her pulse. Instinct told her they were not men of the valley. Had her father sent a search party as far as the gorge? Was rescue at hand?

Europeans were at Kashgar—Donovan had admitted as much. Could not a party from Srinagar, perhaps under Fraser-Carnie, have heard of the affray in the alley, and have traced her from Kashgar to the mountain wilds?

Edith could have clapped her hands with delight. Instead she became suddenly quiet, with a little sigh of suspense.

Up the slope under the pines Iskander and Mahmoud were walking. By the alert air of the *manaps* the girl guessed that they had seen her departure from the village and followed. Iskander moved silently through the brush in his soft, morocco boots, holding up the folds of his burnoose. Mahmoud followed idly as if uninterested in the proceeding.

Whereupon Edith giggled irresistibly and nestled closer to her branch. It was not likely that they would see her in her perch. She felt the pleasant thrill of a fugitive, safe from pursuers, who watches the course of the pursuit.

The two Sayaks moved nearer, evidently at loss where to seek for her. Iskander muttered something angrily under his breath and halted beneath the very tree in which she sat. Mahmoud followed more leisurely.

Edith's bright eyes surveyed the scene with satisfaction. Then her hand flew to her throat as she stifled cry.

Not a hundred yards away from the hemlock, and apparently nearer because of her elevated position, she had seen the Sart. He lay prone behind a low screen of ferns, and his long musket was trained upon Iskander.

There was no mistaking the intent poise of the flattened body, the purpose in the head pressed close to the gunstock. The ferns must conceal the native from the keen glance of the Arab.

Iskander moved slightly, to draw a cigarette from the packet he carried in his girdle. At this, the man behind the ferns looked up, only to settle down to his sight again. A brown hand closed upon the trigger guard.

"Iskander!" she cried—almost screamed—"Look out, in front of you!"

Startling as the girl's voice, coming from directly overhead, must have been, the quick-witted Arab did not look up. He slipped behind the bole of the tree while Edith was still speaking. There he drew a long, first puff at his cigarette and exchanged a low warning with Mahmoud—the *hakim* being still unseen by the slayer behind the thicket. Not even then did Iskander, experienced in the vicissitudes of mountain warfare, raise his eyes from the surrounding forest.

"How many men, Mees Rand?" he asked quickly. "And where?"

"One, that I can see," breathed the girl. "Behind the ferns under the tamarisks. He was going to shoot you with a rifle."

"Good. Is he a white man or a native?"

For a fleeting instant Edith's newly cherished hope flashed at this mention of the nearness of possible rescuers. Then she reflected that a follower of Major Fraser-Carnie or her father would hardly act in the manner of the skulker behind the ferns.

At her answer, Iskander spoke briefly with Mahmoud.

"It was the will of Allah that I should not have my revolver this morning," he remarked indifferently to the apprehensive girl. "But watch! You will see an unbeliever taste his own fear."

He remained where he was. Mahmoud advanced swiftly from the underbrush, his slits of eyes flickering over the ferns in front of him. He seemed to have no fear. Edith glanced at the slayer, who by now had seen Mahmoud. His broad, ugly face changed. His mouth opened and he gaped as if in the fascination of utter dread. The girl noticed that his hands trembled.

Then, with an animal-like grunt, the Sart sprang up and ran plunging through the thickets up the mountainside.

Iskander smiled and placed his hand to his lips.

"Sayak!" he called, in a long, high note that carried far. "Sayak! Zikr!"

As if an echo, a wailing cry answered from the tipper forest. Another took up the word, more distant. Still another voice repeated faintly from a far-off height.

"Sayak!"

"You see." Iskander shrugged his shoulders. "Why should I bleed a dog that flees, when there are those whose task it is? Presently you will hear the death of the dog. Ah!"

He had noticed the telescope. Straightway he swung himself up into the branches, climbing swiftly, for all his loose robe. Edith waited, feeling like a criminal caught red-handed. She wished ardently for John Donovan, but the white man was below in the village.

The Arab swung himself beside her on the branch and took the telescope. Evidently he was familiar with such things. For some time, while the girl observed him and Mahmoud squatted patiently beneath them, Iskander swept the valley. When the tower came within his vision, his dark face tensed. His lips bore a slight smile as he turned to the girl, who was still nervous—an after-effect of the scene just enacted under the pines.

"*Ohé*, my little winged bird," murmured the Arab. "What do you think of those—riders upon the cliff, where you see the tower?"

Edith fancied that he was trying to sound her, to learn what she had seen.

With a snap Iskander closed the telescope and thrust it into his girdle, drawing at the cigarette he had not ceased to smoke.

"A score of years ago to that tower came the beastlike Russians, stupid and without right to the lands. They were strong men, but lustful and very greedy. They put up a flag and made a speech about a boundary. Because of the cold, they stayed close to the *Kurgan*—all but one."

He nodded reflectively.

"All but one. He was like a vulture, and this Vulture and his native allies alone knew of Yakka Arik. They came to our valley—once. They took many of our women who were bathing in the women's pools in the shadow of the mosque. They took my daughter and her mother."

Iskander let the cigarette fall from his fingers. He spoke calmly, but Edith saw the glow in his deep eyes and the veins that pulsed in his temples.

"Yess. It was the Vulture, Mees Rand. When the Sayaks came to the *Kurgan* and asked for their thirty-nine women that had been taken away, the Russian commandant said he knew nothing of the matter. He said that the Alamans and Turkish followers had taken them.

"An Englishman who was hunting mountain sheep—although I think he was never seen to shoot very many—had pitched his tent not far from the *Kurgan* and to him I carried our grievance. He said very little, but he talked with the Russian commandant and after that there was much confusion and sending of messages from the *Kurgan*. And presently the commandant and his men went away from the tower, journeying back out of our sight. The Englishman was Dono-van Khan and although his words were very mild, the Russians feared that he could call upon thousands of sword points from the British in India."

The girl listened eagerly, gleaning for the first time an insight into the character of the adventurer.

"And so," explained Iskander, "we called him *khan*. Afterward, he became the friend of Yakka Arik. Yet he would not admit that he was a soldier, like the Vulture. Nay, but—Dono-van Khan knows the name of the man who is the Vulture, and he alone can tell me the name of my enemy. Soon Dono-van Khan will tell it to me.

"Aie! My daughter had seen fourteen summers. Her eyes were like twin moons and the scent of her hair was like the jasmine flower. Her teeth were white pearls. I did not see her again. It was told to me that her mother was sold in the Yarkand bazaar. But when I traced her to Khotan and the slave house of a merchant, she had died. But I have not forgotten the Vulture. Come, Mees Rand, I will help you."

He assisted her to the ground. Mahmoud rose and stalked down toward the village. Edith glanced at Iskander pityingly and curiously. Then she uttered a stifled cry.

Gunshots had sounded from the mountain overhead. Two quick reports were followed by another. Mahmoud looked up and smiled.

"The dog is dead," said Iskander, with the assurance of one who knew he was voicing the truth. "Come!"

He strode along restlessly, a gnawing fever in his eyes. Edith had to run to keep up, and a slipper fell from her foot. Iskander noticed it.

"Why," she asked, "did that—that man run when he saw Mahmoud ? The *hakim* was unarmed—"

"Fear is sharper than a sword. The dog looked upon the face of him who is master of the caravan, and feared lest he be sent away—"

Iskander broke off. Edith remembered that she had heard him use that phrase before. What did it mean—to be sent away? She did not know. But there was no mistaking the dread in the Sart's face. The man had feared something, and very greatly.

CHAPTER XX
IN THE SHADOW OF THE TEMPLE

That day was the one Edith finished her sewing. The new garment was complete. Alone in the stone room, safe behind the canopy, the girl surveyed it with brightened eyes. She held in her hand a complete Sayak dress, modeled after those brought by Aravang at her request.

This was the task that had kept her busy. Donovan, with a man's ignorance of such matters, had not noticed the character of the garment.

Now, making sure that she was unwatched, Edith slipped out of her old dress into the new.

Putting on a heavy *yashmak* and placing another veil across her tawny hair, the girl surveyed herself in the mirror. To all intents, except for her gray eyes, she appeared one of the women of Yakka Arik. To add to the effect, she touched eyebrows and eyelids with *kohl*, likewise obtained from the obedient Aravang. She still wore the slippers instead of her shoes. The long, black outer garment, which covered the thin shirt and Oriental trousers, fell to her feet and concealed her much-darned silk stockings.

Edith draped several pretty necklaces—gifts from Donovan—about her throat and felt that her masquerade was complete. Then she tiptoed to the door. The hall was silent, and she saw that the outer court with its tiny garden was empty. The Sayaks were either in the mosque or on the way there.

Seeing this, the girl slipped through a postern door in the wall into the larger flower garden beside the house. Once there, she advanced boldly into the path that ran through the village, her little slippers patting the dust diligently until she remembered her new part and endeavored to walk like one of the native women she had watched from the balcony.

Perhaps the attempt was not altogether successful. Edith's young body had never been obliged to bear such burdens as grain sacks, or her head a water jar. But nearly all the women and children of the valley were in the temple. It was the hour before noon and only a handful of belated men were hurrying along the paths, responsive to the wailing call of the *muezzin*.

Edith was going to the mosque. She would see the man Donovan called the *hadji* and appeal to him to keep her friend from danger. Now that she knew Donovan had aided the Sayaks she felt sure that this priest, whatever his nature, would listen to her.

The thought of Donovan removed from her and in danger was intolerable to this girl who had never loved before, but who now loved Donovan with an abiding strength that was part of herself.

Edith skipped along anxious only to be within the temple. Then, as a bent Usbek peasant, withered and toil-worn, glanced at her in some surprise, she moderated her steps to a more sober gait. She did not fear being spoken to. Observation had shown her that the strict privacy of women, a rule among all Mohammedan races, obtained in the valley.

Iskander's tale had aroused her sympathy. She had come to understand—or thought she had—the harassing life of the mountain dwellers of Central Asia, the raids upon settlements by men of other religious faiths, the counter-raids, the fierce religious zeal which led men to slay each other.

But she did not know that Yakka Arik had been inviolate from the surges of intertribal warfare, and this because of one thing. Fear. Nor was she aware of the deep spirit of protection for their womenfolk that dwelt in the hearts of the Sayaks.

Edith, because she did not understand, did not make allowance for the code of these men—an eye for an eye, a blow for a blow, a life for a life.

Her heart was beating clamorously as she slipped past scattered groups of turbaned, swarthy men who scarcely looked at her, owing to the general reluctance to gaze even upon a veiled woman who belonged to another man.

So she walked slowly across the dusty space in front of the mosque. The stone arch rose before her. Armed men, standing beside the gigantic trumpets that Donovan had called the "horns of Jericho," looked down at her grimly from the balcony over the entrance. For a second the girl hesitated, feeling the eyes of the guards upon her.

For the first time she experienced an acute foreboding. Had the watching sentinels who scrutinized each newcomer, fingering their weapons, succeeded in penetrating her disguise?

Then she heard quick footsteps in the sand, and a tiny figure drew near her, running toward the mosque. A Sayak child, seven or eight years of age, had fallen behind the groups of older worshipers. Realizing that her hesitation was attracting the attention of the watchers, Edith took the hand of the boy and advanced beside him toward the arch. He looked up at her playfully and trotted on manfully, perceiving no difference in this tall woman from other Sayaks—glad, in fact, of the aid of her hand.

A moment the clear sunlight gleamed on the white embroidery of her headdress; then she passed into the shadow of the arch—and repressed an involuntary cry. Some steps led into the door of the building itself, within the arch, and on the lowest step a hooded Arab was sitting, scimitar across his knee.

"Peace be with you," the man murmured, not ceasing to look at her. Edith had often heard Donovan employ this salutation and its reply, but as she fumbled for the Turki words in quick alarm, she heard the shrill voice of the child.

"And upon you, also, be peace!"

With that, woman and child passed by the sentry of the steps and entered the outer court where Edith was surprised to see a multitude of slippers of all sizes and colors. While she wondered at this she saw the boy remove his small footgear and go forward barefoot. She did likewise, trusting to the gloom of the inner chambers to conceal her stockings.

The murmur of a sonorous voice reached her. Edith advanced timidly between great pillars and stood within the mosque itself. She saw a lofty space, half in darkness, into which light descended from a single aperture in the roof at the end opposite her. Slender, ornamented pillars supported a balcony with a carved wooden rail. Gold and silver ornaments lined the walls. The light reflected dully from broad gold plates inscribed in a manner strange to Edith.

She had not known that the mosque, which must have been built actually into a cleft in the face of the cliff, was so huge.

Directly in front of the ray of light that fell from the round opening in the dome a turbaned priest in clean robes was reading from a heavy volume, bound in iridescent silk, a gold chain running from the clasp of the book to the neck of the reader. It was the voice of the priest she had heard.

Facing the reader was a silent multitude. Each Sayak, man and woman and child, knelt upon a small prayer rug. Edith had seen them carrying these rolled strips of carpet to the mosque and wondered what they might be. For a moment she feared they might notice that she carried no rug.

But the eyes of the worshipers were fixed on the *hadji*. The girl drew aside softly, walking forward along the side of the nave. Here she was behind the Sayak ranks, and sheltered somewhat by the row of pillars that supported the round balcony. The gloom was deeper in this spot. No one saw the standing girl. While she listened to the sonorous voice, quavering a trifle with age, she had the sensation of being present in one of the old cathedrals of Europe.

Then she noticed for the first time the vapor. So lofty was the opening in the dome and of such small extent that the ray of sunlight moved steadily. When she entered, it had rested on the pages of the book; then it passed over the priest. Now, while still resting upon him, it touched a rising cloud that Edith had supposed to be incense.

Where the altar of a cathedral would have been placed there was a raised latticework of metal—bronze, brightly polished, or gold. It resembled the delicate marble kiosk of the garden of the stone house. Through the apertures of the fretwork a cloud of heavy vapor swirled up.

So heavy was the vapor, it might have been steam. The mosque, in fact, was warmed by it. Edith had fancied for a brief moment that it was incense, rising from a gigantic censer. Then she recalled the hot springs of the lower lake.

Evidently the mosque itself had been erected over one of the sources, and the vapor welled from the hot depths of the water.

The sunlight had just reached the vapor when the priest ceased his reading and lifted both lean arms. A high chant rose from his lips, and he turned to face what Edith still fancied the white incense. And this man, she felt, was the *hadji* of whom Donovan had spoken.

"*Nuri Muhammed s'all Allah!*"

And the multitude responded:

"*La il'oha ill Allah!*"

As one, the heads bent downward toward the breasts of the worshipers. Long folds of the white turbans were detached and laid over the left shoulder. As if performing a well-learned ritual, certain lines of Sayaks rose, with extended arms. Others remained kneeling.

The sight of the concentric rings of multicolored garments, the intent faces, and the lifted hands made Edith draw back, fearful of observation. Utter silence had fallen on the mosque.

In the silence, the worshipers appeared to be awaiting something. She saw that they were gazing at the vapor. By now Edith realized that this was no ordinary Mohammedan mosque.

And then she saw John Donovan.

In the intervals between the Sayak lines he was walking, looking closely at the figures of the kneeling women.

No one molested Donovan. Apparently he was entitled to enter the mosque. Edith felt that he had missed her, and had come to seek her.

Then the lines of standing men began to move from side to side. One voice, then another, took up a refrain :

"Hai—hai! Allah, hai!"

They placed their lifted hands on the shoulders of their comrades and swayed their bodies in cadence.

They seemed to be moving toward her.

"Hai—hai! Allah, hai!"

It was a low chant that rose and echoed against the lofty dome. It grew into a rush of sound, in which the echoes were lost. Edith felt the beat of the passionate cry grip her senses.

Donovan did not halt. He pushed through the moving men toward her position. The chant changed, as the men formed into long, sinuous lines that circled before the priest and the ray of sunlight.

"Yah hai yah Allah. Allah Akbar!"

At this the white man quickened his steps. He almost ran down the side of the nave, looking sharply into the shadows. Edith wanted to call to him, but did not dare. A few moments before she would have wished to keep her disguise a secret. Clothed as she was, how was Donovan to know her?

Yet she wanted him to recognize her. She felt the need of his protection, understanding how reckless she had been in coming. And when he halted to peer at her, she drew a deep breath.

For a long moment John Donovan was a man of stone, so keenly he scrutinized every detail of her clothing and figure. The girl trembled in the effort to keep from speaking. Then he stepped casually nearer to one of the pillars and leaned against it with folded arms.

"Edith, why in the world did you come here?"

"I came—to see the priest, to try to end this war with the Vulture," she whispered.

At that Donovan turned away, so that she could not make out whether he was angered or not.

"Wait," she caught his answering whisper, "until the Sayaks have passed out. The women would see through you."

His face was expressionless as he watched the actions of the priest. Edith saw that the sun's ray had fallen full on the swirling vapor. Color, limitless, impalpable, iridescent, flooded the vapor. A haze of shimmering green and purple and red hung from dome to well. It was as if a veil of supernatural softness and beauty had been dropped from the sky.

And in the heart of the steaming vapor the *hadji* had taken his stand. He had ascended the gold fret-work by some hidden steps and now stood on the top of the grille, with clouds of steam rising on all sides of him.

CHAPTER XXI
A VEIL IS DRAWN

Edith gazed at the apparition in bewildered surprise. The splendor of the flooding color had taken away her breath. She did not understand how the old priest, motionless in the stream of light, could survive the heat. But his aged face was tranquil.

A murmur rose from the throng; dark eyes shone. Then the vapor and the temple itself were plunged in semidarkness. The aperture in the dome had been closed. Edith could no longer see the priest.

Following an interval of quiet, came the rustle of many bare feet as the Sayaks began to pass out of the mosque. Now that her eyes were more accustomed to the dim light Edith could see them gathering up their prayer rugs.

Her quick mind had caught the explanation of the radiant color of the vapor clouds. It could have been nothing less than a rainbow. Light, from the opening in the dome, had fallen upon the steam and gathered strength until the clouds of moisture reflected the prismatic coloring of the rainbow.

But the performance of the *hadji* was still beyond her understanding.

"It is a ritual," whispered Donovan, who had drawn nearer in the shadow, "that occurs only two or three times in a summer. Then the priest of Yakka Arik steps into that confounded steam. It does not harm him."

"Why?"

He hesitated, unwilling to explain further, but anxious not to reveal to her his growing anxiety.

"You chose a bad time to come here, Edith. It is what the Sayaks call 'the miracle of life.' This mosque is their holy spot. The spring underneath has a good deal of sanctity attached to it. Some old legend, you know. Just at noon the sun pierces the hole in the roof."

"It was beautiful," she murmured. "But to see the *hadji*—it gave me the creeps."

Within, the gloom of the vast mosque weighed upon the two. Edith found herself gazing from shadow to shadow fearfully and listening for footsteps that she fancied were moving toward them. Impulsively she stepped to his side and took his hand, surprised to find it so chill.

"Are we in such danger?" she whispered. Then: "You came to find me."

This thought filled the woman with mute delight. She wanted him to understand that she, also, had been thinking of him. "I believed the *hadji* would help us if I told him everything—"

The dome opened again, letting the ray of sunlight stream into the depths of the temple. They had heard no movement, nor had they seen the hands that worked the aperture. Donovan's hand closed on hers protectingly as her eyes sought him shyly, seeing in his clean-cut profile the gentleness and honesty of his race.

"Dear Edith, you must understand. The Sayaks are not ordinary Mohammedans, but are outlawed by the orthodox followers of the Prophet. They are preyed upon by Turk, Alaman, and Buddhist—"

"Why?"

"They worship the sun."

Edith was silent, thinking of the ray of light that had descended upon the priest, and the praying throngs that had raised their eyes to it.

"The *hadji* is their saint, Edith. And they have carefully concealed the location of his temple from their enemies—"

She saw that while he spoke he was watching the folds of the heavy curtain that hung behind the vapor. Seeing this, she felt an impulse to turn and flee from the mosque that seemed to be closing in upon them.

"We know—both of us, now," he went on quietly, "the secret of Yakka Arik. And every fanatical *mullah* from Constantinople to Kashgar would willingly lose his fingers and eyes if he could help tear down this temple of the sun—older than San Sophia, and a thorn in the side of Moslem political power—"

The curtain folds swayed, as if a breath of air had stirred them. The voices outside the entrance quickened and Edith had the fleeting sensation of being encompassed in a trap. She pressed dose to the man, who smiled down at her.

"We'll make it, yet. Come, Edith."

The voices of the worshipers in the court were no longer to be heard. Edith could not help glancing behind her as they started from the shelter of the pillars. She had fancied that the curtains had parted, drawn back by a hand from within.

"How did you follow me?" she asked gently, wishing to hear from his own lips why he had sought her.

"Aravang. Don't fear that he will give you away. He lost track of you and became worried. He hunted me up. I knew if that beggar couldn't find you something must be wrong. Then we learned from an Usbek peasant that he had seen a Sayak woman come from the house."

Abruptly he thrust her back.

"Iskander and two others have come in," he whispered sharply. "Edith, go back to the wall. Hide."

The girl, her heart beating tumultuously, lost no time in slipping back into the shadow of the wall. A slight projection of the granite blocks offered a shallow nook for her slender body.

John Donovan waited, while Iskander, Mahmoud, and another—the Sayak chief—approached. They had seen him and advanced to where he stood. Iskander fronted him with folded arms. To the white man's greeting he returned no answer.

"Where is Mees Rand?" he asked slowly.

Donovan eyed him steadily, trying to guess how the Arab had come to look for the girl and how much he knew of her actions. The presence of Mahmoud and the chieftain was ominous. Still, he was reasonably sure that Edith's disguise had not been penetrated. For a space the two measured each other silently.

Behind them the folds of the great curtain parted.

"Where is the white woman?" said Iskander again.

Donovan shrugged. "Does not Aravang know?"

"He knows nothing." The Arab tugged at his beard, as was his habit when aroused. "Speak, Dono-van Khan. I know that she is here. The guards at the door brought me a pair of woman's slippers, left behind when all had gone. I have seen the slippers before. They belong to Mees Rand."

Listening in her nook a dozen feet away, Edith thought of the pair she had discarded at the gate. Why had she not kept them on ? She had instinctively followed the example set by the Sayak boy.

"The door is guarded," observed the *manaps* softly. "And there is but one door. If you do not summon the woman, we will find her."

Donovan weighed the alternatives swiftly and made up his mind. "Edith!" he called, from set lips.

It was hard for Edith to step from her place of concealment to face the three Sayaks. But she trusted John Donovan.

When she neared the Arab, he tore the veil from her face with his free hand, and scrutinized the native garb of the girl, and his eyes narrowed.

"You came secretly," he said slowly. "You were here during the festival of the sun."

"I was here," she said boldly.

The admission seemed to surprise the two others when it was translated to them. For a moment they stared at her. Then they conferred among themselves. John Donovan stood a little apart, waiting. To Edith the situation seemed not so very serious because the four men were so calm. She now heartily regretted her foolishness in disobeying Donovan. She wondered why he was so silent. Surely he could speak, assure the Sayaks that she had not meant to spy upon their secrets!

Iskander addressed Donovan in the native tongue:

"O Dono-van Khan, this is a woman of your people. You know the law. Perhaps you will think it wise to leave the mosque rather than remain."

Donovan stiffened; but he answered quietly:

"I shall remain."

"So be it. Yet, it is not wise. She is very fair. Why should you see her die?"

At this a short sigh escaped Donovan, the only sign that he had had his gravest fear confirmed.

"Is this the will of Mahmoud?"

"Aye." The *hakim* answered for himself. "Iskander would have let the woman go safely from the mosque, under a pledge of silence. But I have read the hearts of many women, I know that their tongues cannot be silenced."

"Yet I am free to go."

"That is the truth. But you we need. Likewise, it is written that a strong man is faithful to his word. We have no fear that you will voice the secrets of others."

Edith glanced from one to the other, trying to read their faces. All four were speaking quietly, as if discussing some small matter of common interest. Donovan knew that only in persuading the Sayaks to change their minds was there hope for Edith.

It was the Sayak chief who spoke harshly.

"The task of the woman is finished now that she has healed Dono-van Khan. Nay, it was Mahmoud, the all-wise, who lifted the shadow of sickness from your body. The woman did her share, as we intended. Now, she is useless and we will slay her, because she entered where it is forbidden."

"Aye," agreed Iskander moodily. "She is young, and her hair is like the light of the sun as was that of my child. We will not set her upon the caravan. Besides, she is a white woman, and it is best her body should not be seen—without."

Edith touched Donovan timidly on the arm.

"What are they saying, Donovan Khan? I want to know. They seem to be—angry."

By way of answer he patted her hand gently. His alert blue eyes searched the faces of the Sayaks, as a condemned criminal might endeavor to read the faces of a jury, assembling to announce a verdict.

"A spy from without must die," added Mahmoud. He placed a withered hand on the chest of the white man. "Do not grieve: a grave is dug for each of us, and we must lie therein. The woman will feel no pain."

CHAPTER XXII
A PLEDGE

It was Mahmoud who signed for Edith to follow him toward the rear of the mosque. As John Donovan was silent, she obeyed hesitatingly.

Here was the bronze grating, raised some few feet from the tiled floor, and behind it the damask curtain that hung in dark folds from the edge of the dome to the floor. Glancing up, the girl saw that the sun's ray had vanished; overhead, through the dome's opening, a long cleft, dividing solid rock was visible. Only for an hour at midday did the sun strike down this natural shaft in the rock.

Edith heard a dull, purring sound from beneath. Underfoot there was a slight, continuous vibration as the hidden springs seethed and boiled. The heat rose from the vapor and touched her face.

"What is it?" she asked Donovan, her low voice trembling in spite of her effort at control.

"Wait. Do not be afraid."

She tried to smile in answer, as Mahmoud took the veil from Iskander, who still held it, and wound it tightly about her arms and body. Then he looked up and spoke to the *manaps*, who slowly removed his own shawl girdle and handed it to the physician. Mahmoud turned to Donovan, who was watching from smoldering eyes.

"In this way there will be no pain, Dono-van Khan. We will bind the white woman and lay her upon the raised place. Then the hot vapor will creep into her throat Soon she will be dead."

Donovan was smiling—a habit of the man when his thoughts were racing and there was danger to be met.

"Mahmoud," he began slowly, almost painfully, "you must listen to what I have to say. Miss Rand is not a woman of your people. She is innocent of evil. You will not slay her—"

"A woman. No more. What is she but a beautiful slave? Aye, one made for the pleasure of men?"

"I love Miss Rand," said Donovan.

Mahmoud stroked the girdle in his hand gently. "It does not avail. Others you will perhaps love. It is written that a strong man shall have many wives."

"Not a white man, Mahmoud. This is a matter beyond even your knowing. I shall love no woman but Miss Rand. Her life is more than my life."

"Nay, for you have a mission to fulfill in Yakka Arik. If she lives, she could reveal the site of Yakka Arik to our enemies outside. Aye, and the hatred of the wolf for the wolfhound is not greater than the hate of the orthodox Mohammedans for us—who worship the sun. She must be silenced, so that Yakka Arik will be inviolate."

"The wolfhound hunts," smiled Donovan, "and he has need of one who will put him upon the scent of the wolf. The falcon is loosed—but a hand must first release him. I am your friend, and the hour is near when you will hunt. Without me your plans will be like water cast upon the hot sand at midday. You need me." Donovan turned to Mahmoud. "You know that a bargain between two righteous men is like a signed bond. Very well. I will make a bargain. Let Miss Rand live, and I will pledge my honor as surety that she will never speak of Yakka Arik outside the valley. It is in my heart to marry Miss Rand if she will consent."

The Sayak chief shook his head.

"It is not enough. We are no more than servants of *him*"—he pointed to the curtain into which the *hadji* had retired—"and the law of Yakka Arik is binding. Miss Rand must die."

Donovan looked up at the circle of sky framed in the dome-opening. He drew a long breath and his shoulders stiffened. He had lost his point.

He knew that there was no hope in resistance. Hidden eyes were watching from behind the great curtain. Iskander and the chief were armed. A cry from Mahmoud would bring a dozen Sayak guards from the barred door. Even if he could account for the three Sayaks—and, weaponless, this was impossible—he could not leave the mosque with the girl. Fleetingly he thought of seeking the *hadji*, as a last card to be played in the face of the Sayaks' will.

But, knowing the settled purpose of these men, he did not dare leave Edith's side even for a moment. Instead he turned swiftly upon the silent Iskander.

"Scion of Tahir," his words came with the ring of command, "you have drawn sword in the army that once was mine. You have shared the bread and salt of the English. Will you remain passive and see this woman slain?"

The Arab bent his handsome head; his thin fingers plucked at his beard.

"*EfFendi*, it is written and what is written will come to pass."

"Iskander, you are my brother in arms. Once I saved your life in battle, when we followed the trail of him who killed your wife and daughter. Is the mirror of your honor clouded? Or will you grant me the request that I will ask—the one thing I will ask of you?"

Iskander plucked forth his sword; his dark eyes roved and the veins stood out on his forehead.

"Speak!" he moaned. "I will obey. May Allah, the Generous, forgive!"

At this the Sayak chieftain glared, and gripped his dagger in a powerful fist. So deep was the mosque in shadow, so quiet the group by the vapor gate, they might have been five worshipers gathered in prayer—except for the veil that bound the limbs of the woman. Edith was watching Donovan steadfastly, biting her lips to quiet their trembling.

A slight breeze passed through the shadows, cooling the damp foreheads of Donovan and Iskander and touching the yellow curls of Edith Rand.

The white man put hand to belt. But, as the Sayak chief looked up intently, he slipped loose the leather strap at his waist and held it out to Iskander.

"Man of Tahir," he said, "here is a cord to bind me. If they lay Miss Rand upon the vapor gate, you must bind me and put me beside her. This is the thing I ask of you. I will not live if she dies."

Iskander drew back as though a snake had coiled in front of him. Donovan waited, his tall figure erect, the strap in an open hand. While four men kept silence, the balance of judgment was poised. Then someone one spoke.

"The white woman must live."

In front of the damask curtain stood the priest of Yakka Arik. His haggard face, veiled by a venerable beard, was almost invisible under the loose folds of a white turban. He looked from one to the other and nodded slowly.

"I have heard—I have seen."

The chief and Iskander released their weapons. Donovan drew a deep breath.

"I have seen the life of a man offered with that of the woman," went on the *hadji*, his sonorous voice awaking echoes under the dome. "A life for a life. It is sufficient. It fulfills the law, which is not alone of revenge, but of mercy."

Edith fancied that he smiled.

"O, my foolish children! Did you think that the peace of Yakka Arik and its mosque rested upon the tongue of one woman? Let the white man and the woman go free from the mosque."

With that he turned, to disappear through the curtain, and the Sayaks bent reverent eyes to the floor. The master of Yakka Arik had spoken.

At the door Iskander touched Donovan on the arm.

"Do not forget the pledge," he whispered. "Miss Rand must not attempt to leave the valley."

"I will not forget," said Donovan.

They found Aravang striding up and down outside the guards, his broad face harassed. At sight of them, he ran forward.

"Take the white woman to her house," commanded Donovan. "I must go with the Sayaks. There is much to be done."

Edith, once more in possession of her veil and slippers, lingered. Her eyes sought those of John Donovan. "Tell me," she begged. "I know we were—in danger."

"Perhaps." He laughed, at the proscribed word. "After all, the mosque is not a safe place for inquisitive young women."

"I will never do anything you forbid again, Donovan Khan," she promised contritely. "Never. What did the *hadji* say?"

"He said—" Donovan paused. "Well, for a heathen, he said a rather fine thing. Now, you must go with Aravang, Lunch is waiting—"

"Not," responded Edith firmly, "until you assure me that you are perfectly safe. And promise to come *right away* and tell me everything."

His glance rested long on her anxious face. He wanted to take her in his arms, to feel that she was still whole, to press his lips against the tangle of her hair. Edith did not look away. So, Donovan Khan laughed just a little unsteadily.

"'Everything' may mean more—than you think," he whispered.

Not until she had passed across the open space with burly Aravang at her heels, both looking back at him more than once where he stood among the Sayaks, did he realize that he was trembling.

Edith sat on the small balcony overlooking the valley, chin on hand. Her thoughts strayed willfully. Detail by detail the scene at the mosque repeated itself before her fancy; the impress of the light veil still lingered on her limbs; she visioned the flash of Iskander's melancholy eyes—remembered the tranquil words of the priest—words that she could not understand.

"It was some kind of a benediction, I think," she mused.

What had it all been about? Edith was aware that she had been an onlooker at a grim struggle, the meaning of which she would not know until Donovan explained. In the conflict Donovan had emerged victorious. But—so thought the girl—he must have paid some price for his success.

Why did he not come? She wanted him to tell her everything.

"Everything," she repeated, and the watching Aravang saw her face brighten.

The sun declined behind the ridge that backed the house. The coolness of its shadow recalled Edith to herself. She went below and for the second time that day changed her attire.

When she emerged from her curtained compartment she wore the ball dress that had come with her from Kashmir. A scarf covered her bare shoulders. Her cheeks were rosy with the touch of the afternoon sun, and the tawny hair was dressed low on her neck in the manner Donovan admired.

Aravang gaped; then grinned delightedly. His goddess had robed herself in a new aspect of divinity. He announced importantly by signs that he had prepared dinner—an excellent dinner. Edith shook her head.

"Donovan Khan," she ordered. "Find him. Say that I want him to come to me."

The servant hesitated, pretending that he did not understand. But Edith knew better, and waved him away on his mission. Experience had taught Aravang the advisability of obeying her; nevertheless, he went slowly.

Meanwhile Edith bethought her that her hair would need a flower to set it off. She had made her toilette as anxiously as a débutante at a first dance. It was her wish that John Donovan should think her fair when he came to the house.

"The house of the Falcon," she repeated, and rather liked the sound of it.

Smilingly she reflected how once she had dreaded the thought of coming to the house. Now the tiny stone edifice, with its tinier kiosk, seemed to beckon her. It was Donovan's.

It was a poor kind of garden, after all, the roses thin and fast falling to the earth. Weeds overgrew the paths and the stone walls. Edith knew, however, where certain blue grass-flowers were still to be found. She sought for them in the swiftly gathering twilight that falls upon the valleys when the sun is obliterated behind the mountains. That morning she had read Donovan's love in his eyes—truthful eyes that could not lie.

Edith was stooping over a verdant tangle in a corner of the wall when she saw a tall, white-clad figure moving toward her. With her flowers firmly grasped, she rose and extended a hand, smiling not altogether steadily. She had not expected Donovan so soon. Then the blue blossoms fell at her feet, and the hand dropped to her side.

The man was Monsey.

Edith watched, bewildered, as he hastened to her, stooping as he did so under the wall.

"Miss Rand," he said quickly under his breath, "I did not mean to startle you. We must be very quiet. We must leave at once." He was breathing heavily as if he had been running and a muscle twitched persistently in his cheek.

Surprised, she faced him, trying to account for his appearance. Monsey had come from the direction of the small gate through which she had passed to the mosque. She saw him glance toward it anxiously.

"I have been watching you through glasses all this afternoon. Yes, Miss Rand—from the hill behind the hut. Now is our chance. The native guard in the ravine behind the mosque has been slain, but the devils are thick on the mountain side—"

Edith would have given much to read his face. Monsey's coming had at first filled her with expectation. Had aid from Kashmir reached Yakka Arik ?

"Your father sent me." The man spoke impatiently. "I have risked much to come here tonight. Do not wait to get any other clothing. I have horses and men up the mountain. We came through—along a goat path."

He did not tell her of hours spent spying from the heights upon Yakka Arik, or of men slain in a silent struggle where he penetrated the concealed ravine through which he had once before entered the valley—or of the fear that clung to him, close as his own shadow.

"My father? Is he here?"

Monsey swore under his breath and leaned nearer.

"No! He is sick. Come! You do not understand. You must go or these devils will see us, and that will be the end of us all. *Nom d'un nom!*"

Edith strove to think, to decide. She had no reason to doubt that Arthur Rand had sent the Russian. The man's presence in the garden, which must be decidedly dangerous to him, was evidence to back his words. It was her instinctive distrust of Monsey that made her pause—that, and another thought. Donovan had told her of his pledge that she would not leave Yakka Arik without the consent of the Sayak chiefs.

"Your father will be at my camp soon," he urged.

"I have a friend," she said quickly. "He should be here any minute. I will not leave without him. He has given his parole for me."

"A friend!" Monsey hissed angrily. "Some native. Have I come here to risk my neck for any one but you? The valley is guarded—"

Like a clarion from the skies, the long trumpet blast of Yakka Arik devastated the twilight quiet Monsey started, and caught the girl's wrist.

"You hear? Ah." He fancied that he saw a movement on the terrace overlooking the garden. "You must come, before the guard is changed—now—"

"Let me think." Edith was trying to grasp the situation. Reason told her that John Donovan, alone, would find it easier to win free from Yakka Arik than if burdened with her. Because they trusted him, the Sayaks obeyed him. But the girl found that she did not want to leave the valley without John Donovan.

"No," she said, "I can't explain it all"—she was a trifle breathless with the urgent need of the situation—"Donovan Khan will soon be here. I will not do anything without him—"

"A khan?" Monsey, intent on the balcony that was shrouded in gloom, caught only vaguely the name. "Edith, do you want them to find me here?" Under his breath he muttered: "Don't think, young lady, that I also am a fool."

He stepped nearer, his hand rising suddenly to her face. He had caught the silk shawl in his fingers. The girl, startled and suspicious, tried to draw away. But Monsey wrapped the shawl quickly about her head, holding it fast with an arm that he passed around her shoulders. The other arm caught her close to him, lifted her from the ground.

CHAPTER XXIII

THE PLEDGE IS BROKEN

"Excellency, the night was coming and the garden was a place of shadows. Even so, for the trumpets had blown. An owl could have seen. I am not an owl. How was I to know? All unworthy, thou despisest me. Truly, my sorrow has gripped me—here."

Aravang was speaking in his own tongue. As he ended he smote his muscled chest with a knotted fist that made the hollow within his bones echo like a drum. Air escaped his bearded lips in a long, hissing breath.

Impatiently, Donovan moved. He was standing, feet planted wide, at the edge of the balcony overlooking the garden and the gray expanse that was the lake's surface. Under impulse of a fresh breeze the water's margin lapped against the stones.

"From the beginning," he said slowly, "tell me what you did and what you saw. I do not blame you. But I must know."

Aravang squatted on his heels, facing the lake, struggling with the need of intelligent speech. Unlike Iskander, he was a man of few words, and fewer ideas. While the native talked, the white man bent nearer to catch each syllable. His brain was afire with the need of action. Yet men who have commanded others in the armies of the world know the folly of action upon insufficient information.

"Excellency, I am thy *kul*. Did I not slay the pig of a Jain Ali Beg, who betrayed thee? And for the white woman I would give the blood from my severed veins—aye. *She* sent me to seek thee. I passed through the village, looking on all sides. An Usbek told me that the council had disbanded, and so I hastened back, thinking that thou wouldst be again at the stone house, and hungry.

"Two I saw in the garden, but not the faces. One was a woman."

"Are you sure it was your mistress?"

Aravang grunted a disconsolate affirmative.

"Aye. Should I not know the murmur of her voice, even from afar? The other I thought to be thee, for it was a white man. Dog that I am, I waited, listening, and fearful to speak to the higher ones. Then she said thy name, Dono-van Khan, very loudly. The white man made response, then took her in his arms. I was glad. I have known the longing that is in your veins for the white woman. Aye, I have seen the light of desire in her eyes—"

"Aravang!" Donovan felt ashamed, as if he had been caught spying on the woman he loved. Then a hot exultation gripped him, to pass as swiftly as it came and leave him cold.

"Spit upon thy unworthy slave, master! Call me even a dog. Oh, I am unworthy. While I watched, this man took her in his arms and bore her to the small gate, the one that leads to the forest. The gate opened before him and then closed; this thing I heard.

"It was unwonted. Master, I knew thy custom to go always alone. If the gate closed, *thus*, when the white man held my mistress in his arms, another hand must have closed it. So, when I felt of the gate from within and found it fast, I scented evil. Then I climbed the wall. Donovan Khan, there is a small moon to-night. By its light I saw shadows moving into the forest. I followed.

"By the sound of their passage I traced them. After a long time, at one of the upper goat paths I heard the *khanum* cry out, once. Am I not her dog? I ran forward to strike and slay, even though I held no weapon—not a knife. In the goat path where the new moon struck through the trees stood a dozen armed men with horses. They mounted and spurred away, two by two."

"Which way?"

"To the lower valley. The bits of the horses were muffled, likewise the hard leather of their hoofs. For a space I ran behind, seeking to gain the side of my mistress. They saw me and went faster. Then the thought came to me that I should seek thee with the news. I waited until I knew they were riding beyond the valley and not to the mosque. Then I ran down the mountain side to the stone house, where thou wert sitting—"

Aravang ceased, and fell into expectant silence. The balcony was quiet, except for the native's deep breathing and the broken murmur of the lake. Now and then a gust shook the pine branches high over their heads.

For five minutes John Donovan was immobile. In that time he experienced the bitterness that comes to a man with misfortune not of his deserving. Also, with the necessary calmness of a trained soldier, he revised the whole of the plans he had formed with the Sayaks that afternoon, and made others. And, gravely, he prepared to face the consequences of a broken oath.

Edith Rand had left Yakka Arik.

His only information was the story of Aravang. Donovan could not know whether she had gone willingly or not. Yet, he believed she had been taken forcibly.

"Aravang," he voiced the result of his thoughts, "run through the village, to the mosque. Summon Iskander first, to come speedily here. Aye—bid all the Sayak leaders and Mahmoud to come. Say that I must speak with them. Go swiftly!"

"Excellency, I hear"—the servant rose and dropped from the rail of the balcony to the earth, muttering, "It shall be done. I am a dog, but a dog can run—"

Donovan looked at the stars, to mark the hour.

He went below to the empty sleeping room. Aravang had set the table, with lighted candles that flickered in the passing breaths of wind. The sight of Edith's empty chair stirred him strangely, and he moved it away from the table.

The curtained recess that had been Edith's was dark. He could make out vaguely the outlines of soft garments hanging in orderly array beside the bed. A very faint scent of rose leaves came to him. Pushing aside his untouched plate, Donovan buried his face in his hands.

The room was chilly, in spite of the embers of the fire Aravang had kindled in the grate. When the curtains that screened Edith's quarters swayed, Donovan looked up with a start to see only the dressing shelf the girl had fashioned laboriously—the mirror fixed in a chink in the stone, the silk-covered board bearing comb and pins, sewing materials.

Everything that had belonged to Edith was in its place. Could she have meant to leave him ? Had she fashioned her disguise of the morning for this purpose?

"After all," he murmured, "my house wouldn't appeal to her. Perhaps she guessed that I meant to ask her to marry me. I wonder. Did you, Edith?"

Swift, poignant loneliness smote him. And as quickly came the phantom of jealousy to mock at him.

"She knew you had given your word to the Sayaks," gibed the imp in his brain. "Didn't she? Of course, she did!"

"But she wouldn't leave without speaking to me," reasoned the hope that would not forsake Donovan in spite of Edith's disappearance.

"Ha!" mocked the imp. "Wouldn't she? How do you know? Did the girl consult you before she ran away to the temple? And why did she go up the mountain, before that—just when one of the Vulture's Sarts sneaked through the lines? After all, my dear fellow, can you trust a woman? And the Vulture's handsome—Monsey, you know—he's devilishly handsome. Women trust him."

"Edith wouldn't listen to a scoundrel," maintained Donovan's love.

"That's just the point," reasoned the imp logically. "She doesn't know his record, nor that he *is* the Vulture. What did the Sayaks tell you in the council this afternoon? They had information from Kashgar. Monsey spread the news there that he is leading a party to rescue Miss Rand. And that she is engaged to marry him."

"He lied!" cried Donovan, aloud. "I trust her."

"But does she care for you?" The mocking voice became fainter. "Didn't she leave you, of her own accord—"

"No!" cried the faith that was in Donovan. "She was carried off!"

And now the voice was silenced.

Iskander strode in, swaggering and fully armed. When the Arab saw that Donovan would not speak he glanced curiously at Edith's empty chair.

Others of the Sayaks came, among them the chief, and finally Mahmoud. Each one looked at him fleetingly, then knelt on cushions or against the wall, adjusting striped silk robes, and thrusting their hands into the wide sleeves.

"You have summoned us and we are here. The council of Sayak chieftains waits until you speak."

Donovan leaned back in his chair and his glance went from face to face along the wall—dark faces, keen of eye, that did not turn from his scrutiny. His lips moved wordlessly as he murmured to himself: "Isn't it just my bally luck? Every minute we lose before going after Edith is worth—well, there's no price high enough. But I can't act—I can't think of acting—until I've made a clean breast to these chaps who trust me now as they always have, but whose natures won't let them keep from suspecting me if I tell them Edith's gone. Iskander, of course, will back me up a certain extent— no farther. Won't do now to strain his friendship or to bank on my word alone, again."

His lined face was grave, his clear eyes purposeful; but he was tired and his pulse throbbed heavily. Edith's departure jeopardized the fruits of years of work—of the mission that had taken him from the army. Laboriously he had won the faith of the Sayaks. And now—

He had made a pledge to the Sayaks and the pledge had been broken, through no fault of his. Would they understand? If they did not—

"Edith's gone," he repeated to himself, "to the Tower. After all, that's what matters."

The certainty of his love returned fourfold and unsettled his reasoning. He could only think of one thing—Edith was gone and he must go after her, but was kept from doing that very thing. He straightened in his chair and spoke to Iskander.

"Send a rider to the ravine behind the mosque to learn what is to be seen there, where the guard stood. Let the rider report here what he has seen."

Before assenting or refusing, the Arab consulted the other Sayaks with a glance. One, a swaggering Afghan whose evil-smelling wool was belted with a priceless sword, rose and left the room.

From the road outside came a clatter of hoofs. Donovan was gazing thoughtfully into the fire. "The white woman has left Yakka Arik," he said.

The faces of the Sayaks remained impassive, but all eyes turned at once to him. Iskander, leaning against the wall, played with a gold necklace at his throat.

"You made a pledge," he responded softly.

"I have not broken it, Iskander—"

"Speak not in English," warned the Arab, "or these others will suspect and grow angry."

"Bear witness," Donovan slipped easily into Turki, "as to the truth of what I say—"

"If it be truth," broke in one harshly. To interrupt a sahib was insolence.

"A fool, out of an empty mind, questions wisdom, and a jackal yelps from a pack." Donovan fastened the surly speaker with his blue eyes. "Have you not given me the rank of *manaps?* Have you known me to lie, or to speak merely that I might hear the sound of my voice?" The Sayak who had interrupted him looked uncomfortable. "Bear witness, Sayaks," Donovan raised his low voice a little. "Was I not at the council since the shadows have changed (since noon)? After that, you know that I came here, and that I summoned you directly. Is this not so?"

Silence answered him, and Donovan's lips tightened.

"In that time," he pointed out, "I could not have taken the white woman through the guards and returned. Aravang knows that I was here."

Mahmoud spoke mildly, without raising his eyes.

"The *kul* is lowborn, Dono-van Khan: his word we will not hear. Because of our trust in you, because you have aided Yakka Arik, and because your word is the word of Dono-van Khan, we will listen. Tell now how the woman came to depart from Yakka Arik." He paused, weighing his words. "It is well that you have spoken thus. For we knew that the woman was free of our guards. A watcher on one of the cliffs saw her ride hence, with several men who were not sayaks."

Donovan saw into the trap Mahmoud's subtle mind had set for him.

"You ask, O healer of the sick," he observed slowly, "that I tell how the *khanum* escaped. Nay, when I saw it not, nor had a share in what came to pass, what can I tell that you do not know? Only this I know. By force was the woman taken, not by her own will."

Having fought out his own battle and having kept his belief in Edith Rand, he could tell them this with assurance.

Some one—the native who had first matched words with him—arose.

"Dono-van Khan," he said slowly, "well are you named the Falcon, if yours is an all-seeing eye, if you can see what passes upon the mountain slope when your body is within the council hall." There was a challenge and mockery in his words. "Why should the *khanum* be loath to leave Yakka Arik? Does a caged dove struggle against freedom?"

"I will explain that."

A sneer touched the thin lips of the native. Mahmoud's beadlike eyes glittered.

"Does your explaining alter the fact that the veil of secrecy, kept for ten generations, has been torn from Yakka Arik?" he demanded harshly.

Donovan faced him frankly.

"The secret has not been revealed. It was known before this—to the rider who carried off the *khanum*."

Mahmoud looked up sharply. "Twice, Dono-van Khan, have you said she was carried off. Yet the talk of Kashgar has come to our ears, as such things do, through my servants; and we know that the white man who rode hither for the woman claims her as his bride."

"He lied."

"How may we know it?"

"The *khanum* loved no man. And soon you will see that this rider is a master of lies."

The *hakim* looked grave.

"Dono-van Khan, another thing have I heard—a thing that is true beyond a doubt. On the heels of this *wilayati sowar*—foreign rider—who is named Monsey in Kashgar, there came two other *effendis*, one the father of this woman, the other an English officer. From Kashgar they turned their reins to the hills." Mahmoud spoke coldly. "Aye. In the bazaars it was said that Rand *effendi* sent this one who is called Monsey to seek the girl."

At this Donovan rose, carefully concealing the fact that the news puzzled him. It was probably true. Mahmoud had an uncanny way of being aware of all that went on in the near-by hills. The tidings, coming at this point, dealt a blow to his hopes.

Under the leadership of Mahmoud, the Sayaks were beginning to doubt him. Appearances were against him. How could he convince them of his own certainty that Edith Rand had met with foul play? Without the help of the Sayaks he was powerless to aid her.

Any hesitation on his part would be fatal. Swiftly he surveyed the situation. Fraser-Carnie, he was sure, would not ally himself with a man of Monsey's stamp. The fact that the two rescue parties were separate seemed to prove this. But he—Donovan—could not leave Yakka Arik to get word to the Englishman, even if there were time and Fraser-Carnie could be located in the gorges. Nor would Fraser-Carnie be able to find Yakka Arik without a Sayak guide.

Nor would the Sayaks think of joining forces with any outsiders. Moreover, they would hold him prisoner until certain he had kept faith with them. Meanwhile every minute was taking Monsey and Edith farther from Yakka Arik.

Donovan had only one card to play. The knowledge—unguessed as yet even by Mahmoud-that Monsey and the Vulture were the same man. And he had one friend—Iskander.

"Sayaks of the council!" He drew a long breath with a silent prayer for success. "I have said the *khanum* was taken by force from the valley. This thing I know because the rider who came hither is a stealer of women."

He walked to Mahmoud and raised his hand.

"Likewise, O *hakim*, the rider knew the paths into Yakka Arik because he had been here before."

Swinging about, Donovan held Iskander's eyes with his own.

"Scion of Tahir, you, like myself, have felt the evil of the slave dealer. Once a Vulture entered the valley, sinking his talons into the hearts of Sayak fathers and brothers—"

"Aye," cried a Sayak. "He was a *wilayti*, base beyond words, such as Don—"

"Peace!" barked Iskander. "Who should know the Vulture better than I—a father and a husband? Fools! Will you not heed the wisdom of Donovan Khan who has shared our salt?"

The murmurs subsided and the warriors settled back passively, only their dark eyes following every motion of the white man.

At a single throw Donovan cast the weight of his influence against the uncertainty and suspicion of the Sayaks.

"Three years ago during the Great War I came to you when the *mullahs* of the Turks and the Tartars urged the Sayaks to join the standard of war against the Sirdar (the English government). I asked you to keep the peace."

"Aye," nodded Mahmoud, "the *hadji* of the temple added his voice to yours. Thus, the Sayaks kept the peace, and because of the fear of Yakka Arik, the tribes of Central Asia did likewise. Yet the agreement was—"

"That I was not to leave the Hills until your enemy, the man you called the Vulture, was hunted down. And at Srinagar I learned his name."

At this every Sayak straightened and complete silence fell.

"The Vulture and the Alaman, Abbas Abad, were the leader of the slave caravans. And the Vulture was the real head of the slave merchants. He was once a Russian officer: stripped of his rank because of an intrigue with a

Russian woman. Now, concealed behind this name, he directs the activities of his thousand servants, from Kashgar to Samarkand. Oh, he is powerful. When he despoiled the hill villages of our friends—"

"We followed close upon the dust of his going." So spoke a Sayak, a Pathan chieftain, who had been silent until now.

"Aye," assented Donovan,, from the Mustagh Ata to the Caucasus. Yet he escaped us. The *mirs* of the cities sold him their aid. Lawless Tartar and Russian detachments, leaderless after the end of the Great War, took his gold for their services. And he is the friend of Esad Pasha. When fear of the Sayaks came upon him, he fled to America."

"But now he is once more in the hills," murmured Iskander. "And our vengeance—"

"You stood within sword's reach of him in Srinagar, son of Tahir. The Vulture is Monsey, the Russian."

"Ah!"

The Arab started, and his hand went to his scimitar hilt. Fifty eyes turned to him. "Dares the dog return to the scene of his crime, to Yakka Arik?" he questioned harshly, probing the open countenance of the white man.

"Desire for the white *khanum* brought him."

A murmur that was like a sigh answered Donovan. "A-a-h!" Iskander drew his scimitar and threw away the scabbard. "It was written. Oh, it was written. Now the pursuit of blood will be ended and the mirror of my honor will be cleansed—"

"Proof!" said Mahmoud abruptly. "Dono-van Khan, we must know beyond a doubt. Have you proof of this thing?"

Donovan had played his card—had made his appeal to the Sayaks' longing for revenge. Yet Mahmoud and some others had not regained confidence in him. Glancing toward the door, he stilled the rising tumult with a quick command and pointed to the tall figure filling the entrance. Only a moment ago he had seen that for which he had been watching—the return of the Afghan messenger.

"Speak," he nodded at the warrior. "What did you learn at the bridge below the mosque? Where went the riders who entered Yakka Arik?"

"Dono-van Khan," the man growled, blinking at the light, "the Sayak guard at the bridge was slain when he opposed their flight. Yet the venerable *hadji* who was watching from the tower of the mosque saw the riders go, not across the bridge, but up the gorges toward—"

"The Tower!" Donovan cut in crisply. "As I thought, the Vulture has taken flight to his empty nest Mahmoud, who but he would do that?"

While the *hakim* meditated, the Afghan messenger spoke again.

"Dono-yan Khan, the face of one of the riders was seen, by the light of the torches at the bridge. Abbas Abad was with the riders—"

"Do you believe now?" Donovan swung savagely around to face Mahmoud "Have I spoken the truth?"

As one man the Sayaks answered. "We believe. We have never doubted."

He did not smile. Half an hour ago these same men would have killed first him and then Edith Rand—if they could have found her—had not their suspicions been dispelled. Now, as so often in the past, the personality of the white man had won them to him.

Like children they were, jealous, arrogant, cruel, and yet, withal, open-hearted and faithful. As their multicolored robes crowded toward the door, his fist smote on the table.

"Iskander, *bahader!*"

At the familiar command, coupled with his noncommissioned rank in the Anglo-Indian army, the Arab halted and stiffened to attention. Others half paused, to listen.

"Whither go you, son of Tahir?"

"To tear out heart and bowels of the Vulture—Monsey: aye, to sew the arrow stitches of vengeance. The angel of God has opened the gate of justice—we will not turn back. I go to the Tower, and with me all men of the Sayaks who can bear swords. Donovan Khan, those swords will not be sheathed until—"

"I know." The white man cut short the other's eloquence. Now, however, he spoke not as officer to native, but as man to man. "You are the chieftain of the Sayaks; you must follow the path of duty. Am I less than you?"

Hereupon the Arab caught the other's hand and pressed it to his forehead. "Nay, Dono-van Khan," he said softly, "you are the sun of my world."

"And the *mem*-sahib Rand, Iskander—she is to be my wife. If there is a fight at the Tower—and there will be—she will be in danger. I must reach her first. Give me time, Iskander, before you attack Monsey. A little time will be enough."

The Arab's muscular hand plucked at his beard.

"The woman beloved of Dono-van Khan is dear to me as she who was the star of my life. What I may do, I will do. Yet the fury of the Sayaks is like to a torrent and who can stay the course of a torrent?" He lifted somber eyes to the tense face of the young Englishman. "Sahib, we are all under the hand of God."

"It is enough." Donovan smiled, his tired eyes quizzical. He knew that he would need to ride a horse to death to be at the Tower before the Sayaks. "Then I will go alone, Iskander."

"With God," said the Arab sententiously. They passed out together.

In the path by the lake shore Iskander halted with a warning gesture. He could hear footsteps following them. A shadowy figure, bulky and clumsy, was outlined against the silvery-gray glimmer of the lake.

"Aravang," said Donovan.

Throughout the night the servant of Edith Rand dogged the heels of John Donovan, not letting the Englishman from his sight. His broad, good-natured face wore a harassed look, and from time to time he muttered to himself uneasily. When the white man mounted one of the Sayak horses, Aravang promptly laid hold of the stirrup, and trotted silently beside him.

CHAPTER XXIV
THE VULTURE'S NEST

Tash-Kurgan, so called by the tribes of Central Asia, had been erected out of the mountain rock by an Imperial general of the Dragon Throne, to guard the gorge and the caravan track along the opposite cliff against the Tartar foes. This general and his staff, with his foes, were dust in the valleys and gray bones in forgotten tombs long before Tamerlane, the Lame Conqueror, led his armies across the mountains which had repelled so many invasions.

So, the *Kurgan* resembled roughly a medieval stronghold. It was placed almost at the brink of the cliff that led down into the valley with its steaming riverlet. Its only entrance, consisting of a narrow flight of stone steps running diagonally up the wall, was on the western side, away from the ravine. Around it ran a ditch, once a moat but now half filled with pulverized sandstone and debris.

The sandstone walls with their crenelated tops were much worn by rains and snows. In places the stones had cascaded into the moat. The wall itself was some dozen feet high and three feet in thickness. Within, appeared a courtyard of beaten, level clay. Rude stone shelters, roofless for the most part, were built against the inner ramparts.

Only at one end was there a solid sandstone structure resembKng, except for height, the keep of a medieval castle. In one corner of it rose the square tower, much broader at the base than the summit—after the fashion of the Tibetan lamaseries. Once a pagoda roof of sturdy cedar logs had surmounted the tower top. Now this had fallen in.

The *Kurgan* was very much like a bird's nest of many years ago.

In one of the chambers of the hold itself Edith Rand had been placed. It was walled with teakwood that did not entirely keep out the drafts of cold air that swept the *Kurgan*. But a kerosene stove gave out an odorous heat, and heavy Kirghiz carpets had been placed over the gaps in the teakwood.

Candle lanterns, hung from the beams, revealed a hasty attempt to make the chamber habitable—a mattress and disordered blankets in one corner, saddlebags with their contents of cooking utensils and clothing piled in the center of the uneven flooring that was littered with dust and ashes of former fires. In another corner Edith noticed a heap of moldy boots, some rusted tin lamps, and bits of military gear grouped around a smashed samovar.

These, and the carpets, were the only relics of Russian occupancy that had been left by stray plunderers.

"Not much of a boudoir, my lady," Monsey had assured her, "but then we will not be here long. I hope to make you more comfortable."

Edith had not answered. The room was Monsey's, and she compared it without knowing just why she did so with the neatness of Donovan's quarters. She was oppressed by the aspect of the teakwood room.

The ride from Yakka Arik had taken long, involving, as it did, the crossing of the ravine, the climb and descent of numerous heights and the passage through the forest where the girl wondered how her captors could find their way, not knowing that they had familiarized themselves carefully with the lay of the countryside.

Above the low voices of the men she could hear the stamp of horses near by, the crackle of a fire, and an occasional footfall. Not until Abbas Abad had departed—and Edith recognized in him, without especial surprise, the leader of the men in the Kashgar *serai*—did Monsey fling off his belt with its holster and revolver and speak to her, seating himself on an upturned packing case, and drawing another forward for her. She remained standing.

"Still haughty, my lady? Ah, you do not know the pains I have taken to save you from the devils of Yakka Arik. Well, I apologize for using you roughly in what you Americans call the 'get-away.' It was necessary. You are quite strong."

His glance went over her, and Edith turned her head away. Monsey leaned back comfortably, stroking his black, drooping mustache idly. He was well pleased with himself, but he was curious as to what the girl thought of him.

"You remember the dance at Srinagar, Edith—the one you—ah—refused me? You see, it would have been much better to have gone with me than that Rawul Singh. But you did not trust me. Do you trust me now?"

"No."

"That is too bad. Why?"

Edith met his gaze with her honest gray eyes, and Monsey looked away.

"I don't know."

Surprised at this unexpected retort, Monsey's brows went up. Other women had found it good policy to please him. This American, wrapped in her pride, was like an icicle, he thought. Well, he liked her all the better for it.

It would be a pleasant sensation to master her pride. Monsey did not doubt his ability to do it. He did not mean to allow Edith to return to her father for some time. Money payment, even a large one, seemed a small thing when he had the woman herself near him. Life itself had ceased to bore him—and recently there had been certain fears, certain unrest Abbas Abad had said that he was a marked man in these hills. Monsey had taken to using the Alaman's drugs, and this had not helped jaded nerves.

"You fear me, my handsome lady?"

"No."

There was no doubting the sincerity in Edith's low voice. To tell the truth, she disliked and suspected the former Russian officer partly because he was associated with Abbas Abad, partly because he had put aside her own will in bringing her from Yakka Arik, but more because of her own intuition. She read the insincerity in his assertion that he was acting for Arthur Rand.

Monsey's narrow mind, self-centered and suspicious, sought for other reasons. He had the patient, consuming desire for the girl that masters all other impulse in a man of his type.

"Let me see. You spoke of a friend in Yakka Arik—a khan, was it not? So, you stoop to a native's—friendship—"

His calculating words accomplished their purpose. Edith flamed into swift retort, forgetting all caution.

"Donovan Khan is a white man, and I found him very much of a gentleman. He will follow you. Oh, I hope—"

She broke off, at a strange light in the man's amber eyes.

"Donovan Khan? Donovan. By all the images of the Church! Not Captain John Campbell Donovan?" His hard eyes read her easily. "Captain Donovan—in Yakka Arik, alive."

For a moment he considered this, intently. Then he laughed.

"Why, it is fate itself, my beautiful lady. No, not that. It is my luck, my good luck. So, you found a lover waiting in that Sayak pesthole?"

Edith had mastered her impulse of anger as quickly as it came. She wrapped her arms in the end of the shawl, seating herself on the box, her back to Monsey.

"A beggarly Englishman, with a brown beard? The Falcon, as the Sayaks name him? Yes, that is Donovan, who is a leader of these assassins, a renegade, outcast from the British army—"

"I don't believe you!"

"Presently, you will believe." Somewhat uncertainly he studied her, wondering at the change in the girl since Srinagar. "Look here, my fine lady, you can't afford to quarrel with me! Have not I said that Arthur Rand sent me? You choose not to believe? Very well! I have made it known in Kashgar, and the Sayak spies have carried the news that I am your friend to their murderers' nest. So, you will see how Donovan and his allies conduct themselves against the agent of your American father."

Edith shook her head mutely, her faith in Donovan strong within her; but Monsey smiled.

"My luck holds. A few hours and we will see the last act of this little play. I want you to watch it."

Monsey had begun to pace the room. His brown face had been reddened by exposure to the sun; the lines of his jaw were obscured by fat; his heavy mustache fell over the corners of his mouth. Under a bald forehead, the eyes, revealing a network of red veins and set too close together, were prone to wander. This was the only indication of the hashish he used.

His powerful figure swelled under the short black coat with its astrakhan collar. He had grown stouter, more gross. His former careful politeness had altered to an overbearing intimacy. The mask had fallen, now that he no longer needed a mask. Edith saw that he had changed, coarsened. In his face was a faint, unmistakable resemblance to a vulture.

Monsey halted as Abbas stepped into the room without knocking. When the two had spoken briefly, he turned to Edith.

"Horsemen have been seen in the passes around here. I fancy the Sayaks mean to invade the privacy of my abode."

Edith did not reveal the quickened hope that his words aroused. She had learned by experience to judge the events that thronged into this new world. And she reasoned that Monsey expected this to happen. Otherwise, why was he not disturbed?

Presently, with a glance at Abbas, he went out, carrying the holster and belt with him. For some time he had not taken the drug that he now needed at regular intervals. Abbas came nearer at once and peered into the girl's face. He tried to take the shawl from her shoulders, but she would not let him.

"Missy *khanum*," the Alaman whispered in very bad English, "you come with me, sometime. Oh, yas, by God." He pointed after Monsey. "Not him, no. He is the Vulture. Me, I, Abbas Abad, Alaman, *kum dan!* I give you—your fadder, for verree small paying—yes."

Edith shook her head somewhat wearily. Abbas stepped back as Monsey appeared silently in the door. The Russian surveyed him suspiciously. Abbas grinned as he saw the other's hand move toward the revolver in his belt.

"Excellency," he observed in Turki, "would you threaten your slave? Nay, it is not the part of wisdom. Besides, a thrown knife is swift—as you know."

"This is not your place."

"Ah. Yet I came here to sleep." He yawned and went to the mattress upon which he flung his fat body with a grunt. Monsey scowled.

"Those are my blankets."

The Alaman closed his eyes. "And the hashish, my Excellency? That is mine and not yours. If you need some presently, I would not want to deny you. Nay, I must sleep now."

Soon he began to snore, with an open mouth. Edith noticed, however, that whenever there was a noise outside the teakwood room Abbas ceased snoring. Monsey had seated himself near her and tried to take her hand. The drug had warmed his brain and he did not hide his exultation.

"You are beautiful, Edith," he whispered. "You are worth a risk. Bah, what is risk or danger? You do not believe I love you. Well, you will see what I will risk for you. I tell you, there will be dead men lying about Yakka Arik on your account. And you will know how powerful I am."

The girl had met his hot gaze steadily. Her scorn only served to inflame his fancy the more.

"I would not have you otherwise, Edith. When we leave Yakka Arik you will see the garden that I have prepared near Kashgar. I am master there—"

Edith laughed, her nerves high-strung.

"Are you?" She pointed to Abbas. The Alaman had been studying them, one eye wide open. When Monsey turned, the man appeared to be as soundly asleep as before. "Aren't you called the Vulture by the natives? Captain Donovan has been looking for you."

All at once she felt very lonely, very much in need of the Englishman's presence. Her life in the world of Yakka Arik had been built around him. She could not believe that he would desert her.

"Donovan?" Monsey swore under his breath. "We will attend to him."

The sudden set to his full lips left no doubt of the sincerity of this remark, at least.

Time passed. One of the lamps went out. Abbas was snoring in earnest now. The chill that comes with the last hours of the night crept into the teakwood chamber. Monsey, the stimulus of the drug dose gone, paced the floor restlessly, pausing to fiddle with the reeking stove. Edith gave herself up to the inertia that comes with fatigue.

* * * *

Quiet had settled upon the *Kurgan*.

To Edith, this silence was ominous of maturing events. Out of this quiet she felt that something would come to pass. Why had not Monsey tried to leave the castle while the coast was free? He must have expected to be followed. How was Abbas content to sleep when the Sayaks had appeared in the vicinity?

A glint of crimson light pierced one of the cracks in the walls. Edith's ears had been strained for a certain sound. Somewhere, beyond the mountains, the sun was rising, and she had not heard the familiar trumpet blast that resounded in Yakka Arik at dawn. Its absence was vaguely disturbing.

She was conscious of the presence of unknown forces mustering around her. This feeling was not premonition or fear—it was certainty. The world of Yakka Arik had been disturbed. The trumpets were silent. Out of this silence something would come to the *Kurgan*. By and by Monsey noticed the evidence of dawn. He buttoned his jacket at the throat and beckoned her.

"Come! You can see now."

Her limbs stiff with cold, Edith followed him out into the still more desolate entrance chamber of the castle hold. Gray light from the embrasures illumined it. She saw a roughly made ladder of saplings resting against the massive sandstone of the wall. Up this Monsey motioned her to climb.

He followed the girl into a square hole in the ceiling. Rotting timbers on the floor below afforded evidence that once a stairway had penetrated where the ladder led. They stood in a very small, dark space. From above came a glimmer of light.

"The first floor of the tower itself," explained Monsey. "Go on."

A winding stair, broken down in places and illumined only by thin arrow slits in the wall, conducted them to the tower top—a nest of tumbled cedar timbers.

Edith looked out upon the dawn.

Mountain ranges were tipped by vivid, ruddy light. The ravine below was in darkness. The courtyard of the *Kurgan* was a gray square with shadowy corners.

"Look," said Monsey, pointing downward.

On one side of the enclosure some fifty horses were lined with piles of forage at either end of the line. On the other side, the roofless shelters and the open clay of the court itself were filled with sleeping men. Along the walls several sentries paced.

In the darkness, close to midnight, when they had arrived at the castle, Edith had noticed little of this. She had supposed that the only men in the *Kurgan* were those who had been in Monsey's raiding party. Now she realized that the place sheltered no fewer than two hundred or more.

Monsey pointed out a dozen rifle stacks before the shelters.

"A company of soldiers," he whispered. "Tartars, who were once part of the Turkish army. They know that I am a leader who rewards his men. They came with me from the Caucasus region—waited around Khokand. Look there!"

He indicated a huddle of figures in sheepskin coats and black hats, each one sleeping with a musket in hand, their dark faces upturned to the sky.

"Alamans, who came with Abbas from Kashgar. And at the foot of the tower wandering Kurds and Turkomans—all armed. The Tartars have Mauser rifles, with magazines."

The men were sprawled about the clay, around some ashes of fires, between piles of littered garments, bags of grain, some stacks of women's silk garments, and an occasional heap of copper and silver vessels, candlesticks, and glittering cloths.

"All good Mohammedans," said Monsey complacently.

"Then why are not they at sunrise prayers?" demanded Edith coldly, remembering the custom of the devout Moslems of Yakka Arik.

"Prayers?" Monsey stared at her in some surprise. "Oh, my fellows are well enough. They are Mohammedans now, because they are on a religious mission. If need be, I dare say they could be Jainists or other things— anything but Sayaks, sun-worshipers. Every Mohammedan hates a Sayak. Now, look there."

Below the wall on the side away from the cliff Edith could see that the moat had been dug out to a greater depth. In it was a tangle of dead tree branches, with many pointed stakes uprising from the ground.

"A lesson of the war," laughed the Russian. "Openings in the wall command that cursed ditch. My men could dig there without being seen because it is below the level of the surrounding ground. Oh, they made a good job of it—after one or two of the lazy Tartars had the soles of their feet touched up a bit by Abbas. Now, why don't you ask how they got here?"

Edith was silent.

"Well," he went on, pleased with his own cleverness, "you'll notice those *nullahs* to the south. They lead in a roundabout fashion to Kashgar. I brought in my fellows, fifty or so at a time, at night. No one saw them. Only a dozen riders have been seen by the Sayak devils. That's what I want."

As a matter of fact the wooded ravines running between the heights that led to the great southern peaks of the Himalayas might have afforded shelter to many times that number. To the west, facing the prepared trench, was a level plain of some size, rocky at the further end and leading to broken, rolling woodland. At a distance, on all sides, were the mountains.

Nothing could be seen from here of Yakka Arik, the villages, fields, or lake. Edith fancied, as the sun topped the peaks behind them, that she could recognize the snow summit of *Mustagh Ata* standing against the dawn in the direction of Kashgar, across the river's gorge.

"You see I've studied the defenses of this place, my lady," grinned the Russian. "I've been here before, and by the beard of Allah and Satan's hoof, I didn't want to come here again without a bodyguard."

At that Edith drew a quick breath, recalling the tale of Iskander. So Monsey had been the Russian who raided Yakka Arik! But her companion saw no reason for further concealment.

"You don't understand it all yet, my American." He paused at a sound from below and went on in an altered tone. "You were necessary to our plans. The Sayaks will follow you because you know the secret of their mosque. Abbas and I know that, too. And when the Sayaks realize we're here, they will fall the more easily into our trap. Then Abbas and I will settle our reckoning. Oh, I know those fanatics. Their fighting men will attack this castle like mad dogs, thinking only a score of men are here. Then they will find themselves in a pretty mess. I wonder why they haven't tried it already. My outposts haven't seen anything."

Three or four scattered groups were stationed on knolls on the plains. Monsey waved his hand at them, and Abbas grinned.

"Now you understand, my lady. When we have killed off the armed men of those brigands we'll move against the valley. And there won't be so many to kill, at that. Besides some Arabs and a handful of Afghans those Sayaks are not much use in a fight. They do not number a hundred able-bodied men. Then we will take care of the mosque."

Abbas stretched powerful arms.

"Spoil," he grunted, "gold—ev'ryting, by Allah. *Maili barlik!*"

"I thought," Edith faced Monsey, "you came to Yakka Arik because my father sent you to rescue me."

Monsey scowled, then shrugged.

"Why keep up the appearances, *mademoiselle?* I must have something to pay my men."

"And yourself!"

"Yes," he said softly, "myself." He nodded at Abbas. "This merchant needs new goods—"

"I thought slaves were a thing of the past."

"Not in Central Asia, to-day. Gold is power, and women are gold. So much for Abbas. I tell you, I am leader here. And I only came for you." He touched a strand of her hair. "Do you think I would tell you all this if I were not sure of my cards? I want you to understand how you are fixed—with only my word to keep you from these men. Think about it. You won't be so haughty, then." He paused as the Alaman touched his arm and thrust a stocky forefinger out at the plateau. "Now, who is that?" From the rocks at the further end of the level space a figure was advancing toward the castle. Edith saw that it was John Donovan.

He had taken only a few steps before a patrol challenged and he halted while a pair of riflemen examined him. Presently the trio began to walk back to the *Kurgan*. Donovan wore a sun helmet, and was immaculate in his flannels and white jacket beside the short, dingy natives. He strode ahead carelessly, hands in his pockets.

Edith had rejoiced at sight of the man she loved, moving toward her out of the wilderness of rocks. Her heart beat a brief refrain of exultation. Then she bit her lip and repressed a cry of distress.

Apparently Donovan was unarmed. He seemed to take no notice of the two guards. The light of the newly risen sun was dead in his eyes. And he was coming straight into the trap Monsey had set for him and the Sayaks.

The Russian himself was more than a little surprised. Quickly he scanned the near-by woods beyond the rocks, where there was no sign of further movement. "An Englishman, that's certain," he muttered to himself. "No one else would walk or dress like that—here. Now who?"—he glanced at Edith, then peered at the visitor. "By the sacred head of the Prophet, it's Donovan himself without a beard! I didn't know him at first. Look here!" He gripped the girl's arm viciously. "Silence, you hear? Not a word out of you! Or I'll order my men to shoot him down. Besides that. Abbas may skewer you with his cursed knife on his own account!"

He flung a word at the Alaman and scrambled toward the stair.

"I'm going to welcome the *khan* who is your friend," he called over his shoulder to Edith and disappeared. She heard him mutter something about his "holy luck." Abbas drew nearer her.

The girl stared at Donovan in utter dismay. He had looked up coolly at the tower, but appeared not to recognize her. The guards had halted him a few paces from the ditch. She wanted to call to him, to warn him. But she feared—not for herself—that it would be fatal.

Presently Monsey appeared, going down the entrance steps. She watched him join the group and search his visitor for weapons. After a moment Donovan drew a handkerchief from his pocket and one of the men secured it about his eyes. Then Monsey guided the blindfolded man up the steps, across the courtyard where the awakened natives stared at them curiously, and into the *Kurgan* hold.

An explanation of Donovan's appearance flashed upon her. He had reasoned that Monsey would not know him; perhaps, even, her protector was unaware that Monsey was in the castle. He must have hoped that Abbas and his men would not connect the arrival of a well-dressed Englishman with the Sayaks.

And she had unwittingly revealed the identity of the white man at Yakka Arik to Monsey. Knowing the Russian, she understood how great was the peril into which Donovan had walked unarmed. Her heart told her why he had come.

It all seemed perfectly hopeless to Edith. She had been comforting herself throughout the night with the thought that Donovan, somehow, would manage to aid her. Abbas signed to her.

"You come," he grinned. "Don' you talk. No, by God!"

His hand moved swiftly to his girdle and Edith caught the flash of steel. In the same instant, the knife thudded into a beam, across the stairs. The Alaman tugged it out, with a meaning glance at her. He laid his hand on the beam.

"Dono-van Khan," he assured her.

The girl passed down the stairs with Abbas behind her. For this reason she did not see, across the ravine, a horseman riding at full gallop along the cliff path toward the south away from Yakka Arik. It was a native, his long cloak fluttering, bending close to the horse and riding as no one but a hill-bred native could ride. And she heard nothing because, although the opposite cliff was within easy rifle range, Monsey had given strict orders to his sentries not to shoot until he gave the word so that the firing might not reveal the secret of the trap he had set so cleverly with the assistance of Abbas.

CHAPTER XXV
CARDS ON THE TABLE

A rickety table had been drawn against the wall of the teakwood room. On two boxes, facing each other across this table, sat John Donovan and Monsey. A guard stood at the door. Near the stove Edith had seated herself, with Abbas at her side.

"And so you want to know what I am doing with this woman in the castle?" Monsey stroked his mustache complacently and surveyed his visitor. Donovan had hardly looked at Edith. He sat erect, hands clasped over crossed knees. He had been released from the bandage and his tranquil gaze searched the opposite wall, without in the least attempting to watch his enemy.

"Well, I will tell you." Monsey rested solid shoulders against the teakwood, his nervous hand straying about the revolver holster. "It's none of your damn business."

Lower lip thrust out, eyes narrowed, he surveyed Donovan. Monsey, also, had guessed that his enemy came to the *Kurgan* hoping that he would not be recognized.

"Suppose," ventured Donovan, "I should make it so?"

"Oh, fine words. Tell me who you are and what you want."

He smiled, hoping to hear Donovan lie. It rather grieved the Russian that the other had shown no surprise at seeing him. Monsey had fancied his visitor would be startled, afraid.

"You do well to be civil, Mr. Donovan Khan, sometimes called the Falcon. I'll have you know I'm master here. It's very convenient you walked in just now. Miss Rand has been telling me about you—how you deserted the army to be a renegade chief of the Yakka Arik scum. I've heard you have a father who is a knight and an uncle who is a minister of God. They'll be proud of you—"

"I didn't," cried Edith, heedless of Abbas' warning mutter, "say anything of the kind."

"My father is dead." Donovan's words were very cold. His brown, boyish face was quiet except for the eyes that now held Monsey's wavering stare—the Russian had had a sleepless night and his nerves were none of the best.

The self-possession of good breeding was Donovan's; his was the high code of one who has been a law to others for many years; his also was the calmness that comes through long contact with this other world of the Orient.

"Answering the rest of your question, Monsey," he went on, "I have come to ask Miss Rand to marry me."

Sheer surprise made the Russian gape. Edith's glance flew to Donovan's honest eyes, then fell. She had grown quite pale.

"So," Monsey grinned, "you still want her, after she's been in the hands of the natives ? Or maybe you have to marry her?"

Donovan took not the slightest notice of the other's insulting remark.

"Will you do me the honor, Edith"—and his voice quivered—"to be my—wife?"

Not Abbas nor all the powers of the Tower could prevent the girl from answering. "Yes." And she was no longer pale.

"You don't happen to know, Donovan," sneered Monsey, "that Rand, her father, has lost his money—is bankrupt?"

Edith was surprised and could not keep from searching Donovan's face. Money was such a slight thing at this moment, and so Donovan plainly considered it. "Really?" His brows went up. "I was not aware—as you seem to be—that Miss Rand possessed wealth. You, Monsey, and this man, Abbas Abad," he went on, "are marked down by the Sayaks. You know the belief of the Moslems that each criminal has in Heaven a stone marked with his name that will one day fall upon him no matter where he is. The Sayaks have condemned you to death; there will be fighting before long. You cannot leave the tower. I wish to take Edith Rand away from danger."

Monsey broke into a long laugh. "Oh, you are a fool. Well, Edith Rand won't go away. She will stay with me. Is that clear?"

A slight shrug answered him. "I wanted to give you the chance, Monsey, to play the gentleman, you know."

The Russian flushed, biting his mustache. He watched his visitor draw an object carefully from his pocket. It was a heavy jade necklace of many folds, set with some inferior turquoise. Donovan laid it on the table, rolled into a ball.

"You remember this?" His words were crisp.

"Well, perhaps Abbas does. It belonged to the wife of Iskander ibn Tahir. He bought it back, in the Kashgar bazaar. And he has kept it. You know the fate in store for a man who violates the home of an Arab of high birth?" While he spoke, he put his hand on the necklace. Monsey's eyes widened a little, and he licked his full lips. Then he shook his head.

"Not good enough. You can't bluff me."

"I am not bluffing. Whatever happens to Miss Rand, your life is forfeit. It is beyond my saving."

So calmly he spoke, he seemed to be explaining the inevitable. Edith felt this and Monsey was silent a space. As if finished with the business of the necklace, Donovan tossed it, still rolled tightly, into Edith's lap.

"Presents from such a man as Iskander have a meaning," he said.

Donovan had not looked at her. Monsey took the words to himself, but the girl glanced up with awakened curiosity. Abbas would have picked up the necklace, but the Englishman turned to him sharply.

"Mahmoud is coming for you. Abbas," he said in Turki. "Are you ready?"

The simple speech caused the Alaman to draw a long breath and to step back instinctively. Edith wondered whether it was surprise at being addressed in his own tongue. But she remembered the fear that had flashed into the face of the Sart upon the mountain side. The name of the physician seemed to carry a potent spell.

Edith drew the necklace under her lace shawl. Here her quick fingers explored its folds tentatively and she felt a piece of paper crumpled within the jade ornaments. Eagerly she separated the wad of paper from the necklace and thrust it into the bosom of her dress. When the ornament of the wife of Iskander fell again to her lap it revealed nothing but the stones, strung on a gold chain. Abbas later claimed it, with an eye to spoil.

Donovan turned to Monsey earnestly.

"I do not need to conceal my cards, Monsey. Believe it or not, the Sayaks hold you fast. Your men have heard of them, and they are afraid. You know the fear that centers about Yakka Arik."

Sure of himself again, Monsey laughed. He rose, motioning the other to come to the door. There he pointed through the outer entrance that gave on the courtyard.

"Oh, I know the legends. Maybe if I had only a handful of men"—he shrugged—but look out there!"

He watched, pleased, as Donovan stiffened at sight of the numbers in the *Kurgan* and their weapons.

"You see. Likewise, the old moat on the side away from the cliff is dug out into a mantrap. Also, I have had great pine flares made ready to light in case of a night attack. *Vous voyez que je suis en garde*. Naturally, I don't intend to let you leave with this valuable information."

"In spite of your assurance, given me outside the castle?"

"Oh, that. Well, I wanted to let your men who were watching from the wood think you and I were on friendly terms." Monsey's lips writhed and his hand darted to his weapon as Donovan made a quick move toward him. "Stay where you are, my fine gentleman. Now, have you any more cards to show?"

Donovan stared quizzically at the vista of the *Kurgan*. His lips closed firmly under the light mustache." Edith, watching him prayerfully, felt her heart sink. He was her champion, and fighting against great odds.

"I think—not."

"Ah. That is too bad. You have given me a good trump." He grinned, once more enjoying himself. "You are worth more to me alive than dead. And so is Miss Rand. Do you think your assassin friends will attack the tower with the two of you helpless in my hands?"

The lines in Donovan's lean face deepened. "I don't think—I know it."

"Even if they are led to believe I will kill the woman when they attack?"

"It would not change their purpose." Donovan flung out an eloquent hand. "Don't you see, man! Those Sayaks will come, in spite of everything. The *Kurgan* will be a shambles. That is why I came here. On the chance that you, who were once a Russian nobleman, would have enough vestige of honor to spare her that. It doesn't matter, you know, what you do with me if you will release her."

Monsey relished his distress. He stepped back, still fingering his heavy revolver.

"Oh, I don't intend to play the saint—now." He hesitated, as if wishing to say more. Then his eyes gleamed and he smiled. "Besides, I can't afford to."

Edith glanced at him inquiringly. She had been aroused by the scene at the table, where Monsey's character was laid bare brutally. Even now, she could not believe that Donovan was powerless against the men of the *Kurgan*.

"Mr. Rand and Major Fraser-Carnie are approaching these hills," said Monsey agreeably. "They have an escort of a half-troop of one of the native English cavalry. It seems the gentlemen, after comparing notes, did not trust me."

He paused, enjoying the effect of his words. "Unfortunately," continued the Russian, "they will arrive too late."

Edith clenched her hands. Her father was near Yakka Arik! She had felt that he would come if he was able. It was not in the nature of Arthur Rand to leave his daughter's fate in other hands. She knew now that Monsey had not been sent by Rand.

"English troopers in foreign territory." Monsey shook his head. "A grave offense, if any serious fighting results. The—ah—irregulars here might resent it."

"It's a habit," observed Donovan mildly, "of the English border forces to wander to the scene of a—crime, for example."

"Once you paid high for that—habit. And you will pay more."

"Oh, it's in the game. We always blunder in, you know." Donovan smiled a little. "So the major and his Garhwalis are in the hills! As a matter of curiosity, do you intend to face him with your—irregulars?"

Monsey tugged at his mustache, and glanced at Abbas.

"No need, my fine gentleman. As you are a former officer and a scion of a *noble* house"—he tried to mimic the Englishman's irony—"you will appreciate the strength of my position. I don't think the Rand-Fraser-Carnie forces will arrive before a day or two. Meanwhile, the lawless Sayaks will assault a Russian traveler and a peaceful merchant in their camp—to the great loss of the Sayaks. Then, of course, there will be some justifiable reprisals by my men."

"Entirely to be expected>"

"You take the point. Merely one of the mountain feuds, if the worthy drill-book major tries to ask questions. The mosque may suffer, likewise the lawlesss residents of Yakka Arik. But I will not be here nor will Miss Rand."

"And my father?" Edith voiced her anxiety.

"If he is curious, he will be told by some of these natives"—Monsey nodded at the door—"that a certain renegade Britisher named Donovan Khan *alias* the Falcon has disappeared with her. Of course *Captain* Donovan will not be here to cause further trouble. The ravine, to the river, is very deep."

"Five hundred feet, I think," nodded Donovan.

"Exactly. I see you are not altogether a fool. Presently you will be able to judge for yourself."

"I regret that I could not climb the cliff."

"Oh, yes. I believe you. I took pains to investigate that. No, I think you are better apart—so!" Edith had crept to Donovan's side and taken his hand in hers. She was very near to tears. Brusquely, Monsey thrust her aside, while Abbas grinned. "That is well. Now, Donovan Khan, I will ask you to let your hands be bound behind your back and submit to an armed guard, in a corner of this outer room."

"Let me stay with him," Edith pleaded. She felt very weak, very helpless. She wondered why Donovan was so quiet.

"The air in the tower will benefit you. In case you should want to converse, my lady, I will provide you with another of my men. He will have orders."

CHAPTER XXVI

AN HOUR AFTER DARK

It was some time before Edith remembered the crumpled paper concealed in her dress. Then she surveyed her surroundings cautiously. She was in the chamber on the first tier of the tower. An Alaman sat apathetically on the wooden steps over the aperture that led below.

The footfalls of the sentry guarding Donovan below reached her ears. The Englishman himself was not visible. Nor was Edith permitted to look down from the opening in the floor. Anxiously she felt for the bit of paper, drawing near to one of the embrasures.

The guard, leaning against his rifle, kept only an indifferent watch upon her as she slipped the paper into a fold of her scarf where she could see it, and smoothed out the wrinkles tenderly. It took some time before this careful maneuver revealed the whole of the missive to the girl. She saw a small square of worn paper closely written in pencil. Eagerly, with hearing attuned for the approach of Monsey or Abbas, she read:

DEAREST GIRL:

It took hours to dissuade Iskander from launching an immediate assault on the castle. I won my point—a chance to get to you. The Sayaks will attack the night after I reach you. I had no other way of helping you but this.

An hour after sunset, try to be at the eastern wall, nearest the cliff. Aravang will make the attempt at the cliff. He is a regular mountain sheep and none of the other Sayaks would dare it. I don't think A. would, for me. But he will for you.

He will bring my revolver. Take it, if he can't make the climb into the *Kurgan* wall, which is unlikely. Try to reach me with the weapon if you can. If not, use it as you may, and God wills.

Watch out for the sentries on the rampart. Monsey stations two there, I think, as he does not fear an attack from that side. Nothing will keep the

Sayaks from a frontal attack, although I have talked my head off trying to make them see the sides to the north and south are more accessible.

If you can't get to me before the attack, *don't try*. I can look out for myself. Iskander will look for you, perhaps. God watch over you, you blessed woman.

DONOVAN.

If Aravang is not on time, he'll have fallen.

* * * *

Darkness came less swiftly to the *Kurgan* than to the valley of Yakka Arik. Looking from the tower embrasure Edith could see the splendid curtains of sunset drawing about a glowing orb that fired the snow peaks with its life.

The aspect of the mountains, as shadows formed in the ravines and crept up the rock surfaces, reminded the girl of a vast painting—so utterly desolate and so tranquil were these gigantic pinnacles.

It dwarfed her. Since her coming to the valley of the Sayaks, Edith had never felt so insignificant. Life itself was a small matter, here, she thought—and what was life if Donovan was lost to her? Donovan, whose love for her was to be read between the lines of his message?

Edith wanted to sit down and wait. She was listless and chilled. Close beside her the Alaman brooded over his rifle, passive as he had been all the day, except to eat once a meal of fermented milk and black bread. The bustle of subdued preparation, hastened in the last light of evening, came to her ears from the courtyard below. She was grateful that this activity had kept Monsey or Abbas from coming to stare at her during the afternoon.

It was with a start that Edith realized Aravang must have begun his climb. The shadowy vapor of the ravine would conceal him and he could still see after a fashion to find his way up the face of the cliff, clinging to the crevices and spurs of the almost sheer rock.

"If Aravang is not on time, he'll have fallen."

The sentence returned to her mind with the force of a blow. Aravang was on his way and she must be prepared to act. She did not know what to do. How was she to reach the rampart over the cliff? Could Aravang, if he survived the climb, gain the interior of the *Kurgan*? What could a stupid native and a helpless girl manage to do against two such men as Monsey and Abbas and their armed followers?

Edith tried to think. They could not return—if escape from the *Kurgan* were possible—down the face of the cliff in the dark. Even if it had been possible, she would not leave John Donovan.

Iskander, Donovan had said, might aid her. But Iskander would not gain the interior of the *Kurgan*, owing to the trap that had been set for the Sayaks. No, Edith could not plan, could not see any way out of the trap. Donovan himself had—so she thought—merely taken a last chance, heedless of himself—had done his utmost to protect her until the end that would come with the fighting and the revolver.

"He did it for me," she thought.

Edith found that she was unable to realize the truth of the revolver, the *Kurgan*, and her enemies. The whole thing was fantastic, impossible. It was another evil dream, and she must surely waken. She, Edith Rand, could not be so severed from the reality of that other life of home and Louisville and servants.

Was it possible that two men could have talked as Monsey and Donovan had about her—accepting the inevitability of this other world? Could not her father come to help her, as he had always done?

With this, she understood finally that Arthur Rand could not reach her in time, Monsey's guards would see to it. The American and the English cavalry were scouring the hills without knowing the location of Yakka Arik, not realizing that the Sayaks were in a way her friends, nor aware of the events that were shaping about the *Kurgan* that night.

Edith laughed uncertainly, with a twinge of self-pity.

"Daddy," she murmured, "if you could only know!"

The sentry lifted his head. This movement brought the reality of her situation sharply home to the girl. She heard the steps of the guard below once more. John Donovan had need of her!

At this thought Edith Rand entered into the conflict that was being waged in the old tower of this world that was so new to her. She smiled and her pulse quickened.

Donovan loved her! She would be his wife. What else in her existence was so momentous, so wonderful as this? He was not powerless. He—a trained soldier—had taken the one step that would make it possible for him to fight for her. It was not true that he had been outwitted by Monsey. And Donovan trusted her. He had staked everything on her courage. Well, she would not fail him.

Iskander had said that in this American girl was a weapon of tested steel. And he had judged truly.

Thoughtfully she bound the ends of the shawl about her shoulders, thus leaving her arms free. She faced the Alaman with new intentness. After all, she told herself, the native was a witless ruffian. Edith stepped to the ladder, speaking authoritatively to her guard and drawing upon her small stock of Turki.

"*Sa'at,*" she declared. (It is the time to start.) "Take me to"—she pondered swiftly—"Abbas Abad. Abbas, *effendi.*"

The man fumbled uneasily with his weapon. He had not expected this, but the white woman seemed to be certain of her purpose. What was he to do? He rose.

She thrust him aside indignantly, with beating heart.

"Kul!" Edith cried. "I must go to Abbas—to Abbas."

The man hesitated. He was little better than a slave. Greatly he dreaded punishment and the anger of the higher beings, his superiors. And the name of Abbas hinted at both these things. It would be well to take her as she asked, lest the soles of his bare feet be beaten.

Watchfully he climbed down the ladder, motioning her to follow.

It was then that the kindred longing of two hearts came near to defeating the girl's new purpose. Seeing Donovan standing, tied fast by the wrists to the table, brought hither apparently for this purpose, Edith gave a low cry and ran to him.

Her arms went around his neck and his lips pressed hers swiftly. Breathing quickly, her cheeks aflame and her eyes soft, the girl looked up at him.

Donovan kissed her again, incredulous of the nearness of this beautiful woman and more than a little dazed. Her hands touched his rough cheek shyly. The sudden knowledge of Edith's love and the brief possession of her lips were a miracle that rendered him voiceless. Then a rifle stock thrust roughly against his chest.

"Edith!" he whispered. "You must not bother about me. Good luck!"

"Stupid!" she laughed.

Her Alaman escorted her vigilantly to the door. Lanterns were already lit in the courtyard. Overhead, the crimson of the sky outlined walls and tower. Within a few paces of her by one of the lights Abbas was distributing cartridges to a group of men.

"W'at you wan'?" he cried angrily. *"Nakir el kadr!* You go—"

Edith walked nearer quietly.

"Monsey sent for me—Monsey."

Abbas glanced at her and shrugged his plump shoulders. He pointed to the entrance to the courtyard beyond which was the darkness of the plain.

"The Excellency, out there." Monsey was bringing the patrols closer to the walls. "A fool. By God, I am no fool. You stay near, yes, near."

He glanced at the darkening sky and turned irritably to his work. There were certain pine torches to be raised high over the walls. In the daylight these flares had been kept carefully lowered behind the ramparts.

Edith watched awhile as slouching Alamans and Tartars received an allotment of cartridges and departed. She drew back a little from the lantern. Abbas, after satisfying himself that she was accompanied by her attendant, did not spare his attention from his task. The girl, he knew, could not escape from the castle.

So Edith attained the first point in her objective, a tumbled pile of stone blocks against the raised walk that ran inside the parapet nearest the cliff. The Alaman stood before her, leaning on his rifle, well content that there had been no beating of his tender feet.

The eastern wall, together with that of the north and south, was more battered by the weather than that facing the plateau. The parapet was broken at intervals. Edith moved her position casually until she was abreast one of these breaks, and perched herself upon the stone walk that had served as a fire step before the days when guns and cartridges had been invented.

Here, she could look out through a gap in the masonry, and glimpsed the dark space that was the ravine. A distant murmur of running water reached her ears. She watched the two sentinels pacing the rampart and understood why Monsey had not posted a stronger guard. This side of the *Kurgan* was impregnable to attack.

A scant dozen feet of steep incline led to the brink of the cliff. Below was the five-hundred-foot drop to the river. Edith cast an anxious glance at the western horizon. Only a crimson and purple glow was visible. The sun had set some time ago. Across the dark bulk of the cliff facing her a few stars were visible. In the courtyard, the lanterns had gained full strength.

Dark figures passed between her and the lights. Heavy poles bearing a bundle at their ends were being raised into place. Once she saw Monsey, and instinctively shrank closer into her nest of rocks—although he could not now see her in the dark.

She noticed that the two sentries kept to the corners, at quite a distance. The Alaman, however, was very close, watching her. At times she heard the bull voice of Abbas, lowered to a rumble, and wondered if he were seeking her. Without her realizing it, the need of preparation engaged the two leaders, so that they had no time to seek her out, Monsey being unaware that she was not in the tower.

Even the numbers in the *Kurgan* were not free from the dread that the name of Yakka Arik inspired.

On the cliff edge she heard the sound of a bird fluttering its wings. And then a *chirp*. Again came the whirr of wings, like that of a falcon rising, and not until then did Edith realize that Aravang had come and was signaling her. She stiffened and glanced up at the bulk of the Alaman. He had not noticed anything out of the usual.

Whereupon Edith drew closer to the gap in the mass of stones. The sound of the bird—imitated from one of Aravang's falcons—had been some yards away. Nothing was visible in the murk under the wall.

"Kul!" she uttered clearly. The guard moved closer to listen. The noise on the cliff quieted at once, but Edith thought she heard a pebble slide from its place.

Unfortunately, the Alaman had heard or guessed at something moving. He elbowed the girl to one side, thrusting his head out into the opening, with his rifle at the "ready."

"Aravang!" called Edith softly, and as she recollected a native phrase: *"Kaba-dar!"*

The body of the crouching guard was pressed close to her, and she wrinkled her nose at the scent of filthy sheepskins. She thought quickly. Surely the form of the Alaman must be visible to some one without, framed as it was against the afterglow in the west.

So Edith tightened her lips, and pushed suddenly with all the strength of her young arms. Taken unawares, the native, overbalanced, fell forward through the gap. A grunt resounded. He did not fall far.

With strained ears, Edith heard a rifle rattle over the stones. The next instant the legs and scrambling feet of the guard disappeared as though drawn downward. A cough sounded, then the rustle of a heavy body following the rifle. Then silence.

The slight noises had resounded like miniature explosions. But apparently the two sentries still kept their posts. The bustle in the court and the stamping of hordes drowned the struggle outside the wall.

"My goodness!" Edith realized what had happened. "Oh, the poor man—"

She shivered as the powerful figure of Aravang crawled up beside her, climbing over the debris of rocks without. She caught the pungent scent of sweat-soaked wool.

"Missy *khanum!*" Aravang thrust a cold metal object into her hand, fumbling for it in the dark. His own paw was damp.

Edith pushed the revolver back, wishing ardently that she could speak so that Aravang would understand. On thinking the matter over, she realized that it would be safe for her servant to enter the *Kurgan*. No one there knew Aravang, and as far as appearance went he was much like the motley men of Monsey's forces.

"Come," she whispered, laying hand on his shoulder. The man was breathing hard, his giant shoulders tensed, like a swimmer after a long battle with the waves. It had been no mean feat to climb the cliff of Yakka Arik.

"Dono-van Khan," he growled beseechingly, and again: "Dono-van Khan."

"Yes, Aravang," she whispered reassuringly, as she would to a child.

CHAPTER XXVII
SANCTUARY OF THE TOWER

By now the aspect of the courtyard had changed. Alamans, Kurds, and Tartars were lying on their sides behind the ramparts, mostly to the west. Others stood by the horses, and still others by the unlit flares.

The trap was set.

Edith, as she made her way to the hold, saw Abbas, lantern in hand, talking to one of the groups of men. He looked at her keenly, but seeing the figure of a native shadowing her, was content to call out.

"You don' forget me, Abbas Abad. You watch for me, yess, by Allah!"

With a sigh of relief the girl gained the semi-gloom of the room under the tower. In her absence a lantern had been brought to the Tartar on guard—a broad Mongol wearing a round black hat, a bandoleer of cartridges over his shoulder.

Beside him Donovan leaned against the table. Edith advanced toward the ladder slowly, wondering how the armed sentry was to be dealt with. Donovan must be freed. It was for that she had come to the room.

Apparently the prisoner had not noticed her; but his eyes had quickened and he stood with both feet planted firmly on the floor. Here, however, was a situation which Aravang felt himself competent to master without any assistance. He grinned and seated himself on the sizable packing case on which the Tartar loafed.

The man scanned him with some suspicion and without making room for the burly native. Edith paused, holding her breath. She saw Aravang turn toward the guard as if to say something. The man stared at him from slant, cruel eyes that widened and started from their sockets as a steel-like hand flew up and closed about his throat.

No cry was uttered. Aravang still sat on the box. But in his two hands he held the writhing Tartar helpless.

Releasing one hand, Aravang thrust the other's bulletlike head against the stone wall. There was a dull crack and the figure of the guard slumped upon the box.

"Some one is coming," said Donovan quietly, first in English then in Turki. Aravang stood up with knotted hands, as if prepared to face and conquer new enemies for the sake of his mistress. Edith, however, had seen Monsey and a party of his men walking toward the tower. They were armed and seemed in haste.

Urgent need spurred the girl's aroused wit. She could explain nothing to Aravang. Instead, she sprang forward, turned over the box and pointed into its empty depths.

Donovan caught her purpose at once and barked a short command at Aravang. Their powerful friend moved slowly, but with two motions of his great arms he had lifted the unconscious sentry from the floor where the man had slipped into the box. Then he turned the box right side up, over the body, concealing all trace of his victim.

Yet not before Edith had pulled the bandoleer from the Tartar's shoulder, and the round cap from his head. She stripped off Aravang's heavy woolen hat and flung it into a corner, planting the Tartar's cap in its place and the cartridge belt over his arm. Meanwhile Aravang picked up the rifle, which he handled clumsily—not being accustomed to possession of such modern weapons.

Edith faced about as Monsey strode into the door, flung her a quick glance and moved toward Donovan.

"I can spare only a moment," the Russian smiled. "But after I have kept an appointment with the Sayaks I intend to return—" he broke off. "Where is the other guard?"

He looked quickly from Donovan to the giri. His men watched from the doorway. Aravang, not understanding, was mute. Before Donovan could speak, Edith answered.

"Ask Abbas," she said. "He wants me to wait for him—after your appointment."

"The devil!"

"I think he is," Edith smiled.

Knowing Abbas, Monsey did not question her. And then there was the dull report of a rifle from the plateau. The Tartars stirred uneasily.

"Announcing our visitors," observed Monsey. He felt Donovan's bonds, muttering that he liked to be sure of his reception when he called again.

"One can never be too sure," nodded Donovan affably.

The Russian ordered the girl curtly up the ladder to the tower. "And no tricks, my lady." Edith obeyed with surprising readiness. After glancing around and making sure that all was as he wished, Monsey strode toward the door as a scattered burst of firing resounded nearer the *Kurgan*.

When he left the room his men followed. Edith, in the upper chamber, waited impatiently until Aravang's shaggy head was thrust up into the opening. Behind him came Donovan, stroking the wrists that the cords had numbed. The three faced each other silently in the gloom. It was Edith who spoke first.

"Come," she said thoughtfully, "to the tower top."

Donovan had taken the native's weapon and the bandoleer. He jerked open the breech, made sure that a cartridge was inserted, and ordered Aravang to surrender his revolver to Edith.

"Why?" he frowned. "I rather like it here—as a base of operations."

"Because I want you to," insisted the girl.

Familiar by now with the damaged stairway, she advanced up to the open air. Donovan followed more slowly.

Night had fallen. But splinters of light were thrusting into the gloom of the *Kurgan* as the waiting men began to light the kerosene-soaked flares. First one and then another pine bundle crackled and blazed.

By the growing light they could see dark figures running up the *Kurgan*'s entryway, and the line of Monsey's men standing behind the parapet. These had not yet begun to fire. The reports Edith had heard came from the patrols as they were driven back to the moat.

Near the rocks on the further plateau she thought she saw the light robes of groups of men moving. Overhead the stars had claimed the sky and the half-moon was shedding a hazy light Donovan took it all in.

"Monsey is no man's fool," he muttered. "He knows his men are liable to stampede under the old fear of the Sayaks, in the dark. Those flares—"

"Quick!" cried Edith. "We must do something before it is too late."

The man paid her a tribute of admiration in a swift glance. Then his eyes hardened with recollection of the peril below. The whole vista of the courtyard was fast being revealed by the sputtering flares. The door leading to the hold and the tower where they stood must be clearly outlined to any one who chanced to look that way. It would be difficult, practically impossible, to escape from the door into the courtyard without being seen.

Still, that was their only chance of safety, Donovan reasoned. A quick sally, a rush to one of the breaks in the wall on a side away from the Sayak attack—a gantlet of bullets—

He knelt down, resting his rifle on a fallen timber, waist-high, and searched for Abbas. Edith tugged at his shoulder vigorously.

"What, dear?" he asked, without shifting his position."

"Not that, Donovan Khan," the girl exclaimed. "That is not why I brought you here."

"Righto!" he murmured cheerily. "But it will help, you know—"

"No—not that." She crouched beside him, her face close to his. "Don't you see? We can do more than that!"

A ragged volley came out of the gloom, two hundred yards across the plateau. Under cover of the swirling smoke that rose over the ground, they saw groups of Sayaks advancing. Behind the parapet the waiting cohorts held their fire, as Monsey, running back and forth, swore at them angrily. The Englishman knew that when an answering volley came from the *Kurgan* it must do deadly execution among the attackers, who, besides the disadvantage of numbers and inferior arms, had the glare of the pine torches in their eyes.

"We must warn the Sayaks, Donovan Khan."

His eye fixed on Monsey, he did not grasp at first the full significance of her words. She shook him impatiently. "Call to Iskander. Or it will be too late."

"Too late? Ah!"

The instant Donovan understood her purpose, its whole meaning was clear to the mind of the soldier. Laying down his weapon he took the girl's hand in his and studied her anxiously.

"Hurry!" she whispered.

"You do not know it all, Edith. Our warning might check the Sayak attack, but it would bring all these beggars of Monsey's on us, at the tower. It would cut us off. Our only chance is a surprise sally—and we would be throwing that chance away—"

"I understand."

"During the fighting, if we keep silence, we might slip away, Edith, I will not throw aside your chance."

Her eyes held him. He could see every shade of expression in her eager face by the glare below. And he saw no fear—only pride and urgent need.

"Donovan Khan, you told me that the Sayaks would continue to storm the *Kurgan* until they are utterly cut to pieces." She did not wait for his answer. "We can save the lives of a hundred men. And then Yakka Arik—" Edith sighed. "I am thinking of the women of Yakka Arik. We can save them, Donovan Khan, perhaps. Now, hurry." The girl gave him a little push as a second volley—harmless as the first—came from the scattered muskets of the oncoming natives. "Don't you see? It doesn't matter—you and I. We will have each other; they can't change that, now, can they?"

Donovan had seen men, before now, fling their bodies into the face of death. It was something of a miracle to him, this settled purpose of the girl at his side. He rose, with a laugh that had much gladness in it.

"By Jove! You *are* playing the game, Edith."

Donovan, once convinced, was a man of action. He cupped his hands to his mouth and faced the gloom of the plateau in which he could now make out the Sayaks not a hundred yards away.

"Iskander, son of Tahir!" His shout rang out clearly over the bustle below and the confused sounds from the near-by natives. "Go back!"

He had spoken in Turki. Men stared up from the courtyard at the tower in astonishment. Hands were withdrawn from rifles. Monsey seemed turned to a graven image of attention. Donovan continued in English.

"Iskander, Donovan Khan is speaking. A trap has been set. Twice your numbers are in the *Kurgan* with magazine rifles."

Crack-crack! Monsey's revolver spat at the tower summit, the bullets thudding into the beams overhead. Edith fancied that the Sayaks had halted. Donovan paid no attention to the shots.

"'Ware the ditch!" he shouted, in the silence that now held the castle. "It is dug out and staked, in front of you. Monsey has prepared for you. Go back"!

A pause, in which Edith strained her ears. Then came Iskander's answering hail out of the dark:

"Dono-van Khan, I hear."

In response to a command the girl could not distinguish, the forms of the Sayaks began to melt back into the rocks and trees. As if to confirm the warning, a heavy volley burst from the wall of the castle—too late now to do serious harm. Confused firing was kept up by Monsey's men, who seemed to have been startled by the voice from the tower and were emptying their weapons across the plateau. Faintly, Edith heard the Arab's second hail.

"I hear...and will not forget..."

CHAPTER XXVIII
THE VOICE OF MAHMOUD

As Donovan had anticipated, and as might have been expected, the first rush of Monsey's men toward the hold and the ladder leading to the tower was without result except for certain casualties among the attackers.

Aravang, standing over the aperture in the floor through which the ladder led, was armed only with a short wooden pole. But with this weapon—which, indeed, the *kul* favored over others—he sent the first two or three who ventured up the ladder back with broken heads.

Donovan, climbing alertly down the stairs from above, seconded his effort with the clip of cartridges in the Mauser rifle—five shots that drove the attackers back, dragging their wounded, from the ladder and the lower room.

"Ah, that was well. Excellency!" grunted the burly native, leaning on his staff. The reflected light from the courtyard served to disclose the two men and the woman to each other dimly.

"It was but the beginning," responded the Englishman in Aravang's tongue. "We must hold the tower now. This is the only entrance."

He paused to count the cartridges in the bandoleer. Two or three dozen rounds, at the most. The six chambers of the revolver were filled, but extra ammunition was lacking. Aravang, experienced in such warfare, was almost indifferent.

"We may meet another peril, Excellency."

"They may try to climb the outside of the tower?"

Aravang shook his head.

"It may be, Dono-van Khan. But this peril is otherwise."

Edith spoke then and Donovan did not learn what alternative the native had in mind.

"That was splendid," she cried. "Aren't we quite safe in these stone walls—of the tower? If only we can keep them away until my father comes—"

"Our position, Edith," he smiled, "is excellent. Aravang, alone, could hold this floor, at a pinch. And, if you will be good enough to mount the stairs for a flight and watch from the embrasures, we can checkmate any attempt to put ladders against the tower itself." He added, however, to himself: "Of course, we are without food or water, or necessary ammunition, and Major Fraser-Carnie is at least twelve hours' ride from this place—"

"Indeed," Edith reproved him, "I won't think of going upstairs without you. I think you are trying to send me away!"

She pouted and Donovan shook his head guiltily. A new outbreak of firing from the plateau, however, took him halfway up the stairs at her side, to one of the arrow slits in the stone wall, giving on the courtyard.

Hence they obtained a glimpse of an unexpected development resulting from the withdrawal of the Sayaks. Bundles of small pine branches bound together and soaked in part with kerosene—even that poor brand of liquid brought by camelback from China to Kashgar—when once ignited are not easily extinguished. As a consequence, the flares of Monsey were still blazing and crackling away above the courtyard, shedding a bloodlike flood of illumination over the natives who were struggling to haul down the poles supporting the flares and extinguish them. The men worked hastily, with one eye on the tower.

Donovan looked for Abbas and Monsey; but the masters of the *Kurgan* were keeping well without the range of fire from the summit. Meanwhile the horses had fallen into a semi-panic at the blazing masses near their backs and were tugging at their halters, while some Tartars struggled to secure them. This light had given opportunity to Iskander to organize a sniping fire from the branches of trees on the further side of the plateau.

"Oh, do you think it will hurt these—these Alamans and the rest?" inquired Edith interestedly. She felt impelled to call attention to the brief advantage which her strategy had secured for the Sayaks. "Surely these horrid men are worried by our being in the tower and by this shooting—"

Donovan, intent on the panorama of the fight, unconsciously dropped his mask of cheerfulness.

"Hardly, I think, Edith. That long-range fire has little effect. And when the flares are out, the horses will soon quiet down; then we won't be able to see anything that happens."

The girl was struck by the abrupt moodiness of his words, understanding, however, that it was on her account and not his own that the Englishman was troubled. Shyly, she nestled her hand in his, which closed on it firmly.

Realizing that his enemies would soon be in darkness, Donovan jerked his rifle to pick off some while he could still see to do so, Then he sighed. Cartridges were too few for such a maneuver. He must save his fire for defense of the tower. Edith noticed his act, and promptly questioned him.

"It would be unnecessary bloodshed," he parried, not wishing to explain the true reason.

Donovan was silent. He drew her close to his side, his arm around the slender shoulder that pressed near him. Edith's hair was against his cheek, and he felt her warm breath on his throat.

The girl clung to him trustfully, her faith strong that the man she loved would do what was best, under all circumstances.

They watched the flares splutter into smoky gloom as the Tartars pulled down the poles. With this, the shooting from the tree tops dwindled perforce. The horses ceased their plunging, and an unnatural quiet settled upon the castle.

Once Donovan caught up his rifle and took a snap shot at a figure that explored the base of the tower from the summit of the hold. The form sank to the stone flooring and presently crawled away.

Again there was a brief clamor as the men below tried to take the tower ladder by surprise, and Aravang came into action. Donovan did not even think this important enough to go down the stairs, well knowing the advantages of position possessed by their burly friend. Presently this new tumult also ceased, and they knew that Aravang was still master of the stair.

The smoke currents eddied away from the courtyard. The new moon brightened, casting a luminous half light upon the plateau, the walls of the *Kurgan*—a light that blurred all outlines and was more treacherous than helpful.

Edith and Donovan watched it from the shelter of the dismantled beams on the tower top. The girl snuggled close to him.

"I don't like this—this silence," she whispered.

"Oh, it's quite to be expected, Edith. Monsey is checkmated for a moment. Our side had a good inning. His men probably are disturbed by the failure of their plans and our appearance in the tower. These natives are superstitious. They must have been startled by my voice—"

"Please, you are just trying to say nice things. That is what I tried to tell you a little while ago."

Donovan, however, had been reasoning aloud. His mind was alert. He was disappointed by the complete withdrawal of the Sayaks—as the quiet of the plateau seemed to hint. What was Monsey doing? He knew the Russian would not leave them unmolested in the tower.

If scaling ladders were being prepared, he would have heard some noise. And if his enemies did not plan to rush the tower summit from without, what were their intentions? To wait for daylight?

It was not likely, Donovan thought.

Dawn would give an advantage to Monsey, for the defenders of the tower would then be visible. On the other hand, delay would bring Major Fraser-Carnie and Arthur Rand nearer to Yakka Arik. No, Monsey would hardly wait.

Edith did not try to think. She was resting against Donovan, thankful for the interval of peace with him at her side. The peril of the *Kurgan* seemed to draw further off.

"Dearest, this is our hour of peace," she heard him say. "God—it will be short. Brave heart that you are!"

His fingers trembled, touching the soft masses of her hair. She looked up, reading the secret of the steadfast eyes that were close to hers in the darkness.

Sheer triumph thrilled the girl. He loved her. Donovan Khan loved her. No matter how short their hour of happiness, they would be together.

Bitterness was in the heart of the man. He had brought the woman he loved to suffering and the shadow of death.

"Sweetheart of mine, did you really say you would—be my wife? Then I didn't dream it, did I?" His arm tightened around her and his lips brushed her closed eyes. He heard a soft, quivering laugh.

"Donovan Khan, you haven't said yet that you love me?"

"Love you—*you*, Edith? Why, I've done nothing else but that since you came to Yakka Arik. Didn't you know ?"

"But I wanted to hear you say it. Now everything's all right."

"It must be so for you, Edith. This nightmare will end; you'll sail to England with me, won't you, darling? There's a jolly curate, my uncle—a garden that was made for you—" something choked the man's words.

"England is so far. There is an army chaplain at—at—"

Edith's voice failed, and Donovan closed her lips with a fierce kiss.

"Sreenugger, you darling!" He tried to look into the face that was pressed tightly against his shoulder, and, failing, he murmured inarticulately into her ear, his arm straining her to him.

And so did these two voice their love that was to Edith the most splendid gift of this other world of the hills.

At a sound from below Donovan moved cautiously to the edge of the parapet. Edith heard Monsey speak, from the shadows that clung to the stone shelters of the courtyard.

"A truce, Donovan," he called. "Will you hold your fire, while we talk terms?"

The man in the tower considered.

"If your men stay where they are—yes," he announced, keeping well behind the stone breastwork. "No trickery, mind you!"

"Granted." The girl heard Monsey laugh. He spoke like one who held the situation well in hand. "May I compliment you on the trick you played us—warning off your Sayak friends? It was too bad, though, to give your secret away. You will do well to accept my terms."

"I was going to propose some of my own."

"No use, Mr. Donovan Khan."

"I'm afraid not. The Sayaks have marked you for their own," Donovan shifted guilefully into Turki, for the benefit of such of Monsey's men as might be within hearing.

Edith caught an oath from the courtyard below. Then the Russian responded something she could not understand. She leaned back against the timbers, waiting. Into her eyes crept the glimmer of countless stars. The heavens were afire, and in the clear mountain air the jeweled radiance of the sky seemed very close to the wearied girl.

The murmur of the men's voices went on, and her eyes closed through sheer drowsiness. She had not slept for nearly forty-eight hours. It was Donovan's return that roused her from her stupor.

He spoke grimly.

"I must tell you this, Edith. Monsey's men are piling timbers and firewood under the entrance hole of the tower—throwing the stuff in from the door. He says that he will burn us out, if we don't surrender."

"Oh!" Edith sat up with sudden dread. "He wouldn't do that!"

Donovan did not answer at once. "He would, dear, to save his own skin. I wonder if it's come to that? Somehow, I don't think so. Of course, if I were alone here he'd jolly well start a bonfire at once—"

"Then we won't surrender, not a bit. And I'll stay right here, so there will be no bonfire, as you say," she responded promptly. She knew Monsey better than to ask—although she wanted to—whether Donovan could be released, unhurt, if she gave herself up. She dreaded parting with Donovan, even for a moment.

"You must think of yourself a little—" he protested.

"I am. And I don't want you to talk to him any more."

This ended the conference. Donovan reflected that the danger of fire was the one that must have occurred to Aravang. The Englishman and Aravang could not prevent the piling up of wood. A large blaze started under the entrance to the tower would soon catch in the ruins of the staircase and the tower itself would serve as a chimney for the draft. Nevertheless, he fancied that this was Monsey's last card.

With Donovan's arm around her once more, the girl subsided into the drowsiness she was powerless to fight. She tried vainly to keep her eyes open.

In this state of half-wakefulness, the whole aspect of her plight lost its reality. What were the tower, the *Kurgan*, Monsey, but a bad dream, like the one in Srinagar? Only Donovan was real. She rested her cheek against his arm.

Dull sounds from the rooms below failed to disturb her as they did the man. He did not relish hearing an incendiary pyre prepared. But he was powerless to do anything save watch from the tower top.

His arm tightened about the woman. She was his. Nothing must take her away from him now—

Presently he shook her gently into consciousness.

"Listen," he said quietly.

A sound from the plateau had reached his keen ears. He could not identify it. Edith hearkened.

"Why, it's camels," she said at once. "I ought to know their coughing by now. But what in the world are camels doing around here?"

"I fancy you're right." He rose and stepped to the parapet. Something was moving in front of the *Kurgan*. He strained his eyes through the haze of moonlight. Some shapes, clumsy and grotesque, were taking semblance.

The girl was not sure she was not still dreaming—except for Donovan's aroused interest. Camels! Why, that was absurd. Unless a wandering herd had strayed there—

"They are coming here," whispered Donovan.

She could hear the tinkle of rusty bells now, and the protesting cough of the beasts—even the muffled calls of the drivers, still veiled in the haze. Shadows were passing over the ground.

The thought came to her that here was aid; but at once she reflected that her father's party must be mounted on horses. The only camels in these mountain passes were those of Yakka Arik.

"It's a caravan," muttered Donovan. "Now, what does that mean?"

Already Edith was conscious that movement was afoot in the *Kurgan* below them. Men were running to the wall. The *clink* of metal echoed faintly.

CHAPTER XXIX

THE SAYAK FURY

Edith was fully awake, but exhausted by her long vigil and the events of the last hours. It was hard for her to grasp all that came upon the heels of the caravan.

It was not long before she was conscious of a high voice from the plain not far from the *Kurgan*. It came out of the moonlight, wailing and shadowy as the light itself in its substance.

She could not distinguish the words. Donovan, every faculty bent into listening, breathed softly. An attentive quiet had settled upon the castle. Edith caught the drift of strange syllables, intoned after the fashion of a chant. The voice came nearer and grew more distinct.

"By Jove!"

She took Donovan's arm. "What is it?"

"Mahmoud. It is some kind of message. Something about the caravan being prepared. Listen:

"The stars are setting!" he repeated, *"and the caravan...starts for the dawn of...nothing. O, make haste."*

"It's queer." Edith shivered, not perceiving that the night cold had gripped her in her sleep. "Why, he is walking in front of the camels, and coming here."

Donovan was intent on what was passing. The chant went on.

"For the men of faith a fitting grave is dug," he murmured. *"But for some there is no grave.... Their seats are empty, in which they shall ride... The master of the caravan calls, and they will come...when what is written will come to pass—"*

Edith could see Mahmoud now. Wrapped in his long cloak the *hakim* moved through the moonlight like some disembodied spirit. His lean arms were raised. His voice shrilled into the air.

Owing to the waning moon and the shadows cast by the moving forms of the camels, the appearance of Mahmoud, as he shifted from shadow to shadow, from place to place, was illusory. Long watching had strained Edith's sight so that she experienced the phenomenon known to those who have centered their faculties of attention throughout a night vigil—a blurring of outlines and a disturbance of vision that cloaked the vista of the plain with the aspect of a mirage. But the caravan was no mirage.

Edith was not the only one in the *Kurgan* to be bewildered.

Flashes from the rampart lanced into the murk; shattering reports assailed her ears. The firing grew heavier—became thunderous. A camel squealed; the voice of Mahmoud, heard in the brief intervals between shots, went on, although the cloaked figure seemed to have sunk to the ground.

Donovan laughed through set teeth.

"So Monsey's men have nerves," he cried, "even as you and I. That shooting is out of hand."

He watched the scene under them keenly, hands cupped beside his eyes. Swirling smoke eddied across his vision, veiling the courtyard except for the rifle flashes. All the firing seemed to be directed at Mahmoud.

"Not much good bombarding the landscape at night," he shouted to Edith cheerfully. "It excites the men and makes a lot of smoke. I've seen it before this."

She pressed trembling hands to her ears, wondering whether his words were not intended merely to hearten her.

"What is…happening?" she cried. "And Mahmoud?"

"Some mummery of the *hakim*…always means something.… Wait."

His disjointed sentences barely reached her. Then he gripped her arm and bent forward.

New sounds were adrift in the courtyard. Horses neighed—hoofs beat upon stone. Men shouted and cursed. To Edith, struggling with wavering senses, the *Kurgan* and the plain alike were an ocean in which shapes darted and a flood of plunging forms sweptt under the tower. She heard Donovan cry:

"The horses are loosed."

In the smoky murk she could see nothing clearly. A horrid sound rose from the further end of the *Kurgan*—a man's scream. It seemed to her that new forms, white and gray, pressed past the base of the tower, on the broken roof of the hold, and swept over the distant wall to the north.

Surely she caught the gleam of bare steel, against the flash of a rifle. The shooting dwindled, but voices growled and roared.

"Sayak!" And again: "Sayak!"

Then came the words, clearly to the girl:

"Tahir el kadr." And again: "Dono-van Khan—ho!—Dono-van Khan!"

Donovan's lips almost touched her ear. "By Jove! That was clever, what? The Sayaks have crept through the breaches to the north and south and have cut loose the horses. They have launched a surprise attack—"

With the word, he left her. The girl saw him dive down the stairs. A fresh uproar had arisen in the interior of the tower. There was a crashing of wood and the impact of running feet, followed by the swift, regular crack of a rifle.

Stunned, she sought for Donovan. Peering over the parapet, she saw a lantern flicker into light in the mid-courtyard. Monsey and some of his Tartars were visible beside it, the Russian hatless, his face wet with perspiration, a smoking revolver in his hand.

On a pile of stones, Edith made out a Sayak boy, sighting a musket that was longer than his own body; behind the boy cloaked forms waved bare knives. Surely these were women. Edith even fancied that she saw the majestic form of the *hadji* of Yakka Arik moving on the rampart.

Monsey was shouting to his men. She caught the flash of his revolver, before a mass of rushing Sayaks swept toward him and the light went out suddenly, leaving the *Kurgan* in its murk. Cries of pain and anger resounded. Edith recollected that Donovan must have disappeared down the stairs and turned after him, her one thought to find him and keep close to his side.

At the last landing where Aravang had been left a struggle was progressing in the dark, revealed vaguely by a lantern placed on the heap of logs, broken beams, and firewood that had risen close to the opening in the floor.

Bodies thrashed about the stones, dark faces alight with panic peered up into the opening from below, while men fought to push themselves up through the aperture.

On the lowest step of the stairs, just in front of her, the girl recognized Donovan instinctively. He was swinging a clubbed rifle at the tide of enemies. Several bodies at his feet half choked the opening.

Then Edith realized that the men of the *Kurgan* had not waited to light the pile under the tower, but were using it to storm their sanctuary. Two forms, locked in conflict, rolled downward through the opening.

A body was pulled from the aperture which glowed redly like the entrance to some purgatory. She saw the evil face of Abbas peering up, as Donovan was pressed back and grappled by a squat Tartar.

It seemed to the girl that the Alaman had come to seek her, despite the fury that was raging without. His purpose was reënforced by the terror of his men, to whom the tower loomed as a refuge from the deadlier hatred without.

Her heart quickened as she saw Donovan struggling silently with the native on the steps below her. Abbas also had seen the Englishman, and his arm drew back, a knife in its palm. Fire surged through the girl's body and gripped her brain.

She clasped the revolver she held in both hands, pointed it at the Alaman's broad face and pulled the trigger. The report bellowed in the confined space.

Seldom have women, even the bravest, been able to resist closing their eyes when they discharged a weapon. With lids tight shut Edith continued to press the trigger savagely. She was fighting for the man she loved. To save Donovan, she would have gripped Abbas with bare hands. So, since the first ages of man, have women fought when peril faced their husbands and children. And so were native women fighting that night in the *Kurgan*.

Edith, her eyes still tight shut, continued to pull the trigger of her revolver, even after it clicked fruitlessly and all the cartridges had sped from its chambers, even the one that the girl, mindful of the Mohammedan legend, had thought was marked for her. The tower had grown quieter. Presently she was conscious of a cheery voice:

"Cease firing, Edith."

She opened her eyes. The bodies still stirred on the stone floor of the tower room; the lantern flickered on the logs below. Sounds of conflict swept in from without. But the stair and the pile of wood were empty of foes, and Donovan was not to be seen.

"Where are you?" she exclaimed anxiously.

"Present." Donovan emerged from under the stairs, directly beneath her feet and stepped swiftly to her side. He was laughing. "I took to the first dugout handy when you began to strafe the place. Brave girl!"

His eyes were tender as he bent over her. She shivered, staring down at the lantern, unable to realize the truth that he was still well and whole, at her side. Then §he clung to him, burying her head in his shoulder.

"Did—did I kill Abbas?" He heard her choked voice from somewhere under his chin.

"Abbas?, No, you missed him, with something to spare. Aravang was alive and kicking in the mêlée below. He pulled the Alaman down, I think. By rights that native of yours ought to be dead a dozen times before now. But he isn't—thanks to some Providence that looks after his kind. Edith, do you realize you saved my life?" He was talking quickly, anxiously, his eyes fixed on the vista of the room below, with its array of broken men that he shielded carefully from her sight.

"I? How?"

"Well," he laughed again, not altogether steadily, "your first shot knocked the brains out of that Tartar on top of me. The others ran from your barrage after Aravang tackled their chief. So did I—run. You creased the back of my jaw just a little with a bullet, besides singeing my neck. I fancy your last shot got Aravang in the leg. I heard him swear—"

"Oh, dear! I meant to shoot Abbas."

She looked up, her lips trembling with a smile. For the first time she saw Donovan's tired face, spotted with blood—from his slain antagonist—and with a dark line running down from his own injured chin.

"Oh!"

Edith fainted in his arms.

Aravang's mighty strength had held the stairs at the head of the pile of wood until Donovan's rifle came to his aid; but by then the *kul* was grappling with an agile Kurd who slashed at him with a knife and tore at his face with fanglike teeth. The two had rolled to the floor under Donovan's feet and out into the opening through which the men of Abbas were pressing warily against the swinging rifle butt over their heads.

Fortunately for Aravang, his foes were half-mad with panic born of the peril that had overwhelmed the walls of the stronghold. For not alone had the fighting men of Yakka Arik come to the assault under cover of Mahmoud's diversion in front of the tower. Women, boys, and old men, the Sayaks had come, summoned by Iskander during the hours of quiet after Donovan's warning, armed with whatever they could lay hand on and ready to die in the defense of their homes and the temple. And at their head the *hadji* had advanced.

So the men about Abbas felt in their hearts a greater fear than that of the mystery of Yakka Arik—the fear of righteously angered women and aged men led by a priest, of fathers and husbands who cared not for their own lives so long as the marauders were slain—and the struggling Aravang was unheeded until he rose, swaying above the body of his victim, the Kurd.

Just at that moment Abbas, standing above him on the wood, reached for his knife. And Aravang, seeing this, groped for Abbas with teeth agrin. A pawlike hand jerked the Alaman down, behind the pile, and the bloody face of the *kul* glared in his.

"Aid!" Abbas Abad screamed: "Aid—O my worthy friends—leave me not—"

But down through the aperture came the ragged fusilade from the revolver of Edith Rand, and the followers of Abbas fled away from this new peril, crying that the place was bewitched and that there were spirits in the tower. Abbas felt on the stone floor for the knife which had dropped from his hand in his fall and saw that Aravang had set his foot on it. And he read his death in the savage eyes that flamed into his.

"Thou art the man," roared Aravang, "who would have burned my mistress. Taste then what thou hast stored up!"

Aravang had taken a small log in his free hand, and upon this the eyes of the merchant fastened while prayers and offers of money flooded from his quivering lips. In the midst of his begging he flung his stout body forward, seeking to upset the *kul*, his hand clutching for the precious knife. Aravang stepped back swiftly and Abbas reached the knife—only to sink down upon it, his skull shattered by a blow from the log driven down with all the *kul*'s weight behind it.

Then Aravang took up the body of his enemy in his arms and strode over the massed wood, limping under the hurt of Edith's wandering bullet, but inexorable in his purpose.

He staggered forward among frantic horses toward a group of Tartars who had flocked together in the center of the courtyard, while the struggle ebbed about them in the moonlight. He stepped over bodies that writhed on the stones and pushed aside unheeding a Sayak girl who was moaning out her life, a bayonet in her breast—

"Sayak!" he heard the battle cry of the tribe: "Sayak!"

The darkness under the parapets was rife with sound and movement as scattered Tartars and Alamans sought vainly for leaders and gave back under blows from swords that they could not see.

"They are devils!" cried one. "Flee—flee!"

Aravang headed toward where he could see two robed Sayaks standing and a third kneeling. Beside them a figure lay prone on the floor. As he approached, the *kul* heard the kneeling Sayak speaking very quietly.

"*Taman shud* (it is finished)," Iskander was saying, swaying upon his knees. "*Ohé*, my enemy is slain by my hand…as I have sworn…it has come to pass."

Then Aravang saw that the body on the stones was that of Monsey. Beside it he tossed the bulky form that was Abbas, and turned to Mahmoud, who, with the *hadji*, stood beside the Arab chieftain.

"The son of Tahir is dying," said Mahmoud to Aravang.

* * * *

While the fury without ebbed through the *Kurgan* Donovan sat passively on the lowest step, holding the precious burden of the woman close to his chest. Having assured himself that she was uninjured, he waited, stroking the coils of heavy hair that had fallen loose upon her shoulders.

And while he waited, for the fall of the dice of destiny, the battling elements of this world of the hills tore at each other, and parted.

The smoke lifted and drifted away from the walls of the castle. In the heavens, the moon declined behind the cloud bank to the west, and the stars alone looked down upon the mountain top.

To the exhausted watcher on the stairs it seemed as if his life and the life of the woman in his arms were carried onward by a current he could no longer resist. But he held her firmly, joyful in the knowledge that they could not now be parted.

Footsteps approached the tower entrance slowly. Looking down, Donovan saw Mahmoud peering up at him apathetically, a lantern held in a clawlike hand. Behind him Aravang limped, soaked in his own blood, blackened and bruised, wounded in body and every limb, but keeping himself stoically upright.

"*Salaam*, Mahmoud," said the Englishman. "Is the fighting finished?"

"It is finished."

"And the son of Tahir?"

"He is no more. He sought the man Monsey and found him." The *hakim* beckoned. "Come, Dono-van Khan. You must leave the castle. Your work here is done."

With that, he turned away. The Englishman rose stiffly and carried his burden into the courtyard, where masses of Sayaks—men, women, and boys—were gathered about the dark groups of prisoners. He stepped over prone bodies and went down the steps to the plain where the horses were being collected and a string of camels waited. Aravang followed.

They went onward until they came to the edge of the woods, where the native led Donovan to an open ravine where was the bed of a stream and pools of fresh water. Here they bathed Edith's face, somewhat helplessly—being unskilled in caring for the needs of a woman—and sat down to wait until she should return to her senses.

Presently a glimmer of fiery light crept through the screen of trees between them and the plateau, and the crackle of flames came to their ears.

Donovan questioned the native with a glance.

"Mahmoud, the all-wise, has set fire to the *Kurgan*, Excellency. Thus will the bodies, all except two, be buried and the nest of the dead Vulture will be no more."

The white man nodded.

"So, Iskander led the Sayaks into the north and south of the *Kurgan*, Aravang," he mused, while Mahmoud drew their attention and fire to the west? It was well done. Yet whence came these numbers?"

He spoke idly, his gaze on the unconscious girl, as if merely confirming his belief as to what had passed. Aravang was resting his head on his bent arms—both men numbed by pain and the relief from long suspense.

"Excellency, during the pause between the first attack and the end, the whole village of Yakka Arik came to the *Kurgan*. You saw what followed, when rifles were useless before daggers near at hand in the dark. But it was the fear of Mahmoud that brought it to pass."

"Fear?" Donovan dipped his hand into the water and laid it on Edith's curls gently. "I wonder. Then, after all, as Major Fraser-Carnie might say, it was merely a question of morale. But why did the camels come?"

Aravang did not reply at once.

"Soon you will see," he muttered.

CHAPTER XXX
THE PASSING OF THE CARAVAN

It was high midday when a tired American gentleman clad in a long black coat, riding breeches, and a flapping sombrero pushed his horse up the valleys toward the height where a mounted guide conducted him, followed by a string of impatient Garhwalis of whom only those with the best horses were able to keep near them.

Beside him Major Fraser-Carnie was unnaturally cheerful, keeping at the same time an eye upon a faint column of smoke that rose through the trees in front of them and inwardly cursing the reticence of the native guide who had joined them that morning and whose vocabulary, whether by linguistic limitations or personal inclination, was confined to the words: "Dono-van Khan sent me," and "Missy *khanum*."

Even the optimism and doggedness of the worthy major that had enabled them to journey from Kashmir to Kashgar on Monsey's heels suffered when the guide disappeared as if by magic, swallowed up in the underbrush. He glanced back at the half dozen mounted riflemen in their green tunics who were lashing wearied beasts in the dread of being left behind the sahibs should the fighting—for which they had come expectantly half a thousand miles—be near at hand.

"Damn your ambuscades!" swore Arthur Rand.

"My girl is up there on the hill where we saw the fire last night."

He rode very well, this lean American father with the white hair and the slow drawl. He spurred on into a green ravine and the English major, armed only with a valued riding crop, followed, in absolute defiance of all rules of tactics for a small mounted patrol in hostile country.

"Damned if I'll let you lead," he responded irritably.

So the two came bridle to bridle to the bed of a small brook and simultaneously reined in their mounts at sight of Donovan and Edith cooking lunch very carefully over a tiny camp fire, while Aravang stretched his sheepskin-clad body beside them. One by one, the best mounted troopers— all volunteers picked from a native regiment—trotted up with carbines in hand and eyes alert for the treachery which long experience taught them was apt to follow close upon the heels of foolhardy sahibs who rode with no regard for the danger of mountain muskets.

These veteran border warriors—and to tell the truth, their leader also— were astonished to see a tall *mem*-sahib with hair much like spun gold and eyes that gleamed like jewels from a smoke-stained face rise and fly toward the horse of the American who had led them from Kashgar.

"Daddy!"

"My girl!"

Arthur Rand swung from his saddle with an ease beyond his years and took Edith into his arms. Major Fraser-Carnie said "My word!" and coughed. Then he brought his horse up, to interview the tall man in very soiled flannels who waited beside the fire.

"So you had a hand in this, my young rascal!" he accused.

Donovan smiled, without taking his eyes from Edith and her father.

"Not as much as you might think, Major," he said. "Remember, you said at Gilghit I was heading into trouble in the Hills. Well, what are you doing here yourself with an armed force on native soil ?"

Fraser-Carnie looked guilty and muttered something about old ties, and all that sort of thing. "Besides, you see. Captain Donovan, I couldn't let that blooming American—confoundedly game, you know—come up here on his own, of course. Dashed if I could. Wouldn't have been a sporting thing, what?"

"I see." Donovan's eyes twinkled, although he spoke gravely. "I fancy I overstayed the leave given me to go into the Hills. I had to make a bargain with the tribes, and keep it—"

The major nodded gravely, "An agreement, eh? Why didn't you 'fess up, that night at my bungalow? Can I help a bit?"

"Thanks, no. It's ended to-day. I'm free to leave, with Miss Rand, provided we don't reveal certain pet secrets of the tribes—"

Whereupon Edith tripped up to them to demand whether the British army had lunch sufficient for three men and, oh, such a hungry girl. (And to bear Donovan off to her father, while Fraser-Carnie hastened to order up his emergency rations and detail a man from the troopers' mess to cook.)

Before sitting down to the lunch spread on white cloths by the brook, nothing would content the major but an observation patrol sent in the direction of the still smoldering tower. When his men reported nothing at the *Kurgan* except the embers of fires and some camels feeding near by and scattered cartridge shells, the only signs of the recent fight, he was palpably downcast.

"My Garhwalis will never forgive me, quite. I promised them *pukka* fighting, and all we do, my dear chap, is to drop in on you for tiffin. You might at least tell us the whole story."

Donovan looked into Edith's eyes, over the camp fire.

"It might better keep," he said.

Fraser-Carnie surveyed a teacup. "Until the Viceroy hears it, of course. And that means we'll never have a whiff of it. Edith, my dear, you at least will enlighten us as to what happened here."

"M-mh," said Edith, a jelly spoon in her mouth. Flushed and happy and utterly worn out, she sat with her father's hand in hers. "Captain Donovan says I talk too much."

The major shook his head sadly.

"Rand," he observed, balancing a cigarette between two fingers, "do you realize we are snubbed? By our hosts, too. Deuced bad form, *I* call it. A cavalry officer—is it cavalry, Captain Donovan?—goes off hunting in the Himalayas after a confidential chat with the Viceroy of India, mind you. Just before war breaks. And the Central Asian tribes, that we fellows in India expected down on our backs momentarily, by some astounding miracle do not side against us. Then, after this same officer on his utterly foolish hunting trip, which, it seems, was with the Viceroy's consent, is mentioned for promotion he vanishes for a couple of years, to bob up with your daughter—and we are to ask no questions!"

Whereupon he emptied his cup with a sigh. Edith's drowsy eyes glowed and she glanced quickly, proudly at her father. Donovan aimed a covert kick at Fraser-Carnie which the major dodged. Only Arthur Rand remained grave.

"Edith, I haven't told you—we have lost all our money. I am bankrupt!"

He was surprised to see how calmly he could say it and how little effect the announcement had on his daughter. Six months ago it would have broken his heart to confess as much. Here, with Edith restored to him and quite evidently in delighted possession of a tattered, unshaven officer, it seemed a thing of minor importance.

And to Edith herself six months ago the news would have been the collapse of the world about her ears and the loss of her birthright. Now, between mouthfuls of splendid biscuit, it was a meaningless detail of the world she had left long since.

"Yes, Edith," nodded Arthur Rand absently, "you must get away from this inhospitable place. The major will take you and Donovan back, I reckon. Donovan, I hear, has earned a rest on his own estates in England."

But his daughter was staring at Donovan uncomfortably.

"Estates?" She sat up accusingly. "Why—why, I thought you had no money, like me."

Donovan glared at Fraser-Carnie; then his brow cleared.

"I haven't, Edith. Because, of course, the family holdings should go to the wife of my brother."

"My dear chap!" the major observed. "But, of course, your uncle the curate—"

Unperceived by Edith, Donovan's powerful hand closed upon the collar of the major's uniform and he ceased with a cough. The girl was still surveying him accusingly. "Are you certain," she demanded, "that you aren't the least rich?" He smiled, without releasing his grasp on his companion.

"Absolutely—as you can see, Edith."

"Quite so," amended the Major, adjusting his collar.

"Then, that's all right!" She nodded approvingly, and then recalled her father's speech. "Dad! Aren't you coming with us? You are not thinking of staying here?"

Arthur Rand's fine face hardened. "I reckon," he drawled, "I'll look for that cur, Monsey."

Upon the gathering of these four wanderers who had come to the world of the Hills each for sufficient reason, and just now happy at being united, advanced a smart Garhwali carrying a rifle. He stood at attention by Major Fraser-Carnie.

"Sahib, the camels come hither with riders."

They rose, and the major spoke a brief word to his men, seated at their meal some distance away. The troopers took up their arms instantly. In the silence that settled on the ravine Edith heard the *clink-clank* of rusty camel bells and the familiar pad-pad of soft feet Through the trees she saw the moving shapes of clumsy beasts.

Donovan touched her arm, his eyes serious.

"Come, Edith." As he led her away from the brook, he observed quietly to Rand:

"Monsey has been found by—others."

The bells came nearer. Edith and Donovan were out of sight when a cloaked figure came down the ravine from the *Kurgan*, leading a long string of camels walking patiently in the wake of their conductor.

Seeing that only two men were seated on the beasts and they unarmed, the Garhwalis drew back. The two riders who were bound tightly between the humps of the camels, their heads bobbing with the walk of the animals, stared stolidly before them.

"Monsey!" said Rand under his breath.

"And Abbas," nodded Fraser-Carnie.

The rusty bells clanked; the beasts—indifferent as ever—passed majestically by the watchers. Monsey and Abbas swayed in their seats. When the last camel had passed, wending its way among the trees, Fraser-Carnie turned to his friend:

"That was Mahmoud, the Sayak. So my Garhwalis say. Rand, these legends of the Hills sometimes assume the form of rather ghastly reality. I'm glad Donovan took your daughter away."

Arthur Rand replaced the revolver he had drawn. "I know a dead man when I see one—or two, for that matter. Is it a kind of burial?"

"It is," observed the major thoughtfully, "the caravan of the dead. It will go from hill village to hill village. It is the custom of the Sayaks in dealing with their enemies. The tribes, of course, say it comes from nowhere and goes—nowhere. Strange, what?"

* * * *

On a hillock among the aspens that concealed the brook and the passing of the caravan Edith had turned to Donovan, pausing in her walk.

"Was it Iskander with his camels?" she asked.

"The son of Tahir," he responded gravely, "is no more."

Edith made a little, sorrowing sound. Iskander had been her friend, and she had meant to thank him for many things. Now that was impossible. She stood on tiptoe, peering out over the trees, searching for something she could not see among the overhanging mountain slopes. Nothing was visible except the clear blue of the sky and the wandering, white clouds that seemed quite close at hand.

"What, dear?" he questioned gently.

"Our house," she lifted quiet eyes, in which lurked a hint of tears. "We shan't ever see it again, shall we?"

"Why, sweetheart," he touched her face between hands that were not altogether steady, "did you—were you happy there?"

"Too happy to tell you, Donovan Khan—if you don't know."

And her eyes, bright under the tears, smiled up at him.

The aspens at the edge of the clearing parted and an ugly, scarred face looked out steadfastly upon the two who had eyes only for each other. A hand was lifted in yearning salutation. Then a shaggy, limping figure moved away from them through the trees toward the cleft in the hills that was Yakka Arik.

Aravang had said farewell to his master and his mistress.

THE DEVIL'S BUNGALOW

CHAPTER I
THE OTHER SIDE OF THE EARTH

From the wall map behind his desk, Mr. Lee, of Hammerman, Lee and Rambaud, transferred his glance to Trent, who was neither a clerk nor a partner of the well-known investment banking house in Wall Street.

"It's a long trip," he explained, "and something out of the ordinary. But you must know our slogan, by this time."

Malcolm Trent nodded, and as his superior still watched him expectantly, he quoted the phrase that had been impressed upon every employee of Hammerman, Lee and Rambaud. "Unfailing and unquestioning service. World wide service has made our house what it is today. We assume that in your dealings with our clients—"

"Yes, yes." Mr. Lee was never sure just when the former messenger of the firm was making fun of him. He often thought that Malcolm Trent should be analyzed—so that he could be placed in another position.

The twenty-two-year-old who had made his way up from bank runner was much to valuable to lose, and too troublesome to keep in the office. Mr. Rambaud, who liked Trent, said that he never took a job seriously unless there was a fight in it.

Mr. Lee asserted—and when he said anything he asserted it—that Trent, as bank runner, before the war, had a habit of strolling in a minute or so before delivery time with his bagful of securities. Mr. Rambaud countered that Trent might be slow getting about, but he always arrived.

Even the time when he had been pounded on the head with a lead pipe in the subway stairs, and two men had tried to pry his fingers loose from the satchel that contained three quarters of a million in negotiable bonds. That time Trent had been carried in, but he brought the bag with him.

During the months when the notorious bond ring was at work among the boys, they trusted Malcolm Trent. He always did what he set out to do, but in his own way, and Mr. Lee did not approve of his way. After a session of intensive team work in France, he disliked office work more than ever.

So, logically, it fell to Malcolm Trent to undertake—to oblige a client—to carry a certain package from New York City to India, and from there to Kashmir, which is on top of India, and thence to a point in the Himalaya

Mountains, over the border. Mr. Lee had pointed out the place on the map, and it was exactly half way across the stretch of the earth.

"As I said," resumed Mr. Lee earnestly, "Mr. Trevis Haldane is one of our most desirable clients. We are glad to be of service to him, but I confess that I do not understand why he insists you may have trouble in making the trip. It seems that the article he is giving you is no document of any kind. Couldn't be money in any form, or he would have cabled."

"Hasn't he a collection somewhere, Mr. Lee? Curios—ivory and paintings."

"And jewels. I had not thought of that. Yes, he has a priceless collection in London. He said he would take this box—it's in a cylindrical box, I gather—himself, but he must return to London. Just now, he is not feeling very well. Anyhow, he warns us that attempts may be made to buy or steal this box from you. And he is urgent that it must go through to—" Mr. Lee consulted a typed memorandum, but Trent supplied the name from memory.

"Dr. Arthur Bruce, two hundred miles out from Srinugger. on the Tibet road." Trent had wide-set brown eyes that remained perfectly serious when he was enjoying a good joke. He was a stocky man, with square shoulders, and he had the good humor that comes from an untroubled mind and a greater share of physical strength than his fellows.

"You will meet Mr. Haldane tomorrow noon at the Brevoort," Mr. Lee changed the subject. "You know him, of course?" Trent nodded. "Spats and a walking stick. Casts a mean eye."

"And has not advanced more than a minimum of expenses." Mr. Lee permitted himself to smile. "We have made up the amount, Trent. Now, your itinerary is as follows: the Twentieth Century to Chicago, and the Overland to San Francisco, with only about four hours to make your steamer. The *Empress* goes direct to Calcutta from Hong-Kong. So, once you are on the Twentieth Century no one—granting that any one has designs on this packet you are carrying—could overtake you."

Trent was silent, his eyes on the map.

"Mr. Haldane," continued the banker "is eccentric. He seems to labor under some nervous strain, and probably he values this curio very highly—if he is willing to pay a couple of thousand for its safe delivery. You need not take him too seriously, but he said, *if word of what you are carrying leaks out, there are men who will travel the other half of the earth to take it from you.*"

Again Trent nodded. A glance at the printed itinerary showed him that at Calcutta he would take the northern express to a station near Rawul Pindi, and hire a post carriage to his destination. He wondered what a post carriage would be like.

"Have you any questions?" asked Mr. Lee, adjusting his eyeglasses to stare a little curiously at the man who would start off for India. "No? Well, then, we have no correspondent or agent in India, although we do a considerable bit of foreign exchange transfers there. You'll be a long way from—ah, friends, Trent." He stood up to shake hands politely, and Trent grinned at him. "The—ah, best of luck, Malcolm."

At once Mr. Lee plunged into the figures that awaited his scrutiny and promptly forgot Trent and the box he was to convey more than a few thousand miles—except that, in a pigeon-hole of the banker's brain there remained the utter conviction that Trent would not fail, under any circumstances to deliver whatever had been entrusted to his care.

An impulse he did not bother to identify caused him to glance away from the sheets of credit statistics under his hand. His window overlooked the gorge of Broadway, and the glitter of the lower bay, beyond a giant's pyramid of roofs that eclipsed the scanty green of Battery Place. A red girder, on its way to the top of one of the new steel skeletons had slipped in its grapples. A man, riding the girder, lost his footing and caught at the cable.

Then the steel beam resumed its course, and settled into place. The tiny figure that was a man crawled off and signaled down to the street. Mr. Lee studied it, frowning, because it displeased him. Almost, an accident had marred the quiet of his room. Accidents did not happen in the world of Hammerman, Lee and Rambaud.

And Mr. Lee did not know any other world. When his telephone buzzed gently, he took down the receiver and gave it half his mind.

It struck Trent the next day when he lunched with Trevis Haldane at the Brevoort that the client did not look ill. Certainly the Englishman had a good color, and he talked a good deal of the coming trip in no uncertain voice.

He was a thin man, who carried his head thrust forward from stooped shoulders. His grayish hair and the network of wrinkles about eyes and brow indicated a full fifty years, but somehow Trent did not think him so old. Certainly the client was notional, since he talked openly in the midst of tables where more foreigners than native born dwellers of the city were seated. And, the late luncheon ended, he insisted on riding to the Grand Central on the top of a bus.

In the terminal he asked Trent to unlock his valise, to make sure the package was there, although this was not the best place to display anything of value; but to humor the client Trent unlocked his valise and showed Haldane the parcel.

"See if the seals are in place," ordered the Englishman.

It was a rather heavy package, about the size of a coffee tin, wrapped in green silk. Cords had been wound around the silk, and every knot was covered by a seal of red wax bearing the imprint of the owner's signet ring. All of the seals, of course, were intact.

"Look here, Mr. Haldane," Trent whispered, scarcely moving his lips, "either you have two friends who've come to see us off, or they're not friends, and have come along anyway. They don't look like bad actors."

Haldane wheeled, but saw only a pair of slender men in ill fitting black clothes, staring at the clock over the information desk. They appeared to be sunburned, and in their smooth, boyish faces was a curious look of abstraction. He said nothing, but Trent saw him take out his handkerchief and wipe his wrists and neck.

"Know them, Mr. Haldane?"

The Englishman leaned heavily on his cane, and closed his eyes as if thinking, but Trent could not understand his muttered reply.

"Song? Tong capper? What was it, Mr. Haldane?"

But the other said nothing more as he watched Trent stow away the green box and lock the small valise, which he carried, with his heavier bag. A glance at the dock assured the messenger that ten minutes remained before the Twentieth Century pulled out, and he decided to use the time to good advantage. Requesting the Englishman to remain where he was, and not to go near the gate through which people were already pressing to the limited, Trent picked up his two bags and wandered down to the lower level of the terminal, pausing to buy an afternoon paper and some cigarettes.

Then he sought the shoe shining stand, in an unfrequented corner. Here he climbed up into a chair, lit a cigarette and bent over his paper, leaving the two bags on the floor by the boot-black.

A moment passed before one of the studious individuals appeared and walked slowly back and forth near the stand. The other was not to be seen, and Trent knew that he must be on the upper level, watching Haldane. The man seemed restless and his lean face was pinched as if by hunger. The messenger had seen that same vacant light in the eyes of drug users before this, and he wondered fleetingly if Haldane had given him dope to smuggle out of the country.

Then he reflected that opium and coke came from India and thereabouts. It was curious, too, that Haldane, who was palpably uneasy at sight of the two men, should have paraded him through Washington Square and the Brevoort and should have asked him to take out the green box—

A thin hand entered Trent's range of vision, under the newspaper, and closed on the handle of the valise that held the package in question. The messenger, who had been leaning well forward, let fall his newspaper and sprang through the air, using the two footrests for a take-off.

He landed bodily on the shoulders of the stranger, who had turned to run, gripping the bag. The impact of the messenger's muscular body brought them both to the floor, Trent's arm crooked around the other's neck. Seeing that the wrench, or the force of the fall had knocked the breath from his adversary, he retrieved the bag, with his suitcase and ran up the stair to the upper level.

The gateman was glancing at his watch as Trent walked up and surrendered his ticket to be punched. With a quarter minute to spare, he entered the gate and looked back. The other watcher had hurried up and was staring down at him vindictively; but what halted Trent in his tracks was Haldane.

The owner of the green box was half through the gate, paying no heed to the questions of the ticket puncher. His eyes were shining with feverish excitement, and his mouth wide open in a noiseless laugh of joy. The iron fretwork of the barrier, the uniformed official and the hideous mirth of the staring man made Trent think of insanity.

"A nut!" he muttered, and the gate clanged shut. A long drawn call from below and a clamping of vestibules brought Trent leaping down the inclined plane. One porter had seen him and he ran into a vestibule as the Twentieth Century moved out its long chain of Pullmans.

CHAPTER II
A HIDING PLACE

Trent watched the streets of Chicago slide past his window twenty-four hours later, and wished that the Overland were not so crowded. The heat was oppressive, and his car was filled with its capacity of summer tourists, with their children, packages, golf bags, and overcoats. Suitcases were piled in every seat, while the perspiring porter established order, answered questions, opened windows at the request of irritable women, and stowed luggage deftly under the seats of the rightful owners.

"Travel's heavy," Trent remarked. He had taken refuge in the washroom, with the smaller bag that held the green box.

The porter arranged towels in the racks overhead, flicked some dust off the leather bench and shook his head. "Lady in lower eight, cross fum you got a baby and two children, and she wants to know why I don't make down her berth right, so they-all fits. Young ladies in upper three ask' me to call 'em bout four, so they can see the sunrise on the desert. Only desert they'd see, if I did, is co'n fields, near Omaha." He interrupted a chuckle to assure an anxious traveler who poked his head into the compartment that all the train went all the way to San Francisco.

"Does my car go through, porter?" the stranger asked.

"Yes, sir."

"And the dining-car?"

"Yes, sir."

The head disappeared, leaving an aroma of whisky in the compartment. The buzzer sounded and the porter ducked out to see what was wanted. Presently he looked in at Trent. "That gen'leman you just saw, he's got hold of your suitcase. He's sure had some drinks, and the lady in lower eight wants me to change her berth, 'count of him."

"Thanks." nodded Trent.

Tossing away his cigarette, he walked back into the car. In his section the stranger, a plump man in a gray check suit and a shirt with a blue collar, was bending over the open suitcase, running deft hands through the contents. Trent had left the bag locked. He waited long enough to make sure that the other was not as intoxicated as he appeared, then went back to the smoking compartment.

It was clear that the man in the gray suit had looked in a moment before to make sure that Trent was not likely to visit his section for a few moments. Then he had gone to work boldly, reasoning that in the general confusion of the car any one who observed him would think the bag was his own.

It had taken skill to pick the lock in so short a time, and Trent preferred to have the man think he had not been observed. Obviously, he mused, a wire had been sent from New York by those interested in the green box, and the stranger was the result of it.

"Wish I knew what Haldane meant by those Tong Cappers," he muttered. "They must want this package pretty bad."

He glanced reflectively at the small satchel that held his charge—that he always kept under his hand. For three days and three nights he would be penned on the limited with the man of the gray suit. He could not slip off at a stop and take another train, or he would miss his boat.

From his wallet Trent took a new five dollar bill and folded it neatly into a small square. The porter, who had been taking advantage of the brief vacancy of the compartment, to eat a sandwich, stopped munching at sight of it. Trent handed it to him.

"Want you to do something for me, Jack. You know I've reserved all of my section. Make up my lower at ten o'clock. Leave the upper closed—I want the fresh air."

"Yes. I'll do that. Thank you.

"Wait a minute. I'll be there when you take down the upper—shelf, or what you call it. When you take out my blankets and stuff I'll give you something to put under the mattress of the upper berth—the one you won't have to make up. See?"

The porter nodded thoughtfully.

"All right. Just leave that parcel there until we're in the terminal. Then give it to me. And don't happen to mention it around the car. All right?"

The factotum of the Pullman looked at the white man thoughtfully. "Boss, just tell me it ain't dope. Gov'ment persons been powerful hard on anybody handles that stuff. I'se ma'ied——"

"It's not opium; it's not dope—not that I know of." Trent pondered. "It's imported Bismark cordial, with essence of Benedictine, and concentrated Jamaica rum. and worth a dollar an ounce. Likewise, it's sure death for anyone but me to handle."

"Boss," the old porter assured him solemnly, "I've been on this run fo' ten years, nex' November, and I ain't touched no gen'leman's licker."

All the other sections were made up by ten o'clock that night, and Trent had satisfied himself that the interested stranger was playing double Canfield with a drummer in the club car, when he rang for the boy. The porter did his work quickly, and in five minutes the slab of tin mahogany overhead was unlocked, the necessary bedding removed, and the green box hidden. Then the upper berth was locked again, and Trent turned in.

He slept soundly in spite of the heat. The green box was safe. No one but the porter had a key to the upper berth. Skilled though the man from Chicago might be in coaxing locks, he could not pick that one in sight of a car full of people in day time, and at night Trent was in the berth beneath.

It would hardly occur to the other to bribe the porter, and if he did try it, Trent was always around when the section was made up. The green box could not be removed without his seeing it.

The first morning out of Chicago he transferred to the larger bag everything except a roll of toilet articles and some shirts, from the hand hag. "From the way that bird does his stuff," he reflected, I stand to lose this satchel, and I don't want to lose much.'"

He grinned in spite of himself when he noticed just after this that the stranger had gone through his large bag again—apparently having noticed the transfer. The second night out was cooler as the Overland drew up into the high prairies of Utah, and Trent slept from midnight until four when he was awakened by a slight shifting of the satchel which he had placed between him and the window.

The heavy curtains had been unbuttoned at one place and an arm in a gray check sleeve was visible. At the end of the arm was a hand that gripped the handle of the bag. The messenger, fully conscious on the instant, sat up quietly. Drawing back one of the curtains quickly he looked out, squarely into the eyes of the man from Chicago.

"Excuse me," said the other—whose name Trent had learned in the club car, Schmandt—"I got the wrong berth."

"If you do it again," whispered Trent, "pick some other berth."

Schmandt glanced up and down the aisle of the car and slipped inside the curtain, seating himself on the edge of the berth. Trent's right hand closed on the butt of his Colt .38, under the sheet and he sat up.

"I see you're wise." The stranger's pale eyes, half hidden in rolls of fat flickered toward the black satchel. "Lay off the cannon. When I treat you rough, you won't know what's in the air, kid. I want to talk to you, see? How much will you take for that bag?"

"What's your bid, Schmandt?"

The other scrutinized his polished nails. "A hundred."

"Keep the change." Trent thought of selling the worthless satchel, but did not wish to start the man from Chicago to searching elsewhere for the green box.

"Five hundred," whispered Schmandt, "good money, kid."

"Not enough."

"Listen, Trent: you're being double-crossed. The guy what wished that roll of green silk on you didn't put you wise. He didn't say you was risking your life, did he? Well. you are. That's what a big gun in Chicago slipped to me. He said. 'Levy, that kid'll get his in India if you don't pry him loose from that green roll'"

"Thought your name was Schmandt, smiled Trent.

"Ah, have it your way. This big fellow, this gent who's a friend of mine, he asks me as a favor to him to get him that thing you're carrying around."

"Yes," assented the messenger, go on.

"This friend of mine, he stands to pick off some coin, if I do this. I'm glad to do him a favor, see?" Schmandt, or Levy, whispered from the corners of his lips, almost soundlessly—a trick learned by those who had served their time in prison. His neat hand stroked a plump, powdered cheek, already shaved. Apparently Trent's attitude led him to further confidence.

"My friend says the mob that's after you is the original yeggs of the world. They're bad actors, devils—see ? He says, 'If that kid gets through to India they'll croak him sure.'"

Into Trent's mind flashed the address of Dr. Bruce. It was all bunk, he thought; Schmandt was merely trying to throw a scare into him. He shook his head.

"All right." The crook nodded indifferently. "I don't know nothing more than what I've slipped to you, Trent. But I'll have that roll of green silk from you before we get to 'Frisco."

It struck the messenger that Schmandt had caught a glimpse of the roll of waterproof cloth in which he carried his shaving kit, soap and hair brushes. This happened to be green. "I guess you will," he admitted.

"It's a safe bet." Schmandt purred amiably. "Then you should care greatly about India. Your mother will see her only boy again. That's what I wanted to tell you—what I'm doing for you. Don't yap to the bulls, because you ain't got nothing on me and—that's all, kid. That's every bit."

The man from Chicago went away, leaving a strong odor of hair tonic in the air. Trent began to dress, little wiser for the conversation. All he had learned was that a large sum must have been offered for the green box—if Schmandt was willing to part with five hundred to get it without trouble of any kind. He believed the crook did not know the contents of the package, nor the identity of those who sought it.

Events proved that Trent was correct in this surmise.

Trent lost the satchel at Ogden, and he lost it to Schmandt, as the man from Chicago had foretold.

He had strolled through the station, with a crowd from the Pullmans, for a quick walk up and down the main street. After watching the women, in pairs, diving into drugstores for post cards, he turned back. Passing through the throng around the news-stand in the waiting-room, he halted in his tracks. His right arm made a clutch at the bag which had fallen to the floor.

An instant before, something jabbed into the under side of his left arm—something like a needle that sent fiery pain into every nerve of the arm. His fingers relaxed and the bag fell, to be caught up by the man from Chicago who dived away through the crowd.

Running to the door, Trent saw Schmandt enter a taxi and start off into the city. When he was sure the other would not return to the train, he rolled up his sleeve and studied a red pin prick in his arm, surrounded by a spreading circle of brown fluid—iodine, by the taste of it. By the feel of his arm half a pint of the burning stuff might have been shot into his veins by the hypodermic needle the man from Chicago had seen fit use.

In the Oakland terminal a careful inspection showed that the seals of the green box were intact and Trent placed it in his remaining bag before crossing the ferry to San Francisco, to buy a new kit and shirts, and to call for his passport and letters of identification which awaited him at the bank that was the correspondent of Hammerman, Lee and Rambaud.

Once this was done he walked down California Street to the Embarcadero, to go to his cabin on the *Empress*, pausing only to buy a late afternoon extra.

It was while he was leaning over the rail, watching the antics of the tug that was nosing the steamer out of her dock that he had word again of Schmandt. His paper contained, in the box reserved for the red type of the latest bulletins, a brief account of the death of a man calling himself Charles Schmandt, of Chicago.

He had been found, that morning, strangled in his room in one of the Ogden hotels. The only belongings found with the body were some shirts and a black satchel holding a few toilet articles. A cloth dressing case that bore the initials *M. T.* was torn to fragments on the floor.

Twisted around Schmandt's throat was a scarf—a long scarf or shawl of green silk. The local police believed this to be a woman's property; one view of the matter was that the man had committed suicide by hanging himself to the high rail of the bed, and had fallen to the floor.

But, remembering Schmandt as he seen him, Trent could not think that the crook had killed himself.

He tore out the half column story of the tragedy, and put the clipping in his wallet. A roar from the whistle overhead caused him to look up as the tug drew off. The fog of late afternoon had been blowing in, over the hills of San Francisco, and around the giant shoulders of Tamalpais. But a vagrancy of the wind cleared the fog from the channel, momentarily, and for the time that he could draw a long breath he gazed down a crimson path, to the dark line of the sea that marked the limit of his land and people.

CHAPTER III
THE EYES OF THE HILL

Malolm Trent had plenty of time—six weeks—to think over the death of the light-fingered Mr. Schmandt of Chicago, but thinking helped him not a bit. He was shut off from all news of the case. For the first time in his life he could not buy a newspaper to read the latest developments. On board the steamer chess and bridge and the fluctuations of the German mark were discussed with more interest than all of the United States.

No one except a Standard Oil employee, bound for the Yang-tse, cared whether or not the Giants and the Yanks would play for the world's series. At the bar, men talked of rice, hemp and the price of copra, instead of the fluctuations of Wall Street. Unfamiliar figures—turbaned Hindus, and somnolent Chinese—passed in review outside the barrier of the first class deck space.

Trent, left to his own meditations, was certain that Schmandt had not torn up his toilet roll and hung himself in a fit of peevishness. It began to look as if actual danger confronted those who had a mind to the green box. Being a healthy young American, Trent scoffed at this thought, yet could not utterly banish it.

It was queer that Schmandt, who had warned him to stay in the United States if he would escape death, should have lost his life instead of Trent.

At the end of six weeks Trent climbed stiffly out of his compartment in the northern express, into a puff of scorching wind that nearly left him breathless, but did not injure the voices of a dozen would-be guides, interpreters and friends, all natives, and all competing for the privilege of taking his bag.

In one comprehensive glance he took in the heat haze that overhung the white walls of the station, the circle of arid hills on the skyline. The baked clay underfoot scorched his feet through the soles, and eddies of sand rattled the dried plumage of what he took to be palms—the *farash* trees.

"Los Angeles before the boom," he muttered. "That's India."

"Where do you wish to go, sah?" A portly native wearing spectacles elbowed to a place in front of him. "I speak ver-ree good English. I am babu, knowing all things of importance."

"Know the highway to Srinugger, Babu?"

"Sree-ng'r, most certainly. The post road, most certainly, sahib. Will the sahib go by *gharry*, or *ekka*—" the interpreter waved an authoritative hand at several small, hooded carts drawn by patient ponies, and an open four wheeler to which a pair of camels were hitched—"or *doolie*, if the sahib has an illness of the intestines which is quite the fad after the ter-rain."

Trent glanced at the *doolie*, a combination bed and sedan chair, managed by four native boys, and shook his head.

"Haven't you got a motor? No? Then make it a *gharry* without the camels."

It seemed to him as if the babu began a war against the united force of the other grooms and hangers-on, but just as he was preparing to go to the rescue of the man who knew all matters of importance, a vehicle drew up to the station—a contrivance resembling a coffin slung on four wheels. The natives who had fetched it ran off and returned with a pair of horses that reared, plunged and bit as they were forced into the harness.

On getting into the coffin, Trent found that he could not sit up, or stretch his legs, but must recline on some well worn cushions. The babu tried in vain to separate him from his suitcase, then climbed up on the tail-piece, and the throng of natives began to howl at the American.

"They want baksheesh, sahib—tips," explained the interpreter, "so the horses may be made to go."

Trent tossed out some copper coins, and the eyes of the babu glittered. The rabble around the post *gharry* began to turn over the wheels by hand, pulling the while at the team which seemed determined not to move.

"More baksheesh, sahib, and they will bring straw. Then we will go. Will the sahib go to the Club in Sreenug'r, or to—"

"Dr. Bruce's bungalow," growled Trent, tossing out some more coins. "Do you know where it is?"

Glancing back, at an unwonted silence behind, he saw that the round face of the babu had grown sulky and sickly. If ever a man looked frightened, the interpreter was that man. Surprised, Trent saw him drop from the carriage, and shake his head. "No, I have an official position, and I must consider my family. I will not go near the *Tsong Khapa*."

"That's it!" cried Trent, leaning out of his window. "That's the line. What does it mean?" Haldane had used the same words in describing the two who had followed them in New York.

The babu hesitated and while he did so, the *gharry* started off with a jerk. Some of the natives had kindled straw under the horses, while others tugged at the wheels again. Once under way, the post horses apparently made up their minds to finish matters as speedily as possible. The carriage tore through the village and dashed out along a sandy road that wound up toward a break in the hills.

Without the services of an interpreter, Trent was unable to talk with the driver. For three days he was borne upward, out of the heat, into a new country. The post *gharries* made time, and this suited him, although they threaded along hill trails, where rivers muttered and boomed a thousand feet under his eyes, if he chanced to look out. The higher they climbed, the greater the loom of the mountains ahead.

At times they plunged past groups of natives, thin men in gray wool wearing pointed black caps, who scowled and cursed as the carriage forced them to scramble out of the road. But no one molested Trent. Nights he spent in what he called the road houses, the well equipped dak bungalows, where a dinner was made ready as soon as the wheels of the post carriage were heard on the road.

"Such as it is." he reflected, "the service is good. And the movies never got hold of scenery like this. They'd laugh at me in the office if I told them about it."

Perhaps the altitude and the cool nights exhilarated him, or the rarified air acted like a narcotic, as he entered the foothills of the Himalayas, which dwarf other mountains. At the last dak bungalow he was told that he must leave the carriage and take a horse, to cover the thirty-odd miles to the house of Dr. Bruce.

But the American had never straddled a horse, and he had no desire to be carried in a chair by the natives.

"Sell me a blanket and fix me up some grub, and I'll hike," he explained.

To the astonishment of the Kashmiris, he made a pack out of a cotton cloth and several ropes and put together such things as he would need, slipping the green box into it without being seen. Settling his score at the post house, he had the keeper point out the trail he should take to the Bruce bungalow. He was told that he would pass a temple about noon, and should then turn to the right, up the mountainside.

"What's the name of the church?" he asked.

"The *Sheitan ka*. The sahib calls it the Devil's Bungalow."

"Anybody living in it?" Trent grinned.

"Many snakes live in it," the attendant stared at him curiously. "The sahib should be careful not to hurt them."

"Hurt them?"

"The people—the Kashmiris—would be angered." The keeper being a Mohammedan from elsewhere, and in government pay, was scornful of the local superstitions.

"All right," Trent nodded, "I'll spare the snakes. But I'll give you a silver dollar if you'll tell me what the *Tsong Khapa* is."

The Mohammedan pulled at his chin whiskers and looked away. "I do not know," he responded. "The *dakitar-sahib* Bruce can tell you many things. He has lived in the hills for the lifetime of a man."

To the city bred man the walk of thirty miles to his destination seemed possible four miles an hour, eight hours; time out for lunch, say ten hours in all. He lighted his pipe, waved farewell to the staring natives at the dak bungalow, and started on at a round pace.

The thin air of the high altitude sent the blood pumping through his veins, and at the crest of the first rise he paused get his breath. After a while he knocked out his pipe, and changed the position of his pack. His shoulders began to ache, and when the path ascended, as it generally did, he had to bend over and exert every muscle to draw himself up.

The pack was heavier than he had thought possible. By degrees he became convinced that he was being followed.

By this time he had left behind the huts of the Kashmiris. And only an occasional column of smoke rising from the brush in the valley below, or a distant goat herd showed that there were beings in the mountains. But Trent heard a rustling in the glistening rhododendron thickets, and more than once he saw a creeper shake on the boles of the dark oaks. As he pressed deeper into the silence of the forest, these sounds grew clearer—a shaking of the branches overhead at times, and now and then muffled, guttural calls.

Look where he would, he could see no human being. The sun, beating aslant through the screen of branches, made vision deceptive. When he paused to rest, those who were following him were motionless, as if watching his next move.

Trent had quick ears, and where the trail twisted, in a dense network of ferns and vines, he caught a faint stirring in the underbrush ahead. Gripping the butt of his revolver, he strode forward, wary of an ambush.

Rounding the turn he halted in surprise. Beside the trail were grouped a half dozen monkeys, an old, gray beast with a lined, black face and a brood of little ones, squatting gravely to watch him pass.

These, then, had been his pursuers of the morning. Trent chuckled and resumed his march. "First babus then baboons. What next?"

Before long he was convinced that he must have passed the Devil's Bungalow without seeing it. Somewhere behind him the sun sank out of sight. The oaks had given place to giant pines that almost hid the sky, and mists were gathering in the deep chasms. He could no longer hear the muttering of the river. It seemed to him that he had walked much more than thirty miles, and had climbed a dozen, when he came to the end of the trail.

It stopped at the brink of a precipice, and Trent looked down into a narrow gorge that fell away from under his feet to a billowy gray mass that drifted and twined among the trees. Over the main valley to his left, into which the gorge ran, this same rolling carpet of white flecked with gray was spread, obscuring all but the peaks of the mountains—and the highest summits were snow covered, tinted scarlet by the setting sun.

Solitary in the clear air near his head a great lammergeyer floated on motionless wings. Trent was above the clouds.

The gorge was a hundred feet or so across and a bridge ran to the far side from the foot of the trail. He stared at it in dismay, because the bridge was formed of two ropes, one heavy hemp rope attached lo the base of a massive pine, a lighter line, fastened higher up serving as a support for those who crossed.

Trent just had time to make out the portico of a building in a clearing beyond, before the momentary twilight of the higher altitude ended, and gloom overspread the gorge and the clearing.

He sent a hail across, without receiving an answer. There was nothing for it but to venture on the rope before darkness set in. He set his teeth and took hold of the guide line, edging out on the heavier rope.

It bore his weight, but a sudden gust of air from below set him swaying, and started sweat on forehead and hands. He stumbled out on the ground thankfully and made for the building. It proved to be dark, and the entrance was overgrown with weeds. Loose stones covered the steps, and, glancing up, Trent whistled softly.

The house had no roof. Pillars uprose near him, and the ruins of crumbling walls hemmed in a dark void. His day's walk had brought him only as far as the temple which was called the Devil's Bungalow.

CHAPTER IV
TRENT MAKES CAMP

Well, nobody's home." Trent assured himself after a fruitless survey of the darkening ruins. Then he remembered the snakes and moved out hastily. A fresh surprise awaited him in the clearing. Under the nearest trees the gloom was thick as a cellar, but here the earth cast up a pallid glow, as if white fires had sprung to life far down under the roots of the trees.

The faint, greenish glow, made the whole circle of the clearing and stretched in places to the temple. Trent walked over to the nearest patch of illumination and studied it attentively.

"Fungus," he thought, but knew better. Phosphorescent wood was to be found only where the timber was rolling, or damp. He had heard of moss in Australia that glowed with a strong whitish light, but this grew only on rocks.

The glow came from the roots of the grass, and seemed to be out of the earth itself. As darkness closed down on the Himalayas, the light increased. Trent decided to go back among the pines and make camp. He could not go on because he could not see ihe trail. Without a light, it was folly to move along paths where a misstep would plunge him into oblivion. Besides, he might come to another rope bridge.

It did not disturb him to eat his cold chuppaties and chicken within pistol shot of the Devil's Bungalow, and to roll himself up in his blanket where his outstretched hand could touch the phosphorescent—as he insisted upon believing it—fire in the grass. Trent had steady nerves, and he would have slept in the ruins themselves if it had not been for the snakes.

A cold wind, unnoticed at first, pierced his one blanket and chilled his hands and feet, warding off any inclination to sleep in spite of his fatigue. The American had been bom and raised on the city streets, and the surface of the earth to him represented "country"—a place of vacation hotels, trout fishing, and sea bathing.

Yet in his blood was the heritage of ancestors who had cleared away the forests and had built homes on the land they broke for cultivation. He stared up admiringly at the canopy of glittering stars, and fumbled for a match to light his pipe.

Then he stood up, his pulse leaping. The Devil's Bungalow was no longer dark. On one of the inner walls, far down in the ruins, the red glow of a fire flickered. It passed away, and returned, this time to stay.

It was as if some one had opened a door to a subterranean region, ruddy with fire. Trent, on his knoll, could see it, but the light could not have been visible from the trail.

Seeking out one of the smaller pines, he felt for a branch and drew himself up. He climbed cautiously until he could see down into the ruins, and made out a small camp fire—evidently of dry wood from the temple, because it sent out no smoke.

Beside this fire sat a man. Trent judged that he was tall and spare of build. His skin was dark, and he wore a black cutaway coat that did not fit, and a black skull cap. Every minute he turned his head, listening, and seeming to sniff the air.

Trent's eyes were keen, and when the flames leaped up, he could see the wide, loose mouth of the other, and tiny, gleaming eyes under a jutting brow that sloped sharply back.

"Either the janitor of the church or Dr. Bruce," he muttered cheerfully. "Maybe he was expecting me—anyway it's a man in real clothes."

With that he hailed the ruins. The man by the fire leaped to his feet and almost in the same motion disappeared from view among the piles of debris. Left untended, the fire dwindled and the shadows closed in again.

"Dr. Bruce!" called the American again. No response came, and he climbed down from his tree. "Scared him, I expect," he reasoned. "But, Great Scott—what's the fellow to be scared of?" Trent did not feel like going into the ruins to look for the other man. Somehow, the restless, turning head, and the tiny eyes repelled him. The chap in the cutaway had disappeared as noiselessly as an animal, or as an evil spirit.

Realizing that he ought not to let his mind run on in this fashion, Trent caught up his pack and stumbled away, into the network of the forest. When he considered that he was beyond earshot of the Devil's Bungalow, and hidden from it by a rocky knoll, he gathered together enough wood for a fire.

It was necessary, for he was shivering with the cold. Once the blaze was started and his pipe going, be felt better. To occupy his mind, and to drive out thoughts of the figure in the ruins, he tried to guess what was in the green box that lay under his head, with a shirt over it for a pillow. Trent was running no chances of losing it now that his journey was almost ended.

"It's valuable, because Haldane's paying a pile of jack to send it here. And it's not money. He would have cabled that. And it's not papers of any kind—so he says. Family jewels maybe, but why send them to this jumping-off place, on top of the clouds?"

He yawned and put some more wood on the fire.

"Haldane was scared green of those two fellows in the Grand Central, but he was tickled to death when he saw me get off O.K. He said they were *Tsong Khapas*. I've got that line right, by now, but it doesn't mean anything. Let's see; they must have wired ahead from New York to Chicago to some other crooks, and then Schmandt—"

He whistled softly. If the seekers after the green box had wired Chicago, to set a man to trail him, they could have wired San Francisco. Plenty of Orientals there, and some of them could have taken the train east, to Ogden, in time to meet the Overland there.

"That's what happened. The men from San Francisco got their signals crossed. The second relay, waiting at Ogden, saw Schmandt lift my bag.

They didn't know who he was—followed him to the hotel—quarreled over the bag, or killed him in cold blood. That's what."

Who were the murderers? A native interpreter, at the train, had dropped Trent like a hot cake when the *Tsong Khapa* was mentioned, and—Trent reflected grimly—a hard boiled road-house keeper had shut up like a clam when he spoke of it. Evidently, since the words meant something in this part of the world, he had drawn close to the *Tsong Khapa* country when he came to the Devil's Bungalow.

Why should an English physician live near such a place was the question that presented itself?

"If he's the man in the cutaway, he's a nut like Haldane. Well, I don't like it, and when I get my receipt signed tomorrow I'm going to hike out, even if I have to ride a horse."

Trent was more tired than he knew, and drowsiness numbed him, putting an end to his train of thought. The warmth of the fire sent a grateful languor through his limbs, and the scent of the pine branches overhead, scorched by the fire, was the very incense of the forest. He dozed comfortably, waking to stare into the failing glow of the embers, half dreaming of an ancient land where there were no pavements, and no walls, and no plotting of men. He fancied he strode along gigantic heights, and that some one beside him held his hand to keep him from falling. The hand he held was a woman's and she laughed and the sound of it was the merry whisper of the stream in the valley a thousand miles beneath—

It was broad day when Trent woke, and his watch showed nine o'clock. The green box was still in position, the seals intact.

With a sigh of relief he started to stretch his cramped limbs, and straightway forgot his stiffness and everything else, except the girl who was staring at him with frank curiosity.

One of the mountain trails ran within a few yards of his camp and on it was a well groomed pony. The pony's rider struck Trent as something of a curiosity herself. She wore a dark riding habit, and used a side saddle. A wealth of red-brown hair hung down her back—a back erect as a slender pine.

"You look tired out," she said, her scrutiny ended. "Where are you going?"

"To Dr. Arthur Bruce. Does he live hereabouts?"

"You're an American, aren't you? Why in the world did you stop at the Devil's Bungalow, instead of coming on to the station?"

Trent flushed, realizing that he needed a shave and that his camp was not, after all, a commodious one. He suspected that white men in this country rode horses and had natives carry their baggage. Moreover the girl had soft, gray eyes that made him feel awkward all over. He judged that she was about eighteen.

"So sorry I waked you," she rambled on. "I'm Dr. Bruce's daughter, and the way to the station is—to follow the Duke of Wellington's tracks. This is the Duke of Wellington." She tapped the pony's flank. "If you wish, I'll take your—kit, up."

Trent shook his head. "It weighs a hundred pounds—at evening, anyway. Thanks, I'll make the grade. Every one I've met wanted to give me a lift, with this particular bundle."

"Really?" She nodded coldly and gathered up her reins. Trent realized that his joke was a clumsy one. He guessed that the girl did not encounter many visitors.

"How far is it, Miss Bruce?"

"Nearly seven miles."

"Does your—" he started to ask if her father wore a cutaway and a black skull cap, but thought better of it. "Does your grass around here belong to the phosphorous family, or do you fertilize it with electric lights?"

"That is the *jyotismati* grass," she explained gravely. "Some of the roots are luminous, and the Buddhist priests believe such spots are sacred. So this temple was built here a long time ago. It is abandoned now because the priests say that the coming of the white men has offended the gods."

She would have passed on with a nod, when a half dozen men came into view around a bend in the trail. Seeing the girl, they hurried up and thronged around her, elbowing and whining.

They were shining with grease and the dirt of years, so their long gray and yellow garments seemed to stick to their flesh. Every one wore a towering hat, something like a cardinal's cap, ringed around with layers of silver ornaments. Their features were stamped in the same mold—thin, with loose, pendulous lips, and bleared eyes.

One laid a hand on the girl's riding boot, and Trent caught him by the shoulder, sending him whirling among his fellows. At once a dozen pairs of restless eyes scanned him angrily, and the whining voices deepened to snarls.

"You should not have done that," she said quickly. "They are lamas from the upper hills." She nodded across the valley. "On a visit to the temple, you know."

"That fellow touched you."

"They are only Buddhists—priests after money. We try to keep on good terms with them." She tightened her reins, and called over her shoulder as the pony trotted off. "The lamas won't harm you if they see you go up the path to the station."

Trent watched her out of sight, and then started up the trail. The beggars, grouped in the clearing, paid no further attention to him. "Every day seems to be tag day in this country," he thought. "And even the snakes can't be harmed. Hope it wasn't Dr. Bruce I met up with last night. Wonder if I dreamed it, after all?"

But whenever he halted to rest, he looked down, hoping for a sight of the youthful rider who took her morning canter in the wilderness infested with *jyotismati* grass and lamas.

CHAPTER V

THE UNWELCOME GIFT

Trent was relieved to discover that Dr. Arthur Bruce was not the man of the ruins. He found a ruddy, blue eyed Briton who welcomed him to a white walled hospital in a garden overlooking the distant valley and the higher ranges of the Himalayas. Surprised at first, Bruce scanned his visitor's card and stared frankly at mention of Haldane.

"Trevis Haldane? And all the way from New York?" He turned the green box over in his powerful hands, and, after a moment's hesitation ripped off the cords and seals. Under the silk was a cylindrical, ebony box. The cover stuck, and Bruce jerked it off impatiently.

He was just in time to catch the thing that fell from the box. Trent gave a soft whistle of amazement. The object Haldane had sent half around the earth was a woman's head—a head of bronze or lacquer work, almost life size.

The strong sunlight gleamed upon green and white stones that formed the woman's eyes, the necklace about the fragment of throat, the earrings, the eyes of the tiny lacquer snakes that coiled upon the head, took the place of hair. Emeralds and diamonds. Trent thought, worth a small fortune.

"What in—?" Dr. Bruce thrust the head back into the box and glanced around. On the veranda of the small infirmary two native patients had risen to their feet, and a house boy was drawing near, his eyes glued on the thing in the Englishman's hand. "Come into the house."

In the sitting-room of the doctor's bungalow, behind drawn shades, Bruce paced the floor, hands behind his back. Presently he struck a gong and uttered a short command when the native house servant appeared. In less than a moment, a slender, straight backed Mohammedan stepped noiselessly through the door and put the back of his hand to his forehead. Trent noticed that he wore beard and turban like the keeper of the dak bungalow.

"Haidar Ali," Bruce spoke swiftly, "see to it that no one leaves the station before sunset. No one!"

The tall attendant withdrew and the physician took the box to the window, to study the bronze head again in the half light from the lattice. Trent saw that wnat he had taken for a necklace about the woman's throat was a series of glittering skulls in miniature. He had never seen diamonds carved like that before.

And the earrings were tiny men, hanging from gold cords. The face of the woman itself was ghastly, for her tongue projected from an open mouth, like the tongues of the men hanging from the nooses at each ear.

"The head of Doorga!" Bruce muttered. "And half the station saw it."

To Trent's thinking the thing must be worth some tens of thousands of dollars, and he was glad that delivery of it had been made. Some curio, he reflected, from Haldane's collection—Bruce seemed profoundly struck by it.

"Before we forget," he suggested, "would you mind signing a receipt, Dr. Bruce?"

"A receipt? Damn your impertinence!" The physician swung on his guest savagely.

Trent stood up, frowning. "My firm in New York undertook to deliver this for a client, Mr. Haldane, and I've lugged it around a few thousand miles," he drawled. "Is there any reason why you can't give me an acknowledgment of its delivery, doctor?"

Studying the open countenance of the American, Dr. Bruce relaxed, and sank into one of the wicker chairs, calling for a whisky and soda. "I forgot you did not know what it was," he observed more quietly. "And I owe you an apology for losing my temper. Haldane said nothing to you of the contents of the box?"

"He said it was not papers, but something mighty important. Said he would have brought it himself, if he did not have to go to London."

"The infernal liar! Haldane would not have carried this to India for a half million, sterling. Although he 'ud do most anything for that amount."

The whisky arrived and Bruce poured himself out a smaller portion than his guest. After starting up a good cigar and cooling off in the shady room, the American found himself wondering at the strange manner in which the physician accepted such a valuable gift. Bruce tore a blank page from his notebook and scribbled a few lines. He handed it to Trent with the ghost of a smile.

> Received, the head of the goddess Doorga, complete as sent.
>
> Arthur Bruce.

"Best not insert your name." he added. "Have any trouble coming over? Ah! tell me about it."

Trent was glad to relate the incidents that had been puzzling to him, and Bruce proved to be a good listener, questioning him closely about the man he had seen in the ruins.

Perhaps it is just as well you did not strike up a closer acquaintance with him," he remarked. "By your description that was one of the young princes of this district."

"But he wore—"

"A cutaway, precisely. You should see him in evening regalia, dress coat and all that. Prince Markor Lheding was educated in Oxford, unfortunately for everybody—Oxford, and a good deal at Longchamps, Monte Carlo and Nice. A Tibetan by birth, he's improved on his natural arrogance, and scheming. Makes no end of trouble for us."

"Why would he camp in the ruins?"

"To make *pooja*. Trent—establish holiness for himself. He pretends to worship with the old generation of the Tibetans, the Lhassa crowd. They give him money to plot against the accursed *feringhis* that's us—and he spends it at the races, and among the Hindu courtesans. If you ever happen to run foul of him again, drop him over a precipice into deep water, and I'll be confoundedly grateful."

Bruce put the head of the goddess back into the box and sighed.

"It's Markor's crowd, the younger scions of the Tibet barons—ostensibly students—that made things warm for you in the United States. They must have suspected that Haldane had the head, and were watching him. When he passed it on to you, they took up the hunt, and did for that unfortunate operative Schmandt, as you suspect."

"Why?"

"My dear chap, by all the ethics of a religion older than Christianity by a thousand years, we are fated, you and I. The head of the goddess belongs to these people."

Trent nodded. "You could always give it back to them. Not that I—"

"Any one who has had his hand upon the head of Doorga is marked for death."

It took the American a moment to digest this thought. "Sounds like the Inquisition, or—or the movies." He laughed. "They don't do things like that today."

"They did to Schmandt. You were more fortunate."

Something like the touch of icy water passed up the American's back as he remembered the green scarf that had strangled his countryman. "Well," he reasoned. "you can explain matters to the—the Tibet state department, and, after all, Dr. Bruce, you're a British citizen."

The older man smiled coldly. "And you, I take it, are a New Yorker. You know nothing of conditions here—which are worse than usual, just now.

Tibet has no state department, and no dealings with other nations. Protected by these"—he waved his hand at the barren peaks in the distance—"the *Tsong Khapa* can laugh at the British fleet and the American army."

"What is the *Tsong Khapa*?"

"The devil's pope. The head of all the lamas. Powerful, too. Man, the command of the dalai lama is obeyed through all this tribal country, beyond our frontier posts, Mongolia, Siberia and China. The World War loosed the Russian restraint and the pope of the lamas enjoys today the power of medieval times."

Trent thought of Haldane's fright. There was a man who knew what he faced. And Haldane had let him in for this danger deliberately.

"And to think," went on Bruce moodily, "that idle and excitement-loving women in our countries welcome the *swamis* and the *mahatmas* of Asia into their parlors. This good Doorga cult is plain devil worship and these lamas are nothing more than black magicians—conjurers, who deceive their own worshippers."

He looked up as Haidar Ali stepped to the door and waited for permission to speak.

"Sahib," the Moslem said impassively, "one of the house boys has talked to a carrier of wood, who has gone from the station."

Bruce turned to the American. "I fancy we must face the music."

"Look here," Trent began confusedly, "you don't know how sorry I am. I've put you in a tough jam—"

"Through no fault of yours. That is over with. I'd advise you, although you must be beastly fagged, to start down at once. You will be able to get out of the hills safely, if you take a horse and push on to the dak bungalow. Leave the horse there."

The generosity of the other made Trent feel all the more troubled. "I'll wait and go down with you."

Bruce smiled. "My dear chap, do you think I'm going to abandon the station and the work of twenty years ?"

"But if your life is in danger?"

The physician picked up and lit a cigarette, without asking Haidar Ali to leave. Trent noticed that the attendant was listening with increasing interest.

"Haidar Ali," said the Englishman, "is a Pathan of the Orakzai, and my follower for ten years or so. I'm afraid he's going to enjoy himself no end if we have trouble with Prince Markor and his crowd. He likes such things—fact is, he was weaned on feuds, and he becomes homesick when there's no one to quarrel with." The tall native smiled and brushed his short, parted beard.

"You see, Trent, my work has made the station a clearing house for the sick hillmen. They are different from the native Tibetans, although they're under the shadow of the *Tsong Khapa*. It wouldn't do to leave them, you know."

Trent glanced at the small infirmary and the few cots on the veranda. Twenty years' work.

"I've never ridden a horse, Doctor," he observed, "and I'm too stiff to move away from here now. I'm going to stay, for a while."

"Better not." Bruce spoke gravely.

The American leaned back and studied his cigar thoughtfully. "I want to see this thing through, Doctor. My firm has a slogan—service. We're expected to be on the job when a client needs any little thing. I don't get the hang of it all yet, but if you're lined up against this lama mob, I won't leave until the show's over."

With a smile, and a murmur about "quaint Americanisms" the physician studied his young guest a moment. "Good! he nodded at length. "But remember you are not obliged in any way. If an opportunity presents for you to reach the dak bungalow, my advice is to take it." He glanced at his watch. "I operate now—a Pahari cripple with a cataract on both eyes. Then a case of amputation, and then—tiffin is at three, and Helen, my daughter, will return from her ride before that."

He rose, turning back his shirtsleeves, intent on the business before him. "Oh, Trent, you'll want a tub.

CHAPTER VI
THE MAN-TRAP

A bath took much of the stiffness out of Trent's limbs, and clean linen and a second whisky refreshed him. The Moslem, who acted as general bodyguard and helper to the Bruces, unbent sufficiently to comment on the curio in the green box with a few vivid sentences. He accepted Trent as the *dakitar-sahib's* guest, and made it clear that his obligation ended there, for the present.

In other days, he explained, the statue of the devil's dam—as Haidah Ali christened the goddess Doorga—was the center of worship in the temple below them, the *Sheitan-ka* bungalow. During a war of the white men with the Tibetans, the priceless head, with its jewels, had been carried off by a looter.

After that the lamas abandoned the temple, except for seasonal pilgrimages there, to stir up mischief. They complained that the white man's rule on the border, and especially the medicines and surgery of Bruce had polluted the temple.

But the physician's influence with the peaceable hill folk was too great for them to use violence, although the lamas had tried to rouse the district against him more than once. The rest of the statue of Doorga had been carried back to one of the citadels of the hills, and the lamas prophesied that the day was near when the head would be returned to them, and the *dakitar-sahib* done away with.

"They are magicians, sahib, but not true magicians. They say in the villages that they can see in the dark, and put the souls of men into snakes. Also that they have put a deathless fire in the ground by the temple." Trent smiled, thinking of his perplexity when he first saw the luminous roots.

"But," added Haidar Ali, "once you align both sights of a rifle, front and rear, on a conqueror, he is no more than another dead man. That is the best dealing with the lamas. Bruce sahib should keep the jewels of Doorga for the little missi, and clean carefully the sights of a rifle. *Wallah*, the thing is done."

He inquired, and seemed pleased when he learned that Trent had a sharp-shooter's rating, in the service. "In this thin air, sahib,'" the Moslem became confidential, "it is necessary to sight at eight hundred yards, to hit a mark at a thousand. And, assuredly, it is known to you that in shooting down at a sharp angle, the tendency is to over-shoot."

Trent thanked him, and fell to wondering what Bruce meant to do. The Englishman was in a hole, as he saw it; if Bruce returned the head of Doorga to the lamas, it would be evidence that the physician had had it in his possession. Such an act would strengthen the hand of the Tibetans. Moreover, the thing was worth many times the value of the station; and the simple, pine and teak bungalow, with its three or four servants and horses did not hint at wealth, in the mind of the American. Apparently Haldane, knowing the danger attached to possession of the curio, had sent it on to Bruce, to be returned to the Tibetans. Still, it was strange that Haldane had not written.

The last thing that Trent thought possible was that Haidar Ali's rifle practice would be called into play.

Bruce rejoined him at the late luncheon, and was silent through the meal. More than once he glanced at his watch, and afterward Trent saw him talking earnestly with the Moslem, who left the station immediately.

The American strolled up and down the terrace, with the unspoken hope of seeing Helen Bruce come in from her ride. The lawn stretched from the veranda to the edge of a low cliff—a sheer drop of some twenty feet—guarded by a bed of azaleas.

He had about decided to look up the physician again, and had turned toward the bungalow when a soft impact on the arass behind him drew his attention. Stepping to the edge of the flower bed, he saw what appeared to be a round bundle done up in hair on the lawn, near the azaleas. Turning it over with his foot, he started back, in horror. It was the head of a man.

The long, black hair fell away trom a yellowish skin, and the distorted mouth was already hardening upon the teeth. Trent must have cried out. unaware, for a servant looked out from the veranda and presently Bruce stepped to his side and bent down with a quick in-drawing of breath.

"I feared—it's poor Chamar, the groom who went out with Helen."

"It fell down behind me," Trent muttered unsteadily.

"Tossed up, I fancy, from below the cliff." Bruce strode to the edge of the flower bed and studied the underbrush beneath. Presently he rejoined his guest and carried the ghastly remnant into the hospital; when he came out he was frowning.

"Every one of my patients has left. The convalescents and the native helpers must have carried the worst cases off. First time that has happened—"

"But, Dr. Bruce, your daughter—"

"Helen should have been in before now. She is always prompt. Chamar's death points to serious trouble. I'll spare no pains to run down the murderer. Chamar came to me with a bad case of gangrene, and he was a good boy."

Trent stared at his host. "Good Lord, man, Helen must be in the hands of your enemies now, and you stand—"

"Waiting." The eyes of the older man were cold and the lines in his face deepened as he spoke. "Helen might have been on any one of a dozen trails, and Haidar Ali with my hunter has gone in search of her. I can't leave the station, because there is only one house boy left, and because if the lamas actually have Helen they will communicate with me here—"

"There's a band down at the temple now."

Bruce nodded. "The news reached them quickly, then. Markor must have ordered them to come with him."

"I didn't tell you, Dr. Bruce, I met your daughter near there this morning."

"Ah! Did she—touch the green box?"

"No." The American thought quickly. The shadows were lengthening on the lawn, and it would be dark within two hours. The girl must have been intercepted several hours ago, and if so, her captors could be well across the valley and pursuit would be out of the question, even if the Moslem were there to attempt it.

"Dr. Bruce, I've a hunch that Helen is down at the Devil's Bungalow. That seems to be a sort of crossroads, and it certainly commands the rope bridge. Granting that the priests captured your daughter, I think they would be likely to hold her near here, and send for reinforcements. They would take her to Markor, for one thing, and he was down there."

The physician glanced at him quietly. "This head is a declaration of war. Notice that no message accompanied it. If they were holding Helen for ransom, they would not have killed Chamar."

"Can you get word down to the nearest city, and have militia called out—I mean troops sent up?"

Bruce smiled wryly. "The nearest cantonment is two hundred miles away, and the forces in northern Bengal have their hands full with rioting. If word could be sent, and they could come, it would take ten days—too long."

"Then I'm going down to look over the Devil's Bungalow. You stay here, in case Helen turns up, or Haidar Ali."

The Englishman took a turn up and down the lawn. "My dear chap, you'd find yourself in no end of a mess. These Tibetans—"

"They're like gangsters—the same breed all over the world." Trent smiled.

"It's good of you, on my word. Good luck!" Bruce held out his hand and turned back to the station, walking slowly, like a man aged ten years in as many hours. "Watch out for traps, Trent," he called over his shoulder, "and mind the snakes around those ruins."

Trent had not gone far down the path to the temple when he remembered that the Tibetans must have set men to watch the Bruce bungalow. Evidently one at least of the lamas was near, because the head of the unfortunate groom had been carried up. It struck him as certain that this watcher must have seen him start down the trail, and if so—

He quickened his pace, passing over an open level of ferns, and continued on at a trot until he rounded a moss-grown rock where the path neared the edge of a cliff. Not once did he look around, but, under the lee of the great boulder, he crouched back against the steep slope and waited.

Within a moment the *pad-pad* of bare feet sounded upon the trail above him, and the American bent forward, tensing his muscles. A thin figure in soiled yellow rounded the rock and almost plunged into his arms.

The man snarled, and Trent saw that his teeth were pointed, as an animal's. Quick-moving as a panther, the spy evaded his grasp and drew a curved knife from his sleeve, a long, wavering blade, hiltless, with the butt shaped like the head of a snake and ornamented with tiny emeralds in place of eyes.

So much Trent saw in the half second during which the yellow man lunged at his stomach with the dagger. He could not jump back, nor could be draw his revolver. Instinctively, he chopped down at the other's wrist with the flat of his hand, so that the dagger's point ripped through his loose coat, into the earth at his back.

His right hand lashed out at the snarling face of the lama. The blow carried more force than he thought. Knocked back a full pace, the native stumbled on his heels, crashed through the ferns that edged the path—and disappeared.

Drawing out the knife, Trent advanced to the summit of the cliff, and gasped. The body of the priest was just plunging through the branches of the pines a sheer thousand feet below.

A shudder wrenched Trent's shoulders, and he hurled the knife away from him. Then he pushed on, at a trot, knowing that he must hasten if he would reach the clearing and the temple by nightfall. He began to realize that in this warfare of men isolated in this world above the clouds, there was to be no discussion of terms, or taking of prisoners—and that his own life was of no more value than his two hands and his wit could make it.

In spite of his efforts, twilight closed down before he reached the *jyotisviati* region. One moment he could see clearly the boles of the deodars and birches a mile away, the next everything in front of his outstretched hand was invisible. Trent felt like dropping to hands and knees and feeling his way along the path, past the gullies and chasms he knew existed on either side. But he walked forward, using his feet to distinguish the sides of the trail, and more than once drew back hastily when he stumbled against a stone, and caught sight of the stars gleaming beyond a void in front of him. Before he knew it, he was threading through the soft glow of the luminous roots. A stone's throw away, he made out the bulk of the temple.

Trent was glad that he had some knowledge of the lay of the land, but he realized the difficulty of approaching the ruins, where his moving figure would be marked against the phosphorescent patches. A long interval of listening convinced him that no one was moving or talking in the ruins, within earshot. Nor could he make out any telltale glow, as on the evening before.

"After all," he told himself, "I don't know that there is a soul in this devil's shebang. But I know the snakes are there. If I walk up, I'll stumble over some vines or something and give myself away, while if I crawl—"

Sweat started out on his hands and forehead as he thought of a casual warning voiced by one of the dak keepers who asserted that few cobras were found at such an elevation, but a smaller reptile, the *porhu* had its habitat in the region. This species of snake was one of the few inclined to attack a man without provocation and its bite was fatal—or so the native said.

Setting his teeth, he edged forward, to the nearest piles of debris. Here he went down on hands and knees, and crawled to where he thought the young Tibetan had his fire. The deserted temple was larger than he had believed, and it was empty of sound and movement.

Except for a faint, slithering sound, barely perceptible. Trent lay prostrate, his arms outstretched, not daring to scratch a match. Once, over his motionless fingers, a damp, sliding thing passed, and he clamped his teeth until they ached to keep from crying out. A faint hissing, like the hum of a kettle beginning to boil, came from just beyond his finger tips.

Every nerve in him tingling, he drew back and gained his feet.

"That settles it," he muttered, wiping his brow. "If I'm going to be bitten, it'll be in the leg, like a Christian."

It was some time before his nerves were under control again, and he found that now he was prone to start back when the least whisper of wind stirred the vines around his feet.

How long it took him to make the round of the vacant chambers of the Devil's Bungalow, he did not know. But eventually he came out on the side facing the great cliff that formed the wall of the upper valley. Here he stayed his foot and looked down at what seemed to be a dark, round stone directly in front of him.

His exploring hand encountered nothing, where the black patch showed on the earth, and he risked striking a match.

A hole about three feet in diameter, and twice as deep had arrested his progress. Half hidden by a clutter of leaves and mold, he made out what appared to the open jaws of some earth-dwelling monster. Further investigation showed him that the jaws were really wood, fitted with the teeth of some huge fish. Under the spread of the teeth was a board, balanced on a tree limb, sunk in the ground and bent into an arch.

The thing was a trap, although probably rendered useless by age. If he had fallen into the hole, he would have released the rude spring which would have swung the two rows of teeth together.

"Cheerful," he grunted. "Am I dreaming, or is this a museum?"

Suddenly he blew out his match. Beside him a flight of stone steps led down the steep slope toward the abyss, and the steps seemed to be clear of rubbish.

"Must be something down there, if they took such pains to guard the entrance," he reasoned.

Descending cautiously—he did not wish to test out any other man-trap—he found that the stair ended in a kind of terrace where a statue occupied the place of honor. Trent was satisfying himself that it was a stone image, and not a man, when he heard voices.

At the same time he observed a line of light under the wall by the steps. An opening extended back into the hill, here, and across this entrance a heavy woolen curtain hung. A moment's listening convinced him that natives were on the other side of the curtain, and he drew back one edge of it cautiously.

In a stone chamber, or passage, sat Prince Markor Lheding with five other lamas. A gigantic candle of rancid butter or tallow smoked and flared in the center of the place, and although Trent searched every recess with his eyes, he could see nothing of Helen Bruce.

CHAPTER VII
THE PORHU

There was nothing to be gained from listening, and Trent reflected that, as matters stood, he could accuse the Tibetan of nothing definite. True, one of the Bruce servants had been slain, and a lama had attacked him on the path; but this was no valid reason for attempting to hold up the man who sat at ease in the crypt, a blue robe flung over his cutaway.

The American's position was not a pleasant one. If the Tibetans should see fit to come out of the room he could not escape up the stairs without being heard, and he noticed that the five lamas wore the same long knives fashioned like snakes.

The only sensible thing to do was to return and report to Bruce, or to retire to the woods and wait for daylight. But Trent lingered, reluctant to leave his find. And presently he held his breath, leaning forward to hear the better.

"By noon it will be all settled, as I have said. I will restore to my people the thing that is theirs, and the red mark will be on the forehead of the *dakitar-sahib.*"

Prince Markor was speaking in English with a marked accent, and speaking to someone beyond Trent's range of vision in the crypt.

"You would not dare!" The voice of Helen Bruce answered him.

"Would I have seized you, if I had not planned to do away with that meddler, your father?"

"But you have been our guest—you are half an Englishman." Bewilderment and alarm for her parent made the words unsteady.

"No, little lady. I am not one bit a fool of an Englishman. I was sent to your country to learn how to deal with you, and I was what you call a good student." The man laughed, and in the high, guttural mirth there was the delight of a skilled torturer confronted with an opportunity for displaying rare skill. "No, it is you who were daring, to remain so long by the temple that your father plundered."

"He did not."

"Ah, your acknowledgment is small. You are a child, but beautiful—as I have seen."

Peering through the curtain, Trent saw the face of the Tibetan change as if a mask had fallen from it.

"You are a traitor," the girl answered slowly, as if realizing the truth for the first time. "Because you make these priests think you are working for their cause, when you think of nothing but yourself—"

"Why not? You have a saying, 'Only the fittest survive.' But I believe you are worthy of a *depen* of Lheding. As to your father—I shall turn him over to the warrior monks," he laughed, "and the old head of a Lhassa monastery who happens to be visiting the frontier. He is nine times holier than one of your cardinals, and if he gives command to attack your father, his followers will be fired with an unquenchable zeal."

There was no discussion of terms, no threat or appeal for mercy from the girl. Helen Bruce understood the full danger that faced her father. Of herself she did not seem to think at all.

"A dozen men with rifles are at the station," she pointed out. "The lamas would be terribly cut up—"

"Only two are at the bungalow," Prince Markor corrected. "Your father and a worthless Pahari servant. Several fled, and the Moslem fire-eater is being tracked by my friends—and the one with him. Chamar was attended to. The American who spied on me is stupid and panicky; either he has gone away or has sought safety by now."

Silence fell, and the Tibetan spoke to his companions. Three of the lamas rose and disappeared into the darkness behind the candle. When Trent looked at Markor again, the prince had drawn Helen Bruce from her niche in the wall. The girl's wrists were bound, and she flushed when the Tibetan seized a handful oi her brown tresses, twisting them above her ear in the whorl worn by the native women.

Into this rough head-dress Markor fastened a mirror, shaped like a jewel, and some silver ornaments. He surveyed the effect with satisfaction, and spoke to one of his companions. Trent, his eyes on the girl, was startled by a gleam of flying steel that shot toward him from the hand of a lama.

Markor had seen, in the round mirror—the trinket that he had put in Helen's hair—the face of the white man, and had warned his companions. The slender dagger, weighted by its heavy pommel, ripped through the curtain before Trent could move aside. Instinctively he twisted his body and the blade glanced viciously against his hip and whirled on, to clatter along the stones behind him.

Before another could be thrown Trent jerked down the curtain, and swung it into the face of one of the lamas.

Drawing his revolver he shot at Markor and missed. The other Tibetan who was gliding toward him, knife in hand, received his second bullet full in the forehead. Hindered by the girl, Trent emptied the chambers of his revolver after Markor without effect as the prince ran back into the corridor.

"Down!" he cried to Helen Bruce, who was half stunned by the smashing impact of the discharges in the confined space. "They must have guns—"

Look out!" she screamed. "The other—"

Trent had half a glimpse of the remaining native leaping toward him through the smoke fumes. He had not time, even, to face about; instead he dropped to hands and knees, stiffening his body as the flying legs of the native struck him. The man was thrown headlong, and the American was on top of him at once, pounding his head against the stone flooring.

The fight was over in a moment, when the last antagonist lay stunned beside the great candle. Trent could make out a flight of steps leading up behind it. But it was now too late to pursue Markor, and they could not stay where they were.

Without waiting to reload his weapon, or cut the tough hemp cords on Helen's wrists, he caught her up in his arms and ran out to the terrace.

Markor must have gone to rejoin his other men somewhere in the temple above, and if the Tibetans gained the stairhead before him, he would be cut off. Taking the steps two at a time, he reached the main level and plunged to one side, thanking his stars that Helen Bruce was light in his arms. "If we can get to that rope bridge!" he panted.

"Shh!" she warned him. "They have ears like cats and they can almost see in the dark."

To ease the strain of her weight, she passed her arms, tied at the wrists, over his head and braced herself on his shoulders. Trent avoided the man-trap and retraced the way he had come, as well as he could. Although, to move quietly, he had slowed to a quick walk, he did not set Helen Bruce on her feet. There were the snakes.

They soon saw, by the glow of the luminous grass, that they were out of the ruins, and Trent let the girl stand. He was feeling for loose cartridges in his jacket pocket when lights appeared on the walls behind them. Markor and the three other lamas were standing watching them.

Two of the natives bore pine torches, swinging them around their heads to make the flare brighter. The scion of the Lheding family carried a serviceable rifle, and leaped to the ground as he saw that Trent had not succeeded in reloading the Colt.

"Run for it," whispered the American. "The rope bridge is your best bet."

They raced across the clearing, guiding by the flickering torches that kept close behind them. Trent found that he was limping from the cut on his thigh, and the girl, handicapped by riding boots could go no faster than he. The mountain bred natives gained as they moved down the slope toward the gorge.

"Why do you run?" Marker's amused voice came from close behind him. "I could drop you here; I am a good shot. But I will wait, until you climb on the rope, if you are—particular."

Stung by the taunt, Trent sank on his good knee and whirled around, resolved to have the fight out. He was shoving a cartridge into the cylinder, and Markor was taking deliberate aim at him, when a sharp report barked out behind Trent.

By the smashing impact on his ear drums, the American knew that it was a high powered rifle, and fired in line with him, but some distance away. He was aware that one of the torch bearers stumbled and fell.

Again the rifle cracked, and the other priest flung up his arms, letting fall the second pine knot. By the dull glow of the flames on the ground, Trent saw Markor shift his aim to something behind him and shoot twice. The American had his weapon loaded by now, but before he could bring it into play, the Tibetan had retreated out of the circle of light, toward the ruins.

The other lama was not to be seen. Trent started at a touch on his shoulder and found that Helen Bruce had remained by him. "It sounds like Haidar Ali's hunting rifle," she whispered eagerly. "Across the gorge."

Hardly a moment passed before a tall figure loomed up behind them, and Trent heard the voice of the Moslem, warning them to stay where they were. As he passed Trent, he asked him to remain with the miss-sahib, and on no account to leave her.

"Matters have gone ill," his voice came back out of the gloom. "I go to stalk this dog."

Trent placed the two torches together, and added a stick or two to keep the fire going. Then he withdrew to the path near the rope bridge and cut the cords on the wrists of Helen Bruce. This done they fell to watching the fire, listening for sounds from the temple.

They saw nothing and heard nothing until a rifle butt jarred on the earth beside the American, and Haidar Ali made known his presence. How he ever saw them, or how he approached so near without being heard were mysteries to Trent who had never spent nights watching with the Pathans of the western hills, or stalking a village during one of their raids.

Haidar Ali was silent, leaning on his rifle, the white of his restless eyes showing in the glow of the torch embers and the phosphorescent grass.

"What became of Prince Markor?" Trent asked finally.

"Without doubt, he went to *jehannum*. When I circled the Devil's Bungalow, moving cautiously, to take him from the rear, I heard him groaning. He had been bitten by a *porhu*, whose bite is death."

"Is he dead?"

"Sahib, I have said it. A while I waited, then made a light. Already his thigh was swelling and his face—"

"Don't!" cried the girl.

The servant bent down anxiously at her exclamation and asked if she were unhurt. Reassured, he was silent a moment. Then, "Who can tell where his grave is dug? The rascal was a cunning dog, he was lying in wait where even I should have walked into him. But it was written otherwise. Will the miss-sahib listen to her servant for a small moment?"

When Helen Bruce stepped to Trent's side again, it was to report that Haidar Ali had left them. He said he had far to travel before sun-up. and could not stay with them; but he left the advice to start for the station at dawn, and rejoin Dr. Bruce. Furthermore, if a large party of priests attacked them, he counseled surrender.

"I'll be—cussed if we do that!" The American was indignant. "We haven't begun to fight yet. How much do you trust this Haidar Ali?"

"Why, we've always trusted him, Mr. Trent!"

"But he's leaving—"

"I'm sure he has some plan of his own," the girl asserted stoutly. "Daddy saved his life by an operation—removed a bullet from his skull. Besides, he helped us here at the bridge. The lamas wounded Kern Dass, the other servant, but Haidar Ali fought them off and was going to the bungalow when he met us." She rose to her feet nervously. "He thinks daddy is in terrible trouble. If we could only go up to the station!"

But to climb the hill trail without a light was not to be thought of. Trent was not sure he could prepare a torch, even if they dared show a light. So he led the girl to the site of his camp of twenty-four hours ago.

Protected in some degree by the overhang of the rock, they sat shoulder to shoulder, Trent watching the vague bits of lesser darkness where the Devil's Bungalow lay, peopled now only with the bodies of the dead. The presence of the young girl made him forgetful of his own hurt and the increasing chill of the night air, and he racked his brains to think of something he could do for her, without result.

Once he stiffened, hearing a hideous outcry from the direction of the temple, seeing the flickering gleams of lanterns reflected on the branches of the firs.

"A party of our friends the enemies," he whispered. "They've hit on the—the battlefield, and they seem to be leading up the trail."

When all was quiet again, Helen Bruce sighed. "If only some law could punish him. But he is too clever."

"Prince Markor?" Trent grunted. "I think he got all that was coming to him."

"No, Trevis Haldane."

It was a strange story that Helen Bruce told the American in the early hours of the morning, while they waited beside the Devil's Bungalow for the tidings the dawn would bring them.

Twenty years ago a British expedition was sent from India, into Tibet— sent because the Russians were intriguing with the *Tsong Khapa*, to open up a road down into India. Only a small force went into the Himalayas, and its purpose was to march peaceably to Lhassa, and bring about an interview with the dalai lama, the pope of Asia.

Almost at the outset one man broke the implicit understanding against looting. Haldane, a young fellow then, attached to the supply train, succeeded in making his way into the temple of Doorga, and breaking off the head of the goddess.

No white men knew of the act that made the civilian master of jewels worth a large fortune. But the natives knew; an ambush was set in the path of the expedition, and from the border up, the road to Lhassa was opened only by rifles. Men died on both sides, who would otherwise have come through alive.

The natives knew. If the British had slain wounded prisoners and the people of the villages, the mountain road would have been easier for them. But the medical officers who went along, doctored the Tibetans who fell into their hands, and—at Lhassa—hundreds of natives who came to them for treatment. The priests, masters of Tibet, interpreted this as a sign of weakness.

Arthur Bruce, of the India Medical Service, learned from several patients of the looting of Doorga, and the identity of the white man who did it. And Haldane was told, in no uncertain terms, that he knew it.

But Dr. Bruce, the harm being done, kept his own counsel. This did not prevent the news leaking down into India through the invisible telegraph of village gossip. Haldane was exiled from the British clubs, and became no better than a pariah among his fellows. He was forced to leave India. England would have none of him.

As if the crime of the man had opened the way to wealth, he made money at everything he touched—drugs, until the Chinese Government prohibited that traffic, and after—black birding in the Solomon Islands, and finally a tidy list of shipping at the start of the World War, when ships were so much gold in pocket.

During those twenty years he fed his hatred against Arthur Bruce, believing that the *dakitar-saltib* had reported his theft of the image's head. Although his money was able to protect him from occasional attempts of the priesthood to recover the head of Doorga. he was forced to travel from one place to another and could not put his foot on English soil.

"And so," the girl concluded, "he sent the thing by you, knowing that the natives here would see it in daddy's hands, and take their revenge upon him."

Exhausted at last by the events of the day, she fell asleep, and Trent took off his coat, to cover her shoulders. Still asleep, she dropped her head on his arm, shivering with the windy chill of the mountain slope, and he did not move for fear of waking her.

If it had not been for Helen Bruce, the American would have made slow work of the climb to the station, when the gray mists of the false dawn began to thin away under a strong breeze. He was utterly weary, his injured leg was more than half lame, and his head was swimming from lack of sleep. He did not think they would see Haidar Ali again, and as they progressed up the narrow path, he halted to scan the forest mesh more than once. Some instinct, long dormant in him, warned of danger close at hand.

At a distance a rifle cracked, and Trent quickened his pace. Helen Bruce had forsaken the main trail to approach the station by little-known paths, and by the time the sun was over the trees they came out on a ridge overlooking the gardens and the bungalow.

CHAPTER VIII
BRUCE SAHIB'S LAST STAND

Trent's first thought was that they had come too late; his second, that their coming was useless in any case. As the temple of Doorga had been hemmed in by reptiles, hidden in the vines and rocks, so now the bungalow of the white man was surrounded by merciless foes.

Protected by a fringe of azalea bushes, Helen Bruce and the American could see without being seen. Under the cliff, where the lawn in front of the house ended, were several scores of men, brilliantly clad in the red and yellow robes of the lamas. Some bore long, bronze trumpets, others banners, still others had weapons that looked like scythes and pitchforks. But these, Trent suspected, were merely insignia.

"That's their headquarters," he whispered. "Standards and bugles, and regimental emblems—all that and then some. See the fellow with an awning over his head? Bet he's the commanding officer!"

In the gardens beneath Trent, a dozen natives were crawling toward the bungalow, armed with rifles. Movements in the forest on the far side of the station hinted at as many more approaching from that side. The rear of the bungalow was hidden by the stables. But Trent estimated nearly a hundred Tibetans on the scene.

"Where'd they get those Mausers?" he asked. "And cartridges to fit?"

Helen bit her lip, to control its trembling. "Daddy says that the Germans and the Soviet governments have been selling arms to the tribes west of here. Oh!"

A rifle cracked from one of the shutters on their side of the bungalow. A scattered discharge from the lamas beneath them answered it. Again the spurt of fire snapped from the bungalow and a Tibetan rose to his feet, turned around, and fell heavily on his face.

Reports came from the far side of the house, and a Lee-Metford spat back answers. Two men only were holding the station. The Tibetans hugged cover, unwilling to face the marksman.

"That's daddy!" cried the girl, twisting her hands on her breast. Another volley made her flinch, though not from fear for herself. "We must do something!"

"They don't take time to sight before they shoot. Scared. More yellow in them than they wear on their backs. If they hadn't those modern rifles! Our best chance is by way of the stables—"

Even as he spoke a dozen gray figures leaped from the open doors of the outbuildings behind the bungalow, and raced to the wide veranda. Trent heard screens smash down, and then a series of rapid, muffled reports from within the house.

Dr. Bruce appeared on the veranda, and the Tibetans surged forward through the garden. The white man was held by four natives; his clothing was torn and blood trinkled from his lip.

Quickly Trent put his hand on the girl's arm. With the physician a prisoner, Helen Bruce was in his care. He thought of hiding her back in the forest—anything to keep her from the hands of the rabble that swarmed over the station, ransacking it and shouting insults at the captive.

But Helen Bruce broke from his grasp and faced him, cheeks blanched, and eyes over-bright. "I am going to my father—now!"

Pushing through the azaleas, she walked down the path toward the garden, and several of the monks sighted her at once. Someone shouted, and then they stared at her in astonished silence, seeing that she continued to walk toward them. Trent swore under his breath, and took the Colt from his jacket.

A second later he realized the uselessness of showing a weapon in the face of that throng. Thrusting it into the breast pocket of his coat, he buttoned the garment tight and strode after Helen Bruce.

The lamas waited until they were sure no more *feringhis* were coming from the forest, then they closed in on Trent and the girl, hurrying them toward the house. Dr. Bruce winced as he saw Helen jostled by the natives.

"Why didn't you keep off, Trent?" He swung around on the American. "I fired a shot long ago, to warn you, when I saw the bungalow was invested."

Trent made no answer because Helen threw herself against her father, hiding her face on his shoulder so that the natives would not see her sobbing. "It was—my fault, daddy. I—"

"Don't cry, Helen!" He patted her long tresses gently. "We must keep our heads up, you know. Where's Haidar Ali?"

"Gone," responded Trent briefly.

A lama thrust his fingers into the girl's hair, to pull her away from the physician. Trent lashed out with a long arm, and knocked the man over. The nearest monk promptly spat into his face and as he turned, white with anger, he nearly ran upon two long swords, drawn by his guards.

The turmoil subsided as a lane was opened in the crowd, and the fat man came up, walking under the canopy held on spears by four servants. This dignitary of the hills wore a round, velvet cap, resembling Prince Markor's skull cap, and a kind of purple stole hanging from his shoulders.

"A *gylong* counseled Bruce, "a disciple of the *Tsong Khapa*, from Lhassa. One of the heads of the yellow banner sect." Planting himself in front of the captives, the envoy of the chief of the lamas rolled his tiny eyes over them and caressed the heavy jowl that ran from his mouth to his bare chest.

"Pretty isn't he?" grinned the American, folding his arms over the bulge in his coat. "Haidar Ali said that some big politician was coming to see our finish—some one that sounded like a woodchuck-chucking wood, too."

"*Chutuktu* lama?" Bruce looked up quickly. "That would be the head of a temple, or a monastery—holier than this one. Probably a red banner man."

"Didn't know there was more than one kind of devil," objected Trent, talking to keep his mind from dwelling on Helen Bruce.

"The red banners are older, hence more influential; the yellow sect runs more to conjuring. If a *chutuktu* is due here, they may wait until he comes before attending to us. or they may not, if this chap is impatient. Rivalry between the sects is keen."

"Jolly keen—eh?" The fat man caught at the word to display what he knew of English. "Ver-ree keen sahibs, killing one imperial pa-sun Lheding family."

At this Trent turned to him and explained carefully that he alone had handled the head of the goddess, that Bruce and his daughter were innocent of wrong doing, and that Prince Markor had died from the bite of a snake.

"The snakes biting you, pretty soon, by Jove!" The man from Lhassa could not, or would not understand the sense of Trent's explanation.

"No go, America," pointed out the physician grimly. "They have their orders, and it only amuses them to hear us. Money may be his weak point, and we'll have one try at that, for Helen."

"Take the miss-sahib," he observed coldly to the fat man, "to Resident-sahib, Sreenug'r. I will give you a *chit*. It will say that you are to be given one thousand rupees for the miss-sahib."

The eyes of the disciple gleamed from soft rolls of flesh, and he pondered a moment. Just then, however, his followers brought out the prize for which they were searching, the head of Doorga.

Instantly all the crowd but the *gylong* fell down and pressed their foreheads on their clasped hands. The disciple stood aside from his canopy and the bearers placed the head on its cover of green silk where he had been.

"*Om mani padme houm!*" chanted the fat man, eyeing the prisoners sidewise. "Not much!" he confided under his breath to Bruce. "She bitten by snakes bimeby. Ver-ree pretty, by Jove, what?"

CHAPTER IX
THE END OF THE TRAIL

Evidently the disciple from Lhassa did not care to wait until his superior came to take charge of the prisoners, and certainly the crowd of monks and hangers-on did not want to wait. They stared at Helen Bruce and smiled, and their smiles were worse than curses.

How many of them believed that Bruce had stolen the head was not easy to decide. After looting the bungalow and rounding up the animals, their passions were to be let loose on the captives. Those among them who had claimed to cure the sick and drive out devils remembered that the hospital had mocked at the powdered lizards' skins that they used—and they cried that they would set fire to the hospital.

But first they would attend to the prisoners.

They proceeded to build a rough square of stones, on the lawn. Around this the lamas ranged themselves, red on one side, yellow on the other. The *gylong* himself came up with a brush and color pot and painted three horizontal red marks on the foreheads of the white men and the girl.

"The mark of Doorga," said Bruce slowly. "The devils aren't going to wail for the abbot. Seems to me that this chap from Lhassa is taking a good deal on himself."

"What are they going to do?" asked Trent.

Bruce glanced at his daughter and the muscles around his mouth quivered. "If only Haidar Ali had found Helen!" He stiffened his shoulders. "Sorry for your sake, old man. Why, the usual ritual in slaying sacrifices is to—" he lowered his voice—"tie them hand and foot, and stake them down by the knees, lying across that altar. Then their clothes are stripped off and their limbs are sliced gradually—"

Trent felt the blood drain away from his face, but he managed a smile. "Never thought I'd pine for snake bite. Thought they were going to toss us to the *porhus*."

"No, the snakes are the knives, fashioned like reptiles."

Until now Trent had been watching the preparations with a tired interest. It had not seemed possible that these men were planning to end their lives before the sun reached another noon. But the calm words of the physician, preparing him for what was to come, struck into his brain and numbed his thoughts for a moment.

"Afterward," went on Bruce, "they'll throw the bodies into the bungalow, and burn the whole station. No one in the village around 'ud dare betray them to the sirkar—the government—on account of that Doorga thing."

Glancing at the fat disciple, Trent whispered, "We have one trump to play. I've a revolver under my arm, loaded."

No one had troubled to search him for a weapon, in the center of a ring of a hundred armed men it mattered little, anyway. The Tibetans were excited, and they must have assumed that Trent was unarmed, to have given himself up as he did.

"I'll turn it loose on the bunch between the altar and the terrace edge," he continued, "as soon as they try to tie one of us up. You and Helen break through the line there, and jump from the flower bed, into the brush below. I'll stage a fight and—"

Bruce touched his arm. "No use. They'd hunt us down in a few moments. Stand close to Helen. Use your weapon on her when the time comes." He swayed on his feet and straightened with an effort. "And then, we'll fight—God, how long will they take!"

The ring of men pressed closer, as the disciple began a long harangue. Their beardless faces, and seamed eyes were fastened on the prisoners, and the reek of their garments was nearly suffocating. Trent stepped closer to the girl, who had taken her father's arm.

He looked at her head, on which the sunlight played, and tried to tell himself that he could point the revolver at her and pull the trigger. And he knew that he could not do that.

Feeling that he was looking at her, she turned her head and smiled, "I'm sorry," her lips murmured.

The disciple stopped his flow of denunciation, and a sudden silence fell upon the ring of men. On the ridge beyond the garden, where Trent and Helen Bruce had stood an hour ago, an old man came into view, pushing through the azaleas.

An old man with lidless eyes and a head nearly bald, who leaned on a staff and gazed at the throng impassively. He was clad altogether in rags, tied upon him with other rags, and left there for years. His wrinkled countenance was strangely pallid.

Later, Trent learned that the *chutuktu* had submitted to be placed in one of the hermit caves at Lhassa for ten years. His first appearance was greeted with a murmur of respect from the lamas of the red sect—respect that changed swiftly to amazement.

Behind the *chutuktu* walked Haidar Ali, rifle at the "ready" and the muzzle of the rifle between the shoulder blades of the monk.

At the edge of the garden the Moslem halted his captive. Already Haidar Ali had taken in the situation on the terrace and his deep-set eyes blazed. "Ha, sahib!" he boomed. "Bid the sons of four-legged devils stand back from the miss-sahib, or I will blow this one to all of his fathers in *jehannum*."

His usually immaculate turban was disarranged, and there was blood on his sleeve. Trent found out that the Pathan had stalked the high priest, had come up behind his half dozen followers, had tumbled two off the path, down the cliff, had used his rifle on the next two, and his knife on the last. The American knew it because the Pathan who had the blood lust strong upon him, shouted it out at once.

But just then Trent had his eye on the fat disciple who was thinking swiftly, and, whose thoughts were reflected in the evil twist of his lips.

"Go through the reds—quick!" Trent whispered to the physician. Bruce nodded and drew Helen back with him.

At last the American was facing a situation he could handle, because he knew all the cards on the table. He knew what the *gylong* was thinking, because the fat man was a politician, and a conjurer—a juggler of words and a plotter. So much Trent read in his face, and he beat the Tibetan by three seconds to the conclusion that if Haidar Ali killed the abbot, it would leave the disciple in command, with a hundred armed fiends hungering for vengeance.

He saw that the fat man had no reverence for the *chutuktu*. As the abbot made no sign either way, the red lamas allowed Bruce to thrust himself into their rank.

Then the fat disciple whispered something to his own followers, and began to shriek with rage, pointing to the white men, and foaming at the mouth. He whipped a knife out of his sleeve and several of his men drew their clumsy swords as the *gylong* started toward Helen Bruce.

"Don't shoot!" Trent shouted at Haidar Ali. Standing squarely in the path of the Tibetan swordsmen, he did not move his folded arms until two of them swung up their weapons to split his head. Then he withdrew his right arm from under his coat.

The fat man was not slow to slash at him, from the side, as the revolver gleamed in the white man's fist. But Trent's first bullet ripped through his chest and he squealed. Stepping back, Trent emptied his weapon into the yellow lamas.

Wheeling in his tracks, he dived through the men behind him and brought up beside Bruce.

"*Shabash!* Well done, sahib!" roared the Pathan.

"Back to the bungalow!" Trent cried at the physician. "Pick up a rifle if you can, but take Helen out of this." Reloading his Colt, he faced the crowd.

So swift had been the burst of firing in the center of the ring, and so unexpected had been the gunplay of the American, that the superstitious lamas were staring at the dying and wounded on the ground. Some began to shriek and shake their weapons, others pointed at the *gylong* who had fallen across the altar.

A shrill cackling burst from the lips of the old abbot, who felt the cold muzzle of Haidar Ali's rifle digging into his back. The mob stopped to listen to him, and some of the red sect struck at those of the yellow priests who were clamoring to rush against the white men. Trent saw from the corners of his eyes that Bruce had come out on the bungalow veranda with a repeating rifle, and Helen had disappeared.

The Englishman's head was up and his step was firm as in former years when he had walked unharmed in the heart of the Himalayas.

"Don't shoot, sir!" warned Trent, who saw how to make the most of the advantage they had gained. He pushed deliberately back into the crowd of red lamas, knocking down two of the yellow robes who seemed to be leaders of that party. Trent knew crowds. To draw off and try to hold that mob under three rifles would mean death. He kept them stirring, signed with his Colt for the red priests to form in a line apart from the yellow.

Meanwhile the *chutuktu* had come down and was holding in his hands the head of Doorga. The Tibetans fell silent as they realized what he was doing, with Haidar Ali—who had obeyed Trent's warning—at his back.

Trent thought quickly. All their lives hung on what the *chutuktu* would do now. And he did not act like the disciple: he was not afraid of death—the fire of fanaticism burned in his shrewd eyes as he gazed intently at the thing in his hands.

"Haidar Ali!" called the American softly.

"Here, sahib—"

"Whisper to the old faker. Tell him that head is not the real one, but one I brought, to fool 'em. Say if we die he will never have the real head of—what's her name—Doorga."

"*Atcha*, sahib. I—"

The Moslem tightened his grip on the rifle, and Trent did not see his lips move, because just then the Tibetan did an amazing thing. He flung down upon the grass the head of Doorga and spurned it with his toes.

Then he raised both arms over his head and howled like a wolf, pausing to snarl and chatter in the gutturals of his race.

"By Jove!" cried Bruce, who had drawn nearer. "He's saying that this head is an imitation—false jewels, and lacquer work where it should be bronze. He says he's disgusted with the business. There he goes."

Just in time Trent caught Haidar Ali's wrist as the *chutuktu* started to walk away. Some of his own sect followed. One or two others came and stared down at the trophy on the ground, and the white men watched them keenly. Bruce stepped forward, rifle over his arm, and motioned the others back. Something he shouted at them, and the throng began to drift away.

Told 'em to tend to their own bloody affairs after this, or their monastries would be torn down by the sirkar's troops. Hullo, they've left their wounded for me to patch up. Jolly crowd, aren't they?"

Bruce denied, point blank, Haidar Ali's request to shoot down a dozen before they could take cover, and the Pathan twitched his beard, deeply disappointed. But presently he brightened, and turned to look at Trent.

"Ha, sahib, it was otherwise in the Devil's Bungalow. There you and I left no more than one on his feet. That will bear telling about."

And the American was glad, because in the other's voice there was deep respect, and the confidence of one man in another.

It was evening, when he remembered that the head of Doorga had disappeared from the terrace about the time the Tibetans had left. Thinking that someone had rolled it off the terrace, meaning to hide it, he was searching the garden below when Haidar Ali came swinging up the hill path, chanting a song.

"Nay, sahib," the Moslem took in Trent's purpose with a glance. "It is not there. It is not anywhere."

"How so?"

"It caused much evil, although the fighting was good for us men who have not marched with a regiment for two years. So I carried it hence and dropped it over the cliff, and told what I had done in the nearest village." His white teeth flashed in the gloom. "Perhaps the dogs from the hills will carry the feud to me, for my touching it."

Trent laughed. He did not think the lamas would want any feud with the Pathan. "They went away mighty quick, this afternoon."

Haidar Ali spat at a shadow. "That is the way of the dogs. Their chiefs claim to be magicians, and when the mob sees them whipped it loses heart for bullets and slashed skins. But I do not understand why the old one threw down the head."

"You told him to. of course."

The Pathan, leaning on his rifle, shook his head. "Sahib, I was about to explain to you that I knew not their dog's language, when the chief devil cast the head away and cried that it was a counterfeit."

Puzzled, Trent stared at the Moslem. His advice to Haidar Ali had been a bluff, and it had gone through. But the head, he thought, was not a counterfeit.

"Perhaps," suggested the native, "being a magician, the lama read what was in your mind. The devils are cunning at such things."

And that was the only explanation Trent arrived at, because just then Helen Bruce came to the veranda and called him.

"Coming!" he responded, with such eagerness that Haidar Ali grinned under his beard, and continued on his way singing his chant, which was of women beloved by warriors.

Have any trouble on the trip?" asked Mr. Lee, of Hammerman. Lee and Rambaud, when Trent presented his receipt at the desk of his superior, some two months after the fight in the hills of India.

"Well"—Trent smiled, and then noticed that Mr. Lee was fingering some sheets of statistics impatiently. "Well, nothing to speak of. But I'm convinced that you need a representative in India, and I know just how I can give you one. And I'll explain in detail why you need a man there."

"Yourself?" The second partner adjusted his eyeglasses and pursed his lips, more than a little surprised at the care-free manner of his employee. "Hhm. Oh, I see this receipt reads *"for the head of the goddess Doorga."* Then it was some curio Mr. Haldane sent."

"*Some* curio," assented Trent grimly "is right. I'm going to talk to him about that."

"Mr. Trevis Haldane died a week ago in his apartment in London."

"Then he—" Trent broke off, reflecting that he did not care to lay bare the crime of a man who had passed beyond earthly justice. Bruce had kept silence. "How did he die?"

Mr. Lee put the finger tips of his two hands together and shook his head disapprovingly. "Ah, that is the curious part of it. Sad thing. One physician reported apoplexy—Haldane had been very much run down, as you know. Others said something about poison."

"Suicide ?"

"No. He was found locked in his study—his private study. The safe in it had been opened, by use of the combination. The body had slipped from the chair and the head lay on his desk, beside some barbaric bit of jewelry. Ah, I remember, the curio was called the head of Doorga."

Trent whistled, and was silent, thinking.

"This head," went on Mr. Lee, "was ornamented with scores of emeralds, and diamonds, worth close to a hundred thousand, as an appraiser reports. Some of the ornaments were miniature snakes, and some unusual kind of poison was on their fangs. It was hard to analyze, because most of it had worn off."

Trent nodded.

"The servants," concluded Mr. Lee, "reported that this curio was the prize of Haldane's collection—something he would never part with." He put down the receipt Trent had given him, and then frowned at it. "Curious that you should have been given another head of the same kind."

But to Trent the thing was clear enough. Haldane had, even at the last, been unwilling to part with the thing he craved. He had ordered a replica made, and it had been skillfully done—well enough to deceive everyone except the former master of the Doorga temple, the *chutuktu* lama The real jewels and the real trophy he had kept, and because of that he had died.

All that Trent said was, "How soon can I get the appointment in India? My wife is waiting for me there."

Mr. Lee looked surprised. "I did not know you were married."

"I'm not." Trent smiled brightly. "I said my wife was waiting for me. And so she is, though she doesn't know it, yet."

THE DESERT DRIVER

CHAPTER I

AN ACCIDENT

No Traffic cop has a post in Donkey Meat Street. A jumble of rambling motor cars, bullock carts, carriages and jinrickshas use their own judgment and the result is chaos. Donkey Meat Street is in Pekin.

If there had been a traffic cop at the crossing, Tim McMahon would not have had to jump for his life out of the way of a big red sedan that swung around a mule cart. As luck had it, he jumped backward—a good, healthy leap that propelled him against the chest of the man behind him.

Tim McMahon is stocky, big-boned, and sturdy in the leg. The man behind was knocked into the gutter. McMahon turned around with a muttered apology ready on his lips, and saw a round-faced Chinese youth in a suit of Americana tailoring. It was a costly suit, and just now, smeared with mud from the gutter.

There are a lot of things Chinese do not like to have done to them, and one is to be shouldered out of the way. The young man who climbed out of the gutter could speak English and did speak pointed, vitriolic English.

Now Tim McMahon had missed three meals in the last twenty-four hours; his clothing was shabby, and a sandy growth of hair covered his bare head, chin and upper lip. He was out of a job and broke and his temper was none of the best. His left hand snapped out at the insult.

The head of the tailored man flew back on his shoulders, and when McMahon's right followed to his jaw he rocked on his heels a second time and sat down on the curb. He put his hand to his lips, and saw that his fingers were bloodied. Slowly his face turned red, and he rose on one knee, his right hand feeling his thigh tentatively. The next second a blue, Colt six-shooter was in his hand, and a shot bellowed through the shouts and peddlers' cries and creaking of wheels on Donkey Meat Street.

The bullet, instead of striking the surprised McMahon, soared harmlessly up into the air. A man had stepped from the watching throng, had caught the young Oriental's wrist and jerked up the weapon The Chinese looked up into a pair of gray eyes belonging to an American foreign devil.

A moment of twisting and straining, and the revolver was in the newcomer's possession. At once, and as if familiar with such operations, the man of the gray eyes snapped open the Colt, shook the six cartridges into his left hand, transferred them thence into a pocket of his jacket, and handed the Chinese youth back his weapon.

Then the American nodded significantly to where a gray uniformed soldier was peering from a sentry box across the street, and the Chinese gunman faded back into the press of his countrymen. The stranger turned to Tim McMahon.

"Come away," he said.

The two white men walked around the mule cart, stepped out of the way of a laden coolie, crossed under the horns of a pair of bullocks and passed from the sight of the sentry, who returned thankfully to his box. The crowd moved on, pursued by a smattering of peddlers, and Donkey Meat Street came back to normalcy.

In this way began the very strange history of the teakwood box; a history that had its prelude in the alleys and hotels of Pekin in the year 1923 the Christian era, and its end in the vast spaces of the Gobi desert. That is, if a tale that goes back to the first ages of Time itself can have a beginning.

"You act," said Tim McMahon, "like I done wrong. How d'ye get that way?"

"No," responded the stranger, "I merely said that when you strike a Chinese, you have to watch out for trouble, and keep on watching out for months or years. That young snake in the mail order clothes was probably the son of a wealthy merchant or official of the mandarin class. Have you any friends in Pekin, McMahon?"

Tim, of the sandy hair and deep-set blue eyes, sat down on the stranger's cot, asked for and got a cigarette, threw off his coat and opened the collar of his flannel shirt. It was hot in the room of the small hotel.

No, he said, he had no friends west of Jersey City. He was a mechanic by trade, had once had a berth as driver of a motor repair lorry in France. He had stoked his way across the Pacific, had looked for work along the railroads in the coast district of China, and had grabbed a rattler to Pekin. So he had come to learn that of the few jobs open to white men in China, the good ones were filled by men sent from the United States or Europe, and the poor ones by half a dozen Chinese to every job.

"What's your line?" he asked.

The stranger smiled wryly. He was a slender man, quietly dressed in a way that made McMahon think vaguely of an artist or a foreign chap. Perhaps because of the close-clipped reddish beard and the high, bald forehead over the alert gray eyes.

"Selling typewriters," he answered. "I'm Robert Warner. Came across from the States a year ago."

Over his cigarette McMahon considered the acquaintance who had "got him out of a jam." But for the quick action of the stranger, his wanderings might have ended at Donkey Meat Street.

He reminded McMahon of men who had been to college, or army officers. There were black boxes under the cot that looked like filing cases, and several queer Oriental paintings on the wall, with an ancient Chinese repeating cross-bow.

"Any luck, Mr. Warner?"

"Rotten. 'Most every merchant in Pekin has a typewriter." Warner grinned, his short beard bristling. "Yesterday I called on a big name of Fu Cheng, curio dealer. Talked to him half an hour in my best Pekinese; then found out he spoke English as well as I—had come over a few months ago from a ten years' stay in San Francisco, and had three of the portable typewriters I'm selling. Fancy his listening to me for half an hour, and reading through all my credentials!"

Now the cigarettes were of a good, American brand; the ash tray was real ivory. Tim wondered how Warner had lived for a year. "This line," he said, "about the heathen Chinee is bunk. It's all wrong. These Chinks are wise; they've changed their skin. Look at out there."

He indicated the electric lights and trolleys of the Pekin streets, and the big radio tower that loomed over the old city wall. "I ask you, Mr. Warner, ain't that so? I ask you, does the young cabaret hound I knocked down on—"

"Donkey Meat Street."

"Does that cabaret hound slink around after me and give me a shot of feng shee or—"

"Feng sha? Magic?"

"You get me, Mr. Warner—yellow magic, or poison or any of that line of stuff? No, he goes for his gat. These Chinks is up to date. They don't have no tong wars, or ancestor worship, or opium—maybe they do sell that to the dope dealers in the States. No, these fellows are out for the jack and Chicago-made clothes."

For the past minute Warner had been extracting a folded Pekin newspaper from a pile on the table. It was printed in English, and he handed it to McMahon, pointing out a marked paragraph. "Read that."

MOTOR ACCIDENT

On Donkey Meat Street near the British mission yesterday a large gray limousine ran into and seriously injured a smaller car belonging, it is alleged, to the Cheng Curio Company. The driver of the damaged car was thrown out and escaped death only by a fortunate chance. The police of Pekin are trying to trace the ownership of the sedan which sped away after the accident, with its cut-out open.

"I said it," grunted McMahon. "Why that jam might have happened at Forty-Second and Fift' Avenoo—only there wasn't no traffic cop."

Warner's quiet eyes blinked. "No, there are no traffic cops. No one interferes. And accidents don't happen, in this part of the world. They are made to happen."

"You can't tell me!" McMahon thought of his recent escape. But his companion, who had been observing Tiim closely, noticed how husky his voice was and how weakly his hand moved. He judged that McMahon had not had a square meal for some time.

"Look here," he said. "You can help me out. Are you handy with machinery?"

"You said it, Mr. Warner."

"I know you can scrap, and keep your mouth shut. But can you—or rather, will you—obey an order, McMahon?"

The mechanic thought this over seriously. The qualifications Warner had enumerated were not those of a typewriter salesman's assistant. "If I'm minded to, Ican that, Mr. Warner."

"Well, consider yourself hired—if you're willing to bunk in with me and willing to run the chance of the ghost never walking—no pay day. And, my name's Bob, to my friends. And the first thing on our program is tiffin."

"What's that?"

"Eats."

But before the two white men could wash and go down for a late luncheon there was a knock on the door, and McMahon sat down on the cot again with a sigh as a black-suited Chinese appeared in the entrance with a succession of bows. "Mlister War-ner?" he asked, smiling.

"Yes," said Warner, and took the note the man—who might have been either servant or clerk—held out. He read it through carefully and nodded. "Very well."

"All light—you come plitty soon?" The messenger bowed himself out, and Warner sprang up, whistling cheerfully as he plied comb and brush on his sparse hair, considering the result critically in the cracked mirror.

"Looks as if we're going to make a sale, McMahon. Letter from Cheng, the merchant I called on, asking me to come around again this afternoon on a matter of business. On the strength of that we'll have chicken."

McMahon extinguished his cigarette promptly. "Nothing could be fairer than that. Say, Mr. Bob, my name's Mac, to my business partners. D'ye get me?"

"All light, Mac."

CHAPTER II
CHENG MAKES AN OFFER

The curio store of Fu Cheng resembled from the street a junk shop. In fact, there was nothing but odds and ends of junk in the shop entrance; in the second room were common articles presided over by a tattered and wrinkled guardian who ushered the two white men into the third room, filled with a fine stock of curios. Here the English speaking clerk took charge of them and conducted them up a flight of steps to a chamber where the daylight did not penetrate and Fu Cheng sat under a large yellow lantern amid the sheen of silks, the glimmer of strange jewels and the glint of splendid, ancient china.

Fu Cheng rose and bowed courteously. He was a man, unusually handsome, clad in a mandarin robe. Warner noticed that his mouth was firm, and his muscular hands well kept—a successful merchant, who had sold out his business in San Francisco at a profit.

For a half-hour, as custom prescribed, they talked, in English, about everything but Cheng's summons. Then the mandarin glanced gravely about the room, listened for a moment for sounds from the shop below, and observed, "I venture to ask, Mr. Warner, if you will be able to undertake a commission for me, involving some time and great care?"

As the American did not reply, he went on.

"You may be able to make some sales for yourself at the same time. Unfortunately, as I said yesterday, I have all the typewriters that I need. What I desire is that you should deliver for me a certain piece of goods to a business friend who is not in Pekin. At present I can not spare any of my men. I have taken the liberty of looking up you. It is your intention, you said, to leave Pekin for the interior?"

Warner nodded assent.

"By extending your journey somewhat you could deliver my package, and you would find yourself in a locality where"—he smiled politely—"typewriters are not in such supply as in Pekin."

"Where, Mr. Cheng, is this place?"

"Chagan, outside the great wall."

"In the Gobi desert?" Warner's brows went up.

"The Gobi desert, Mr. Warner, covers a great deal of ground. It is made up of mountains and plains as well as sand stretches. Between the great wall and Chagan—a distance of about four hundred miles west by northwest—it is a high Prairie, treeless and flat as a table top. It is like your Wyoming, or Kansas, but perfectly level, and the climate is—"

"The best in the world!"

"Like California," nodded Fu Cheng, who had a sense of humor, "according to Californians. A highway runs from the wall through the Great Kinghan Mountains, and beyond there you can strike across the plain along the route I will give you, outlined on a map. You should be In Chagan in five days after leaving the wall."

The two white men looked up in surprise. Four hundred miles in five days, even by a fast camel, was impossible—if there were mountains to cross.

"I would advise," explained the merchant, "hiring a light car in Peking. The rent of the car will be paid by me; you can leave the money I give you as preliminary payment on deposit with the automobile company as security for the return of the car. I will give you a hundred dollars in American currency now, and as much again when you bring me the signed receipt of the friend to whom I am sending the box, in Chagan."

"Better say a hundred now and three hundred later," suggested Warner. "I will have to take Mr. McMahon with me to drive the car and make repairs."

To this Fu Cheng assented after a moment's thought, and Mac had much ado to restrain a whistle of delight. He wanted to whisper to Warner not to say anything more, lest Cheng change his mind. But his friend looked thoughtful.

"I take it there will be some danger in it, for us?" he observed.

Fu Cheng nodded promptly, and asked if either of the white men were married—whether they had close friends or dependants in China, or were known to the American consuls. To all of these questions Warner responded in the negative. Then the Chinese admitted frankly that the mission was dangerous, because the article they would take was valuable, and his enemies in Pekin would know that he had sent it. Attempts would be made to harrass the messengers, and to steal the box.

"Then why do you trust us with it?" demanded Warner quickly.

Fu Cheng spread out his hands and smiled. Two Americans, bound presumably on their own business, would be allowed to go, especially in a car, where Chinese might be—killed by Fu Cheng's enemies. "You have weapons, I assume," he concluded, "and once out on the plain in your motor you will be able to go faster than any pursuer."

For the first time Mac spoke up. He liked Fu Cheng's manner and way of doing business. Warners hesitation annoyed him. "Look here, Mr. Cheng, this is all right with me. Get that? If Warner backs down I'll do the job and glad of it."

A sharp glance from his friend silenced him, and Warner considered a moment. "To whom is the—box, consigned?"

"To my old acquaintance, Mr. Li Yuan Kow. No street address is necessary. There is," Cheng's fine eyes twinkled, "only one street in Chagan and one Li Yuan Kow. Do you accept the mission, Mr. Warner?" He did not look at Mac.

"Yes, if I may ask one question." As Cheng assented readily, the American asked quickly. "Has Kow a car?"

"*Pu chih tao*," said the merchant, explaining, as he perceived he had spoken in colloquial Chinese, "I do not know." Mac thought he seemed a little puzzled by his companion's irrelevant question.

"Then we will deliver the package," Warner agreed.

Whereupon Cheng struck a small gong hanging by his head and in a moment the clerk appeared, bearing with him an oblong box about a foot long, half as wide, and some four inches high. It was done up in heavy rice paper bound with supple-reeds knotted in an intricate fashion. These were sealed in one place by red wax, stamped with a signet, the pattern of which resembled, Mac thought, a bird like a crow.

Warner glanced at this seal twice and took the package. It weighed several pounds and Cheng suggested that Warner carry it to the hotel in the typewriter case he had brought to the merchant's house, leaving the typewriter to be sent around later.

"I do not want you to be seen carrying the box from my house," he pointed out, and Warner, agreeing to this,, signed the merchant's receipt for a package, contents unknown.

Warner took out the small typewriter, and placed within the empty case—which was of the portable variety with a handle—the package Cheng handed him. Then the clerk gave him a hundred dollars in American bills. As they were leaving the shop he asked to see the automobile that had been damaged in the collision recently, explaining that his friend, McMahon, was an expert mechanic and might be able to repair it for the merchant.

Shaking his head doubtfully, Fu Cheng took them to the garage opening into a court at the rear of the shop, where two cars were standing. One, a big touring car, was in good condition; the other, a roadster, was hopelessly smashed, as Mac saw at a glance.

"It's a job for a half-dozen new parts, Mr. Cheng, and a month's time. Was it a head-on smash?"

While the merchant was making clear that the roadster had been struck a glancing blow by the other car and had swerved against a stone wall, McMahon noticed in a dark corner of the court by some packing boxes, a figure that he thought he recognized. When they were back in the hotel room he mentioned this to Warner.

"That flash guy, the one I handed a sock to, was hanging around Cheng's garage."

"And followed us here," was the reply.

* * * *

Fu Cheng had pointed out that their best course was to leave Pekin for the wall and the west as soon as possible. So McMahon spent a contented afternoon selecting a car for the trip, putting up the money by way of surety, and buying equipment from the automobile company and a general store where Cheng had asked him to order what he needed and charge the things to him.

It was a pleasant task indeed for the mechanic who had wandered, broke, into the city that morning. He had the car and took his purchases home with him—canvas, ropes, tools, three spare tires and tubes with a pump. Also large tins for gasoline and oil. Also a demijohn for water.

For himself and Warner he took a pair of heavy corduroy jackets, gloves, and blankets. For food he had a good stock of American canned goods, coffee, evaporated milk, sugar, and a good-sized box of *pao ping*— thin bread cakes. Meat, rice and fruit he knew could be purchased on the way. He added a kettle, fry pan arid two tin plates. Finally he indulged in a shave and a box of fifty first-rate Manila cigars which he succeeded in charging to Cheng.

Satisfied with what he had done and feeling hungry, he made his way back to the hotel where he found Warner sitting in his shirt sleeves by the open window, the paper bound package on his knees: On the cot, amid a clutter of newspaper clippings, a compass, and field glasses, was a Colt forty-five, loaded and well oiled. Mac surveyed it with appreciation. "Where's mine?" he asked.

Warner glanced at his companion quizzically. "You've got us in for this thing, Mac. I was half-minded to decline Cheng's offer, when you said you'd go through with it anyway. If you had, you'd have been uncommonly good buzzard meat out in the Gobi in five days."

Mac shook his head. "First you say Cheng is square, then you make out he's crooked."

"He's merely Chinese—like his store, that has the worst things on view in the windows and the best things hidden away where nobody sees 'em."

But the mechanic was convinced that his friend was wrong. What could be fairer than the way Cheng had treated them—two strangers? No, the Chinese were good Americans, up-to-date and business-like. The talk about feuds and trickery was the bunk.

He was more sure of this when Cheng's clerk looked in at their room that evening, after supper, to return the typewriter and deliver the map the merchant had promised. Also a message to the effect that they could get petrol at a town a hundred miles out from the wall (indicated in the map) and that they should watch out for marauding bands of Mongols in the Gobi.

The clerk said good-by very politely and went out. Mac listened to his steps dwindling down the corridor, and yawned. His own labors were ended some time since: the car with its load was waiting in a side alley, and Warner had not offered to assist. He had sat smoking in the chair, and now showed no signs of turning in. Mac was sleepy and a little irritated.

"You didn't strain yourself, helping me with the stuff, Bob, but it's all fixed now. What you been doing?"

"Thinking."

Mac grunted. "Forget Cheng. We're in four hundred bucks. Ain't that enough for you? What's eating you?"

"I don't know."

The mechanic swore under his breath, and Warner looked up sharply, his reddish beard jutting out.

"Wonder what's in the box?" muttered Mac, stretching himself out on the bed.

"We'll know in a few minutes—as soon as we open it." Warner rose, moved the one chair in front of the keyhole after locking the door, and hung his coat on the back of the chair. Then he produced several lengths of reed cords, similar to those that bound the box. These he laid on the table beside the box, and pulled down the shade, turning up the gas jet full at the same time. Mac sat up, no longer drowsy.

"Listen, kid," he observed after a minute. "I know darn well you're boss of this outfit, but I got a hunch. It will be unlucky to open that box." As Warner proceeded calmly to work the seal loose with the blade of a pocket knife, he added, "It ain't square to Cheng to do it."

CHAPTER III
THE CROSS-BOW

Robert Warner had taken Tim McMahon under his protection because he knew that if the mechanic was not looked after he would suffer inevitably at the hand of the young citizen of Pekin whom he had struck in Donkey Meat Street. Warner could not explain this to McMahon. He had come to like the sandy-haired wanderer.

McMahon, however, had been a law to himself for years. Naturally, he did not relish being given orders that he did not understand. In hardship or a fight he would stick by a friend as long as he lived. But when everything was peaceful on the surface, he would grouch like the ex-soldier he was, at being told to do things that seemed unnecessary.

So Warner, being wise, left the table and the package, still unopened, and sat down on the cot by his companion, drawing out his packet of cigarettes.

"It's time," he said quietly, "that we understood each other. Mac. I know that we are in danger this minute. We may not leave this room alive. You can't see it, of course. I've got to make you see it, so we can work together without a hitch."

McMahon accepted a cigarette without comment. They were in a locked room in a good hotel under European management; under their window a trolley car jangled. They were safe enough, he reasoned. Why not?

Reaching up to the wall, Warner took down the ancient cross-bow. Its hard teak had withstood the wastage of time, and the crude iron catch and winder had been carefully cleaned and oiled. The salesman produced a short, heavy arrow, and fitted it into the groove, explaining that he had made it himself out of a small javelin head—another curio—and a long screw driver.

Interested in spite of himself, McMahon watched his friend wind up the bow with a wooden lever and set the catch, so that a touch on the trigger would release the bolt. Then he laid it down carefully on the cot, its head pointing toward the locked door. "Might come in handy, especially if we had some more bolts. It's a repeater. Do you know that bow—the parts I haven't had made over—is a thousand years old? The Chinese used these weapons at a time when our ancestors were scrapping with iron swords and leather shields. And they are still wiser than we are—if we only knew it."

The blue eyes of McMahon went to the Colt the salesman carried, and his friend saw the glance. "They have better weapons than that."

"You'll have to show me."

"They'll attend to that." Warner's beard bristled in a grin. "Your Donkey Meat Street friend trailed us to Cheng's, and then to this hotel. He must have seen you loading up the car. But there were too many people standing around watching, of course, for him to do anything to you then." He rubbed his forehead thoughtfully. "Cheng knows that something is up. He showed it in two ways—drawing out of us that we had no friends in Pekin who would miss us if we didn't turn up again; and by doubling his offer so quickly, provided payment was made *when we come back*. For some reason he thinks it's a good risk that we won't show, up to collect."

A slight sound in the corridor made him pause, and he went on in a whisper. "Cheng sent his clerk around to see if we—and the box—were still intact. Clever chap, Cheng—I remember his name appearing in the San Francisco papers once. I used to hold down a reporter's job with the *Bulletin*. As soon as we open the box, I'm going to dig into those old clippings"—he nodded toward the litter on the cot. "Perhaps Cheng knows that young gunman is camping on your trail; perhaps he knows there's a string tied to this mission of the Gobi trip. Anyway, he's held something back, and I'm going to make sure of what he has given us to deliver." He looked at the mechanic squarely. "I promised Cheng to take his property to Li Yuan Kow, and I will. I didn't say I would not look at it."

Mac nodded slowly. "That seems fair. Go to it, Bob."

"Good. Shut the window, please, and watch the door for me." As Mac obeyed, Warner finished removing the seal, which cracked in the process, and—after studying the knots a moment—slashed off the thongs with his knife.

The rustle of paper had not ceased before the key that they had left in the door fell to the floor matting without attracting their attention. It could not be seen, as Warner's coat was in the way.

When the layers of rice papers were removed a strongly made box of polished black teak was revealed to the two Americans.

"Damn!" exclaimed Warner. "A puzzle box."

The surfaces were all covered with beautifully carved figures of animals, and in the center of what might be the top was a circle containing a replica of the raven that appeared on the seal. But not a trace of keyhole, crack or hinge was visible. It seemed to be a square of solid wood, smelling strongly of some spice.

"It's hollow, because something is loose inside. I've worked out a number of these things before, and—yes, this chap works by mechanism." Warner had been tapping it all over with his closed knife. "One place doesn't sound like the rest. That's where the spring and catch are fastened to the wood. Now to find what operates the catch."

Patiently he began to push and tug with two fingers at each raised figure on the wood. The smell of spice became stronger. The air in the room was close and McMahon's eyes grew heavy, in spite of his determination to watch the door while his friend worked.

Once the mechanic started up, at an exclamation of irritation from Warner who was intent on his task. Mac's sleep-drugged eyes turned toward the door and observed vaguely that the room had changed in one detail. The coat had fallen from the back of the chair.

He saw this, and told himself that he should tell his companion. When he opened his mouth to speak he discovered that he could not utter a sound. In spite of his efforts, his eyes began to shut, as if an invisible hand were drawing the lids together.

The room seemed to Mac to be full of rosy colors; the dim form of the salesman swelled to enormous size. He observed that puffs of brown smoke came through the keyhole in regular succession and formed a kind of pall over the cot. The hotel must be on fire.

This thought filled Mac, curiously, with great amusement. The hotel was on fire and Warner could never escape out of the window, he had grown so large! He chuckled, without a sound. Of course, the red glow was the reflection of the fire. What had Warner told him? To use the cross-bow. Why, whoever had heard of putting out fire with a cross-bow a million years old!

The fire smelled very pleasantly of spice. McMahon waited in delightful suspense until the flames should touch him.

* * * *

From a vast distance he heard the voice of his friend.

"Mac! I've got it. Now—what in blazes? Mac!"

He was conscious of being lifted and carried out of the roseate glow— of hearing the window open. Then cooler air struck his face, and he saw the row of street lights under him. Mac wondered if he were flying—an exhilarating feeling. He laughed, and this time heard the sound of it.

"Hotel's on fire, Bob—see the smoke?"

"Steady, Mac, as you were." Warner's face was anxious as he peered back into the clouded room and saw that his coat had disappeared from the chair and that puffs of brown vapor were coming through the keyhole. "Can you stand? Wake up, man, they're after us!"

Slowly Mac planted his feet and rose, gripping the window ledge. Warner had been holding him out over the sill. His motions were awkward and his lips still twitched with reasonless laughter, but the red glow was fading from the room. Passing his hand across his eyes, he saw Warner step to the cot, catch up the cross-bow and press the catch, sending the iron bolt through the thin panel of the door over the keyhole. An exclamation from the corridor, then the *pad-pad* of slippered feet, then silence.

A revolver shot would have brought a crowd to their door, and this was the last thing Warner wanted just then. He kicked his coat aside, picked up the key, unlocked the door and looked up and down the hall. It was quite empty. Directly under him lay a kind of wand made of strong iron wires twisted together and bent slightly at one end—evidently the implement that had been passed through the keyhole to remove his coat.

Coughing, although the fumes were clearing from the bedroom, he made his way back to the mechanic, who was examining the box.

"How do you feel now, Mac?"

"Grand, my boy! I can't stop"—with a chuckle—"laughing. What's in the box?"

Together they bent over it. An irregular segment had come out of the top, and through the opening came the strong spicy odor. Within was a single object that gleamed brightly.

"Gold!" said Mac, stifling a giggle.

"In the shape of a hand. That's strange." Warner frowned. "Don't touch it. If it's gold, it's harmless; still—we must leave this place."

They looked at the gleaming hand in the black cavity and both men felt a sudden sense of repulsion. Warner believed this aversion came from the scent in the box. Mac shivered slightly as the lid was fitted back, clicking sharply into place. "It's unlucky!" he said.

When the teak box had been put into the typewriter case, and the suitcase packed and closed, and their coats caught up, Warner threw the cross-bow bolt under the cot, with the bulk of the newspaper clippings, stuffing the remaining clippings into his pockets, and sniffing the air dubiously.

"The place is quiet, Mac. Certainly there was no fire. Judging by the smell of the smoke we were being doped by burning *hasheesh*—the fumes blown through a tube into the room. That was what gave you the laughing fit. The man or men outside were Chinese, no doubt of that. You were nearer the door and sleepy, I guess. When they had put us both into dreamland, they could have forced the door easily. And," he smiled wryly, "my Colt would have been as much use to us as a bucket of water."

"God, I'm thirsty," muttered the mechanic. "I don't know what you're talking about."

"Whoever was in the corridor is not far away. Stick by me, and when we reach the machine start it up at once, and get going. Do you understand that?"

Locking the door after him, Warner led Mac out into the hall, and down the stairs to the lobby. Leaving the key with the drowsy night clerk he said briefly that he would be away for two weeks. No one else was in the lobby, and the side alley where the light touring car stood appeared deserted.

"Now for it!"

* * * *

The alley developed life as the two men ran out to the waiting car. Shadows moved toward them from the rear of the hotel, voices clucked, and when Warner tried to thrust Mac into the front seat, the slapping of feet on the cobbles became audible.

But Mac caught up a crank from the driver's seat and wrenched free from his companion's grip. "She starts with a crank, Bob." Feeling his way to the front of the engine, his feet moving unsteadily—for his head was still swimming and the night was red before his eyes—he braced himself and jerked the engine into throbbing life.

A shot was fired at them from the alley. Warner's Colt answered almost in the same instant and for a brief space smoke and spitting flame rent the quiet. Mac calmly climbed into the driver's seat and pulled down the gear shift. "Bus starts for Chagan," he shouted. "All aboard, Bob. Whoop—"

The windshield crashed under the impact of a bullet, and a spare tire exploded as McMahon stepped on the cut-out. Warner swung into the seat beside him, and the car, gaining speed, turned out of the alley. At once the shooting ceased, Mac released the cut-out, and they darted through the lighted streets, under Warner's directions, in silence except for the muffled tapping of the engine valves.

"You pass cars to the left, not to the right, Mac," he warned. "And," as the driver kept glancing over his shoulder, "don't worry about traffic cops. There aren't any."

CHAPTER IV
THE GREAT WALL

Within an hour they had left the city wall behind and were on the main highway to the west, almost deserted at that hour. The road was good, and Mac was able to average over twenty-five miles an hour with the heavily-loaded car; so when the sky paled behind them and the world took on color and form they drew up at a large village near the Kalgan gate of the great wall that guards the heart of China from the desert country.

Mac felt that they had left any pursuit far behind them, but his companion pointed silently to the telegraph poles that stood beside the highway. There would be a detachment of soldiers at the Kalgan gate, and they must pass through the wall without delay.

"Here's a tea shop"—pointing to what looked like a combination pig and chicken farm centered around a rambling wooden shack—"and you'd better get some, while I see if the local telegraph office is open yet or not. It's probably closed, and if so, we're all right."

"Tea—hell! Say, can't we cook up a shot of Java, while the bus is cooling off?" The radiator of the car, in fact, was steaming. In that season on the flat, lowland of Pekin, the night was almost as hot as the day, and the road was thickly carpeted in dust.

"No." Warner glanced at the mechanic appraisingly and went off, followed by a queue of half-naked urchins and snarling dogs. Others gathered around the car to gaze at the "no-horse cart" and the foreign devil who dismounted therefrom stiffly and went to the inn to return presently with a pail of muddy water. This water Mac strained two or three times, giving the watching children the instant impression that he was making magic in a foreign devilish way.

When the pail had been emptied of all but dregs into the radiator, Mac climbed to his seat, crossed his arms on the steering wheel, laid his head on his arms and was asleep at once.

He wakened at Warner's touch, and blinked blood-shot eyes.

Ding-dong—ding-dong-ding! Rusty bells chimed monotonously, and dust swirled around the machine. The air was permeated by a stringent animal odor. Beside him an endless line of laden camels was moving past him, a caravan bound for the Mongolia trail. It was broad daylight, the sun well above the horizon.

"A message came through ahead of us," said Warner anxiously. "The telegrapher has gone to deliver it, and the coolie helper at the office couldn't read—good luck for us. For a penny he let me look over the copies of recent despatches for Cock Crow Post City—that's this village. One of 'em was an order to the officer in command of the gate guards to hold up any foreigners until further instructions were brought by car from Pekin. I'm not quite sure of the wording, but I read enough of the official language to gather that much."

He considered a moment. Evidently their enemies in Pekin had influence, and money—equally important. In that case bribery would not help the white men. Haste, too, was imperative, if a car was on the road behind them.

"Give me a pill, fellow," muttered Mac, arriving at a decision simultaneously with his friend. "We got to crash this gate."

Warner nodded. They must reach the wall before tidings of their arrival in the village could spread as far as the gate by rumor's invisible telegraph. "If the doors are open," he conceded. "They are built of wood and iron four inches thick and locked with a bar that weighs about a ton. I think the head of this caravan will be passing through by now—"

"Leave it to me."

Mac went along by the camels, the car half-hidden in the haze of dust. When he could see the loom of the thirty-foot wall, he speeded up. The great gates of Kalgan were open.

Without sounding his horn. Mac held the car on the edge of the road, almost grazing the snarling and grunting beasts. When they were a hundred yards from the arch, he saw men in gray uniform run out and stand in the highway, waving their arms and shouting at him.

They were a dozen yards from the high arch when an officer wearing a sword stepped in front of the car, brandishing a yellow paper. Mac stepped on the accelerator.

The officer jumped in among the camels, and the soldiers rushed back to the guardhouse, barely escaping the fenders of the car. Before they could return with rifles, Mac had side-swiped a camel, gone down into the ditch, swerved back into the ruts of the road and passed under the arch.

A wild clamor from the bells, a shouting of men, and a thick, impenetrable cloud of dust. They were through the great wall.

* * * *

Head that dried up the sweat that soaked through their shirts. The glare of a mid-summer sun on a dry, caked plain. Ruts, worn deep by the wheels of wooden carts. Dust that sifted into eyes, ears and throat—

Without stopping that day except to replenish the gasoline tank from the spare tins, McMahon nursed the light car along over a trail where ten miles an hour was speeding. He had been without sleep for forty hours, and doped into the bargain. Sometimes he sank into a half-doze, waking mechanically at some obstacle, or at a warning jolt from the front wheels.

Warner could not have kept awake and did not. Once when the radiator was boiling, Mac turned aside under a plane tree. "Sufferin' hell cats," he muttered, "who said this was Kansas and Wyoming? It's Southern California in the dry season! You get your sleep, Bob"—as Warner, aroused by the halt, started up—"nothing's happened except the engine is almost as hot as we are. I'm going to make me some Java. Won't be long."

He ransacked the back of the car for the new kettle and the two pint-size tin cups. Dumping a double fistful of ground coffee into the kettle, he crawled under the radiator and unscrewed the pet-cock, letting a quart or so of scalding water shoot down into the kettle.

Then, sitting on the running board, he fell to pouring the brown fluid from the kettle into the cups and back, over the coffee grounds until he had a hot liquid, tasting of iron rust more than coffee. He drank a cup of this, shook Warner up to give him one, tossed the kettle back into the car and started off.

Now he could see a blue line of peaks on the western horizon—the Kinghan Mountains—and during the afternoon he crawled nearer, passing among the villages of the foothills. By twilight he was guiding the car up winding grades, and over stone bridges standing shakily across rock gullies. Before long he sniffed the familiar scent of pines, and felt that the air was cooler. Setting his jaw, he kept on until the huts by the roadside thinned out, and the mountain slopes closed in. Although he was passing alone up the higher levels of a deserted road, it seemed to Mac as if the forest on either hand were alive. Although it was dark, he could see rivers rushing through the chasms.

But these were not phantoms inspired by drugs. Mac's eyes were fatigued to the limit, and the illusions were bred of tortured optic nerves. Aware of this, he forced himself to center his attention on the strip of light cast by the headlights along the rough road.

Up and up the car climbed, the chill of higher altitude keeping down the heat of the laboring engine. Then, when he was barely crawling forward, Mac fancied that a wide highway, lighted by a double row of arc lamps appeared under his front wheels—a smooth, inviting street, wide as Fifth Avenue. He started to press the accelerator, but, warned by some latent sense of danger, jammed on the brakes instead.

He passed his hand over his hot forehead, looked, and shivered. The avenue had disappeared. The trail here made a turn, and the front wheels of the car were halted at the edge of the cliff. In the distance, above the trees he could see the crimson streak that was the last of the late mid-summer sunset.

"Can't be that! I'm seein' things." He reached swiftly back for his heavy mackinaw and a blanket, and nudged Warner, who sat up, alert, at once. "I'm through. Don't call me, boy, until you've got the breakfast cooked. And say, make it bacon and biscuits and boiled coffee. Get me?"

"Great Scott almighty!" breathed his companion, observing the glow in the western sky. "You've reached the pass in the Kinghan!"

"So?" Mac grinned. "Well, you can take it from me that other car won't reach us tonight." With that he pulled the blanket around him, lay down, rolled himself up in it within a hollow filled with pine needles and lost interest in the world.

CHAPTER V
ROBERT WARNER

Two days passed before the white men had a chance to replace on the package the seal, broken in the hotel in Pekin. The night after descending the western slope of the Kinghan range they spent at an inn in the village where—as Cheng had assured them—gasoline and oil was secured to fill up the spare tins. But at such inns privacy is unknown, and it was only after another day's run over the tableland of the Gobi that they could make camp and take out the teak box.

During this day they had left the Mongolia trail and headed out across the first plain, steering by compass. Here Cheng's prophecy proved to be true, for they found themselves alone on a vast, brown, bare prairie, where the air was crisp and cool and the white clouds seemed to hang directly over their heads—so great was the altitude.

Although they used the field glasses that afternoon, they could see no indication of any car following their trail. The air was remarkably clear and any landmark on the plain stood out with startling distinctness. When they camped that night it was with the conviction that they had shaken off pursuit, for the present, at least. Warner, however, took care that the car was halted in a hollow where the small fire that they made out of wood bought in the last village would not be visible. And they rigged up the canvas shelter, stretched out from the car top so that it almost covered the flames.

When dinner had been cooked and eaten, and the dishes washed in warm water from the radiator, and Warner's pipe and Mac's cigar were glowing, they inspected the teak box silently. From it, more faintly in the open air, came the familiar odor of spice that repelled them so strangely.

"I vote," said Warner after a while, "we do it up without looking at the thing inside?"

"It's gold, ain't it?"

"Probably not. It looks like gold. But if it were, it would be a whole lot heavier than it is. Plate, likely."

"Then, let's get it over with. Don't open it again, Bob. My hunch was right—the thing's bad luck to us. Look what happened when you opened it up the first time!"

He watched with interest while Warner carefully gathered together the pieces of the seal and laid them aside. Then the salesman wrapped the paper around the box, tied it with the new reeds, knotted roughly as before.

This done, he heated a spanner taken from the tool-box of the car in the embers of the fire, placed the portions of the seal in place, face down on a little mound of moistened, sandy earth and heated the reverse side with the red hot spanner.

When the wax softened a trifle, Warner dropped the spanner and pressed the bound box on the reverse of the seal where it would adhere to a crossing of the reeds. After a moment he turned the box over and inspected it. The seal was stuck in place, the cracks obscured by the softened wax— the image of the raven a trifle blurred, but still visible.

"Fair enough," commented Mac. "You've done that before. You ain't a salesman, Bob, any more 'an I am a stenographer. What's your real line?"

Before answering, Warner took the package on his knees and seemed to be studying the seal. "A man has to have some business in this world, Mac. He must be able to say he's a brick-layer or a broker when people ask questions. And they do. Besides, selling typewriters enables me to go places I want to."

"Uh-huh. What are you—a detective?" Warner laughed. "Not at all. I'm a collector."

"Bugs?" Mac was surprised.

"In a way, yes. I pick up queer things out of life."

"How d'ye mean, queer?"

"Well, I used to paint and read a bit; then I worked for city editors; used to wander all over the map. In nineteen-seventeen, I wandered into the intelligence department of the A. E. F. Gave me a taste for the world. The only fun a man gets in life is finding out things. I've always hankered after the queer things—suppose you'd call them horrible. But I wouldn't trade my experiences of the last years for a gold mine. Secrets have turned up that never will be told about in books—

"Take the case of Cheng," he broke off, thoughtfully. "Here's the gold, or rather gilded image of a human hand, sent by Cheng, a wealthy Pekin merchant, to a friend, by two white men—you and me, Mac. A Chinese *never entrusts his affairs to foreigners*, without a special reason. What was Cheng's reason?"

He felt in his pockets and emptied out bunches of newspaper clippings on the box. "We'll look for that paragraph that appeared in San Francisco ten years ago. Hm. It was something about a woman, I believe—I have it!"

While Mac put the last of the wood on the fire, and the flames leaped up, Warner studied the clipping. "Fu Cheng, curio merchant, was tried by the city authorities for smuggling into the country a female slave, from China. The Salvation Army people actually obtained speech with the girl, who was young and extremely pretty. She claimed that she had been kidnapped from her home in China, and forced by Cheng's agents to come to him in America. After that interview she could not be found, so the case fell through from lack of evidence. No one to appear against Cheng, you see. It was shown that he had bought and sold slaves in the past, but nothing definite could be proved against him."

"Slave merchant," muttered Mac.

"Probably. What bearing has that on this box?" Warner surveyed it curiously. "That seal bears the raven token. The ancient Chinese believed that the raven was a bird of evil omen. Its presence foreshadowed danger."

"It sure did," assented Mac heartily. "Why did you ask him to show me his car?"

"Wanted to see if his machine had actually been damaged in the collision, as the newspaper reported. Remember the news clipping? It was correct, but I don't think it was a full report. For instance, the explosions of the exhaust were more than likely shots. While he talked to us I had a vague idea he was sending us with some unpleasant surprise for the man who ran into him. Accidents don't happen in Pekin—they are made to happen. That was why I asked if Kow had a car, and Cheng forgot himself and answered in Chinese, before he thought. Granting that a feud existed between Cheng and Kow—but Cheng wouldn't send his enemy any gold. Damn! I half see the whole thing!"

"You're a nut about that, Bob." Mac cast the stub of his cigar into the fire. "Just because a merchant gives us a piece of business, and I have a hop dream in the hotel, you start collectin' bugs."

Warner shaded his eyes from the glare of the fire, and replaced the clippings in his coat. Thrusting the box under his knees, he said thoughtfully, "Unless I'm mistaken, this piece of business, as you say, is going to be a ghastly surprise." As he spoke his hand flew up and the heavy Colt appeared. "For one thing, you might look behind the fire, there."

Aroused by the change in his friend's voice, Mac sprang up, and saw, outlined against the stars, a circle of horsemen about their camp. He had not heard them come up, but now one of them advanced slowly to the car and stared at Warner curiously.

It was a squat old man, with a wrinkled, good-humored face, and garments that were a medley of deerskin and soiled wool. He smelled strongly of sheep and camel and carried at his back a long pole from the end of which hung a lassoo.

"Sai-bei-nah," he said, or rather croaked. Warner lowered his weapon and seemed relieved. "Mongols," he explained to Mac. "Desert men. Harmless, but curious. They've come to look us over. Let them—they won't steal anything."

In fact the nomads, who must have been attracted by the glow of the brightened fire, drew nearer, to stare for a half-hour at the camp and the two white men. Then, as if satisfied, they galloped off, laughing and shouting.

But Warner, using his glasses, believed that they halted for the night a short distance away. "This is our last night out, Mac," he observed. "We'll be in Chagon tomorrow, a day ahead of time. We'd better take spells on guard."

Nothing, however, happened before dawn. When the car got into motion again, shortly after sunrise, the Mongol riders showed up again and raced the white men for a mile or so over the prairie before pulling up.

* * * *

By noon they had covered more than half of the eighty-odd miles that had separated them from Chagan. Then they sighted the gray car.

Rains had freshened the Gobi here, turning the grassland green. The ground, too, rose and fell in long, gentle slopes that made the white men think of swells upon a motionless sea. The other car, appearing over one of the crests a mile away on their right, had been going in the opposite direction; now it changed its course and headed toward them.

They quickened the pace of the light touring car. No sooner had they done so than the long, gray machine began to glide over the prairie, rocking from side to side gently and bobbing over obstacles, as if it were a schooner entering a mild head sea.

By using the glasses Warner made out, in the clear air, that the other was a limousine type—an open seat for the chauffeur and a closed compartment at the rear; that two men sat in the driver's seat, and one carried a long rifle.

At this time Mac had coaxed his motor to a speed registered on the instrument board at thirty miles an hour and Warner was forced to hold on to remain in his seat. "Can you get ahead of him?" he asked. "That's no pleasure car; it wants to hold us up."

Mac glanced fleetingly at the gray machine, gliding nearer on a tangent. "If it's what I think, Bob, it can run circles around us. If we keep on, it will cut in ahead of us."

Taking advantage of a dip in the ground where they were out of sight, Mac whirled the steering wheel and headed off at right angles, to the left. For a moment he could run along the bottom of the gully. When they came on the sky line again, the gray car speeded up, turning until it was directly behind them.

Mac pushed down on the accelerator and the four cylinder engine throbbed and knocked anew. Guiding it with an expert hand he tried every possible means of throwing the pursuers off their trail, only to see, as he shot over the long slopes, that the limousine was within gunshot and drawing nearer rapidly.

"I think it's slowing down!" exclaimed Warner. "Look out!"

Only for a second had Mac taken his eyes from the prairie ahead, but they topped a rise and plunged over a four-foot drop into a sandy pocket. Mac flung his weight on the wheel, and kept the front wheels steady at the impact by a miracle of skill. The car crashed, plowed forward, and slewed around, the racing engine roaring as the rear wheels slipped in the sand. The front tires jammed in a fissure and the engine stalled.

"Jump!" Mac yelled. "They'll come down on us!"

The two men left the car at the same instant and ran back, to peer over the low bank that had caused the disaster. The other machine, however, was slowing to a stop in a jerky fashion, a hundred yards away.

"Keep down," whispered Warner. "I'll watch," He had placed himself behind a clump of daisies, standing where the bank concealed all but the top of his head. He observed that the two men—Chinese—climbed from the driver's seat and stood gazing about as if trying to locate them. Then they moved to the engine hood of the limousine and began to talk excitedly.

"Can't make out their lingo—mixture of western Chinese and Mongol," Warner whispered. "But the radiator of their car is steaming all over. Certainly, they don't seem able to start it up"—as the driver of the gray car climbed back and did things to the controls without result. "The tall chap with the rifle is standing guard. Mac, get our machine going again, and take it where we can make a getaway. Then wait for me. We can't go on with that outfit loose behind us. I'm going to stick up the limousine."

Still with his eyes on the Chinese, Warner heard the mutter of Mac's engine behind him, heard it draw away and quiet down. Waiting a moment, he climbed over the bank and walked forward, his Colt in hand.

At once the thin rifleman dropped on one knee, stuck into the ground in front of him a forked staff attached to the barrel of his weapon, and, steadied by this rest, took aim at the white man, fifty yards away.

There was something disconcerting and business-like in the steadiness of the rifle that warned the white man to halt where he was; moreover the rear of the limousine, although showing no signs of life, might be tenanted. Then, watching narrowly, he saw the head of the Chinese shift toward his left, and the rifle barrel waver.

"Carry on, buddy," Mac's voice reached him. "I've got a good, shiny jack from the tool box. At this distance the Chink doesn't know if it's a Luger or a sawed-off machine-gun. Make 'em yell kamerad!"

"Sai-bei-nah!" shouted Warner, using the only Mongol phrase he knew. "Good day!" He held up his left hand, and advanced a few paces.

The rifleman seemed undecided, but the Chinese chauffeur climbed down and spoke to him earnestly. Warner caught the words, "Inglis devil." Reluctantly the other nodded and motioned Warner to advance—which he had been doing all the while. Coming up to the gray car, and hearing Mac's step at one side, he signed for the tall Chinese to lay his weapon on the ground and step back, which was done. Then he made the chauffeur of the gray car go over to his companion. "Look into the tonneau, Mac—carefully."

A moment and Mac swore roundly. "Just as I thought, an American twin-six. But I'm damned if it ain't more like a tank. Machine-gun stand by the driver's seat—no gun on it, though. Good thing for us, I'll say. Get wise to those steel shutters. What are those straps for?"

Warner, out of the corners of his eyes, saw that the rear compartment of the big car was sheathed in steel shutters that could be moved up or down.

Outside, about three feet above the running boards dangled a series of short straps, clamped at the middle to each side of the car.

"Look in the tonneau," he said again impatiently. A pause.

"Come and look for yourself, fellow," remarked Mac presently. "Never mind those guys. They won't bite now."

The interior of the tonneau was finished in crimson broadcloth, and there was also a top light. In the darkest corner of the seat somebody sat, a slender somebody clad in blue silk tunic and trousers.

A girl it was, with blue-black hair knotted over each ear, a peony peering out of the coiled tresses. She sat very straight, looking out calmly at the white men, her cheeks a little flushed, or touched with the customary rouge.

"Why do you threaten me?" she asked angrily, in educated Chinese. "Foreign devils have no manners. Why is my no-man cart not going?"

Warner responded in his best Chinese. "What is your name?"

"If I tell you that," her slant eyes half-closed, "you must first show me your visiting card."

This was not an unusual request. People of any importance in what used to be called the Celestial Empire were expected to produce cards. Not to have one was equivalent to admitting that one was a shady character. Warner produced a card and the girl scanned it. She could read. That she was carefully brought up was shown by the fact that she did not raise her eyes to the faces of the white men, after that first startled glance.

Woman-like, instead of answering his question she asked another. "The desert Mongols brought word to Chagan that your car was coming. Why did you run away?"

"Why did you follow?" he smiled.

Her delicate lips drew together firmly. "From what place did you come?"

Warner explained that they were from Pekin, bringing to one Li Yuan Kow a gift from a friend. Did she know Mr. Kow, an honorable person of Chagan? He was surprised to see how she shrank back, as if he had struck at her. But her lips repeated readily that she knew the esteemed Mr. Kow of Chagan and would take the white devil to his home as soon as her servants could find out what had bewitched her no-man cart and make it go.

This said, she lifted a tiny fan and held it in front of her eyes. This was not coquetry—merely a sign that the interview was at an end. Mac, coming to his side, Warner closed the door.

"This is some sport model, fellow," remarked the mechanic. "While you was chinning the lady I talked some with the sho-fer, pidgin brand, and a little of that. The car's a cross between a town-model limousine and a tank. Those shutters are quarter-inch steel; and those slits are for the boys inside to unhitch their artillery through. Those straps are to hold a line of coolies on the running boards. The coolies carry gats, and there ought to be a machine gun on the stand, but it didn't arrive from Pekin. Can you imagine?"

"How did it get out here?"

"From the States, of course. Made to order for the owner. Must have set him back a few bucks."

"Who owns it?"

"The gun over there said Mr. Puchito."

"Pu chi tao," Warner grinned, "means 'I don't know,' and is usually a lie." He considered a moment. "What's wrong with it? Somehow I don't hanker to jog on into Chagan and leave this young lady loose."

Mac made a quick survey, tried the starter, looked into the carburetor and reported. "It's been treated something awful. Battery's down, although she's only gone a thousand miles. And—great, jumpin' wildcats!—she's *out of oil.*"

"Can you start it—take it into Chagan?"

"Sure," Mac grinned, "I'll take the lady in, if you want to follow in the jitney with these two wops sitting in your lap."

While the mechanic went after the other car, Warner explained matters to the lady of the limousine. "Miss Peony, your car is bewitched. My—er, man servant can drive out the devil that is in it, and make it go. I will tell him to do it, if you will lead me at once to Mr. Kow, and speak to nobody else."

From the depths of the tonneau came a muffled "Yes."

* * * *

Mac's system of counter-devilment consisted merely of pouring in about two gallons of oil from the spare tin of the touring car, and twirling the crank of the gray limousine until the powerful engine started up— uncertainly at first. The "sho-fer" looked chagrined. He had been given a few lessons in driving the car from the agent in Pekin, but had not bothered about anything except gasoline, as the untouched tool kit of the big car proved.

Meanwhile Warner had disposed of the rifleman and the native driver, hitching them up on separate running boards by the convenient straps. This done, the touring car was secured behind by a make-shift tow rope.

Guided by the tall Chinese they reached Chagan by mid-afternoon. It proved to be a rambling village of Mongol skin tents and thatched cottages on the edge of a small lake. Behind the village on rising ground was a sizable wooden house with a kind of pagoda roof. It had a garden of plane trees and rocks, and established its superiority to the average dwelling by the fact that the stables and the sheep folds were separated from the house.

The gray car wound around the lake—a pretty, reed-bordered spot—and the tall Chinese directed them to go to the larger house on the hill, where they stopped at the front entrance. Some women peered at them from latticed windows and two or three men servants trotted out, followed by the usual assortment of dogs. After Warner had released the two henchmen from their straps he asked the girl if this was Mr. Kow's house.

She nodded and said that she would take him to the master of the house.

Warner removed from the car the package Cheng had given him, and handed Mac the long rifle—a Russian piece, dating apparently from the Crimean War. "This place looks harmless, but keep your eye peeled until we've met Kow and passed him his box. Then we'll hike right out."

"It's a crime to leave that there twin-six to these heathen," grumbled the mechanic. "At least until I've taught 'em a little about its works."

"Save your brains, Mac," grinned Warner. "The minute you're gone they'll most likely burn paper prayers under it and the whole thing will go up in smoke."

Mac groaned and followed Warner and Miss Peony, as they called her, and the two retainers. They went through the rock garden instead of entering the house, and the Chinese girl stopped by a tall tree under which was a miniature edifice of stone built in a freshly dug bed.

"Where is Li Yuan Kow?" demanded Warner. "We have not come here to be tricked."

"My venerable father," responded the girl, raising her eyes to his, "is sleeping in the terrace of everlasting night. This is his illustrious grave."

The white man stepped back, and, after a moment's bewilderment, took off his hat. "I regret the misfortune of the daughter of the worthy Li Yuan Kow," he said gravely. "How long ago did your father go to his distinguished ancestors?"

"Fifteen days ago this sorrow came upon the house of Kow. I, unworthy, live alone in the house. My elder sister is not here. Did you say you brought a condolence gift to my father from a friend?"

"That is true." Warner remembered the package, and handed it to her. As she knelt to place it on the stones of the grave, and to open the wrappings, he thought that Cheng might have known of the death of his friend, and that the raven seal might have been placed on it as in keeping with the occasion. He watched curiously when Miss Peony held the black teak box, frowning a little.

She tried one or two ways of opening it, but in a moment more had discovered the catch that had caused Warner two hours mental stress. Lifting the cover she looked inside.

Suddenly she bent her head and gave a little cry. When he could see her face again it was white as tinted ivory, under the rouge, and her eyes were wide with horror. Her hands, rigid fingers bent, tore at her hair.

This silent manifestation of agony was more pitiful than any amount of screaming or wailing. Even Mac turned away eyes. Warner, seeing that Miss Peony was beyond speech, knelt to look again at the gold hand in the box—half-expecting to find something different.

Again the familiar odor of strong spice greeted him, and he touched the beautifully shaped hand with a tentative finger.

"God!" he cried, springing up. On the tip of his finger was a tiny particle of stuff the color of gold. The hand in the box had not felt like metal, and it was covered with gold leaf, very skilfully.

Then Miss Peony spoke to him. "Who sent this—gift?"

"Fu Cheng, of Pekin," he answered.

She bit her lip, trying to keep from showing her emotion before strange men. But her tongue would not be silent. "*Ai*—it is the hand of my sister! The hand of the pretty and virtuous Tsi Yan has been cut from her arm and sent to her father!" Suddenly she sprang up, her eyes flashing. "Dogs of Cheng! I will have you killed!"

CHAPTER VI

ONE OF THE NIGHTS OF THE GODS

"And now," calculated Mac, as they walked back to the car, "I guess you're thinkin' what a fine, dandy bit this is for your collection—hey?"

"I think," responded the adventurer gravely, "that I feel a lot meaner than one of the dogs down in the village."

"You said it."

"But not all of it, I've been blinder than a drunken mole. Great Scott—not to know mummified human flesh when I saw it! There are hundreds of bodies sitting up in the temples and vaults hereabouts, treated in some way, with spice among other things and covered from the air by gold leaf."

Mac shivered, and undid the tow-rope, casting it into the light car vindictively. For a moment he surveyed the long, gray car with genuine regret—a perfect example of the builder's art. He hated to leave it.

But they had no alternative. Already the girl of Li Yuan Kow and her attendant had disappeared into the house. Delay would be dangerous to the white men. No amount of explaining would save their faces in the eyes of Miss Peony. Why should she believe that they were not aware of what was in the package sent by Cheng? Or that they had run away from her car on the plain because another machine several days ago had been on their track? Or that they had bound her retainers and taken away the rifleman's weapon from motives of simple prudence?

"Well, let's go, then," he observed grudgingly. "We can have Cheng arrested."

"A mandarin merchant of his influence? On what charge?"

They could do nothing. Although neither man had doubted that the sorrowing girl had uttered the truth at the grave, they had no proof to offer in a law court. Even the hand was not in their possession.

They were morally certain that Cheng expected they would be killed in Chagan by the angered retainers of the Kows—possibly by Li Yuan Kow himself, for Cheng might not have known that the girl's father had died. But they had not the slightest proof of all this.

"We can beat him up, anyway," suggested Mac hopefully.

"You hit one Chinese once," said Warner grimly, "and you remember what came of it. Cheng would have the law on his side, if we laid hand on him—especially after signing the receipt for the package in his office. We would be lucky to get off with a heavy fine and not go on a personally conducted tour of the Pekin jails."

"Speaking of receipts—are you going back for one from Miss Peony, for her poor sister's hand? No? Well, neither am I! Why'n hell's blazes did Cheng send it out here?"

"Must have had a feud with Kow, after all. The slave merchant got hold of Kow's other daughter—maybe she was the one sent out to Frisco—and cut off her hand in revenge for something that Kow did to him. Shouldn't wonder if this gray limousine was the one that rammed Cheng's car. We couldn't drag the truth out of Miss Peony by torture. Only stress of emotion made her say what she did before us at the grave."

They climbed into their seats, and Mac began to back the car down the hill, watching the house the while for signs of hostile activity. But it remained silent, apparently untenanted. Halfway to the village, he stopped and laid the long rifle by the road. Warner was sunk in a brown study.

"Mac, do you see the deviltry of it? If we had not happened to meet Miss Peony out on the prairie, we would have driven up to the house and sent in the package, and cooled our heels for an hour or so on the threshold, until someone came and stuck a knife in our backs. Someone would have done it, too. I'd give anything for a chance to get back at Cheng."

The village was mildly occupied with its evening tasks—a herd of cattle was driven in from pasture by a barefoot girl astride a buffalo; several hunters, carrying long muzzle-loaders with wooden props on which were strung strings of geese and quarters of antelope, loitered by the lake side, gazing at the white devils in the no-horse cart; women, lumbering up from the water carrying armfuls of dripping cotton clothing, grinned at them. A pungent smell of smoke and cooking was in the air, and Mac sniffed, feeling very hungry and a little tired.

"Can't stop here," Warner observed, as the machine came to a stop. "We'll have to camp fifty miles out on the plain. I don't think the Chagan men can start the big car, but—"

"What's that bird over there doing?"

A Mongol was trotting toward them, riding with the effortless ease of a desert man raised in the saddle. The fingers of one hand held the reins lightly in front of his chest; his other hand held gingerly a square of white paper.

"Sai-bei-nah!" said Mac, on a sudden impulse, and pointed at the letter.

The thin, cracked lips of the Mongol gave forth some chuckling gutturals and he showed them the missive he carried, as he passed by, smiling like the child he was.

Both men in the car saw that the letter had a seal of heavy wax, stamped with the sign of the raven. They waited until they saw the rider head up the path toward the house of the dead Kow before driving on.

"That pony was fresh," said Warner reflectively. "Looked as if it had not come far."

He glanced back as they topped the first swell of the plain. Above the lake the mist of evening was gathering, and through it the setting sun gleamed red. On the surface of the water a crimson path extended from the sunset toward them, as if marking a trail of blood. For perhaps a half-hour they drove in moody silence. And then, when Mac reached down to switch on the lights, Warner stopped him with a gesture.

They were threading through the murk of a gully. On the skyline at one side was a ruined *caravanserai*—a rough enclosure of stones that had served as a stopping place for the caravans of a by-gone day, perhaps before Chagan had been built. From this a spiral of smoke ascended, penetrated by darting sparks. Beside the old wall was the bulk of a large motor car.

"Sufferin' cats!" grumbled Mac. "Do buses grow in this country?"

"Not by any means," whispered Warner. "That's why I'm curious enough to go and look at those people. Shut off the motor and wait here."

It was a simple matter, in the gathering darkness, to climb up to the rise, over the grassy slope, and—on hands and knees—to work his way to the stone wall, which was no higher than his waist. Crouching where he was for several moments, Warner made out that the men around the fire within the roofless enclosure were cooking supper, quite oblivious to his presence.

When he looked cautiously over the stones, the flames had gained strength enough for him to see six men squatting and lying near the fire. All were Chinese, although three wore European clothes; those in native dress were thin-faced, sharp-eyed fellows with rifles near their hands.

Two of those in modern dress were throwing dice on the bottom of an upturned pail. One of these was the pockmarked clerk of Fu Cheng—the one who had been so proud of his English; the other was the young sport Mac had affronted in Pekin.

Warner noticed that this individual wore over his sack coat a cartridge belt with a holster, from which peered the butt of a large caliber automatic. For some time he listened, trying to catch something in their conversation that would explain their presence in the Gobi. They spoke little, however, and then in a slang that was too much for his understanding.

Only once did one of the men glance at the stars that were glittering into life overhead and remark, "Tomorrow night is one of the nights of the gods."

Whereupon they all glanced at the youth, intent on the dice, who looked up sullenly. "Is it so?" A day of the gods was one marked by either good or evil omens, set apart often as a festival. "But tonight my luck is not good with the dice."

The clerk smiled. "Yang, the son of the wise Fu Cheng is always fortunate." After this they gave themselves over to dice or sleep, and Warner crawled away, taking the trouble to pass by the car outside the *caravanserai* entrance. It cost him some labor to retrace his way to where he had left his companion, but eventually Mac's voice hailed him softly.

Warner did not want to take the chance of starting the motor in the vicinity of the other party, but Mac solved this difficulty by letting the car slide back for several hundred yards, while Warner walked by it to feel for chuck holes. When they had put a knoll between them and the camp, the descent ended, and the adventurer described what he had seen.

"Fu Cheng's son and a friend, and Cheng's clerk with three armed retainers are up there. Also Cheng's touring car—the one we saw in the garage by the damaged machine. Yang—Cheng's hopeful—is the one who has a grudge against you."

Mac swore long and fervently. "D'ye mean," he ended up, "that that flash guy trailed me all the way out here to hand back my sock?"

"Probably not. I rather think he came expecting to plant flowers on your grave. Don't forget that we ought, by rights, to be corpses by now. Cheng wanted to avenge his son on you—which he couldn't do safely in Pekin—and to get in a knock at his enemy, Kow, at the same time. Mac, I'd stake a lot that Cheng's men made that attack on us in the hotel. The clerk fellow had been hanging around; when they saw us open the box they were afraid we would raise a row if we discovered that a woman's hand was in it. That was why this car chased us through the great wall. I wonder why it came out here—and why the hand was sent in the first place—"

"Bob, for the love of Peter, let's go up there and mop 'em up!"

"On what pretense?" Warner shook his head. "Those chaps are about as harmless and easy to handle as snakes. We've got one gun against six—"

"This Yang fellow must of sent the letter we saw delivered in Chagan."

"Right. And that means he has business with the girl—nothing benevolent, either, judging by the looks of their outfit, and the way they stick outside the village." Warner thought this over a moment. "Mac, you and I don't know beans about what's going on, but it's black and shameful work without the least doubt. The Kow faction has only Miss Peony and a scattering of minute men; Yang has automatics and repeating rifles. I think we'll have to go back to Chagan and investigate the merits of this row."

"Nothing," assented Mac heartily, "could be fairer than that."

"It's dam foolish and infernally danger—"

"Ain't that what you collect?" chuckled Mac. "Hop in."

* * * *

Not even Warner, who knew many things, expected what they discovered in the house of the dead Li Yuan Kow, at midnight.

They had maneuvered the car as near to the village as they dared, on the side of the—as it might be termed—mansion house. This was made easier by the lights that gleamed from every aperture of the large building. They had eaten a cold supper before leaving the machine, and made their way cautiously toward the dark stables. Although the house was brightly lighted, no one seemed to be moving within, and this apparent quiet was more suspicious than the wildest outcry. Warner, not liking to go ahead until he had investigated more carefully, had Mac help him to the roof of an outbuilding from which he could see into the second story of the house.

He saw that a kind of balcony or upper porch was screened in, and here the lights—candles, by the flickering shadows—were brightest. Through the slits in the bamboo screens and numerous breaks he could make out that somebody was seated in a chair; that this somebody was dressed in white and did not move, although he watched patiently; that a table top was visible on which stood the teak box he had brought with incense sticks smoking beside it.

"I don't like it," he whispered to Mac, coming down. "Servants asleep, apparently, all lights going, and one person—Miss Peony, in all odds—performing a real ceremony of some kind up there. Safest thing to do is to break into the upper room."

They searched in vain for a ladder, and finally Warner, disturbed by what he had seen, planted Mac against the corner of the building and climbed up on his shoulders. Holding to the fissures in the rough boards, he worked himself erect and found that he could reach the beam ends that projected through the wall at the upper floor.

Swinging himself up quickly, he got one knee over the projection and clutched at the hanging lattice. It came down with a splintering rustle, but he was able to seize the railing of the open room, and pull himself up to a level with the person within.

What he saw made him draw in his breath sharply. The girl he had christened Miss Peony sat facing him, clad in loose garments of white silk, on her small head an elaborate, towering head-dress with jade pendants hanging down each cheek. Her hands held a short, slender dagger and the breast of the white robe was stained with blood.

"Dog of Cheng," said the woman calmly, "when I heard you climbing upon the side of the house, I thought it was Yang, come to claim me ahead of his time. My hand was weak—"

"Daughter of Kow," interrupted Warner, "you must not strike yourself again. Tonight is one of the nights of the gods. Would you revenge yourself on your enemies, if you could?"

He had said the one thing that might arrest the attention of the girl. Her dark eyes glowed, but she sat erect in the chair, a pallid image of disdain. "The ignoble Cheng took my sister into slavery, and slew my father, the righteous Li Yuan Kow, at the end of the last moon. Now his son, Yang, is at Chagan with many men and guns. I cannot withstand him. Leave me, so that I may stand before the soul of my father with a clear face."

The *pad-pad* of slippered feet drew nearer the balcony. Warner thought quickly. The servants had been aroused by the noise of the falling lattice, and if they found him here they would attack him like so many wild beasts. He had his revolver, but knew how swiftly men like these could throw a knife.

"I can help you to drive away Yang and his men," he said. "Because Cheng tricked me, I have lost face. If I were the friend of Yang I would not be here. Order your servants to keep their distance!"

Several house boys had appeared in a doorway, drawing their knives with exclamations of anger at sight of the white man. Warner made no move to touch his revolver. Miss Peony watched him, swaying a little in her chair. "How could you help me?"

Warner did not know, exactly. Hesitation however, would be fatal. "No one except my friend can start your big no-horse cart. If you could use that against Yang, the issue would be even."

"That was why my honored father bought the foreign devil cart."

"True," nodded the white man, and added, "Order your boys not to use their weapons, and I will not harm them. There must be truce between us. I will tell you how I brought you the gift of Cheng, thinking it was gold, and you must tell me the story of the wrong done by Cheng. Do you agree?"

For a moment Miss Peony thought, a spasm of pain closing her eyes. Then she nodded and spoke a few words to her retainers. Warner gave a sigh of relief.

But it was not the girl who told him the story of the desert feud. She had cut herself deep under the arm, the knife blade catching against the upper ribs, and bleeding made her lose consciousness. An old woman bound up her hurt and began brewing some herbs to administer to her mistress. Reluctantly at first, she answered Warner's questions, and the house servants squatted down in the doorway scowling at him. Not until the white man had related all that happened in Pekin did the nurse confide in him.

* * * *

Centuries ago the nobles of the court of Pekin had been accustomed to send for women slaves to the province of Chagan, then well populated and noted for the beauty of its girl children. In time it became customary for the inhabitants of Chagan to give each year a quota of girls to the rulers of Pekin.

Among others, the ancestors of Fu Cheng, the merchant, had obtained women, and the fathers of Li Yuan Kow had given them. Even in the last century some slaves had been bought by merchants, and Fu Cheng insisted on this right as hereditary.

Some ten years ago, the merchant had sent men to carry off the elder daughter of Kow, who refused to agree to the old custom. Tsi Yan, the captive, was sent to San Francisco against her will. There Fu Cheng, taking a fancy to her, kept the girl instead of selling her. A year ago he returned to Pekin, and demanded that the headman of Chagan sell to him Miss Peony, his second daughter, who was much younger than her sister.

Kow—a well-to-do owner of sheep and cattle, tended by the Mongols— refused, and ordered the heavy motor car from the States. When it arrived in Pekin he went with one of his followers to claim it, and to learn to drive it. One day, in the street, he encountered Cheng's car with the merchant's son at the wheel and two cronies in the rear seat.

Then Kow tried to smash into the other car, but—being a clumsy driver—only succeeded in grazing it; while he himself was riddled with bullets by the three Chinese. The gray limousine had plunged off, had been brought under control by the man with Kow, who carried back to Chagan the body of his master.

"That young snake Yang," observed Warner to Mac afterward, "was in the car that chased us through the wall, I think. The letter he sent to Miss Peony this evening was a request that she surrender to him before noon tomorrow, or he would come into Chagan and get her."

"That girl's had a hard life," remarked the mechanic.

"If Yang happens to get the better of her men, she'll kill herself."

"How you going to help 'em?" Mac asked.

"I don't know. They're suspicious of us, won't obey orders from me. The house can't stand a siege—walls too thin to stop bullets, and Miss Peony can't be moved. Wouldn't leave her father's grave if she could."

"Think Yang would carry the fight here, if she doesn't show up within the time limit?"

"Certainly. He'd like nothing better. He knows Kow's dead, thinks we're gone, suspects the limousine is out of order. With his high-power repeating rifles and automatics he could whip a hundred of these hicks."

Mac turned this over in his mind and assented. "What Miss Peony ought to do is to send her men out to tackle the tong-men in their camp."

"Good idea, but if she did that, Yang could pack his gang in the car and drive through the desert men and beat them into Chagan." Warner looked at his friend thoughtfully. "Mac, it looks as if you and I'd have to take charge of the war against Yang."

"Why, Bob," the mechanic closed one eye, as if in great surprise. "I'm ashamed of you! A collector, too—and me a peaceful man. What else might you be thinking?"

"We'd better take the armored car."

"Listen to the boy," remarked Mac to no one in particular. "Ain't he bad? What next?"

"We'll decide that when we get out there. Meanwhile we'd better hunt up our blankets and get some sleep."

But when they had found their car and rolled themselves up in the blankets, with canvas packs for pillows, Mac lit a cigarette and smoked for a while in silence. "Bob," he observed after a while, "you awake? You're the blamedest fool I ever hitched up with. I told you back there we ought to go and mop up that bunch, when we could have done it nice and easy. No, you wouldn't think of it. Now you're going out on the warpath against six killers with good guns in broad daylight, and I'll bet you're going to yell out to them what you're comin' for, like one of these here night errand boys."

"Knights-errant?"

"You get me. Ain't you really got any more plan than that?"

"Not a bit. Except that the house boys are devoted to Miss Peony and they are good knife fighters."

"Hell! They'd do fine, throwing knives at repeating rifles behind a stone wall!" He sighed. "Well, it's too late to reach Yang's dugout before sunrise, now."

* * * *

Warner slept soundly during the hour or so before dawn, but Mac remained wakeful, the tip of a fresh cigarette glowing as soon as one went out. And he took no heed of the glory of the sky that spread over his head. He did look up when he noticed, squatting a hundred yards away, the thin antelope hunter who had been in the car with Miss Peony.

The man, however, merely watched Mac as he set about getting breakfast. He cooked enough for two and ate his share while Warner slumbered on in the shadow of the car. Then he wakened his friend.

"Now, Bob, you feed yourself while I give the big bus a look-over. I've got an idea. You listen careful, and go and have Miss Peony explain it to her men. Watch your step, because this Beanstalk bird here, is keeping tabs on us."

For a moment more the two talked together, and then separated, Mac going around to the twin-six, to examine the carburetor, gas feed line, and the motor generally. He worked away for several hours, because, as he explained to Warner when the latter strolled out of the house, he did not want anything to break down when the time came to run away.

It was nearly noon when Mac at last was satisfied with his labor, and climbed into the driver's seat. The three Chinese who had accompanied Warner, and who had waited patiently for the ceremonial that was to make the no-horse cart go to cease, got into the rear compartment.

"They don't look like much," grunted Mac, testing out the engine.

"They can use their knives, and that's what you want. Miss Peony took a long time making up her mind about us, but when she did, all the village wanted to go along. I wouldn't hear of that, of course." Warner grimaced. "The girl's as white as her dress this morning. Thinking of that dagger of hers gives me the shivers."

As they passed the house, turning to go down to the village, they saw at an opened window in the second story a face look out at them, and a tiny hand wave a greeting.

In the village itself every living being, apparently, had been waiting patiently along the one street to see the car and the foreign devils that were going to fight the enemies of the honorable, dead, Li Yuan Kow. Midway down the street, the taciturn rifleman stopped them, and insisted by signs that he was going along, with three friends, who proved to be some of the hunters the white men had seen the evening before.

"Why not?" said Mac briefly.

He was silent as they drove out to the *caravanserai*. In many ways he was more experienced than Warner, and he knew that the task before them was a difficult one.

CHAPTER VII
THE CARAVANSERAI

Arriving within sight of the stone shelter on the knoll that rose above the swells of the prairie, the two white men were surprised to find that on every vantage point within view of the *caravanserai*, groups of Mongols were sitting, looking on eagerly. Even as the gray car rolled forward, groups of nomads came galloping up, halting at a discreet distance.

"Inviting themselves to see the show," grumbled Mac. "Well, it ought to be good, at that."

He made the hunters dismount from the running boards before the car came within gun-shot of the stone wall. Thereafter he proceeded more slowly, Warner, at his side, waving a white handkerchief. When they were near enough to hail the men from Pekin, he halted.

After a moment Yang himself climbed over the wall and advanced a few steps. Warner, in turn, moved out from the car, although Mac warned him to stay in his seat.

"We know why you have come to Chagan," the white man announced. "Go back, Yang, son of Fu Cheng, without doing further harm. If you and your men leave in your car within an hour, you will not be molested."

The reply of the young Chinese was strident with anger. "If you are wise you will not meddle in what is not your affair. Taker of my father's money! Leave the car that does not belong to you, and go away!"

"One hour," repeated Warner, "you have to start east. We are not going to leave Chagan for several days."

"Stay here forever then!" Yang dropped to the ground and started to crawl back toward the wall. At the same instant three rifles flashed from the *caravanserai*.

Mac, however, had been expecting this, and had the big car in gear. Starting forward with a jerk, he turned in a wide arc, picking up his friend who jumped for the forward seat. The sides of the car were high, and were made of steel. Stooping down, the two were pretty well protected from the bullets that whined overhead for the most part.

Once Mac had completed his turn they were safe. Two or three shots clanged against the rear, without penetrating the steel plates.

"Now you've got that off your chest," muttered Mac, "we'll start the hunter's barrage."

But the men from Chagan had lost no time in selecting cover of sorts on neighboring knolls and were blazing away at the stone shelter from their long-barrelled pieces. Mac drove behind a convenient rise and chuckled at seeing the spectators hurrying away to get beyond range. For half an hour the rifle duel continued, and Warner, who had crawled to the top of the rise with his field glasses shrugged his shoulders when he came back. "I think one of the tong-men was hit in the head by the antelope hunter, and one of our Chagan allies got his back scratched over there."

"Time we started something," Mac pointed out. "Here comes Beanstalk with a busted shoulder."

From up the gully the tall rifleman was walking toward them calmly, his gun in his left hand, and his right chest stained with blood. He shook his head slightly and looked inquiringly at Warner.

Mac whistled softly between his teeth. Under the circumstances, the shooting was unusually accurate—especially on the part of Yang's men. Somewhere near them the two remaining hunters were keeping up a slow fire. "If you have any sense left at all, Bob," he remarked, "we'll travel right back to Chagan. If not we'll do our stuff and get it over with. Any time now Yang may get wise to the fact that all he has to do to queer our game is to crowd his car and rush us."

"Then we'd better be starting."

The three boys who had been peering from the window behind him sank back on the rear seat as the big machine wound along the ravine, keeping out of sight of the men in the *caravanserai*. Mac turned into another gully that circled the fight around the knoll.

In order to reach the far side of Yang's citadel they were forced to twist a mile or so through the depressions, keeping down from the skyline. Then, when they decided that they were near the entrance side Of the *caravanserai* they turned in toward it sharply. In front of them, judging by Warner's observation of the night before, should be the wide gateway in the stone square.

But now there were no friendly depressions to cover their approach. Mac increased the speed of the car, and, over his shoulder, he could see the three Chinese, knives in hand, peering from the steel shutters. The gray machine sped up a slope and shot forward toward the *caravanserai*.

Mac had been praying that none of Yang's men would be keeping watch on this side. Squarely in the opening of the wall, however, a rifleman was seated, smoking. He sprang up with a shout as the car appeared, out of the grass of the prairie.

They were closer than they had expected to Yang's citadel, and before the solitary sentry could begin firing the car swept to within a hundred yards of the gate. The white men crouched down. A shot ripped through the top overhead, and another smashed into the radiator. Then, with four thousand-odd pounds of metal bearing down on him, the man with the rifle jumped aside.

Mac released the accelerator, and, as they passed through the entrance, jammed on both brakes. He had been in more than one mix-up in Mexico, and wondered if the appearance of the armored car within the *caravanserai* would not be a signal for Yang and his men to throw up their hands. But as the car skidded forward over the slippery grass, a fusillade of shots roared at them.

Luckily, the heavy machine skidded to the side where three of the tong-men stood, and they had to jump to escape being run down. The instant the car slowed up the three Chinese sprang out of the rear doors, and Warner stepped out of the front, Colt in hand.

The space inside the four walls became a very bedlam of snarling, shrieking men and roaring guns. The smoke wreaths, split by orange flashes, thickened to a murk. A bullet clipped Mac's shoulder muscle. He saw one of the Chagan boys run full into the discharge of a tong-man's automatic, halt as if he had encountered an invisible wall, and—before sinking to the ground—hurl his knife. The long blade imbedded itself in the other man's stomach and he began to walk around slowly in circles, holding his revolver up stiffly as if it were a strange thing in his hand.

Warner had dropped another of the tong-men. But a stray bullet passed through the lower leg of the white man, toppling him over.

"Sufferin' cats!" yelled Mac, climbing out of his seat. Crouching, he ran to the side of his friend, only to see Warner sit up and look around, revolver poised. The shooting had ended.

Two of the tong-men had fallen, and one had been dead when the car rolled into the *caravanserai*. In a corner near them one of the Chagan boys was rolling on the ground with the pock-marked clerk of Cheng, who had gripped his hair and was trying to use the butt of a revolver to brain his foe. But the boy's knife, already crimson, was slashing at the other's body, and presently Yang's henchman ceased to struggle.

Another of the boys was sitting against the wall, holding his chest where a dark stain was spreading. The remaining ally of the white men was chasing through the entrance of the wall Yang, who was loading his automatic with a fresh clip as he ran.

Nothing was to be seen of the erstwhile sentry. But as Mac helped Warner to his feet and moved toward the wall where the air was clearer, he saw the tong-man who had been at the entrance climbing into Yang's car. There, too, ran Yang, jumping into the driver's seat and catching at gear shift and ignition plug frantically.

The boy with the knife was some distance away. Warner levelled his Colt, and then let it fall. "Can't pot that beggar Yang like that!"

"Fine for us if he gets away," grumbled Mac. "See, the car's off."

"Look there!" Warner pointed outside the *caravanserai*.

A hundred yards or so down the slope the tall rifleman Mac had christened Beanstalk had been limping up the knoll. As Yang started, on a course that would take him within range of the hunter, the man from Chagan sat down, and propped up in the grass the rest for his long rifle. Using his one good arm, he pushed in a cartridge, sighted his piece and waited.

Yang's machine was gathering speed, and in another moment would be beyond range. When the car reached the skyline the tall hunter pressed the trigger.

The two white men saw that Yang sat as before in the driver's seat, but the car swerved. Presently it stopped, and the remaining tong-man climbed down and held up his hands. Yang remained motionless—shot through the body under the arms. Meanwhile the hunter had loaded again and was calmly proceeding to shoot down the last of the foes, when Warner shouted at him and shook his head.

The fight was over.

* * * *

Three weeks later, Robert Warner and Tim McMahon were sitting in their room in the Pekin hotel, when they heard a knock at the door, and presently there entered a wrinkled old Chinese in native dress, who, bowing politely, held out to them a sealed envelope.

After a moment's hesitation, Warner took it. The aged messenger—whom he recognized as the keeper of Fu Cheng's outer shop—withdrew, closing the door after him. Warner opened the envelope, glanced at what was within and whistled softly in surprise.

"Mac, a month ago you said the Chinese had changed—that they were like us. Do you still think so? Because, if you do, I'll let you guess what Cheng has sent us in this letter."

"No. I've quit guessing. I'm wrong." Warner held out to him a certified check for three hundred dollars, drawn by Fu Cheng and made out to Robert Warner. The letter enclosing it stated that the merchant had learned that they had delivered his package and took this opportunity of settling his debt to them.

With a questioning glance at his friend, who nodded assent, Warner tore the check into small pieces and tossed the fragments of paper out of the window.

www.ingramcontent.com/pod-product-compliance
Lightning Source LLC
Chambersburg PA
CBHW020751250626
47155CB00003B/1027